VULTURE PEAK

VULTURE PEAK

JOHN BURDETT

Alfred A. Knopf New York 2012

THIS IS A BORZOI BOOK
PUBLISHED BY ALFRED A. KNOPF

www.aaknopf.com

Knopf, Borzoi Books, and the colophon are registered trademarks
of Random House, Inc.

Library of Congress Cataloging-in-Publication Data
Burdett, John.
Vulture peak / by John Burdett. — 1st ed.
p. cm.
"This is a Borzoi book."
ISBN 978-0-307-27267-6 (alk. paper)
1. Sonchai Jitpleecheep (Fictitious character) — Fiction.
2. Police — Thailand — Bangkok — Fiction. 3. Organ
trafficking — Fiction. 4. Bangkok (Thailand) — Fiction. I. Title.
PR6052.U617V85 2011
823'.914 — dc23   2011041047

Jacket image: Picture Hooked / Michael Szebor / Alamy
Jacket design by Chip Kidd

Manufactured in the United States of America
Published January 10, 2012
Second Printing Before Publication

For Nit

What you do to yourself, you do to the world.
What you do to the world, you do to yourself.

—Buddhist proverb

If a living donor can do without an organ, why shouldn't the donor profit and medical science benefit?

—Janet Ratcliffe-Richards, *Lancet*
352 (1998), p. 1951

AUTHOR'S NOTE

As a point of information, for reasons of atmosphere the Patong I have described is pre-tsunami. Vulture Peak the mountain, like the book, is entirely fictional, as is the Golden Goose temple.

PART 1

1

In the golden age of conspicuous consumption—it must be more than twenty years ago now, although it seems like only yesterday—someone rich and famous from Hong Kong built a stately pleasure dome high on a hill in Phuket overlooking the Andaman Sea. They used the finest Thai architects, who produced a lyrical palace with curving roofs under which teak pillars of great girth support high ceilings over vast play areas where pools of limpid blue are linked by tiny streams that tinkle over smooth pebbles selected by a feng shui master, and enormous bedrooms offer ocean views to make you gasp. The developer named the hilltop they had thus colonized Vulture Peak, whether in homage to the Indian mountain upon which the Buddha gave his celebrated sermons, or to the buzzards they had evicted, is unclear.

It's as good a place as any for a triple homicide, although access is complicated. I came by taxi, but the driver lost us in a complex of single-lane roads that led to other mansions. We could see the place clearly enough—it's the biggest and swankiest of them all—so in the end I climbed up an iron ladder from the sea and have arrived a good fifty minutes after the forensic team, which is led by our senior pathologist, Dr. Supatra, a diminutive figure in white coveralls, mask, and gloves. We press our palms together and *wai* each other from a distance. She is accompanied by a team of about eight, for the news that it is an atrocity of the more serious kind preceded our arrival and the good doctor likes to be prepared. More than the size of her team, the heavy silence and glum faces—only she and her chief assistant are wearing masks—portend a crime scene lurid with bad luck. Not a one of us will not spend an hour or so making merit in a temple before the day is out. In my mind's eye I stand before a Buddha image with a bunch of smoking incense and bow three times.

Dr. Supatra leads me to the master bedroom, where three human forms lie on a giant bed. In an attempt to minimize the bad joss as much as to express respect for the dead, Supatra has covered them from head to toe with an equally extravagant white sheet. She pauses for a moment before inviting me to share the labor of removing it. The rest of her team have wandered in to observe my reaction.

The Buddha taught that the distinction between subject and object, the self and other, even between you and me, Dear *Farang Reader* (may I call you DFR?), is illusory. This lesson is brought home with perhaps more drama than the Master intended when the human forms before you have been stripped of faces, eyes, genitals, and—as the good doctor indicates by pointing to gaping wounds in each cadaver—kidneys and livers too. To call them anonymous would be to evade the issue. Stripped of every vestige of personal identity, they are all of us, as anyone knows who has ever flown economy. With so much surgery to absorb, it takes me a moment to notice that the finger and thumb tips of each victim have been snipped off. Supatra follows my gaze.

"Any first impressions regarding cause of death?" I ask.

"Gunshot wounds to the back of the head. A single shot in each case. Everything points to a carefully planned execution prior to pillaging the bodies for organs."

"Obviously no print identification," I mutter. "DNA?"

The doctor shrugs. "If any of them committed a serious crime over the past five years, maybe. We only have DNA records for convicted criminals."

"But prints could have been checked on the national ID bank." I shake my head. "Someone is being unusually shy about who they killed. We have to go on the likelihood they were all Thai residents who could have been identified if they still had fingertips." I scratch my jaw. "That leaves sixty million possibilities."

Supatra allows herself a smile bordering on the coquettish. "I may be able to help, Detective. Just last week I sent off for some fancy software that will allow us to reconstruct the faces on my laptop. The government won't pay so I'm buying it myself."

"Really? That will be helpful. By the way, what genders are the victims?"

"Two men and a woman."

Now I notice something else. "No blood?"

"Somebody cleaned up meticulously. They even used some chemical that neutralizes our tests. I tell you, whoever did it were professionals. There were certainly more than one." I nod.

"Any ideas?" the doctor asks when we have replaced the sheet.

"You mean whodunit? Only in the more general sense." She raises her eyes. "Ronald Reagan, Milton Friedman, Margaret Thatcher, Adam Smith. Capitalism dunit. Those organs are being worn by somebody else right now."

She stares at me for a moment and, good Buddhist that she is, shivers. "Oh, yes. Of course I saw that from the start."

I leave her in the infinite lounge to step out onto the balcony, which offers a plummeting vista of rocks and ocean of the kind that invariably provokes thoughts of suicide in even the healthiest psyche, and fish out my cell phone to call my assistant, Lek. I ask him to go straight to the Phuket land registry and give him the address of the crime scene, which should be enough for the registry to work out the lot number. I don't bother to check the rest of the house—what's the point?

Despite my evasive answer to the doctor's question, I already know too much. I need to clear my head and my heart. I also need to consider how to break the news to my partner, Chanya. All of a sudden I need to do a lot of things that form no part of crime detection. The iron ladder I climbed up starts at a corner of the balcony and hugs the massive rock all the way down. I jump the last two steps to land on soft shale that releases an inelegant sea stench, which I suck in with some relief. Despite the impossible heat I decide to follow the shore all the way back to the main road. I'll find a cab or a motorbike taxi there.

Lek, a transsexual permanently on the verge of the operation that will equally permanently turn him into a woman, is waiting outside the thoroughly modern land registry, a refugee from the glacial air-conditioning that our bureaucrats have come to expect as a perk of their employment. He shivers as I open the door for us, and we are braced by an arctic breeze. "The clerk's a *katoey*," he complains. *Katoey* means transsexual, which is to say one of his own tribe. Is it too early in the narrative for a dark observation on the human condition, namely that to know well is often to loath well? To put it another way, the fishwife inside all men is liberated when the goolies are cut off—or about to be.

But he's right, the clerk is a *katoey* of the kind who did not find consummation after the operation. Dark, paranoid eyes seem in endless doubt as to whether life without a cock is even worse than with one. When I ask politely if he cannot find the lot number of the address I give him—it is after all the biggest, most prominent, most overblown mansion on the highest rock in the locality—Lek interjects loudly with faux hurt, "I already asked him exactly that question, and he said, 'What do you think I am, a private detective?'"

I catch the clerk's eye and smile glacially as I present my police ID. Caught, he goes into a classic *katoey* sulk. It's the full show with pouted lips, tuts, and well-I-supposes, but he magically finds the logbook under the desk. He must have retrieved it from the shelves while Lek was outside sheltering from the cold. Perhaps fearful that I will make a formal complaint, he tuts and frets his way through the pages until he finds the lot we are seeking. He also runs his finger down the column that records the various parties who have owned the pleasure palace over the years.

It seems that a famous and now deceased Hong Kong Chinese woman, the widow of an equally famous land development tycoon, bought the lot through a local company without disguising her identity. This we may take as an act of flamboyance, proving she was so rich she didn't much care if one day she would have to pay tax on the resale or, more likely, that she would one day be cheated by her Thai shadow shareholders. On her death the property was sold and resold through a succession of shell companies until the present owner, B.C.A. Company, bought it officially for one hundred million baht, which at the present rate of exchange works out at roughly $3.5 million. The recorded price doubtless reflects a strategy to evade transfer tax; we can assume the actual sale figure was at least double.

As is proper, the details of B.C.A. Company are also recorded in the register. I am not surprised that the eight shareholders are Thai; I would be surprised, though, if any of them invested any equity at all in the company. Whoever is the true owner of the mansion has made sure someone searching the registry—a cop like me, for example— will not so easily discover their identity.

I thank the clerk. He has transformed into a female doormat who fawns and moans as he hefts the heavy tome and tramps slope-shouldered down the aisle between shelves that hold the larcenous secrets of a real estate boom more than thirty years old, while Lek and I retreat gratefully to the heat wave that awaits outside.

I try to avoid Lek's eye while we look around for a taxi, but he grasps my arm.

"It's part of the other thing, isn't it?"

"Too early to say," I reply. He treats me to a fishwife leer of disbelief.

2

I shall tease you no further, DFR, but straightaway tell you what I know. It all began on an inauspicious Thursday last week.

"I looked into body parts about five years ago," Police Colonel Vikorn said, and gave me one of his dangerous smiles. We were in his spartan but spacious office, where he sat at his desk under a great anti-corruption poster of which he is inexplicably fond. "But the logistics seemed too nerve-wracking. In the end I decided to stay with what I knew. Smack never goes bad, especially if you keep it in morphine bricks during a bear market."

My Colonel stood. He is of average height with gray hair almost cropped. As on most days, he was dressed in an informal version of the Thai cop's brown uniform, a worn cotton combination that looks like military fatigues. It is one of his idiosyncrasies that he never walks but only prowls. Now he prowled to the window to look down on the cooked-food stalls that line the street below. "So many things you have to set up. The surgeon to harvest the parts from the donor or the cadaver. The other surgeon to pop them into the donee. Nursing support for both. And if you do it right, you probably need a specialist in whatever organ you're transplanting—kidneys are the gold standard, but there's quite a lot of liver, heart, lung trafficking these days, and they say that whole eyes and faces are now viable. Then there's the clinic to set up. If you've got some *farang* calling the shots, he's not going to expect it all to happen in a third-world garage."

He pursed his lips. "And you have to have a good organ hunter to work the supply side in the first place, not to mention the nurse to take the blood samples to check compatibility." He turned to face me. "But I could see the point, of course. Suppose some rich little shit on Wall Street needs a new heart. Is he going to wait in line in the hope that the health system will find him a replacement before he croaks—or is he going to buy himself one on the black market? If he's on the point of dying, obviously he'll pay whatever price the organ hunter demands. If he's worth eight hundred million, surely a mere million is not too much to ask in return for another twenty years of bleeding the world white? See, the hunter is the key to it all." He paused and frowned. "Sure, it would be a first-class racket if it wasn't for the short shelf life of the product. Did you know that lungs and hearts only last six hours? After that they're useless."

"No," I said, "I didn't know that."

Vikorn flashed me a glance and nodded thoughtfully. "Eyes, of course, last longer. Just pop them out and chuck them in a fridge, they're good for a week."

"I thought you said eyes were only just coming onstream."

"I said *whole* eyes. Corneas are entry-level stuff—you don't even need a real surgeon, a well-trained nurse could do it—but the corneas are kept intact on the eyeballs until they're needed—it's called an *eye bank*. No civilized country is without one." He covered his mouth to cough. "The United Arab Emirates is one of the big markets for corneas. It's all that sun, burns them out. How long do you think human testicles would last on ice?"

"I have no idea. I've never heard of transplanting testicles."

"There's an incredible demand for them in North Korea, did you know that?"

"No."

"Of course, with North Koreans you never know if they're going to transplant them or eat them."

He let the moment hang for a few beats, then said in a suddenly formal and almost public tone of voice, "Organ trafficking is a deplorable thing, don't you think? It's outrageous that people use our country as a staging post for such an appalling crime. Someone needs to do something about it. I spoke to the deputy secretary yesterday, he's right behind me. He's given me tacit approval to lead the charge."

Now I'd lost the plot entirely. Vikorn lead a law and order campaign? In your mythology, DFR, that would be like Judas running for pope. Stranger still, this was the first I'd heard of Thailand being a world organ-trading center. Shrewdly, my master gave me a few moments to adjust to the new reality. Then he said, "So I'm appointing you as lead investigator."

"Huh?" In more than a decade of feudal service to my chief, he has never asked me to perform a socially useful task. On the contrary, my contribution to the community has largely consisted in modifying his personal interpretation of Western capitalism. "You started out admitting that you looked into the trade for personal profit. Now suddenly you want to wipe it out. May I ask why?"

He turned to stare me full in the face. "Why d'you think?"

"I have no idea . . ." My voice trails off, then I emit an "Oh."

"Right," Vikorn says, and turns to the window.

"Uhh, how long has General Zinna of the Royal Thai Army been in the business?"

"Ever since that car accident he got all twisted out of shape about. Five years or so. I turned a blind eye to it for a while, because it was relatively small bucks, but now the business has exploded. Organ trafficking today is what personal computers were in the eighties. I can't let him get too rich. Before you know it, he'll be trying to wipe me out again. You know what a competitive asshole he is."

I stared at him. "Why me?"

"Who else? You speak English. You are the half-*farang* bastard son of an American serviceman and so can pass for near white. You are also accustomed to international travel. That's already three qualifications not owned by anyone else in District Eight. If you must know, there is a fourth." Predictably, he paused with his eyebrows crooked. When I refused to rise to the bait, he added, "You're actually interested in truth and justice. I had a feeling that might come in useful eventually."

I was not in the mood for those kinds of games, so I scowled instead of smiled. This modest symptom of insubordination used to be enough to get you traffic duty at the Asok/Sukhumvit interchange in the old days; it still was in most cases, but when the Master has bigger fish to fry, he can be amazingly tolerant. Now he was grinning into my bad mood; not a good sign. Still standing, he reached down to pull out the top drawer of his desk, from which he extracted what looked like a scroll about eighteen inches in width. Now he was holding one edge of the document in his left hand next to his left cheek, while unrolling it with his right. Okay, now I saw it was not a document. It was a poster showing him in a brilliant white military-style uniform with brass studs, which is the identity of choice for any Thai man who needs to make an impression on the community. But it was the caption underneath his picture that was drilling holes in my psyche from every direction.

I went gray, because all the blood had drained from my face and an attack of nausea had begun rolling something around in the depths of my stomach. "No," I said, "you can't be serious. Please tell me this is an elaborate joke to humiliate me, I can live with that. Just put that damned thing away before I puke."

Even these strong words failed to dent his amused stare. "It's official. You can check with the electoral commission if you like."

"You as governor of Bangkok? You're really going to run?"

"That's what it says, isn't it? There's going to be one of these on every third lamppost in the city. I've already booked and paid for all the television time I'm allowed under the rules." He rolled up the poster and threw it on his desk. Now he was rubbing the left side of his nose with his left index finger, a sign of unadulterated triumphalism. "Actually, I can hardly lose. None of the other candidates has the dough to beat me. My political counselors tell me there is only one element missing, only one minor flaw that could trip me on the way to the top."

Now I was beginning to understand. "In twenty years as a colonel in the Royal Thai Police, you have never done a single thing to fight crime, while doing a great deal to contribute to it."

My words really should have had him in a rage, but instead the grin just got bigger. "That's not entirely true. I have done one very important thing to fight crime, something that has cost me dearly over the years." He paused for effect, then continued, "And now it's pay-back time."

"What are you talking about?"

"You. I've put up with you and all your sniveling, bleeding-heart conscience, your holier-than-thou posture that gets up everyone's nose and has had half the payroll moaning to me about you on almost a weekly basis for the past ten years. I'm not just talking about your monk manqué attitude, I'm talking about the number of man-hours you've wasted on forensic trivia when you could have been earning your keep. I'm talking about more than a decade of mollycoddling at considerable expense, taking into account how much money you would have made if I had listened to other voices. But I didn't, did I? You're still here, aren't you? I knew I'd find a use for you in the end, though even I never thought it would take a whole decade."

I was flushed, now; raging blood and a thumping heart replaced gray with near crimson. Suddenly the words were out: "Fuck you. I resign. Right here and now. You'll have it in writing as soon as I get back to my desk."

I was stunned that I still had not penetrated his impossible compla-cency. He was even shaking his head while smiling tolerantly. "Oh, no you don't. You can't."

"Why can't I?"

"Because this is your big moment as well as mine. I'm giving you the highest-profile criminal campaign in the country, and your goody-two-shoes Buddhist conscience will drive you till you drop. All I ask in return for bestowing upon you such glory, such cosmic opportunity to mend and improve your karma to the point where, if you're obliged to reincarnate at all, it will be as a prince or captain of industry or even, Buddha help us, a holy and revered abbot of a great monastery—all you have to do is tell the truth."

"Which is?"

"That your soon-to-be-world-famous crusade to put an end to the nefarious practice of illegal trafficking in body parts, which is so vilely exploiting the poor and the helpless, et cetera, is driven by *me*. You don't even have to confine yourself to Thailand—the Philippines is a world center for organ trading. You can even extend beyond Southeast Asia—in Moldova human kidneys are the staple of the economy. They grow them for cropping the way we grow rice. You're going to be our first World Cop. It'll put us on the law enforcement map like never before—we'll get to be more self-righteous than Western Europe and the States put together. We'll be the Mr. Squeaky Clean of organ sales."

My jaw dropped. "You're going to plaster it all over the media, aren't you? I mean, the international media? You cunning bastard. The surest way to get the respect of the Thai people is to get the respect of the rest of the world first, especially the Western world. You're going to give exclusive interviews to CNN and the BBC, which will run endlessly on Thai TV. Damn it, you can't lose." I was scratching my jaw furiously. "And you get to nail Zinna into the bargain. It's two birds with one stone."

"Right."

I slumped. "And it's true, I can't refuse."

"See, you agree with me on every point."

"It's also an easy way to get myself killed."

"There is a risk factor, I agree. But how long do you think you would live if you resigned from the force?"

Stress now had me all curled up in my chair—if I were alone, I would have been in a reality-denying fetal position on a bed somewhere. Of course, he had anticipated this moment, just as he had stage-managed the whole interview. Now in one seamless action, he took out his wallet, extracted something small and black from it, sat on his chair, leaned back, and chucked the credit-card-sized black object across the desk. It landed in front of me. I refused to pick it up or even look closely at it. "What is it?"

Now he showed the first sign of irritation. "What does it look like?"

"A credit card."

"What a genius detective you are."

"A black one?"

"If you pick the bloody thing up, all will be revealed."

Correction: if I picked it up, it would be a symbolic act of defeat. Well, he'd already defeated me, so I picked it up. "Amex? They make black ones? Is it for people with poor repayment records?"

He smirked. "You jerk. If you had one atom of street sense you would know you could buy a jumbo jet with it."

I turned it over a couple of times and shrugged. "So congratulations, I already know you're filthy rich. What's it got to do with the price of human testicles?"

"Look again, mooncalf."

I looked again and gasped. "It has my name on it."

"You've no idea how I had to lie to get them to put you on the account. They checked you out—they told me things about you that were truly shocking, but I battled on. It's a supplementary card. Just don't tell any of my wives—they've been on at me to get them one ever since they found out what it is."

"You mean—"

"Of course, I put a limit on it—a very generous one, actually."

"How much?"

"Not telling you. Let's say, if you find out, it will be because you've gotten uncharacteristically extravagant—or because the case has taken one of those turns that only money can control."

All I could do for the moment was to stare, as if the sinister black piece of plastic had arrived from a distant planet. "But why do I need it? If the case requires cash, I can just come and ask you for it."

He sighed. "You've missed the main clue, Detective."

"Okay, I'm just a dumb monk manqué—what clue?"

"In the old days you would have got it in an instant. I deliberately let it drop early on in this interview. I'm very disappointed. And don't say 'fuck you' again—you only get to play that card once in a lifetime."

Now I shrugged and made myself look even dumber than he was making me out to be. I let my jaw hang and gave him a slack-eyed stare.

"The United Arab Emirates," my Colonel said with heavy patience.

"That's where you're going. Start with corneas, and work your way down till you get to testicles. I want the list of contacts as it develops."

"The UAE? I can't just land in the middle of the Arabian Desert and start selling corneas."

"I know. I already told you I looked into the trade a few years back. I have contacts who will be interested in taking on a Thai apprentice organ hunter."

I scratched my head. "What are the names of the contacts?"

"D'you know the Chinese for 'Old Hundred Names'? Never mind. Just say 'the Vultures,' and everyone in the business will know who you're talking about."

"Where are they based?"

"Everywhere. The ladies speak a thousand languages, own a thousand faces. I think you'll have a lot of fun with this case. Don't worry if you have to do things that threaten your marriage. I'll corroborate it's all in the line of duty."

3

My first thought after leaving his office with shoulders slumped was to rush home to my partner, Chanya, a former whore who'd worked in my mother's bar, the Old Man's Club, where we fell in love. We're not legally married but went through a Buddhist ceremony, which is what counts in the country area where Chanya hails from. A few years ago our only child, a son, died in a traffic accident, and the event changed my darling forever. She grew serious, studied sociology from a distance-learning institute, followed up with a master's in the same subject, and now works day and night on her Ph.D. thesis, which, naturally, is all about prostitution in Thailand, with a special emphasis on Bangkok. Let me be specific: she conducted almost the whole of her research in Soi Cowboy, where my mother's bar is situated. All was going well until the university in its wisdom replaced one of her Thai supervisors with a *farang* woman, with whom Chanya did not get along. For a year it had been one long High Noon between the two of them, each trying to outresearch the other. I didn't think I was going to get the reception I needed by going home right now.

Instead, I checked the open-plan office where I have a desk to see if my assistant, Lek, was still there. But it was six-fifteen in the evening, and he'd long since left work. I doubted that he'd gone home, though. I pressed an autodial number on my cell phone. When he answered, I could hear a plaintive Isaan folk song in the background and a lot of semifemale voices. When he is among his own kind, Lek turns pretty much totally fag.

"Where are you, Lek?"

"Master, *darling*, is it really you? *Soo* wonderful of you to think of me."

"Lek, I have a new case you're going to have to help me with."

"Anything, Superman, anything you say."

"Be serious for a moment. You have a good connection in the army, don't you?"

A snigger. "I do love your discretion, master."

"There's a General Zinna angle to the case. I need to talk to you."

Lek dropped his fag performance. "Zinna?"

"Just tell me where you are, I'll come."

"I'm in the Lonesome Cowboy in Nana Plaza. Do hurry, I can't wait to show you off to my friends."

Now I was outside the police station, facing the long row of cooked-food stalls, which would be illegal if they didn't cater to cops, and I was of two minds about whether to grab a cab or walk to Nana. I knew that if I decided to walk, it would start to rain, and that if I grabbed a cab, it would not. Just to prove that I could predict the future, I started to walk. By the time I got to the end of the *soi*, the heavens opened; call me Nostradamus. The drops were light enough at first, and of course it was about thirty degrees Celsius, but this was the remnant of a typhoon that had been lashing Vietnam for four days, and now the sky had turned black and all of us on the street were hit with great plashing drops of warm water that soaked you from top down and also from bottom up because the rain bounced off the sidewalk to a height of maybe twelve inches.

By the time I reached the Sukhumvit/Soi 4 interchange, the calves of my pants were wet rags. The roads had started to flood and turn into shallow brown rivers. I decided to wait in a doorway with a clear view of the traffic jam. Cars, trucks, and buses pumped carbon monoxide into the warm rain; an old diesel bus with no air-conditioning stopped right in front of me. Rows of Thai faces stared implacably into the bad weather. A couple of whores and a *katoey* who were hanging around looking for customers had also taken refuge in the doorway, so it was quite cozy. The *katoey* was by far the most beautiful of all of us, but given to pouting. By the time I decided to make a dash for it, I had offended all three of my new friends by declining to hire any of their bodies.

I reached Nana soaked through. *Farang* don't like to get wet, not even in the tropics, so the plaza was almost without customers, the outside bars awash with water, the girls huddled together under the extended roofs that are supposed to look like country pavilions. I knew the rain wouldn't last long, though, and even if it did, lust and loneliness would bring the white men out to play sooner or later; anyway, these were mostly Isaan girls, conditioned from childhood to take a contemplative attitude to life: they have a hundred ways of passing the time, mostly by grooming one another. At the Crazy Elephant three girls were looking for lice in the hair of three other girls, and the remaining "waitresses" were making up in mirrors. The Isaan hairdresser in the corner was doing a roaring trade as usual, and as the girls wandered in for work, they *waied* the Buddha shrine next to the Forbidden City bar, sometimes bringing lotus and other offerings to lay under the saffron-robed statue. As recently as five years ago there were only heterosexual bars here, but the *katoey* market has grown inexplicably in recent times. Is something happening in *farang land* you need to tell me about, DFR? Don't you like girls so much anymore? Is it feminism that has turned you off or something latent in the soul, so long denied, that is emerging in this new century of enlightenment?

I'd not been to Nana for years, so for me this was a trip down memory lane. When I saw that the Lonesome Cowboy was on the ground floor at the back of the plaza, I had to smile to myself. It used to be called the Catwalk; my mother, Nong, worked there when I was about twelve years old. I used to take a motorbike taxi early in the evening to come and ask for money for food; sometimes, when I got lonely, I would arrive in an emotional mess as late as one or two in the morning. If Mum was with a customer, her friends would take care of me. According to the head experts, I should have quite a few problems, shouldn't I? Well, I can report that in my case I do have one unusual quirk: I adore whores. Generally speaking, they are the most honest and generous of women, and the only ones who have a clue about men.

The entrance to the bar was covered by a red velvet curtain and guarded by four *katoeys* (in shimmering silver body gloves or gold one-piece swimming costumes with white daisies at the bosom). They gazed upon me as a prospect and undressed me in their imagination as they let me in; I saw about twenty more *katoeys* in bikinis and faux-ermine shawls busy eating their evening meal. They were using the stage as a table and discussing silicone inserts with reference to the price/quality tradeoff. There was no sign of Lek. I nodded at the *mamasan*, a *katoey* in his midforties who remembered my mother from the bar's earlier incarnation; he nodded back.

Now I saw that Lek was sitting at a table in a dark corner and had been watching me with an excited grin on his face since I walked in. The other *katoeys* watched jealously as I strolled over, just as Lek intended. He was right to be discreet—all *katoeys* are compulsive gossips; but they are also a sub-subclass: no one listens to them, no one accords them the right to be taken seriously. I'm fond of Lek, perhaps I love him, but I don't appreciate his fag persona, so I went stern, just as he started to tease me about being in a *katoey* bar.

"General Zinna," I said, and he immediately got the message. He nodded humbly. Now he was a doormat who would take any punishment from the master he loved. "I only heard the story about his accident tenth hand. He's into body parts, all of a sudden?"

"It was such a terrible shame," Lek said with a sigh. "That young fellow was tall, strong, and handsome like a dream." Lek shook his head. "The most beautiful soldier in the army, they used to say. And an ace marksman."

"Zinna was driving?"

"Of course. He used to love to drive his Ferrari down lonely country lanes with his latest beautiful boy by his side. He doesn't do that anymore. They say he sold the Ferrari."

"A cement truck?"

Lek nodded. "It was all General Zinna's fault, he admits it himself. He didn't lie or punish the truck driver—he just paid off the cops.

They say he really was broken up about it. He tried to buy the boy a new face, even went up to China to arrange for the surgery, because there was that case in the news in Beijing where they transplanted a whole face from a brain-dead person to some guy who got attacked by a Rottweiler—but you can see from the pictures the surgery didn't really work. He still looks like a monster."

"He bought his lover a new face?"

"Tried to. The Chinese sold him one fresh from a prisoner they had executed, but it didn't take so well. The poor boy had to go through months and months of surgery and drugs, surgery and drugs, and he still ended up with a hideous mask. In the end he told Zinna he was going to dedicate the rest of his life to the Buddha. He found a forest monastery in Cambodia that would have him—the Thai Sangha wouldn't take him. They say he's achieved happiness. Maybe he's an *arhat* already. With that kind of suffering, I suppose you progress pretty quickly. You know the saddest thing of all? He wasn't even gay, just doing the right thing to get promotion in Zinna's brigade."

"Your soldier-lover told you the whole story?"

Lek smirked. "He's not my lover, darling. You know I'm no good at sex. He tried to rape me that time when we were on the Tibetan case, and then he had a change of heart. He won't stop asking for forgiveness, he says it's at least partly my fault for being so pretty. What a charmer!" He giggled. "You see, I don't think he knew he was gay until that day." Lek laughed. "Boys are funny."

"So what's the connection with organ trafficking?"

"Zinna is all bent out of shape from the accident and what he did to the love of his life, but Zinna is Zinna and always looking for a way to get richer than Vikorn—and it's like in the midst of the greatest misery, he's suddenly found El Dorado. He's blown away by the Chinese—he thinks it's unbelievably clever the way they sell organs from executed prisoners—and of course the more executions the better for business, so there's a lot of people on death row who shouldn't be there. It's like natural resources with legs that deliver themselves to the factory. He admires that. His first idea was to set up as a broker. You know, matching the supply side from China with the demand side from the West and Southeast Asia. It's exactly his kind of capitalism: brutal and profitable."

"Why did you say it was his first idea?"

"Because a lot of people were already in the racket. There wasn't that much opportunity left. You can't compete with the Chinese when it comes to business—they never sleep. So he takes his idea a bit further."

"How?"

"How d'you think? He's got connections with Burma that go back decades—that's where he's got his meth factories. A lot of Burmese would line up to sell a kidney, a piece of liver, an eye, to get their hands on a few thousand dollars. Especially mothers trying to save their babies from disease and hunger. And there are all those executions the generals carry out. Zinna sells Burmese and Chinese body parts, and business is booming. They say it's better than methamphetamine, and the best news is there's no law enforcement, not even from the West. Smuggle a little marijuana, and they jump on you. Smuggle a liver that's been ripped out of a political prisoner, and they wave you on."

While we were talking, the *katoeys* came and went through the curtain. It was dark outside. That meant it was after seven o'clock and almost at the end of the rush hour. Now a *farang* in a business suit slipped in. He was the first genuine customer, so the *katoeys* made a fuss over him. He had been there before, though, and someone started calling out for Shirlee. Shirlee was a young *katoey*, perhaps twenty-two or -three, very slim and feminine looking. He was wearing a single-piece fawn-and-gold swimsuit and looked more vulnerable than any girl. He sidled up to the *farang*, who must have been some kind of lawyer or businessman in his late twenties. The young man in the suit grabbed and hugged the even younger man in the swimming costume. "I've been looking forward to this since nine this morning," the *farang* said in a voice ripe with lust. He wiped out the dreary reality of the day with a great sigh.

"Are you going to pay my bar fine?" Shirlee asked in a cute-submissive voice.

"Tonight and every night, love."

Lek, too, had noticed the romantic moment and smiled at me in a provocative way. I shook my head, laughing, and paid for the drinks. While I was waiting for change, a short, bald, and very nervous *farang* came in. Lek said, "Oh, my," because it was obvious from his body language the new customer had never been in a *katoey* bar before. This was a closet breakout.

The *katoeys* were salivating. Two of them, one in a silver body glove and another in a leopard-skin tunic with short skirt, went up to him. They stroked his shoulders as if he'd been out in the cold too long; he immediately bought drinks. Lek's eyes said, *Insecure, lonesome foreigner fleeing callous whores and worse wives for the twilight world of transsexuals.* In your language, DFR, you say, *Out of the frying pan into the fire.* We say, *Escape the tiger into the mouth of the crocodile.* By the time my change arrived, the little bald guy was on his third whiskey-and-Coke and was starting to believe the endless flattery he was getting from the two *katoeys*.

"Your tits are coming along," I told Lek as I was leaving. "Better not let them show too much, I'm getting heat from Vikorn about you."

"I know, I know," Lek said.

My mind flipped back to the case. I paused for a second. "Zinna must have a go-between. He's too brutal to work directly with Western surgeons and clients."

"Sure. I even heard the name once, but I can't remember it."

"The Vultures. A two-girl team?"

"Yes. How did you know?"

"Vikorn told me."

Outside the plaza was starting to hop. Just as I predicted, the rain couldn't keep the johns away for long. The girls who were grooming one another before were grooming white men now, and those who'd bought new hairdos from the coiffeur at the corner were showing them off behind the bars. A dozen TV monitors were showing a dozen different shows, most of them soccer, and all the sound systems were blaring. Still the rain from Vietnam was flooding the streets; still the girls paused to *wai* the Buddha shrine and leave lotus buds.

4

I found a cab fast enough, but we got snarled at the mouth of Soi 4 where it exits onto Sukhumvit. In terms of human sexual activity, this is the busiest corner in the world. Traffic from Nana Plaza, consisting of older *farang* men accompanying girls they've just hired, meets traffic from the other brothels and street pickups, making toward the short-time hotels. Simultaneously newly-mets are arriving from the bars farther up Sukhumvit in the Pleonchit area, looking for somewhere air-conditioned where they can get horizontal for an hour or so.

To me, sitting in back of the cab waiting for the lights to change, the answer to the world economic crisis was obvious: legalize prostitution and tax it. At 15 percent per bang, deficits would shrink overnight. It would be safe to leverage as well. The worse things get, the more people bury their problems in sex. The better things get, the more people celebrate their good fortune with sex. It's a tax revenue for all seasons, and with ever more sophisticated surveillance coming onstream, it won't be long before governments will be in a position to tax sex between married couples. Hey, Obama, are you listening?

Out of boredom the cab driver switched on his radio. One of the chat shows reported that five women had complained separately about a stalker on Sukhumvit. It seemed a man with a grotesquely damaged face had been approaching women and scaring the hell out of them.

Two complained to the police, but the police told them there was no law against being ugly. Now a bunch of people called to say they agreed with the police: *What was Thailand coming to when people showed no tolerance for the afflictions of others? We were supposed to be a Buddhist nation, after all.* Then one of the stalked women called in to say, "Have you any idea just how ugly this guy is? We're talking about extreme mutilation, worse than any horror movie." The story made me think of Zinna's lover, whose face was smashed in that car accident; but of course he was in a monastery somewhere in Cambodia, so it couldn't be him.

By the time we emerged from the jam, it was nine-thirty. A few more holdups kept me in the cab until we finally arrived at my little *soi* where my little hovel was waiting. I saw from the lights that Chanya was home, working in the corner of the room she calls her office. I called out "Hi," and she said it back to me, without looking up from her monitor. I tried not to feel lonely, isolated, and rejected. I tried not to think of the nervous little bald guy who'd come into the Lonesome Cowboy a couple of hours before and was probably this minute being initiated into his new world in some upstairs room by those two *katoeys* who would have his money one way or another. I tried not to think of Burmese mothers selling their kidneys and their eyes to keep their babies alive for a few more years, or of all the other Asian women and men who had tried to help their families by selling body parts after the tsunami. It's a beautiful, global world, so long as you keep your eyes shut.

The first thing I did when I arrived home was to grab a bunch of incense, light it, and hold it at eye level while I *waied* the electric Buddha we keep on a high shelf in the northeast corner. He's quite gaudy with purple and red lights, which are kitsch enough to remind me it's only a symbol I'm bowing at. On The Path, symbols are functional things, DFR; you really don't want them to seduce you with their charm or resale value.

So I was practicing a gritted-teeth kind of husbandly tolerance when I went to the other corner of the room, picked up a bottle of red wine, poured her a glass, and set it in front of her keyboard, then poured another for myself. She was not a natural drinker; I'd started to insist on one glass per night, just to bring her down from that high-stress war with her supervisor whose name, inevitably perhaps, was Dorothy. I knew that if she didn't have wine, she would hit a wall and slob out in front of the TV to watch her DVDs of *Ice Road Truckers*. You'd think there wouldn't be much for a slender Thai girl to relate to in a series about great hairy white men driving massive trucks across frozen lakes in Alaska; the attraction of opposites, I guess.

She got the message and looked up apologetically. We clinked glasses. I said, "I have a new case."

She struggled to emerge from her world into mine. "Really? What?"

"Vikorn's decided to abolish illegal organ trafficking worldwide. At least while he's running for governor."

She searched my face for an explanation. I told her all about Vikorn's election strategy and the latest ploy in his war with Zinna, and the black Amex card, which made her grin. "But isn't it dangerous? If there's so much money in that kind of trafficking, someone's sure to try to kill you."

"If I resigned, Vikorn would probably feel he had to bump me off. I know too much, and now that he's running for governor, the stakes are much higher. Anyway, I'm a cop, how could I refuse a case like this?"

Talk of my death sobered her. Suddenly the war with Dorothy wasn't so important. Suddenly she remembered she loved me. She shook her head, then started to caress me. I understood because I felt the same way. The likelihood that one will be hanged in the morning can make you horny as a rattlesnake.

We were lying naked together now, in the other corner of the room where the bed was. We'd finished talking about how we could get the most out of Vikorn's credit card before an enraged organ hunter sent an assassin to kill me—half joking, half not—so now it was my turn to listen. But it was not a new story, it was an old one that kept pressing on Chanya's mind like a thorn. An earnest look appeared on her face that signaled she was about to go intellectual.

"Dorothy just can't get it out of her head that all Thai whores are slaves. It's amazing. The idea that a woman would go on the game voluntarily, accept it like a challenge even, test herself that way to show she's tough enough, beautiful enough, clever enough with men, sometimes even enjoy it—sometimes *really* enjoy it—it's like it would destroy one half of her worldview. I've shown her all the evidence, but she goes blind when she sees anything she doesn't like. A *farang* like her thinks that a prostitute is some kind of being, an entity in her own right, whereas it doesn't really occur to the girls that *prostitute* as a word is any more than a nominal convenience—not even a description; what they *are* is women, daughters, mothers, farmers, and members of a rural community—all those things that traditionally form the sense of *being* in the ontological sense."

She paused for breath, then continued, "I know of at least thirty girls who had breast transplants during their working lives, then had them removed the day they retired. They hung up their tits, you could say, washed their hands of the whole city, and returned to their home villages as if nothing had happened. Therefore they do not lose their identity when they sell their bodies, so that the profession of prostitution is never more than an economically driven distraction. *Farang*, on the other hand, are unable to see the sale of real biological sex—as opposed to fantasy sex in movies and pornography—as identical in nature to the sale of any other commodity like tomatoes or mangoes. It doesn't make any sense. If one were to impose any *logical* value system, one would have to say the *farang* position is schizophrenic in that it encourages and exploits an obsession with sex but at the same time denies consummation to anyone who wants the convenience of paying for it with cash. Which is a lot more honest in most cases than pretending the flavor of the month is the lover of a lifetime. But for me the question is, why do *farang* get to live in a science fiction universe while the rest of us have to deal with reality for them? I finally told her she had to spend a night with me sitting in a corner at your mother's bar. I called your mother, and she said it was okay, so long as Dorothy doesn't scare off the customers."

I said, "What does *ontological* mean?"

She looked at me, laughed, and said, "Sorry. You didn't want to hear that mouthful when you've just come home."

She let a couple of beats pass, embarrassed maybe to have

intimidated me with her big words, then gave a little jump and said, "Look at what an anonymous admirer sent me today." We went to her PC, and she clicked on an icon so we were looking at her e-mail window. Then she double-clicked on one of the items. Now we were looking at a screen that was blank save for two naked feet. While we watched, the feet slowly grew legs, then knees, then thighs. Chanya threw me a glance, grinned, and turned back to the screen. A further unscrolling revealed a tan penis and testicles, pubic hair, a mass of highly developed stomach muscles, an impressive hairless chest, terrific pecs, biceps, and triceps—a more perfect figure of a man you could not hope to find in your electronic inbox. But the scrolling stopped at the neck. It was a beautiful body without a head. Now a message in crimson Thai script was slowly spelling its way across the screen where the head should have been: *I love you.*

I said, "Who's it from?"

She shrugged and used her mouse to point to the sender's address, which was a collection of numbers. "Anonymous."

I said, "I didn't know they'd started targeting women like that. I get about a hundred a week. Women, I mean."

"Naked without heads?"

"Nope. They all have heads, as far as I can remember. Some have dicks in their mouths. One two weeks ago had an erection in both ears, and she was holding two others in her hands."

Before we fell asleep, Chanya said, "Do you care about dying?"

"In some ways yes, in other ways no. How about you?"

"I feel the same. It's a filthy world. I went to temple today—I think I had a breakthrough."

"How?"

"I finally understood—but it's unnamable. Afterward I realized I didn't mind dying. Even if you weren't there, I could handle it—I never felt that way before."

"Sounds like the real thing."

"But when I came home, I got angry with Dorothy, and the Unreal grabbed me all over again."

"I know the feeling. Try being a cop."

"Yes, I thought about that. I thought about how the more you get involved in the world, the lonelier it gets. I understood you a bit more, maybe. Is it like you're in some underground cave system and only connected to the light by a string that could snap any minute?"

"Exactly like that."

"And for you I'm that string?" By way of answer, I slipped my hand between her thighs, right up to the top: the origin of life. There was nothing erotic about the gesture, it was too childlike for sex. She responded by holding my cock in the same way. "But if you rely on me too much, then you've lost your own center—your whole life will depend on the whim of the unknown, namely me."

"Did you get all this from a book?"

"That's what you're afraid of, isn't it? That you've lost me to books?"

I withdrew my hand. I did not say, *Not only books*. This was not a good moment to mention the rumors.

5

In the morning I woke to feel the world on my shoulders, which is where it normally sits. I know there are other cops all over the planet who feel the same way. The steady accumulation of human dirt—let's call it evil—makes it a little harder, day by day, to find the light. On the other hand, I also felt a new thrill: this case was a big one, whatever way you looked at it. Maybe it would be the trump to get me out of the hole forever? Remember that Leonard Cohen song: *"The card that is so high and wild he'll never need to deal another"*? For a second I allowed my ego to inflate; I saw my name in headlines: foreign media flashing my mug around the world; the Nobel Prize for law enforcement. I also tried to see the good I might be doing—but that detail eluded me.

Chanya was already up, making coffee called three-in-one: the sugar and creamer are included in the little sachet with the coffee. She handed me a mug while I was still in bed. "I've been thinking about your new case. Isn't it kind of—ah—"

"Morally ambiguous."

"Yes, that's the phrase. Isn't it?"

"A crime without a victim, most of the time. Most of the time the illegal organ sale is voluntary. The real crime is letting people get that poor. The real crime is capitalism, of which this trade is an inevitable product. Yes."

"I hadn't gone into it that deeply. I was thinking of the beneficiary—I mean, lives are saved, right?"

"And ruined. There are young men all over the third world, from Manila to Rio de Janeiro, who were conned into selling one kidney for a thousand or so dollars, usually to some Caucasian old person who abused their body in their youth and wasn't going to live more than another five years anyway. Now those young men have lost their youthful good health, they fall sick easily, suffer from diminished energy, and are unable to do heavy manual work, so they get rejected by their tribes. Girlfriends and others know what the saber-shaped scar on their abdomen means. Shame and a sense of deep self-betrayal dogs their lives. Organs are very personal things. You sell one, it's the same as saying you don't really exist except as an economic unit. They become very angry young men."

Chanya listened with wrinkled brow. "I think Dorothy gave me a paper to read on organ trafficking. It was her second specialization after prostitution in Southeast Asia—they sort of go together in her mind. Maybe we should consult her. She claims the trade might have altered the whole rhetoric of gift, especially in India."

"Then there are the cases where the donor doesn't agree to donate at all. It's a feature of modern wars. Civilized man doesn't take scalps—he strips POWs of organs, like an environmentally aware butcher, not wasting a single valuable item."

"Really? That happens?"

"The Kosovar army harvested human organs like rice in October."

Now Chanya was ready to go to her computer, which would trap her spirit for the rest of the day. I asked her to first try to book me a business-class ticket to Dubai. The task interested her, and in a few minutes she'd found out the prices, the flight times, and how to register for air miles. We sat together at the monitor to see how well the black Amex card worked. It worked fine. Now we printed out my ticket on the rickety little printer that always seemed on the point of dying. We exchanged a glance.

After breakfast I called Vikorn to tell him I had the ticket; now I needed some way of contacting the Vultures. Vikorn had it at his fingertips: "The name the lead vulture is using at the moment is Lilly Yip. Here's her cell phone number." He called out a ten-digit number with a Hong Kong prefix, which I wrote down. "When you get to Dubai, call her. She'll come to your hotel to check you out. She does a lot of work for Zinna, but she also knows me. I might send her a little something she'll like."

"Really?"

"You'll understand when you meet her. She's a pro."

"You've already given her immunity, if this thing really takes off?"

Vikorn coughed and ignored the question. "What time is your flight?"

"It's a red-eye tomorrow morning."

"Okay. Listen. I mentioned you to the election committee. They're happy for you to do this, but they want to meet you."

I looked into the mouthpiece of my phone as if it were malfunctioning. I repeated his words slowly. "Your election committee is happy for me to carry out a law and order assignment? Well, I'm certainly relieved about that."

"If you keep on being sarcastic, I'll take away your black Amex and replace it with a parking ticket. Get your ass over here at eleven A.M."

Chanya caught the expression on my face when I closed the phone. "I have to go see Vikorn and his election team at eleven," I tell her. "I think they're going to brief me about my law and order assignment."

"Wow," Chanya said. "This is getting seriously Californian."

As I was knocking on Vikorn's door I heard American voices that suddenly stopped. Instead of the usual "Yeah" from the boss, Manny opened the door. I remembered that Manny spoke English and often interpreted for Vikorn when he needed to talk to Miami.

What was shocking to me at this moment was the new sofa. It was beige leather and looked Italian and quite incongruous. Vikorn prided himself on his bare wooden boards and couple of hard chairs for hard cops to sit on while he dished out orders. I think he must have told Manny to go buy the most expensive sofa she could find, and now here it was supporting two American bottoms, one female, the other male. There was a third stranger, an older American man who had been given a chair that, though old and retrieved from some store-room somewhere, nevertheless had arms and therefore could be said to be the equal in protocol of Vikorn's own chair, which also had arms. The two armless chairs had been relegated to a position in the corner, but now Manny brought me one to sit on.

The two men and the woman owned in common a specifically North American seriousness, which seemed to freeze nerve endings in the area of the cheeks and mouth. I knew instinctively not to appear too human around those people.

"Sonchai, how nice to see you." Vikorn beamed.

I threw him an incredulous look, which I had to modify immediately. "Great to see you too, Colonel," I said. We had spoken in Thai, but Manny was under instructions to translate everything into English. "The Colonel said, 'How nice to see you,' and Detective Jit-pleecheep said it was nice to see the Colonel too," Manny explained. The three guests allowed their lips to part in nanosecond smiles that bloomed and self-erased while Vikorn told me everybody's names. The woman was called Linda, the older man was Jack, and the younger man sitting on the sofa with Linda (I decided he was older than he seemed: one of those John Kennedy–type faces that look thirty when the owner is at least forty) was called Ben. Vikorn told me he had outlined the bare bones of my trip to Dubai and the basic strategy of making contact with the global organ-trafficking community.

"The Colonel just explained to the detective that he had already outlined to you the bare bones of the detective's forthcoming trip to Dubai and the basic strategy of making contact with the global organ-trafficking community," Manny said.

Now we were waiting for the Americans. The woman and the man on the sofa waited for the older man in the chair to speak. I thought, from the way he was twisted in the chair with his long shanks drawn up like Abraham Lincoln, that Jack must be very tall. He remained immobile, then turned to the woman with his brows raised and said, "Linda?"

Linda nodded thoughtfully, prepared to speak, coughed, remained silent. Nevertheless Jack treated this as a useful contribution and passed on. "Ben?" he said.

"Yeah," Ben said, "I can see the point. The detective here discovers that Thailand is being used by unscrupulous organ traders as a center from which to conduct their evil trafficking. The Colonel busts them — it's like the gold ring. The Colonel not only puts himself on the international law enforcement map, he makes Thailand into the squeaky-clean, non-organ-trafficking, righteous Buddhist center of humane governance of the world. Sure, I can see the upside."

The older man said, "Linda?"

"I don't know, Jack," Linda said.

"Don't know what, Linda?" Jack said from his arm chair.

"I don't know if it would be a plus or a minus for us."

"Surely a plus?" Ben said.

"Take us through that," Jack said.

"Bust someone big in this trade, and you get the attention of the world," Ben said.

"Sure," Linda said, "I got that the first time. But the downside?"

"Take us through the downside, Linda," Jack said.

Linda frowned, then sucked in her left cheek while leaving the right one inflated. "You know," Linda said.

"What?" Jack said.

"It's like, you start to give specific examples of what could go wrong, you end up arguing about the examples?"

"A forest-for-trees thing?" Jack said.

"Exactly that."

"So give us the forest, forget the trees," Jack said.

"Okay," Linda said. "So, it's the whole unknown of this industry. There are no responsible papers on public reaction to organ trafficking, but anecdotal reports indicate we're in serious voodoo territory. I don't mean the science is voodoo, I mean the ordinary uninstructed human reaction. We have to forget the professional oversight for a moment and look at it from a personal point of view. Think about your own favorite organ, Ben," Linda said.

"Bet we know what his favorite organ is," Jack said.

"Okay," Ben said, struggling with a blush. "So, we're talking about my liver."

Linda and Jack smiled wryly at the joke. "No," Jack said, "let's make it your—wait, which is your favorite testicle?"

"My favorite testicle?" Ben said.

"Yeah, the one you're most fond of," Jack said, winking at Linda, who smirked.

"I don't have a favorite testicle," Ben said.

"Sure you do, Ben," Jack said.

"Yes, Ben, sure you do," Linda said.

"It's the one you most like the lady to jiggle and bounce around a bit when you get laid," Jack explained, and looked at Linda.

"Don't look at me, Jack," Linda said, "I don't have one."

Jack looked at Ben and said, "Well?"

"The left," Ben confessed with a pout.

"So, think about all the possessive, tender, and above all proprietorial feelings you have about your left testicle," Linda said. "Then think about someone taking it away from you and giving it to another man."

"Or woman," Jack said.

"Or woman," Linda said. "Now, hold that moment—the point where it's lost and gone forever, that oh-so-very-important part of you—"

"Wait," Jack said. "I think we'd better make it his cock, now I see where you're going."

"We're already committed to the testicle," Linda said.

"Oh, okay. So, your left testicle," Jack said, looking at Ben and jerking his chin. "Close your eyes. Right." Jack looked at Linda.

"Go deep into that very specific personal proprietorial male agony, that nightmare of nightmares, far worse than dying, right?"

"Right," Ben said, keeping his eyes closed.

"Now project that over the population of the third world—like, say, four billion people divided by two gives two billion males with those kind of feelings."

"What kind of feelings we talking about here?" Jack said.

"I already got the message," Ben said, opening his eyes. "Yeah, so what you're saying is, this could all backfire badly owing to the very powerful and unpredictable feelings this new industry provokes in people. Instead of associating the Colonel with a major law and order breakthrough, we might end up with a labeling problem where he gets associated with a Frankensteinian experiment, even though he's the good guy trying to fix it, or, even worse, as the guy preventing people from undergoing life-saving operations by busting the racket. The disgust, loathing, and paranoia could spread to all parties. At the same time you get a medical lobby kicking in defending the industry, and you end up with a public relations oil slick. Yeah, I get that."

"But we do need to at least pay lip service—" Jack murmured.

"Oh, I think we can pay lip service, so long as we all agree we might have to finesse it," Linda murmured back.

As if by common tribal programming, the three Americans seemed to have come to an agreement indecipherable to the rest of us. Now they were looking at me again. The two men kind of glazed over me with their eyes: I was not a member of their secret society, not an initiate, therefore I hardly existed except in the field of basic courtesy. The woman, though, double-checked my face and saw that I had indeed picked up on certain incongruous phrases: *might have to finesse it*; *need to pay lip service*. She gave me a split-second chance to ask the question, but I hadn't decided which way to jump.

"Can we move on to the next item?" Linda said.

Now we were all waiting for Jack, who nodded and put his elbows on the arms of his chair and pressed his palms together at the same time as he kissed the tips of his fingers. He let a lot of beats pass before he said, "What we don't want to have to deal with is a Noriega-type situation."

"Right," Linda said.

"Those photos of the younger Bush on a certain island not a hundred miles from the west coast of Panama—that little punk in jail after Big Daddy's invasion and threatening to tell all—how toxic was that, for Chrissake?" Ben said.

"Bush was a cinch compared to Yeltsin. I never saw so many skeletons in one cupboard," Ben said.

"Yeltsin? This is a breeze in comparison," Linda said. "Try getting instructions out of a terminal alcoholic."

"Yeah, Ben bore the brunt of that one," Jack said with the ghost of a twinkle. Linda coughed. "Except the time he came on to Linda," Jack added.

"If he'd been able to get it up, I woulda shot the creep," Linda said.

"Well, what do we do?" Jack said.

Silence. Now Linda coughed again. Jack looked at her. "We've got to have more detailed data, so we can analyze the risks," Linda said.

"That's right," Ben said.

"So, do we have a conclusion to this meeting?" Jack said.

"Well, I think we let the detective follow present instructions from the Colonel and keep a close eye."

"That's just the present issue—what about security in general?" Jack said.

"Like I said, we need all the relevant data—all of it," Linda said.

"Like with Yeltsin?" Jack said. He shared a dirty grin with Ben, who was delighted.

"You boys," Linda said.

"How'd you get out of it again?" Jack said.

"Chrissake, Jack," Linda said.

"How'd she do it, Ben?" Jack said.

"Kicked him in the balls so hard she nearly killed the client."

Jack's eyes took on a new life. "Yeah. The one time they rushed him to the hospital for non-alcohol-related injury."

"Okay, okay," Linda said.

"So," Jack said. "We stand pat for the moment and let the detective go to Dubai on business as usual, but that doesn't mean we necessarily take the thing any further than that. Good. What was the detective's name again?"

"Jit—plee—cheep," Manny said.

"Right," Jack said.

There was a kind of satisfied pause. The three serious Americans seemed to have talked themselves into a mood of indomitable optimism that made Vikorn smile. There was one more item on the agenda, though, something that had perhaps been alluded to so far only in code. I had a premonition of a knotty problem they were about to share with me. Linda mumbled something impossible for me to catch. Jack mumbled back. Ben said, "Better you than me, Linda." Linda gave him a stern glance but prepared to speak.

She looked at me. "Ah, I wonder if you could help us with this, Detective. Thing is, we know the Colonel here is a genius-level administrator, but—ah—put it down to American insecurity, but it bothers us the way nothing at all is *visible*. I mean, no docs, no computer program—there's nothing for us to look at. How can we know what's supposed to happen next in any of his multiple operations? To do the job properly, we have to know everything he's up to to make sure nothing goes wrong. I mean, with Bush we knew exactly how much coke he did and who he screwed when he was wild, and with Yeltsin we actually took control of his vodka supplier for two months prior to the election. What we thought was—"

"Some kind of project management software, with full security, firewalls, et cetera, that we could have access to, the three of us, or maybe only Jack, whatever, just so we're not working in the dark," Ben said.

"So far the Colonel has been kind of resistant," Linda said.

Manny translated everything to Vikorn, who went on smiling like a gnome.

I spent the rest of the day shopping for clothes to wear in the United Arab Emirates. They say it's one of the richest countries in the world, and I needed to look like a successful organ trader, so I went to the swank men's shops at Chitlom. At Armani, Zegna, and Yves St. Laurent I wanted to pay with my shiny new black Amex, but none of the Thai sales assistants had ever seen one and wouldn't take it, so I had to use a bank machine to get cash. (The machine had heard of black Amex and delivered pronto; if it could have spoken, it would have called me *sir*.) I have a thing about shoes: I can almost never find ones I like, and when I do, I tend to wear them out in months. It took me hours to settle on a pair of Baker-Benjes and some chamois-soft Bagattos. The shopping spree took all day, and I think there must be quite a lot of woman in me because I enjoyed it; we still think like that over here, by the way, DFR. We still have freedom of speech too.

By the time I reached home, I had to take Chanya to the One World Hotel, because she'd arranged to meet Dorothy there for supper; then the three of us were to visit my mother's bar on Soi Cowboy. I wanted to wear my new Zegna pants with my new black Armani shirt with silver studs and my cream linen tropical jacket that comes ready crumpled, but there wasn't time, so I wore generic jeans and a short-sleeve shirt instead. Chanya was wearing tight denims that squeezed her gut and clearly delineated her vagina. She looked deceptively casual in a man-style shirt that was one size too big; but she left the three top buttons undone and every second man we passed tried to see her breasts; she wasn't wearing a bra. Normally retired prostitutes don't play that kind of game, they know too much, but Chanya wasn't dressing for men, she was stealing a little of each man's power as he tried to look down her shirt. I was starting to feel sorry for Dorothy.

Who was already waiting for us in the lobby when we arrived. When she stood up, I thought I understood the problem. When she spoke, I was sure I understood it. Dorothy was about six feet tall and pear-shaped. Her hips were wide and her breasts not large; she liked food too much, so her thighs were fat, and so was her face, which neverthe-less was pleasantly regular, with sky-blue eyes and topped with bright blond hair. She spoke London English with an estuary accent and car-ried with her that unmistakable odor of English depression, which passively asserted that despair was the only reality—but lest you think me cruel, DFR, let me right away explain that, like my partner, I also found myself irked by her for reasons that had little to do with physical appearance. Does the phrase *pretentiously depressed* ring a bell in regard to a certain kind of Brit? (*Clinical chic?* I'm not an expert, although I visited Harrods once with Mum; the john was a member of the Hooray Henry tribe whose net worth was not commensurate with his nasal vowels.) It was mostly her posture that was unattractive; indeed, her face possessed all the charm of an English daisy, with, alas, the droop of a sunflower.

She was dogged though. She doggedly stood to greet us, doggedly smiled at Chanya as if she loved her, doggedly tried not to be afraid of me when Chanya said, "This is my lover. He's a cop and a pimp, he multitasks. Now he's working on a big international case about human organ trafficking—the biggest suspect is a two-woman team."

Dorothy took this not-so-subtle jibe as a mule takes a whipping: just part of being alive. Now I led us to the buffet area, and one of the waitresses showed us to the table Chanya had reserved. Chanya left Dorothy and me at the table while she went to get hors d'oeuvres for all of us. She wanted me to bond with her supervisor to see what I could discover.

Now Dorothy and I were staring at each other across the stark white tablecloth. Dorothy looked down. I said, "So, how do you like working with Chanya?"

"She's very bright. Maybe she's too clever for me. I don't understand her."

"How so?"

"All the progress women have made over the past thirty years. She seems to just want to throw it all away." Dorothy made her blue eyes plead. "How can she accept that any woman would willingly commodify her body?"

"Newton discovered gravity," I explained. "He didn't invent it." Dorothy didn't get it, so I had to say: "She decided to study sociology because she has a scientific mind. She's only interested in the truth. It's important for her. She was on the game herself, she's interested in an accurate description, not . . ." I let my voice trail off. Dorothy was looking more miserable than ever, so I didn't want to say *feminist fantasy*. I didn't want to point out that there were women who knew very little about women. If I could have, I would have gone deeper. I would have explained that Chanya was a country girl who left school at fourteen years old with an exclusively Buddhist worldview, which she found beautiful and comforting. She was on the game for nearly ten years and traveled to America, which made no impact on her views—if anything, it confirmed her Buddhist faith. After our son died, she had nothing much to do, so she studied sociology because I told her it was about people and society. She has an excellent brain and was at the top of her classes. The price she paid was that she had to think like a *farang*. It seemed to her there was something seriously missing in *farang* logic: it only dealt with measurable things and had no way of incorporating the Unnameable—or even basic human nuance—in its calculations. She let that pass, at considerable cost to her peace of mind and personality—you might say she sold an organ, metaphorically speaking. What she demanded in return was that *farang* thinking be faithful to its own terms. Things were fine up to her first and second degrees, but when she started working on her thesis, which required personal creative input and direct fieldwork, she began to discover she had been right all along: *farang* social science was mostly propaganda for *farang* dominance. In former times, DFR, you used exactly the same double-talk to justify the opium and slave trades. She went back to Buddhism and challenged the Western world from there. Starting from Emptiness, it is not so difficult to see clearly: one has less of a stake in fantasy. When Dorothy arrived on the scene, the English sociologist became her favorite pincushion.

Now Chanya was back with hors d'oeuvres for all of us: a little smoked salmon for me, some *somtam* for her, and a great pile of potato salad with smoked salmon for Dorothy. For a second I thought Chanya had gone too far with her sarcasm, but Dorothy tucked into the potatoes with gratitude. For the first time since we met, her mood rose above room temperature, and she was almost beaming. We ate in silence. When the time came for the second course, we each went to serve ourselves. When Chanya and I were alone, I repeated what Dorothy had said about a woman commodifying her body. "For Buddha's sake," Chanya said, "human beings have been commodifying our bodies since the first tattoos. What are mascara and lipstick if not commodifying agents? What about hair dye? *Farang* are so far gone, they are blind to the obvious."

I didn't want to say I wasn't sure exactly what *commodifying* meant in this context. Dorothy returned with two plates, one with roast beef and roast potatoes, the other with oysters and prawns from the seafood bar. She ate quickly, putting it all away within about fifteen minutes. I paid the bill and led the way across the bridge to the Skytrain station, then down again to the other side of Sukhumvit and the tunnel that took us to Soi Cowboy. As we approached the *soi*, we collected more and more participants in the trade, so that now we were in a crowd of middle-aged *farang* men and working girls aged somewhere between twenty and thirty-five. They were on their way to work in denims and T-shirts. Some arrived on the back of motorbike taxis. When we reached the cooked-food stalls at the entrance to Cowboy, a number of the girls eating at the tables had already changed into their working gear, bar uniforms that emphasized busts and buttocks; they were about as naked as they could get without breaking the law. Dorothy turned gray, as if she'd never seen anything like it before. Chanya claimed that Dorothy had done her thesis on Thai prostitution in a pub in South London.

My mother Nong's bar, the Old Man's Club, was about halfway down the street, opposite the Suzie Wong, and when we arrived, the place was hopping. As a former player herself, Nong knew how to pull in the customers. Her advantage over all the other bars was that Colonel Vikorn owned most of the shares, so no cop was ever going to bust her. Consequently she allowed most forms of sexual activity, barring actual intercourse, in the corner of the bar known as the Office. (Johns could call their wives to say they were stuck in the Office and might be late for supper.) My mother's girls tended to make more money than their rivals in other bars, so they were pretty content. The most attractive came here because we paid more: we were surrounded by beauty at its smartest and most avaricious. Chanya went up to Nong, giving her the high respectful *wai* due to the mother-in-law. I kissed her and introduced Dorothy.

Nong led us to a table in a dark spot at the back wall, which nevertheless gave unobstructed views of the Office and the rest of the bar. She called one of her serving girls to bring us drinks and resumed her place on a stool at the end of the bar, where she ostentatiously broke the law by chain-smoking Marlboro Reds. She still looked pretty sexy in black leggings and a bright checked cowboy shirt, with plenty of gold jewelry.

Chanya told me in Thai that she was going to call a girl over to talk to Dorothy and asked me which one would be most suitable. I said it would be better to let Dorothy choose the girl—it would look more objective that way. Chanya agreed and was about to speak to Dorothy when two *farang* men in their early fifties walked in and took up stools at the bar just in front of us. One of them, a blond, owned an Errol Flynn moustache, a flat stomach, and a blazing smile. Immediately two girls in bikinis slipped in between them, but they were quite small, so the *farang* could continue their conversation over their heads. They seemed to be civil engineers and were discussing a project up in the north, near the border with Laos; they were on leave in Bangkok for a few days.

While they were talking the girls went to work on their flies and scooped out their cocks, taking care not to damage the merchandise on the zips. (How many times in my life have I seen that search-and-seizure operation with half-cupped hand that always finds the love object sooner or later, even if it requires excavating as far as the biceps femoris?) The *farang* continued talking about the project for a while, each one shielded from the other by his girl and perhaps not wanting his colleague to see what was happening. Then they broke off for a moment and looked down simultaneously, then up again at each other, and burst out laughing. The girls burst out laughing too. My mother grinned sardonically. Chanya and I both checked Dorothy to see if she had seen the humor, but she was looking at Errol Flynn's erection. Cocks don't age the way faces do, and this one could have belonged to a much younger man, especially considering its apparent virility; it was even bigger than his smile. The glans appeared and disappeared under the brown girl's tiny hand. Dorothy's eyes were like gimlets.

"I guess I better go home and pack," I said. I nudged Dorothy. "Drinks are on the house."

But out on the street I asked myself: *Do I really want to go to the UAE tonight?* I told myself to pause, think about it. The way Vikorn suddenly laid the new case on me, which so far wasn't a case at all, along with his sudden declaration that he was running for governor of Bangkok, and those three very serious Americans—it was all too unreal. And wasn't Dubai Muslim? I looked up and down the famous

soi. Exterior air-conditioning was making misty rainbows in the tropical night, along with a half mile of neon; near-naked girls with welcoming smiles; unresisting johns: and not a girl, man, or *katoey* who
wouldn't have qualified for a stoning under Sharia rules. I imagined
Mum, Chanya, and me tied to stakes at one end of the street and a
gang of yobs in flowing white *kanduras* at the other taking aim, a
builder's truck laden with Halal crushed rocks behind them. I
shrugged. A continuum is a continuum, after all.

6

So there I was at the airport in my new Zegna pants (metallic gray with a sheen; they fell from my hips perfectly, as they should have considering the price). I had decided on a black T-shirt under the cream Armani crushed-linen jacket, Bagattos to pamper my feet. I looked the very model of a modern organ trafficker. At check-in I told the girl under the scarf I had only carry-on, and I made sure she recorded my air miles.

She smiled the way she'd been trained to and said, reading from the computer monitor: "Mr. Jitpleecheep, your medical supplies were safely placed in our refrigerated storage facility at four twenty-three this morning. In view of the emergency, they have already been cleared for customs in Dubai. You have no need to pick them up yourself, our staff at Dubai have arranged for a refrigerated truck to collect them and take them to your hotel." She checked the name of the six-star hotel with me, and although the color had drained from my cheeks, I said: "Yes, thank you." I did not say, *What emergency? What medical supplies?*

When I left the check-in area and passed to air-side, I tried to call Vikorn, but he was not answering his mobile or landline. I sent him an SMS: Emergency medical supplies? When I cooled down a little in the CIP lounge, I realized that the medical supplies were just as ambiguous as everything else. Sure, he could have been using me for a piece of personal trading, but equally the medical supplies could have been part of my cover. Or they could have been both and neither. It was quite possible Vikorn hadn't yet decided whether he was the hammer of organ profiteers or an organ profiteer himself. He liked to keep his options open and maybe he was waiting to see if he would win the election and become governor of Bangkok. This speculation didn't arrive at a conclusion either: As governor, would he drop all his criminal activities and become squeaky clean, or would he use the office for even more personal gain? Was the either/or dichotomy relevant here? Was it ever?

At Dubai the theme was stars: stars on the stainless-steel handrails, stars on the carpets, stars on the ceiling. I should have understood immediately, but I didn't. Only after I'd passed through immigration did I remember: desert stars. When I saw a Bedouin in full flowing white *kandura*, I thought I would have liked to be one such: a life under *les belles étoiles*, the good clean emptiness of the desert, a wholesome existence dedicated to Allah; but he arrived in a big new four-by-four and wore a lot of gold around his neck and wrists. At the six star I let them take a copy of my black Amex and enjoyed the full six-star treatment; I was reminded of a well-run brothel where, once they're convinced of your value, they'll do anything for you, anything at all.

The girl under the scarf told me my box of medical supplies had already arrived and they'd taken the liberty of leaving them in my suite, plugged into an electric socket. She spoke of my mysterious package with respect, as if she'd guessed what it was. I wanted to ask her what *she* thought was in the box. The six-star made me feel like I'd arrived in the future, as I took the noiseless elevator, which whisked me up to the thirty-first floor in about a second without a jolt, so I was left thinking, *How did I get so high so fast?* The medical supplies played on my mind; they made me feel hyper-important and hyper-crooked at the same time. Ever feel that way yourself, DFR, like you're simultaneously winning and losing?

• • •

The suite was all about minimalism and silk: vast with floor-to-ceiling windows that featured sand and sea plus two sailboats with white sails, which had perhaps been hired by the hotel to hang there in the middle of the view. Now the house phone rang: it was the deputy manager; he wanted to know if the suite suited me, or did my taste tend to the more luxurious? He ticked off the names and themes of some of the other suites, and I wondered what this was all about, until I realized someone at reception must have told him about my good friend BlackAm. They probably had a rule: black Amex gets deputy manager treatment. If you were *famous* and owned the dark card, you'd probably get the manager himself, who was certainly a sheikh; you had to be in that country only an hour to realize everyone at the top of a pyramid was a prince.

I told him the suite was fine, then even before I checked the medical supplies, which I couldn't find for a moment, I had a panic attack and called Chanya so I could remember who I was. All I got was the Thai voicemail system, which meant she'd turned off her mobile so she could concentrate on her thesis. Or was she having an affair? Was she glad I was out of the country so she could bang someone she had got the hots for? I didn't want to believe the rumors that she'd developed a friendship with a handsome young cop; that she'd been seen with him. (Every cop shop in the world is a gossip city.) But did she really need a male nude as a screen saver? Why? Was she trying to tell me something? The psychology behind my paranoia was subtle: I'd been finding other women attractive for quite some time; my wisdom body was maybe pointing out that I was not the only one who might be suffering from seven-year itch. Now I saw the box in a corner of the business lounge area of the suite.

It was not of the dimensions I had in mind. When the check-in clerk first said *medical supplies*, my imagination had flashed up a discreet box about two feet long by six inches by six inches. I didn't know where I got the idea that medical supplies would come in boxes like that. I also thought the box would be red or white, or both, with maybe a red cross on it. Then when she talked about a truck, I immediately thought of something huge, maybe the size of a large fridge. Now I had to reprogram: the box was gray with stainless-steel bands and stood about two feet high. It seemed to be a perfect cube with a thick black electrical cable, which emerged at the bottom and was plugged into the wall. When I put my ear to it, I couldn't hear any whirring. Its lid was locked down with combination locks on all four sides, and wherever you looked, you were affronted by black block capitals that said: HEAT SENSITIVE MEDICAL SUPPLIES, KEEP REFRIGERATED, TO BE OPENED BY AUTHORIZED PERSONNEL ONLY. There were other block capitals in other languages which I suppose said the same thing.

In my anxiety about Chanya, I'd changed the profile on my cell phone so that on receipt of an SMS or phone call, it gave a huge space-age whoosh and vibrated at the same time. Now the thing went off in my Zegna pocket and vibrated the hell out of my left testicle:

Honey, sorry I'm not answering the phone. Dorothy has been plaguing me all day about last night, and I just can't listen to her anymore. I have to get on with my work. (Basically she now believes in the re-empowerment of woman through inversion of the public imaginary of the brothel as exclusively male playground. In other words, I seem to be winning, but she's stealing my idea. Yes, something happened, but I don't have time to tell you right now.) I'm so glad you arrived safely, have a great trip. C.

Now I felt terrific (except that she didn't end with *love* C, and I didn't know what a *public imaginary* was); I was ready for the authorized personnel. When nothing happened for an hour, I called Vikorn again, but he was still not receiving calls. I tried out all the sofas and chairs, forced myself to stare at the unreal view, which really existed on the other side of the window (or did it?), and wondered if I should tour Dubai. It occurred to me, though, that this was one place in the world where the tourist DVD might reflect the reality, so I extracted it from the hotel's welcome package and shoved it into the state-of-the-art Sony player.

Here we go: desert music from Arab pipes by someone in New York; now we're playing in the sand with a four-wheel bike—ATVs or all-terrain vehicles, according to the commentary, and don't forget your designer crash helmet. Now it's the crocodile show with a reptile too doped to remember to shut its mouth when the trainer puts his head in it, even though you *really* wish it would—hey, let's take the amphibious bus to the other side of the river, after all, none of the locals do—or maybe golf in the sun for those who want to grow some melanomas? Oh, no, not the monotonous water scooters up and down, round and round the artificial lake—let's go to the airplane acrobatics with the colored smoke, bet you've never seen that before—and to finish, how about the ten-story water slide—don't worry, the brawny slave with the perfect smile is waiting to catch you at the bottom, it's all safe and clean here.

Thank Buddha for DVDs—now I didn't have to do any of that crap. Finally the phone rang. It was reception. "Sorry to trouble you, sir. You have a guest waiting downstairs named Madame Lilly Yip. Do you want to come down to collect her, or shall I have someone bring her up to you?" A cough. "Or shall I tell her you are indisposed?"

Something gaped in the middle of my stomach. I said, "Please bring her up," and closed the phone.

I couldn't stop looking at the perfect cube squatting in the corner of the room. A bell rang softly and sonorously; I went to the door. The first person I saw was a burly bellhop in hotel livery; someone was standing behind him. He made sure I wanted to receive the woman I couldn't see—he didn't mind being rude to her, she wasn't a guest.

"Yes, please let her in." He stood aside.

7

She was younger than I expected: early thirties, jacket and three-quarter-skirt combination, Chinese of the tall willowy kind—I could imagine her leaning on a humped stone bridge in one of the gardens of Suzhou; sophistication to freeze an erection on any man except a horny aristocrat; beauty worn like a personal fortune that is implied in every detail. She liked the impression she was making on me as she extended a perfect product of the manicurist's art: "Mr. Jitpleejeep? Lilly Yip. I understand you have something for me?"

"Yes."

When I didn't say anything else, she smiled approvingly, as if I were a fellow professional who knew the ropes. Now she took a piece of paper out of her designer handbag. It was an irrevocable letter of credit to the value of $200,000, payable to a corporation registered in Geneva. I supposed the corporation belonged to Vikorn, but I didn't see how I could let her have the box until I'd got approval from the Colonel, and I could not understand why he hadn't returned my calls.

I allowed an awkward pause to intervene, covered up by closing the door; I became fascinated by how smoothly it shut and opened, noted that I'd not dented her perfect poise, and said, "I'm afraid my principal hasn't been in touch since I arrived an hour ago." When she frowned, I said, "Maybe you'd like to check the merchandise while we're waiting?"

An unplanned twitch corrupted the cosmetics for a moment. Irritation? Excitement? It was impossible to be sure. "Yes, of course."

"You have the combination?" I said. She looked at me as if something were wrong, as if I were stupid. I said, "Of course you do," and led her to the cube.

She quickened her step as she approached, apparently forgetting me. When she reached the cube, she stabbed in the combination numbers from memory. I was surprised that every lock had a different number and that she seemed to know each one by heart. I walked over to help her with the lid. She seemed excited. Together we lifted. I took the full weight of the lid and stepped back. Now I was seeing her at an angle that caught the hollow of her left cheek from behind; I was looking at the jaw of a Manchurian wolf.

Under the lid there was a layer of high-tech packing material, and under that a layer of smaller cubes. Something in the main cube started to whirr, and some wisps of condensation collected on the surface. She took out one of the smaller cubes, which seemed to be made of plastic, opened the lid, removed some more packing material, gave a soft gasp, and nodded at me to look. I leaned over her. It was a perfect human eye with dark iris: moist, almost tearful as if on the point of telling a sad story. "It's beautiful," she murmured and looked up at me for confirmation. I wanted to puke, but I said, "Yes, perfect."

"Where is your fridge?"

I jerked my chin in the direction of the six-star fridge. It seemed she must examine each eye, so we stored the examined ones temporarily in the hotel refrigerator, crowding out the Evian and the tinned caviar. One thousand seven hundred and sixty-four human eyes, none of them blue, gray, or green. To break the monotony, I leaned over her shoulder halfway through the quality-control exercise and said, "Chinese?"

She cocked her head, peered more closely with her lips quivering. "Korean. From the North."

Now we put them all back in the mother cube one by one, each in its own jewelry box like a gigantic gem, and closed the lid. We'd been working for more than an hour, and I was exhausted by the tension. Lilly Yip hadn't broken a sweat. My cell phone whooshed.

"What's happening?"

"Where have you been?"

"In a traffic jam. I forgot I'd turned off my cell phone. Everything okay? You've made contact with Lilly?"

"She's here now."

"Good. She's given you an ILC?"

"Yes."

"For two hundred thousand dollars payable to my corporation in Geneva?" He gave the name of the corporation.

"Yes."

"Okay. Let her take them away."

"Not until you tell me where you got the merchandise."

"Don't worry, it's a cadaver-only trade."

I wanted to ask how the former owners of the eyes became cadavers, but Lilly Yip was listening while pretending to look at the view. I didn't put it past her to understand Thai. I closed the phone. "That was my principal. It all seems to be in order."

She nodded and fished her phone out of her handbag. She spoke in fluent Arabic. Then, without asking, she went to the house phone on the desk in the business end of the suite and again spoke in Arabic. She turned to me with a smile out of *Vogue*, Shanghai edition. "A security team will pick them up in thirty minutes. If you confirm with reception that they are allowed to remove the container, we can take a stroll through the Gold Souk. I think this is your first visit to Dubai, no? We can have some lattes at Starbucks."

Her English was finishing-school perfect. I lifted the house phone to call reception.

8

In Dubai's Gold Souk all that glittered was at least eighteen carat. I strolled side by side with Lilly in my top-of-the-range trafficker's kit, so we looked like a brace of beautiful Asian billionaires (probably childless by choice but who might adopt a half-dozen third-world orphans for the cameras), at the same time wondering if some of the local eye problems didn't originate here; I was looking forward to the muted colors of Starbucks. Wherever you put your elbow, there was some garish yellow object demanding attention: window after window, shelf after shelf was crammed with that highly polished kind of gold that, from a distance, is indistinguishable from brass. To our left were ten-chain necklaces laden with heart motifs that surely only a weight-lifter could wear; to our right, browsing Muslims examined the very latest in superfine yellow webs to patch on any remaining area of unadorned flesh. It was one of those terraced malls popular in the East where you can look up at level after level of distilled ostentation designed to burn your retinas into submission.

Now here was the coffee shop: good old corporate identity, I would have recognized that couch anywhere in the world. It was midday and most good Muslims were on their knees in the gilded mosques, so Starbucks was almost empty save for a *farang* couple with two brats who were moaning about the size of the swimming pool at their luxury hotel. I didn't know why Lilly had brought me here, but I was sure it was not for a romantic interlude.

Or was I? I'm a humble, self-effacing Buddhist, but I was brought up in the flesh trade. Lust does subtle things to women's faces, and the light around Lilly had shifted from ultraviolet to something lower down the spectrum. She seemed younger, more impish. This was a shape-changer for sure, with the dough to buy a lot of enigma. In the circumstances I had to wonder which, if any, of my organs she might be interested in. Maybe it was shrewd of her to have chosen Starbucks: you could be anyone you liked in a place like this. Dropping the French-style hauteur, she insisted on carrying our tray, commanded the milk and sugar stand—I told her two packets of Equal and a nuance of nonfat, please—and led me to a sofa where we could sit and watch the gold go by.

"So, how did you get into the business?"

She had sipped at her soy latte, dabbed her lips with a napkin, and dropped the opening question without looking at me; but she followed up with a stabbing glance that seemed to penetrate under the flesh, right to the gristle. I had to walk a middle path here. If I claimed to be a fellow professional, she'd nail me with a whole load of science that I wouldn't understand. On the other hand, I did just sell her 1,764 human eyes.

"Actually, I'm not really in the business, but I would like to be. I found a principal, talked him into using me as a go-between. I guess I'll just take it from here. You know, whatever comes through the door?"

She sipped the latte, gave the table her full concentration, and said, "Come off it, Detective," and sipped some more latte, then looked up at me to see what effect she'd had.

"I, I, I—"

"You're working for Vikorn, you've got to be. There are only two men in Thailand who could have delivered that merchandise so quickly, and the other one always calls me direct. Your Colonel got mad at me five years ago because I won a bet with him, and he's a seriously bad loser." She looked me in the eye and laughed. "Asian male pride is quite as ridiculous as Western male pride."

I said, "Oh. Yes. I suppose that's true." Her laugh was gay, hearty, sincere. Or was it? *Like a wolf she looked, when we lifted that lid.*

"So tell me, has the price of smack gone through the floor, or is the DEA up his backside so he needs to diversify? There are plenty of drug barons who are seeing the light and getting into the organ trade, where there's practically no law enforcement and no tax. I could give you the names of twenty mid-rankers from Colombia who sell kidneys, livers, and eyes these days and sleep better for it."

"He says things have changed since he last looked into it."

Perhaps I had pressed a secret switch of some kind. She gave me the naked look of appraisal, then said, "You don't know a damned thing about it, do you? He picked you because you speak English and know how to dress? You're a peasant boy from up-country?"

"He wants you to teach me the ropes. That's what he said."

I thought I had at last surprised her. She pondered for a moment. "Why not? So long as Vikorn delivers, I can find a use for you."

We both paused when two men walked in dressed like lawyers who spoke in British accents. They were discussing a local real estate project and how difficult the sheikh-in-charge could be. Lilly stared at them for a moment, seemed to categorize them precisely—I could almost hear her ticking off the points: net worth, personality traits, sexual preferences, corruptible or not—and turned away. "I can't initiate you here. Let's meet at my hotel in an hour. It's the other six star, you know the one I mean?"

At the other six star the staff uniforms were not the same, and you beheld the sailboats in the bay from a quite different angle. In the lift I stood behind a burly bellhop until we reached the highest floor. He rang Lilly's bell, keeping his body between me and the dear valued guest until she had confirmed she wanted to see me.

Up until this moment I had been quite interested to discover what theme of suite she had chosen. Had she gone for minimalist, or overblown Oriental, or something in between? Now I lost interest in the suite because for a second I did not recognize the woman who was welcoming me into her sanctum. She was wearing an après-tennis short-sleeve V-neck cotton pullover, a pair of white shorts, and hotel slippers that revealed her toenails, which had been painted with individuated flower patterns. Now I saw she had done the same to her fingernails. She could have been ten years younger, and there was even a twinkle of preppy mischief in her eyes as she welcomed me in with a French kiss on one cheek, then offered her own for me to reciprocate. Even more impressive than her genius for shape-changing was her intuition: her persona of an hour ago I had found intimidating and sexually off-putting. Now I thought her sexy as hell.

"You changed," I said.

She produced a smile and led me gaily into the suite.

I could have kicked myself for not coming as someone else and wondered if my days as apprentice organ hunter were not already numbered. Meanwhile I was impressed with the suite, which didn't go at all with the new Lilly. It was perfectly executed belle époque, exactly like the interior of Maxim's, in Paris, where my mother's client Truffaut used to take us for lunch at least twice a week. I was so hit with nostalgia, I could have raised the hots for one of the lady lamps. I wanted to play the girl, tell Lilly the eyes and her personality change had left me feeling dizzy. I needed to sit down but was afraid to show weakness.

She led me to a giant sofa and a low glass table with a fruit bowl big enough to breed sharks in. She was imitating the snake in *Jungle Book*, with its deep-throat gurgle—not to mention Eve herself—when she asked, "Would you like an apple?" I couldn't help it, I broke into peals of laughter.

A Mozart sonata suddenly erupted from her cell phone. She listened for a moment, then spoke in impeccable French: "Yes, tomorrow, first-class, three in a row, one window, correct." She pressed a couple of buttons on the phone, said, "Excuse me," then spoke again, this time in a language that sounded Chinese, although I could not tell which dialect. She closed the phone, chucked it playfully to the other end of the sofa, and cocked her head to see if I had any questions.

I did have one. As a semilinguist myself, I was jealous. "Tell me, Lilly, how is it you speak so many languages fluently?"

Lilly picked up an apple—not a golden delicious but a big green one full of juice—and took a bite. She spoke with her mouth full. "It's all thanks to Dad and Granddad. The old man was a big industrialist in Shanghai. When he saw Mao was going to win the civil war, he put his entire factory on a ship and moved everything and everyone to Hong Kong. He was an old-style Confucian. Appreciated bound feet on women, especially his wives and his mistresses, and liked to relax with an opium pipe on a Friday night." Lilly looked at the apple, perhaps at the big chunk she had taken out of it with her perfect teeth. "He brought my father up very strictly, which is to say Dad learned how to obey and that was about it. When the old man died, my father didn't know what to do about anything, so he imitated the British. He got a British nanny for my sister and me when we were hardly more than zero years old. When you grow up bilingual, you can pick up languages very easily, like picking up shells from the seashore.

"We didn't like the British nanny much—she was built like a bulldog and went all red and blotchy when she was angry. She believed in spanking, so when we wanted to get rid of her, we exaggerated and told Dad she was a sadistic lesbian—we were very precocious and loved learning about weird things from the *Encyclopaedia Britannica*. He was so shocked that lesbianism existed that he sacked her on the spot without making inquiries. Anyway, our English was better than our Putonghua at that stage, so we didn't need her.

"In those days the Brits thought the French were the top of the cultural league, so we got a French governess. She was a total pain in the ass with rules for everything and this nasty high-pitched arrogance. She always dressed impeccably, so we found ways of messing up her clothes and hair. Over time the sustained disorientation sent her psychotic—literally. She called it *Chinese torture*. They had to take her away in an ambulance, but we were pretty much perfect in French by then.

"Next was a German, a hyper-hygienic bitch with an enormous bosom. When we'd learned the language, we told Dad about the Nazis. He only knew about Japanese genocide during the war, so he freaked out and got rid of her. Next was an Italian. She was great. Unbelievably lazy, very soft and indulgent, but she had to have sex with a new man every month to prove she was irresistible. Unfortunately, Mum found out and sacked her." She proceeded to munch. "Actually, the real center of our family—the *foyer*, as the French say—was the Fukienese maid. She was mum, dad, sister, grandmother all in one. We adored her and took care of her in her old age. She died a few years ago, and we gave her the big Chinese funeral with tons of hell money and cognac. We cried for a month. Fukienese is our real mother tongue."

Lilly gave an exaggerated toothy grin and made rings around her eyes with thumbs and index fingers. I guessed the idea was a caricature of the Chinese face, which might have been crude from anyone else but from her was hilarious. Her new persona—call it Lilly II—was a lot of fun. I shook my head.

"And the Arabic?"

She threw me a knowing look. "That came later. We were in our twenties before we realized that the big money wasn't necessarily in the West anymore. As I said, Daddy was very out of touch. Standard Arabic isn't difficult, we cracked it in six months, and you get access to the whole of North Africa."

"Am I going to meet your sister?"

Lilly took another bite out of her apple. "How d'you know you haven't already?"

I must have been getting slow. It took quite a few beats before I saw the answer to the conundrum. "She's your twin?"

"Got it in one, Captain Kirk."

I felt a shiver run down my spine, as if I were penetrating a mystery that was not really mine. I didn't believe Vikorn ever got this far. "What's her name?"

"Polly."

I let a few minutes pass in silence. "Which one are you?"

She took another bite out of the apple. "Not telling you."

I groaned. "Just tell me this, are you the same woman I met this morning, sold one thousand seven hundred sixty-four eyes to, and went to Starbucks with?"

"Excuse me one minute," she said, and stood. I watched her walk through an arch at the other end of the suite, I supposed to the master bedroom. I was left alone with the giant fruit bowl and the view. Those two sailboats were starting to seriously get on my nerves: Why didn't they move? Didn't mankind invent sail for exactly that purpose? Was everything upside down in toy town?

There was a movement beyond the arch. A woman appeared. So far as I could tell, it was the same woman I met this morning, done up in the same *Vogue* costume, exhibiting the same HiSo hauteur, but with a sly smile flickering over her face. So now I had to restate the conundrum: Was this one woman posing as two, or two women posing as one? And what did it all have to do with the market price of kidneys? Nothing in my background had prepared me for this kind of challenge—perhaps if I'd gone to an Ivy League college or a Swiss finishing school, I would have had the appropriate social response at my fingertips. (*Is that you, darling, or are you the to-die-for little doppelgänger?*) As it was, I simply stared like a spaced-out peasant.

She walked over to me in an exaggerated catwalk gait, carefully smoothed her backside, then sat demurely next to me, laid an impeccable hand on my forearm, and said, "Forgive us, but if you want to work with us, you'll have to get used to our little *jumelles* ways." Then she broke out into a grin that belonged to the other one—if there was another—reached for the apple she—or the other—had half-eaten, took a huge non-*Vogue* bite out of it, and burst into hysterics.

All women are aware of the debilitating power of subtle mockery; this one (or two) had it down to a fine art. In my preferred persona as police officer, I have always known how to handle it: male authority figure trumping female frivolity with a higher, realer purpose. As apprentice organ trafficker, though, I had to confess it was doing my head in. Somehow she'd managed to shrink me, and I thought it best to retreat and regroup. I stood, as an inevitable response to my own thought process, without having figured out an excuse to leave. "Ah, I, ah, forgot something—I'd better go back to my hotel," I mumbled like an embarrassed kid.

"Oh, if it's only *something*, surely it can wait?" Lilly said, also standing.

Now she blocked off one avenue of retreat with her tall, elegant form. I turned to walk around the coffee table in the opposite direction, and was just in time to slip past her as she tried to head me off. It seemed we were engaged in a noncontact form of martial art in which each protagonist occupied an inviolable personal space, which was to be used as a kind of colonizing gambit. Lilly was very good at this silent game, which had me searching for a nonviolent way of getting out of there, and her cleverly dominating the ground zero of the door. We had chased each other from the tropics of the coffee table to the northern reaches of the fridge before I was able to slip away and walk with huge strides (running would have been an admission of defeat and probably against the rules) to the door. I had the latch under my finger when she arrived and jammed the door with her foot. I cannot do justice to the expression that flickered across her face for a split-second, as though she had been taken over by an ungovernable rage, which nevertheless passed in a flash. Now with a sudden change of heart, she opened the door and said with a big chummy smile, "Please do come back this evening about nine o'clock. All will be revealed. Sorry about our little game. You're so incredibly cute, we couldn't resist. After all, we're only girls, you know."

As I was leaving the hotel's atrium, the heat socked me in the head and my body went into shock. My lungs had trouble with the superheated air they were trying to process. To cover the half mile between the two six stars seemed an impossible task. It dawned on me that after a lifetime in the tropics I was experiencing the first symptoms of heat-stroke: there is no heat like desert heat at two in the afternoon. It all added to the surreal feeling of the place, along with a pair of twins who could have been one schizophrenic female organ trader. Instead of grabbing a cab I started to run, in a panic, and my mind flipped. I saw Lilly Yip holding a human eye in the palm of her hand as if it were a living creature and crooning over it: *It is sooo beautiful* . . . Then I saw an army of eyeless ghosts marching reproachfully toward me.

Back in my room I drank cold water from the refrigerator, which is supposed to be the worst thing you can do when you overheat, and checked my e-mail. When I saw there was a message from Chanya, I immediately started to feel better, at the same time feeling pathetic that my well-being should have depended on a few lines from her:

Sorry to take so long to write to you darling, I got so caught up in Dorothy's new thing and trying to finish my f**cking thesis at the same time I even forgot to be jealous of your exotic new case in exotic Dubai—thank Buddha all the girls are Muslims and risk getting stoned to death if they look at your beautiful face the wrong way— yes, I'm missing you and feeling horny. Speaking of which: did you brilliantly interpret my cryptic SMS? Well, this is the fuller version. You remember that middle-aged blond farang with the moustache who was sitting there having a cock massage with D's eyes on stalks? Well, he noticed and being obviously a Don Juan was quite flattered and also assumed D was on the game, so he came over to our table and bought us drinks, told us his name was Jimmy Clipp, and after about five minutes he asked D if she would like him to pay her bar fine—and she said yes! Just like that! Your mum of course is a total pro and kept a straight face while he paid D's imaginary bar fine (which your mum gave to me to give back to D because D's not on her payroll—yet!) and D didn't look me in the eye again but just sat there with that dogged look on her face like she was waiting for a bus while your mum gave the john his change and then D followed Jimmy Clipp out into the street (I got up and went to the door to watch) and across to the short-time hotel and I had to put my fist in my mouth because I was literally hysterical with laughter. Got to rush, more in a couple of hours when I take a break. Love love love, C.

9

Ever do something you absolutely know is going to lead you into a whole heap of trouble, DFR, but you just cannot seem to stop yourself? I don't mean the kind of thing you're forced into against your will—say, doing something illegal under pressure from the boss—trading in human organs would be a good example. No, I mean something you are quite free to refuse, where the pressure is minimal to nonexistent? Something that from one perspective makes the hair on the back of your neck stand on end, but from the other possesses an irresistible attraction? So the answer to your question, DFR, is: Yes, I did get myself tarted up and took a cab to Lilly's six star to arrive fashionably late at about twenty past nine that fateful evening. Standing behind the bellhop outside her door, I was all in a dither about which one she would be. Would I at last find out if there were indeed two of them? Or was I dealing with a total psycho here, albeit a psycho of genius?

The door opened on a chain, a soft female voice spoke in Arabic, and the bellhop nodded at me and strode off down the corridor. I watched the door close so the chain could be unlatched and waited. The door remained slightly ajar. After thirty seconds I pushed and—feeling like a jerk—called out: "Lilly? Oh, Lilly!" No answer. I pushed harder. The door did not resist. Lights were tastefully dimmed. I closed the door behind me and made my entrance into the vast lounge area. I was pleased that it was too dark to see the sailboats, assuming they were still there. Instead I fixated on a tall, slim female figure standing by the window. The woman by the window did not move, and neither did I, for I was suddenly in the grip of an intense speculation of the erotic kind. It went like this:

I pray in aid the ancients who meditated on the erotic possibilities of twin sisters. (Don't ask me which ancients—we all know what horny and imaginative buggers they were.) Suppose, for example, Twin One (let's call her Lilly) stood before you in a man's long-sleeve white shirt and nothing else. And suppose, further, that one made passionate love to her, after which one became, so to speak, mere putty in her hands. Now, by presenting appropriate proof, she demonstrates beyond reasonable doubt that she is not Lilly but Polly: Are you head over heels in love with Polly or with Lilly? Or has the whole experiment busted the great taboo of courtly love by demonstrating existentially that crotches do not differ much in quality and kind from one lover to another, so what/who exactly were you in love with anyway? Don't answer unless you intend a voyage into the mysteries of the *I* versus the *Not-I*, DFR.

Well, I have news. The lady standing at the window turned to face me, and guess what? She was wearing a man's shirt with all the buttons done up except the top three (the shirt was black, not white) and was this very minute tapping the glass-top table with her finely manicured left index finger, transmitting a nerve-wracking mixed message of impatience, disdain, vulnerability, and impenetrable cunning combined with a most convincing and charming invitation for sophisticated erotic adventure expressed in the faux innocence of her eyes and the pleasing scent of musk, which may have been her own or that of a butchered doe, it was hard to say. Now what?

The bathroom door opened, and—yes—an identical woman appeared wearing—yes again—a man's shirt with all the buttons done up save the top three and apparently nothing else. No prizes for guessing this shirt was white.

I must have still been disoriented by the eyes, and by the association of 1,764-divided-by-two-equals-882 cadavers with these two beauties. My knees turned to jelly. I grabbed the back of a chair to steady myself, then decided to accept defeat and sit down, thus fatally lowering myself before the two of them, who were now transformed into Giant Female Powers towering above me. I felt a twitch in my left cheek, a frown disfiguring my brow, an erotic-neurotic sweat both cold and hot causing my body to shiver while my eyes flitted from Blackshirt to Whiteshirt. "Will you please tell me who is who?" I gurgled.

Whiteshirt walked slowly toward me on exquisite bare feet, her shapely thighs appearing and disappearing under the impeccably laundered shirt (I'm pretty sure it was of the Arrow brand) until she reached my chair, whereupon she bent over me in a way that ensured an unobstructed view of her breasts. She passed her fingers through my hair. "Stop pretending it matters. Do what we want, and we'll be yours for the weekend."

"What do you want?"

"You have to guess. One clue: we've booked three first-class seats to Nice for tomorrow morning."

It was one hell of a moment for a quiz. Fortunately, as a Bangkok cop I had had a great deal to do with Chinese from the Swatow region, and on the flight over I had studied the airline's most popular routes. The reason why Dubai–Nice is a favorite in the Muslim Middle East did not escape me. I had the answer in less than a second. "You want me to take you to Monte Carlo?"

Four black Chinese eyes opened wide with delight, and the two women burst out laughing. "Smart," said Whiteshirt, "very, very smart."

"Of course we could go on our own, but we're old-fashioned."

"It's the way we were brought up."

"We're strictly Confucian."

"And you are very, very cute when you're horny."

More laughter. The erotic moment dissolved. They both disappeared for a moment, then returned, one, whom I shall call Lilly, in the preppy uniform of late afternoon, and the other, Polly, in the *Vogue* business kit.

"Shall we go into the business area?" Polly said. "I wanted to show you some e-mails."

The thirty-six-inch monitor sat on a teak credenza under a window.

Polly clicked on her black wireless mouse, while Lilly sat at the coffee table and dropped large black grapes into her mouth. On the monitor the Yahoo e-mail window opened:

Dear Dr. Black,

I know that's not your real name but that's the one they told me to use. I'm desperate. My husband is all I have left in the world after our only child Sebastian died in a car crash last year. My husband Abe was also in the crash—he was driving the car—and they amputated his left arm from the elbow and both his kidneys and liver are damaged. They won't put him anywhere high on the lists because they're jerks and blame him for the accident because there was alcohol in his blood and since the accident he drinks a lot to bury his sorrow so they decided he wasn't worth saving, even though they would never admit that in court. We have lots of money and we'll pay anything, go anywhere to get our life back. Abe made his first fortune in pornography and the second in Internet gambling, so you can be sure we're good for the dough. I know you maybe can't do much about the arm right now, but that can wait. I can't tell you what misery we're in, otherwise I would never write to anyone like this. Please, please help us, I am on my knees to God every day, I love my husband like no modern woman would understand, he's taken care of me all my life and if he goes I go too. Please, please, Dr. Black, just say the word, give us the account number, whatever, we'll get on a plane yesterday, anywhere, anytime.

Yours very truly, Rita Smith (okay, that's not my name either but I'm scared of the FBI)

Polly was watching my face. I looked up. "What do you think?"

I tried to work out what the question was getting at. She had to prompt me: "How would you rate them as potential clients?"

I shrugged. "How would you?"

Her lips tightened; I seemed to have failed this part of the test. "Triple A."

"How so?"

"Pampered, sentimental, self-pitying, semicriminal, rich, no qualms." She tapped the e-mail. "Generally, women are safer to deal with—they put survival of the family before survival of the species and survival of the ego above everything—but we cover up so much better than men. Now, take a look at this."

She was on the point of showing me another e-mail from another Yahoo account, then paused to lean back and appraise me. "You're so brand-new, you don't know about the cyclosporine revolution, do you?"

"Cyclosporine?"

"Yes. The reason why trade is booming and the likes of Vikorn have decided to give it a second look." She was standing next to me where I sat at the computer. Her white hand of the perfect manicure flicked to take in the view, then came to rest on my shoulder for a moment. I was surprised. With a subtle, almost imperceptible jerk of her chin toward her twin, she lifted the hand from my shoulder. Without a word she clicked on the mouse.

Dear Dr. Pink,

I am in pain. I've been in pain all my life, I couldn't have done anything to deserve it because I've been too sick since childhood to hurt anyone. I am innocent and now I'm forty-two years old and I can't take it anymore. I don't care what you have to do, I don't care who has to die, it's my turn to live a whole day without pain. Get me the fuck out of here. I have the money. Do you hear me? I HAVE THE MONEY.

Yours very truly,

Michael James Conran

She was looking at me, waiting for my reaction. "Well?"

"How would I rate it? I would say a perfect client. Rich, desperate, no qualms."

A shrug. "Sure, but he doesn't tell us what is wrong with him. We only do organ transplants. If he's been in pain since childhood, it's likely something incurable, in the bones, perhaps, or the immune system itself. More likely it's psychological. Someone else's body parts won't help." She tapped the e-mail. "You get lots like this, lots and lots. Whoever thinks life is wonderful doesn't practice medicine. How about this one?" She clicked onto yet another Yahoo account:

> Dear Doctor White,
>
> Sorry I don't speak Inglish so good. I am mother of Chad. My husband bring us to America but he dye. My little girl need diyalisi for kidneys. We don't have insurance. I heard you help poor people, you very good woman. Doctor White, my little girl she need kidneys. We love you Doctore White.
>
> Abena Abeni

We remained silent for a moment. Finally she clicked back to the first e-mail and smiled her *Vogue* smile. "So, do you think you and Vikorn can find a liver for poor Abe?"

A *liver for poor Abe?* "I'd have to ask Vikorn," I heard myself say.

She nodded. A grin, then she cocked her head. "But however rich Abe is, he won't expect to pay more than a few thousand dollars for half a liver. You want to hang on to clients like that. After a few years the second liver starts to fail—that's when you get into the serious money. Second transplants are a serious business and generally you need a whole liver, a perfectly healthy whole liver."

"From a cadaver? Or someone brain-dead?"

"Then you're talking about waiting lists, priority allocation, just-in-time contacts with traffic police or some other authority. That's hard for us in the parallel trade to set up. Perhaps impossible." I gasped. She noticed how I recoiled and scrolled back to the e-mail from Michael James Conran. "You read what the man says. *He doesn't care who has to die.*" She stood up. "If you really want to be a player, this is what you have to realize. All human beings are cannibals when it comes to brute survival. That is really what the trade is all about, no matter how they care to dress it up for the folks at home. Think about it, Detective. But don't take too long. I can get over three hundred thousand dollars for a good-quality whole liver from a recently deceased donor, whether brain-dead, volunteer—or otherwise."

I walked out of the business suite into the silk rugs and damascene chaise longues of the sitting area. The door to the master bedroom had been left ajar; I saw a brilliant white pillowcase, a Turkish bedspread turned back, a pair of naked white feet. Polly caught my gaze and stopped moving for a telling moment. The hairs on the back of my neck stood up; somewhere under my skull prohibited synapses were making a thrilling connection between sex and death. Then I seemed to hear Chanya's voice: *One move, one hint that you're ready for sex, and you're done for. They don't care who dies.*

I coughed. "Cyclosporine," I said. "You were going to tell me about it, then we got distracted."

She nodded, as if conceding that the moment had passed. "Modern solid-organ transplant is decades old. You could date it from the first-ever kidney transplant in 1950 in Illinois, or from the first heart transplant by Christiaan Barnard in South Africa in 1967, but there are plenty of other landmarks. What's new, though, and what has transformed an exotic sideline into a global business that is about to explode, is the discovery and commercial production of cyclosporine. Before, there was the laborious task of matching organs to try to avoid rejection by the recipient's immune system. The new drug changed all that—it suppresses the immune system. It's not quite a case of throwing any working kidney into any body that needs it, but almost. In fact, at the seedier end of the trade, that's pretty much what happens. Of course, the recipient dies in a few years. Even if the new organ functions properly, the immune system is paralyzed by the cyclosporine and the patient starts to grow every kind of tumor imaginable, but without the transplant they would have died sooner. That's an important factor that can't be disputed. Actually, they're kept temporarily alive by the cyclosporine as much as by the new kidney, but who's splitting hairs?"

10

Next morning we shared a limo to the airport. Lilly dressed down in jeans, designer T-shirt, and sandals while Polly, in a navy dress suit, decked herself in gold, especially in the form of bracelets on her wrists. On the plane Lilly took the window seat, Polly took the aisle, and I was the meat in the sandwich. Not that it really mattered: in first there was so much space between pods, we could have been flying solo. There were buttons that, when pressed, sent screens up from the armrests to shut out the neighbors on either side. Being friends, none of us used the facility, which enabled me to make what may have been a key observation. Lilly said something to Polly in one of their Chinese dialects—I fancy it was Fukienese—which attracted her twin's attention. A stowaway fly had infiltrated First and was free-riding on Lilly's window. I assumed a HiSo fastidiousness had been invoked, and I looked forward to an indignant word from one or both of them to the purser.

Wrong. Polly said something back to Lilly in an excited voice. Lilly responded with still greater excitement. All six of our eyes were now fixated on the fly. I had no idea of the odds or the sums agreed on, but something told me neither was minimal. The fly made a dash toward the top of the window—a move in Lilly's favor for sure, to judge from the glee in her eyes and the glum in her sister's. True to its nature, though, the fly would not be so easily predicted and made a series of jerks in a W pattern, which left it pretty much where it had started in terms of suspension between earth and sky.

More hurried punting. I had a feeling the stakes were getting serious. A middle-aged woman in the seat behind me looked up from her video and understood; now eight eyeballs awaited the fly's next move. The fly jerked a couple of inches skyward. To my right Polly fidgeted unhappily with one of her solid gold bracelets. Lilly pressed her palms together and wrung her hands. But the fly was nothing if not a tease. He decided to give himself a body wipe with his legs, all over from head to feet, about a dozen times with extra attention to face and eyes. Who said flies are dirty?

Unable to resist, I leaned toward Polly. "What's the betting so far?"

She glared. "Don't ask."

"I ask."

She slipped off her gold bracelet to invite me to heft it. More than two ounces, that's for sure. Maybe five. I remembered the figures from the Gold Souk. Well over a thousand dollars an ounce, close to twelve hundred if I remembered correctly. We were talking about a six-thousand-dollar fly. Now Polly lost it and said something fast— desperate, I would say.

Lilly turned to stone but nodded her head.

"How much now?" I asked.

Polly refused to answer. The woman behind me got up to lean over my pod. She had an American accent. "Please tell me how much they are betting on the fly?"

"About six thousand dollars, I think."

"If it gets to the top of the window before flying away?"

"I think so."

"If it gets to the *bottom* of the window before flying away, *she* pays double," Polly hissed.

Lilly remained stone-faced, silently urging her fly heavenward.

Now the fly was clean as a whistle and good to go. In a sudden burst he shifted four inches up. Only about an inch and a half more, and Polly's gold bracelet changed owners.

I stared at the bracelet for a moment. Polly understood my thought. "It's gone up a lot more than that."

"Oh, please tell me how much you're betting," the American woman said.

"You wouldn't believe it," Polly said.

Lilly broke into a grin. "Tell them."

"Fifty thousand dollars," Polly said.

The American woman turned pale. "You're serious?"

"We're Chinese," the Twins explained in unison; without humor, though. They were still fixated on the fly.

"That's a lot of kidneys and livers," I exclaimed, and covered my mouth. Polly nodded as if she'd had the same thought. The American woman stared at me, then sat down.

Without a second thought for its audience, the fly took off, having failed to reach either border. The sisters relaxed. Polly played with her bracelet.

I took the opportunity to ask a question that had been on my mind since last night. "Is Monte Carlo the only reason for going to France, Polly?"

"Actually we're on our way to Lourdes."

"Ah, why Lourdes?"

Polly picked up a pack of roasted almonds the flight attendant had placed on the arm of her pod. She pulled it open and slipped a couple into her mouth. Despite her mouth being half full, she answered in precise English, with a touch of the schoolmarm in her manner. "Of the world's three universal religions, one is based on a profound insight into human psychology and one is based on a profound insight into the kind of social structure that is necessary for people to live in peace and harmony. Got it so far?"

"I think so."

"The former is Buddhism, and the latter is Islam. The other world religion is an insane collection of primitive magic and mumbo-jumbo, with cadavers resurrecting and walking around with holes in them, lepers suddenly healing and the blind suddenly seeing, virgins giving birth and snakes that talk. Since it's all a blatant lie, something has to be done to keep the faithful dropping coins onto the plate, or the economic model on which the whole pious edifice is based will collapse in less than a generation. It needs miracle machines. Lourdes is the most important. Of course, since there are no miracles, you have to have a large collection of people willing to lie to themselves. We are talking about the terminally ill, of course."

"Okay. Why are we so interested?"

She made a gesture of impatience. "Terminally ill—not every organ is busted—need money for real medical treatment when the abracadabra fails—sell something—anything—find a close relative to sell one of theirs—alternatively need a new organ—will pay anything, ask no questions."

"It's your marketplace?"

"One of them."

At Nice a guy in a business suit was waiting with a sign: MADEMOI- SELLES YIP AND PARTY. He led us to his limo, which was a big, dark Benz with automatic gearshift and tinted windows. In a few minutes we'd joined the motorway system that goes all the way to Italy. We turned off at Monaco, and suddenly we were in a Ferrari jam: any color you like, so long as it's red or yellow. They were driven by middle-aged men wearing cravats, all of whom had women beside them wearing Hermès scarves over their heads, along with sunglasses, which could be worn on the scarf or nose, according to taste. When we got to the hotel, which was almost as famous as the casino, the staff all knew the Twins. They didn't try to distinguish between them, simply called them both *Mademoiselle Yip*.

My room was king-size with a view over the Mediterranean, which didn't strike me as much different from the other seas I'd seen. I was wallowing in the king-size tub with faux-ancient tap fittings circa 1920 (you could turn them on and off with your big toe, but it was quite a stretch—the gel was out of this world: lime and thyme with a touch of primrose and great bubbles), when a deep gong announced someone at the door.

It was housekeeping with a complete casino-goer's rig: tuxedo, black pants with shiny stripe down the outside leg, plum bow tie ready-tied (a handy hook-and-eye catch at the back for bumpkins like me), shiny black patent leather shoes, and dress shirt with frills down the front and pearl buttons. It all fit perfectly. It was ten P.M., the hour when serious players start to make their way to the tables.

At the top of the steps to the famous casino a footman in livery bowed at Lilly, Polly, and me.

"The best of France is a museum," Lilly whispered.

"The more you pay, the better behaved the exhibits," Polly said.

"They think a vagina is masculine, and their patron saint is a transsexual roasted in a suit of armor," Lilly said.

"No wonder they're so screwed up," Polly said.

I didn't know much about gamblers, but I knew vice when I saw it. The Twins, both in black evening gowns with pearls, silver earrings, and icy diamonds that glittered, owned all the signs, including fetishism. These two wealthy heiresses who took limos and six-star hotels for granted swooned over the casino's old brass and worn carpets, while a delicious tension came and went in their eyes, and they clasped and unclasped each other's hands. "Every time is like the first," Lilly said.

"You remember the first?" I asked. I imagined Maurice Chevalier introducing them to champagne right here in the velvet lobby.

"We won twenty dollars. Daddy wouldn't let us bet more."

"I remember the roulette wheel, how big and heavy and silent, and how everyone seemed to hold their breath."

"One of the Beatles was here, I forget which one—he lost ten thousand dollars in a bet on black."

I already knew that roulette was the star of the show, and we would proceed slowly toward the wheel by way of lesser pleasures. They bought a bunch of chips from the tux behind the grille, and we paused at the slot machines. These were not serious bets, but both women had serious faces. I understood: this was the reading of the entrails before the invasion of Troy. How well or badly they did would determine how recklessly or conservatively they played on the grown-up tables.

Lilly gasped, squealed, giggled: three oranges in a row. The machine coughed up chips as if it had taken an expectorant, but the total win was hardly more than a hundred dollars. Polly didn't fare so well, but she was happy enough with a couple of pineapples and a carrot, which delivered about five dollars. They gazed into each other's eyes like newlyweds, then remembered me and held my hands on either side.

Let's face it, every man likes to be king for a night. I was feeling like a million dollars myself when we finally took the steps up into the main hall. All the guys in tuxedos envied me. The more generous shared humorous grins, while the meaner spirits would have liked to spit on the carpet: *two* beautiful women, and I wasn't even Italian! Hey, I was having a ball after all. These startlingly beautiful, rich, young(ish) women were spoiling me here. I was almost skipping while I hummed:

> As I walk along the boulevard with an independent air
> I can hear the girls declare
> He must be a millionaire
> He's the man who broke the bank at Monte Caaaaarlo.

(Okay, so I am a tad bipolar, but there's no need for anyone to get judgmental: what do you do for variety yourself, DFR?)

We spent an hour or so on blackjack, then finally took the short set of steps up to the big table. The Yip party will only play *French* roulette, messieurs—don't even think of imposing *English* rules, *merci* all the same.

"*Faites vos jeus*," the croupier said, but like all pros, Lilly and Polly waited until a nanosecond before the ball fell into the last two rows of the wheel, which is to say just before the implacable Frenchman said "*Rien ne va plus*." Lilly put a thousand dollars on red, which was an even-money bet. Polly also put five hundred on red, and a hundred dollars each on 9, 11, 13, and 15. Focus on the spinning wheel was total. The table was silent. A public hanging would not have produced greater concentration in a crowd. The ball stopped on red, which was good for Lilly, but—even better for Polly—it landed on 13. At 35 to 1 it was a serious win. Lilly and Polly exchanged glances. Did I detect a certain reticence in both sets of Chinese eyes?

"One and three add up to four," Lilly said, "the number of death. I can't believe you did that."

"Me either," Polly said, "I just wasn't thinking." She seemed seriously penitent, as if she had inadvertently made a pact with the devil.

"You knew what you were doing. You did it because of the fly."

"You didn't win with the fly."

"No, but I almost did. You were scared shitless. You bet on four to get even."

"It wasn't four, it was thirteen."

"Even worse. Even *gweilos* know it's unlucky. And it adds up to four. You've ruined the evening."

Polly made a face, but she was shaken. Lilly looked as if she were about to cry. "I brought the shrine," Polly said, and put an arm on Lilly's elbow.

"You did?"

Polly opened her handbag to show something to her sister.

Lilly collared one of the supervisors. "We want to go to the prayer room," she told him.

"Certainly," he said.

"Excuse us for a moment," Polly said to me.

I watched them disappear into some private room of the casino—and never saw them again. I hung around for about an hour and a half, then grabbed one of the supervisors. When I mentioned the name *Yip*, he shrugged and allowed himself a slight smirk. There was no message waiting back in the hotel, and reception told me the sisters had not returned to their room.

Next morning a message was waiting for me on the hotel's system. It gave the reservation number and other details of an e-ticket in my name: a single seat, first-class, Nice–Bangkok via Dubai.

11

Back in Bangkok, Vikorn's mug was everywhere, just as he had promised: every third lamppost. His undisguised intention was to crowd out the competition, which was numerous. It's one of our paradoxes: we are a shy people who love to run for public office. Men and women, who cannot hope to get votes other than from family members dress in their Sunday best—white military costumes for the boys, serious colors and high necklines for the girls—so they can share lampposts with the likes of Vikorn, whose life and times had begun to be discussed in a discreet way by the media. One brave journalist hinted that a Bangkok cop might not be the wisest choice for governor when you thought of how creative former holders of that office had been with those purchasing contracts for buses and police cars, not to mention the multibillion-baht extension to the Skytrain. I was not comfortable, either. The man who had controlled my destiny for more than a decade now loomed at me from every corner: master crook of the universe.

Those three Americans had checked out my people's value system and decided to present Vikorn on the street as Father Wisdom, with gray hair whitened a shade, a confident smile (which had triumphed over deep suffering), right hand held slightly palm up, in a subliminal reference to a Buddha image, the sparkling city behind him as if it had elected him already. Voting day was more than a month away, though, and he had not yet gone public with his "Stop Organ Trafficking Now" campaign, although I'd seen some of the advance publicity: "Devout Buddhist police colonel who has worked steadily and self-lessly on his own time for more than a decade to stop this ghoulish trade and, now, thanks to meticulous detective work headed up by his hand-selected protégé, Detective Sonchai Jitpleecheep, can humbly reveal that a vast international network, which uses the sacred soil of Thailand as an organ depot, has been broken and busted."

He hadn't debriefed me yet, however, because I'd taken a day to recover from the Yip sisters. Apart from Vikorn's election campaign, the other news on the radio and TV was all about the Sukhumvit Rapist, as he'd come to be known. Early sympathy for the deformed stalker had evaporated since he sexually assaulted two women and attempted to rape a number of others. Sergeant Ruamsantiah of District 8 had declared that he personally would not rest until the streets were safe again for respectable women and girls.

I intended to take a motorbike taxi to the station, but Vietnam was getting one hell of a lashing again, and the skies were black all over the eastern Pacific. (I bet boat people make good organ donors: I imagined them hanging on to the gunwales, a saltwater gargle every twelve seconds; now a luxury yacht shows up with a pair of Chinese twins in bikinis and wrap-around sunglasses: "*One kidney each, and your troubles are over, my little chou-chous.*") I would have taken a cab if there were any available, but each one that passed carried a passenger, its red *wang* sign turned off.

It just happened that one of my favorite *kao moo* cooked-food stalls was around the corner on Soi 51; it provided an overhead tarpaulin, so I made a dash for it. And now I was sitting at the rickety iron table with the braised pork leg with rice in a bowl steaming before me, liberally loading up on *nampla* fish sauce with enough granulated chili to melt the spoon, when my eye caught things floating just under the surface. Of course, they were only eggs cut in half with the yolk visible, but for one psychotic moment I was seeing human eyeballs. It was a genuine hallucination, the first I'd experienced without dope, so in addition to everything else, I was wondering if I was not—you know—a total loony.

I was sweating, the blood drained from my face. Talk about karma. I'd lost my appetite and to hell with the rain, I needed to get to the station and safety. I wanted to feel bored, because bored seemed the opposite of crazy.

Sure enough, when I was at my desk and logged into my personal e-mail account, I opened two spam offers to enlarge my penis and five to send me improbably cheap Viagra by anonymous post: serenity had returned. I was pushing my chair back and waiting for Lek to bring me my first iced lemon tea of the day when Manny, Vikorn's secretary, called: the Old Man had heard I was in the office and wanted me upstairs, pronto.

Now I was sitting in the hot seat opposite him on the far side of his huge desk. To avoid his gaze, I stared at the anticorruption poster above his head and wondered when it was going to include a reference to human organ trafficking. I'd just told him the whole story of my trip to Dubai. We were in the midst of one of those silences: he looked almost stupid while his criminal genius worked deep down in the brainstem.

Finally he came out of his trance. I saw that I might have succeeded in shocking him. "They're twins? Identical?"

"Yes, sir."

"I didn't know that." He stood up, stumped, turned on me, said, "Twins?" again, then went to the window, held his chin, and nodded to himself in the way of a man who was once badly burned but has only this minute understood how the scam had worked. He turned on me again with the same aggressive sweep. "They're compulsive gamblers, you say?"

"The type they call *whales* in Las Vegas. They bet fifty thousand dollars and a gold bracelet on a fly walking up a window." I saw a deep reprogramming taking place somewhere in the depths. When he turned again, his eyes said, *So that was it.* He returned to his seat, sat, and nodded to himself again. I watched in fascination as that special thing geniuses have—that extra half inch of willpower the rest of us lack—started to stir at the back of his retinas.

I said, "Sir, may I ask a personal question?"

"No."

"I'm afraid I need to, sir, if my investigation is to proceed." He raised his eyes. "About these twins, sir. They are very mischievous—somewhere between bad and evil, it seems to me at this point—but girlish at the same time. Rich and out of control, sir. Without any moral compass at all. I don't think they're really into sex, but they know how to project it. Manipulative to a degree that's hard to believe." He was daring me to continue. I continued. "I wouldn't put it past them to make a bet—a pretty big one, I would guess—on whether or not one or the other—or even both—could seduce a man—say an alpha male of the Asian type—say a—"

"Get out, Detective," he whispered. "Get the hell out of my office, right now."

"Yes, sir."

Well, now I've brought you up to date, DFR, and told you all I know. Nothing neat and tidy, I'm afraid, only a collection of fragments that may or may not be related. A few days after I reported to Vikorn, which is to say about a week after I got back from Monte Carlo, I received the call to Vulture Peak, where lay the three anonymous cadavers with every salable organ missing. Am I the only observer who does *not* see the Colonel's hand in this? Call me naïve, but it's just not Vikorn's style—and anyway, he already has the election in the bag. On the other hand, anyone who doubts that organ theft happens on the sacred soil of Thailand will soon be considering voting for the Colonel, once the story breaks. Very interesting, think about it.

12

Meat scares me and makes my flesh crawl, even when it doesn't resemble anything human. Am I getting soft or are the cases getting harder? Why do I see three faceless corpses whenever I close my eyes? Why does my mind keep fixating on the deep gashes and the floppy blubber where livers and kidneys used to be? And no eyes, sweet Buddha, *no eyes*. The worst was this morning just before waking: an army of the blind and faceless moving in a dogged mass toward rebirth and revenge.

I'm curled up on my bed sucking my thumb and trembling. If anyone asks, I'm going to say I caught a touch of fever in Dubai. This case has got to me like no other, and I'm not even convinced it's a case. To make matters infinitely worse, my partner, my darling Chanya, doesn't seem to have noticed there's something wrong. She watched me drag myself across the room after only a couple of hours on duty, blinked at me without losing that glazed look she has for everything and everyone except her computer monitor, seemed to have a bright idea while I limped broken and shattered to the bed, and started stabbing ferociously at her keyboard just as I collapsed.

I called Lek on my cell phone to tell him to get me a supply of dope from Sergeant Ruamsantiah. I'm going to smoke until I forget who I am, and I'm not coming back to earth until they've improved it. Really, this time I've had it with everything. I can feel it, that thing that happens to your mind when they add that extra few ounces to your paranoia and you sink under the weight. Every time I close my eyes I see someone with a curved knife aiming for my vital organs with an expression of insane greed. I see monsters from the deep, breaking the surface after billions of years in the lightless zones: blind, hideous, eel-gray, voracious for human flesh. I'm trembling.

"I'm just going out to buy some more printer ink. D'you want anything?" Chanya calls.

"No," I groan.

She comes over to the bed. "You okay?"

"Fine."

"Good. Listen, I just wrote this brilliant paragraph. I've nearly finished my thesis, and I had to get the ending right. I know you won't understand much, but you can get the idea:

> Thus the comodification of bodies, whether superficially in the sense of a prostitute painting herself in a way designed to send the required signal to prospective customers, or in the more extreme sense of a person selling, or having taken from them, a vital organ such as a kidney, is obviously and unavoidably a consequence of the present economic system which relies on what has been called "the promiscuity of objects." This system carries with it the unspoken implication that once something has been defined as an "object," it is automatically assumed to be "promiscuous" in the sense that it may be bought and sold like any other object, even if the object in question is somebody's kidney or liver—or whole body. This kind of thinking is exactly what underpinned the slave trade for hundreds of years: as soon as a captive West African was defined as "property," then he could be treated as a "promiscuous object," that is to say an object whose human rights have been magically transmuted into a money value in the accounts of the property owner. What is unclear, however, is why modern Western culture has continued to target prostitution by adult volunteers as "immoral" (i.e., in Professor Smith's definition "the enemy"). Consider the manner in which both Hollywood and the advertising industry have been comodifying bodies for the purpose of profit (i.e., treating both male and female

models as "promiscuous objects" to be traded). At first glance it seems strange that the line should be drawn at what one might call the "cottage industry" of street-level prostitution, especially in Bangkok, where the practitioners are relatively free of exploitation by pimps and can therefore fairly be described as choosing to commodify their bodies on their own account for the purpose of survival. It may be that the answer can be found in a parallel paradox: the obsessive repression of "soft" drugs like marijuana, despite the wealth of data which proves that the "hard" drug alcohol is far more dangerous to health and responsible for almost an infinitely greater number of diseases and deaths. It is not difficult to see what the private trading of marijuana and street-level prostitution have in common: these are industries any private person can develop on their own account without being squeezed out by big business or falling liable to tax. Thus it is in the suppression of prostitution and soft drugs that we see the hypocrisy at the heart of the culture. It is in the interests of government and big business to appear to uphold a "moral code," the true purpose of which is to ensure that impoverished individuals cannot escape their poverty except by becoming fiscally and commercially useful: read slaves. In other words, it is a "code" driven by exactly the same dynamic as the slave trade. But, as Professor Steiner points out (op. cit.), the peculiar reverence we have for moral codes depends exactly on their being founded on something beyond functionalism. A money-driven morality is no morality at all.

"That's just amazingly brilliant. You're a genius," I say. I do not add: *I just hope I'm still sane when you get your Ph.D.* In my insecurity I want to ask about the rumors, but in my insecurity I don't have the courage. She's basically a very honest girl, and I don't think I could handle any form of toxic truth right now.

While she's out, Lek comes with a sizable package, takes one look at me, asks where I keep my skins, rolls me a big one, shakes his head, and leaves. Now Chanya is back, and I'm quite high. At least I've got control of the demons. Thanks to the power of cannabis, I'm able to shrink them with my brand-new green demon-shrinking gun, which sort of grew out of my right hand after the third joint. Chanya smells the dope, gives a mildly disapproving glance, shrugs, goes back to her computer. Time passes (it could be a minute or a couple of aeons, this is export-quality stuff).

She comes back over to me. "You sure you're okay?"

This time the floodgates open. "No, I'm not fucking okay," I bawl. Now I'm blurting, mostly about the eyeballs I sold that won't give me any peace, but also about those three anonymous corpses in Phuket.

She raises her eyes to the ceiling. To complicate matters still further, I am horny. I can just about reach her left breast, thanks to the way she's leaning over, which suddenly seems to offer solace in a cruel world, so with the directness of a monkey I grab it. I wouldn't call it a lecherous gesture, myself, more like a dash for safety by a threatened psyche.

She sighs. "Oh, Sonchai, it's always the same."

"What is?"

"When you smoke too much. You go space traveling for a couple of hours, disdaining the earth and everything on it. Then when you finally get back, you're like a horny sixteen-year-old."

I release her breast like a drowning man releasing a straw. "I'm in a state," I admit. "I'm kind of scared, but it's not that exactly." She frowns, because she sees I've gone into that mood of meticulous self-analysis that often accompanies a comedown. "It's more like fear overlaying something fundamental. I mean it *is* fear, but it's mixed in with something more general, like *what's happening to the species?*"

"What species?"

"Humanity."

She curses. "It's Vikorn who's done this to you. That old bastard. I hate him. I hate having to look at his hypocritical bloody mug on every third lamppost. I hate the way he's going to win the election and bleed Bangkok white." She pulls her cell phone out of her jeans pocket and stabs at one of her autodial numbers. "Get me Vikorn," she snarls at the reception.

Well, I may be a basket case and on the verge of terminal catatonia, but Chanya going for Vikorn in a toe-to-toe standoff is too good to miss. I perk up a bit. Unfortunately, our cell phones don't work so well in the hovel, so she has to go out into the yard. I see her walking up and down, her left hand flaying while she yells at the phone. I have no idea what she's saying, but I'm sure of the psychology: she and Vikorn own me jointly, and there are clear demarcation lines. He has tres- passed on her turf, and the she-wolf is in a rage. She comes back into the house fuming and shaking.

"What did you say?"

"I let him have it," she says in the tone of one who might have gone a tad too far.

"What did he say?"

"He just asked where you were."

"What did you tell him?"

"That you were stoned out of your brain on the bed killing demons with a big green demon-killing gun."

I scratch my head. "How did you know about the gun?"

"Have you any idea how stoned you were half an hour ago? You kept telling me about it, over and over." She pats my head, then cud- dles me a bit the way she did in the old days. After a while, she says, "D'you want to hear about Dorothy?"

"Yes," I gulp.

"Well, the man she went off with that night, this Jimmy Clipp, she's crazy about him. Totally gaga. I checked him out with the girls at your mother's bar. He's a regular there. Very popular. He's gener- ous, considerate, never hurts anyone, and they say he's quite the fin- ger artist. His cock isn't too big, and it's not crooked. You know how superstitious the girls are and how they think a crooked one is seri- ously bad juju. Best of all, he's funny. He doesn't take sex seriously at all and makes jokes in the middle of boom-boom that crack every- body up.

"But he's a total *jao choo*—a butterfly. Even when he's got the hots for a girl one weekend, he dumps her next time he's in town, because he's got curious about another, or he decides to go back to one of his old lusts. And he likes to do two at a time. He's an engineer on some road they're building to Laos. It's China-driven—you know how they want trucks to run from Beijing to the Gulf of Thailand within the decade?"

For the record, DFR, my darling does not normally describe life in quite such mannish terms; she's doing it to amuse me and somewhat succeeding. I've managed a wan smile or two already.

"I haven't told Dorothy this—she's in blind lust at the moment. She sort of confided in me she's never really had good sex in her life before. A few gropes here and there, a night now and then with an incompetent or, even worse, an alcoholic. She tried to be a lesbian like all the other female sociologists in her circle, but it just doesn't work for her. Most of the men in her life have been male feminists, and everyone knows what cockless wonders *they* are—now this new guy of hers is a world-class player. For her he's like nirvana itself. She can't believe sex can be such fun. That's why she decided that brothels can be good for women too. He's back up north working on his road, and she e-mails and SMS's him all the time." She pauses for breath. "See, so long as she's in this state, she agrees with my whole point about prostitution, and she's going to pass my thesis with full recommendations. That's why I'm working my buns off to get it finished. You understand, darling?"

"You mean when he dumps her, she'll change her mind, and brothels will be wicked engines of exploitation all over again?"

"Right. And she'll start giving me a hard time with my thesis all over again."

We are discussing how bad it's going to be when Jimmy Clipp forgets to contact Dorothy next time he's in town and what we can do to cushion the blow (find Dorothy another john in another brothel?), when we hear a police siren in the distance. We exchange a glance, and Chanya goes pale. This is District 8, after all, and in normal circumstances only one cop in D.8 is allowed to use his siren. Sure enough, the siren gets louder, and Chanya gets paler. Now the siren is at the beginning of our *soi* and quite deafening.

Chanya has gone to the window and pulled back the curtain. "Sonchai, where's your gun?" she asks softly.

"Don't be silly. You can't kill a cop, especially not a colonel, especially not Vikorn."

"Not to kill *him*. For myself. I don't think I can stand it. Oh, Buddha, it *is* him!"

I'm still in bed, so I have to imagine Vikorn in his fatigues getting out of the car and prowling to our front door. There is a knock. It is neither loud and arrogant nor soft and humble. Nor is it anything in between. It is a Vikorn knock, the kind no one ignores.

"Can you go, darling?" Chanya says. "I don't feel so good."

So much for equality. The first sign of trouble and she hides behind her man. "No," I say, "I'm already stoned, terrified, catatonic, and hysterical at the same time. I'm staying in bed. Anyway, in bed is exactly how he should find me."

She goes to the door and opens it. It is a feature of our luxurious apartment that I can see the front door from the bed; see Chanya back away while giving Vikorn the high *wai*; see his polite *wai* in return; notice how he hardly seems to notice her, prowls toward me. He is about three inches shorter than me, but he fills the hovel like a giant. Chanya has retreated to a corner, half bent over in some kind of groveling posture.

Now he is staring down at me. He is accompanied by two armed cops in uniform who have been with him long enough to be telepathically sensitive to his every gesture. When he jerks his chin, they retreat and close the front and only door behind them. Chanya draws up our only chair for him to sit on. She backs away as soon as she has placed it next to the mattress.

"How stoned is he?" Vikorn snaps without sitting and without looking at her.

"He's coming down."

"Has he asked for sex yet?"

"Yes," in the tone of a witness for the prosecution, "about ten minutes ago."

"When did he last smoke?"

"About two and a half hours ago."

"So he got out of his skull as usual, did a tour of Andromeda, then the blood sank back down to his balls, and he wanted to screw you?"

"Yes."

He examines me. "You look awful," my Colonel says. "What's the matter? Wouldn't she fuck you? I can't say I blame her."

"Everything's the matter. Especially the eyeballs." I look at him. "I hate you for making me sell them. And I want to know about those bodies in Phuket—did you do it as part of your election strategy? Yes or no? I don't care if you kill me, I'm not working for you anymore."

He rubs his jaw, decides to sit on the chair, then makes an almost imperceptible jerk of the chin toward Chanya behind him. I say, "Darling, why don't you get yourself a hairdo?" Chanya never has hairdos, but she says, "Oh, yes, oh thank you, darling," and gives me a high *wai* in the mode of dutiful wives of yesteryear, then leaves the house in a rush.

Vikorn has stood up and is watching her disappear down the *soi*; now he turns to stare at me. "Suppose I told you I don't know."

"Don't know what?"

"Who did it."

"Don't know? What kind of godfather are you? You're supposed to know even if you didn't order it yourself."

"Aren't you taking everything a little too seriously, Sonchai?"

"What, the eyeballs? What can be more serious than a thousand human eyeballs staring at you resentfully every time you close your own? *Oh yes, you can still see with yours, you can open and close your eyelids, aren't you the lucky one!* That's what they say."

Vikorn has never had a hallucination in his life, so my state is exotic to him. He frowns in concentration. "Really? They talk to you?"

"All the time."

"What language do they use?"

"What language? Thai, of course."

"But none of those eyeballs were Thai. They were mostly Korean."

"From the North?"

"North, South, what's the diff? They're more likely to speak Korean than Thai, aren't they?"

"How would you know? They don't talk to you."

He pauses to look at me for a moment, he seems to hesitate, then asks, "What's it like to be loony? I've always wanted to know."

"I'm not loony. I'm suffering from aftershock. It can kill—there are *farang* statistics."

"People in shock don't hold conversations with eyeballs."

The discussion seems to have reached a wall. Vikorn turns away to look out the window, then examines the room for a moment. His eyes come to rest on Chanya's generic computer, her old printer, tubular steel chair, and collapsible desk. After a few beats I say, "Come on. You can tell me, whodunit? Was it Zinna?"

Vikorn shakes his head. "Unclear. That's the problem. I need something to go on." He shakes his head again and repeats, "That's the problem." He looks me in the eye. "Zinna's even more psycho than you. He comes out with threats that make even my blood curdle. Then the next day he's in a different mood, quiet as a kitten, keen to make peace. That's queer love for you. I've never understood it, the way they get so intense—how can you be so hung up about another man's hairy asshole? You surf the Net—what's the explanation?"

It's not a real question. I don't reply. He goes to the window that looks out onto the street where his cop car is parked. "Policing," he says to the glass, then turns to me. "You think you've got it tough. You don't have any idea how it was when I joined the force. The whole cake was divided down to the last crumb. The big boss got seventy percent, and the portions got smaller as you descended the totem pole. I got maybe half a crumb. And I was damned grateful for that." He prowls back to the chair, holds it by the back. "And no complaining. You learned to keep your mouth shut at all times—*you* wouldn't have survived the first week."

He sighs. "You see, what nobody tells you about capitalism is that it's warlordism in disguise. That leaves the only job in the jungle worth having as apex feeder—the rest is slavery at various levels of discomfort. Socially, psychologically, we're still in the rain forest. I feel sorry for you, but I didn't design the system, I simply learned to win in it." He sighs again. "I think I've tolerated you because you're the opposite to me. Sometimes I don't think you're interested in survival at all— then the next thing you're in bed sucking your thumb, thinking you're scared shitless. That's what you think, isn't it?"

"What kind of question is that? I know if I'm scared or not, don't I?"

"No. I've seen you in firefights when you didn't even break a sweat. Bad men don't scare you. What scares you is the thought you might not be on the side of the angels. I think you're staging this whole drama because you fear for your karma."

"How could anyone work for you and not fear for their karma?"

"Easy. You stop believing in karma."

"An unstructured, cause-free universe where evil always prevails?"

"Now you're sounding like a grown-up."

Time passes. We stare at each other for a moment; then when that becomes embarrassing, we look away. "I'm sorry," he says.

"Sorry for what?"

"That I let you get away without the full initiation. Maybe it's because you're half *farang,* so you won't get promotion anyway—what was the point?"

"The point of what?"

"Making you see." He rubs his jaw. "The rule of law is just another piece of *farang* hypocrisy—a piece of theater designed to dazzle the masses while the movers and shakers clean up. As a cop, you are expected to participate in this theater. That's your real job—play the game as if it's real."

"What are you talking about?"

"But nobody can stop you from writing your own script. That's all we have, Sonchai. Our real privilege as cops is that now and then we get to write the screenplay. Any cop who doesn't grab the chance while he has it . . ." He doesn't finish the sentence.

"That's what you're using me for, to clean up?"

He gives me one of his wise-old-man looks, even makes his eyes twinkle. "You know what my own mentor told me, after I'd seen a few things that scared me? I was a lot younger than you. He said, 'Think about it. What is the easiest crime in the world to solve?'"

The Colonel stops strategically. I say, "Okay, okay, I'm hooked. What is the easiest crime in the world to solve?"

"The kind you plan yourself," Vikorn says. He puts a hand on my shoulder and chuckles as he pats me. "That's policing. He said he got it from the British. What did they do when they wanted to impose law and order in India? They invented Thugees. Amazing. You invent a massive crime wave, then you get the kudos for suppressing it, and you end up with a docile populace and a few thousand dead down-and-outs. That's real policing."

He straightens himself. "All my professional life I've earnestly striven to do what the British did a hundred years ago: sell an opiate to make enough money to keep the peace. It may not be pretty, but as the Brits demonstrated, it works worldwide." He stares at me. "You've already made the point for me. With my black Amex card and my money, you've found out more about worldwide organ trafficking in a couple of days than the FBI has managed in ten years. Let me be plain: the dough you spent in Dubai comes out of the smack habits of inadequate, narcissistic *farang*. That's the way this world works. If you can find a better one, let me know—I'll be right on the spaceship with you."

"What do you want to do, exactly?"

"I'm not telling you yet." He prowls to the window again to stare at the *soi*. "I want you to follow up on your contact with the Twins. They're based in Hong Kong, right?"

"Yes."

"Good. Visit if you have to. Find out everything you can." He nods at the street. "Your wife has come back."

The door opens. Chanya walks in. I know exactly what has happened in her inner life. She felt disgusted with herself for running from Vikorn and has screwed her courage to the sticking point instead of having her hair done; now she is all ready to confront him in the flesh. Her eyes are twin blazes of defiance in an honor-retrieval exercise, but she is taken aback by the father-and-son atmosphere.

"Darling, would you mind booking me on a flight to Hong Kong next week?" I say.

"First-class," Vikorn says. He turns to give her a polite *wai* and takes his leave. At the door he seems to remember something, looks at her, smiles: "Great hairdo."

Chanya stands at the window with her hands on her hips and watches as he collects his goons and ducks into his car.

"I have to go back to Phuket," I say, when his car has drawn away.

"I thought you said Hong Kong."

"Next week. If I'm going to have any questions to ask in Hong Kong, I really need to start in Phuket. All I've done so far is stare at the crime scene for ten minutes and talk to Supatra."

13

Patong, about two miles from Vulture Peak, is the down-market play area in Phuket. On the right night it's a lot more festive than the Bangkok hotspots, which tend to have a no-frills air in comparison. Here on Bang La, Patong's main street, you get the full *farang* fantasy of unrestrained orientalism. Adolescent elephants come up from behind and lay their trunks on your shoulder, begging for sugarcane, which you can buy from the mahout. In one of the pavilions you can watch some kind of snake-charming gag with a full-size cobra, which has had the venom removed, naturally. If anything, the *katoeys* on Soi Crocodile are even more flamboyant than in Nana, and there are girls everywhere. *They* don't have to exaggerate anything, they are young, beautiful, and friendly in bikinis and will do anything you want so long as it doesn't hurt and you use a condom.

I arrived a couple of hours ago at about eight P.M. and spent time at a few bars watching the street and deciding what to do. I came on a hunch. My reasoning is simple: Vulture Peak was built for pleasure, but it's high on a hill, a good couple of miles away from any live entertainment. Soi Eric here at Patong is the nearest center for fun, including takeaway. What I can't figure out is exactly who to ask, or how to frame the question. Naturally, I checked in with the local police force and received mostly a stonewall. I have a feeling the entire station has taken a vow of silence with regard to Vulture Peak. The best I can obtain is the promise of an interview with two constables before they go out on patrol tomorrow morning. Now after two hours on the street I've made no progress and I'm starting to feel restless, so I take a stroll.

Things have livened up. They were pretty lively before, so I guess you could say the place is reaching that strangely predictable level of hysteria typical of a certain kind of mass-market *farang* tourism at around eleven-thirty in the evening. Couples with teenage kids they don't know what to do with hang out in the less outrageous bars while small gangs of drunken young pink men, who can hardly believe the good time you can hire for a thousand baht, are nevertheless daunted by the feast of flesh and instead channel their nervous lust into a familiar drinking routine with their mates who support the same soccer team. Maybe tomorrow they'll take the plunge and get laid. More serious older men look for the perfect female form on which to spend the sperm they saved up during the boring flight over, while longer stayers hang out talking to the girl they know they will eventually take back to the hotel, because that's what they've done every night since they arrived and they don't really like change.

The mahout and the elephant still tramp up and down, and there are three snake shows at the open-air pavilion instead of the former one. The *katoey* quarter is farther up the street, where lack of authenticity is compensated for by elaborate stage costumes with long ostrich feathers that soar over hairdos of every color except black. It's noisy, cheap, but not unfriendly. The trouble is: so many bars and so little time.

I buy a beer at a tiny place served by one pleasant-looking young woman who I suppose will have to close the shop if ever she finds a customer who wants her body. I take out a five-hundred-baht note and ask where slumming millionaires are most likely to look for someone to love, and without hesitation she jerks her chin at one of the bars behind the first cobra show.

"Any particular reason?"

"It's the first big bar you come to if you're arriving from the hill, and they pay more, so the girls are more beautiful and speak better English. Also, they have a takeaway service." She giggles. "I mean they have a van with a driver. If somebody knows which girl they want, they can call or e-mail."

The name is Chung King House, so I guess they get a lot of Chinese customers, or maybe the owners sought the advice of a seer who read the future. It's twice the size of most of the other bars and lacks the personal touch. I order a beer and ask about the takeaway service. The bartender tells me that anything can be arranged, but I need to speak to Khun Nong. He picks up a cell phone, presses an autodial number, and hands me the phone.

A soft voice from far away says, "Good evening, sir. How can I help you?"

"By meeting me at the bar in five minutes."

"I'm sorry?"

"I'm a cop. I have some questions for you. If you cooperate, I won't be any trouble."

The phone goes dead, but a door behind the bar opens and a woman in her forties appears. She flips up a section of the bar top and comes to sit next to me on a stool, just as if she's expecting to be picked up. Her face is blank when she says, "Do you have Colonel Naradom's permission to ask questions? My bosses make a lot of contributions to the Phuket police retirement fund."

"I don't need permission to investigate a triple killing with bells and whistles."

She seems relieved. "Oh, yes, I heard about that, but it hasn't been on the news."

"We're keeping it under wraps until we've had a chance to investigate."

She nods, thinks about it, then gives me the phoniest smile I've ever seen. "How can I help?"

"You send girls to hotels and private homes in a microvan. You're the only bar that does that. The house on the hill is a couple of miles away. It's built for pleasure." I stare at her.

She touches her hair. "I've only been in the job a few months. I've never had a call from any of the houses on Vulture Peak. Most of the business is to hotels hereabouts. It's all about *farang* men who think they're respectable and don't have the guts to be seen leaving the bar with one of the girls. So they pay the bar fine, give the name of their hotel and the room number, and I arrange the rest. Usually in such cases the hotel is upmarket, so we have to negotiate. Most of my job is keeping up friendly connections with the concierges. Generally the van takes the girl to the tradesmen's entrance, and someone leads her to the lifts." She shrugs. "Discretion pays."

"But there must be occasions when a *farang* or some other foreigner who owns a flat or house requires your services. How about parties with dancing girls?"

"It's rare, but it happens."

I think I understand her body language and take out my wallet, but she puts a hand on my wrist. "I promise I don't know anything. Nothing like that has happened while I've been here, and most of the girls don't stay more than six months, usually less. Either they find a *farang* husband in that time, or they go back to their villages. There are only two girls who have been here longer than me. I think one of them may be able to help. Her name is Om, and you can get her number from the barman. Please don't tell anyone you got her name from me."

She gets up, stone-faced, and retreats to her office behind the bar. I signal to the barman and ask for Om's number. He gives me a business card with a heart on it: OM, AT YOUR PERSONAL SERVICE.

I call the number. "Hi, Om, I'm Sonchai, I'm at the Chung King and wondered if you'd allow me to buy you a drink."

"I'm off duty, darling. Time of the month, I'm afraid. If you haven't found a friend by Monday, please call. Thanks for thinking of me." She closes the phone. I press the repeat button on my cell. Now she sounds a little weary. I say, "It's worth a thousand baht. I don't want your body, just your company."

There is hesitation in her voice when she says, "It's late, honey, and I'm very tired."

"Two thousand, just for a half-hour chat, any bar you like."

"Okay, but not the Chung King." She gives the name of another bar down the street.

· · ·

Now I'm sitting with my third beer in half an hour, waiting for Om. When an attractive woman in her late twenties appears in jeans and T-shirt, no makeup, hair clean and combed but without coiffure, I don't make the connection with the voice on the phone. Even when she sits next to me, I can't believe this is the professional I spoke to a few minutes ago. There seems to be no side to her at all. A good clean Buddhist girl.

"Hello, Mr. Sonchai. I'm Om. How can I help?"

She's so normal, so much the Thai girl next door, no frills, confident of her beauty but modest just the same. I guess when she says off duty, that includes the personality. It's always a dangerous sign when you like someone you're interviewing with respect to an atrocity.

"Somebody told me you once did some entertaining up on the hill, more than a year ago." I flash my cop's ID.

She takes in the mug shot on the plastic, flashes me a glance, and says, "Up on the hill?"

"Vulture Peak."

Another change of personality. Not paranoia exactly—let's say a sudden attack of extreme caution. "Not here. Meet me on the beach in twenty minutes."

"Where on the beach?"

"The big T-shirt stand next to the green parasols."

It doesn't sound like a very precise direction, but when I reach the beach, I see what she means. The T-shirt stand is still doing a roaring trade at nearly midnight, and although the green parasols are all folded like cypress trees, you can't really miss them. There are plenty of people about, mostly *farang* couples who came for romance in the exotic East, some *farang* men with Thai girls with whom, I suppose, they are trying to have a relationship, and some young Thai couples holding hands. You can't see the stars for the light pollution from the town, but the moon is up and bright.

I feel a slight flutter when I see her making toward me. I suspect I wouldn't give her a second glance when she's on duty and dressed like a tart, but that no-frills naturalness is quite a turn-on. And it is a beautiful evening. When she sees me, she nods faintly toward a couple of deck chairs that have yet to be folded and stacked. She sits in one. I play along by letting a few beats pass before I join her.

She takes a pack of Marlboro Reds out of a down-market black handbag and puts one in her mouth without offering the box to me. She lights up at the same time as she says, "What did you want to know?"

"I want to know everything you know about Vulture Peak."

She takes a long toke on the cigarette, inhales like a true addict, exhales, and starts to talk. "The owners of the Chung King House have connections with travel agents in China—that's why they called it the Chung King. But it didn't really work out. Maybe they're ten years ahead of the curve. Most of the business is still *farang*, with some Japanese and Korean. But they keep up the connection with the Chinese, and every now and then a tour group comes to town. Usually they stay in one of the midrange hotels. Often the group is so big, they take over the hotel.

"Mostly it's genuine sightseers, but sometimes it's all men on the loose, looking for a good time. When we get the call, we girls pile into the van, sometimes up to five or six of us. One night about two years ago we got the call for eight girls. Eight is a lucky number for Chinese, right? But it wasn't to a hotel. It was to that fantastic palace up on the hill. From the start everyone told us we would be well paid but we had to keep quiet about it. Never tell a soul where we went that night."

She shrugs. "I don't know why it had to be so secret. When we got there, we found about twenty Chinese men, all drunk. There were crates of cognac stacked up against a wall, and it looked as if they were having a stag party. There were also a lot of roulette wheels, mahjong tiles, and stacks of playing cards. A lot of banknotes all over the place, but not Thai baht—I suppose it was all Chinese money. They didn't speak any Thai or English, but we managed to work out that one of them had recently had a serious medical operation and was celebrating his recovery.

"They were noisy with bad manners, but they weren't really obnoxious. They wanted us to undress, to hang around naked. So we did. Of course we got groped mercilessly, but they were the kind of men—middle management with wives and kids, I guess—who are scared of girls like me. They didn't want to screw any of us, just the endless groping, like curious boys.

"Then someone said it was time for a show. A woman appeared—a Chinese woman—who took us all into a big bedroom and gave us silver and gold bikinis to wear. Then she gave one of us a big solid gold ring which had to be hidden in one of the girls' vaginas—she didn't care who. She gave us all numbered buttons to wear. I was number seven. Then she led us out to the big room with pools and little streams of water, and someone turned some music on. It was a disco tune, and we all started to dance. The men were staring at us and gabbling furiously to one another, and a lot of money seemed to be changing hands. I got the feeling this was the high point of the evening.

"The Chinese woman told us to take off our bras, then our panties, so we were naked again. All the men were staring at our pussies, of course. And betting. They were more interested in the betting than in our bodies. Finally the music stopped and the Chinese woman who spoke English said that the girl with the gold ring in her vagina should come forward. The girl walked up and took out the ring, and the men went crazy. Those who had bet on number seven cleaned up. Some of the men looked really depressed, like they'd mortgaged their houses and lost everything. Then we were led out, told to dress, and the van took us back to the bar. They paid us all five thousand baht each, and the girl was allowed to keep the gold ring. That was quite a tip."

She has finished the cigarette, which she stubs out on the sand. When she reaches into her bag I think it is for another cigarette. Instead she takes out a solid gold ring, which she hands to me to heft. It's small, solid, and heavy. "I had it valued. It's real gold, twenty-three carat. More than three baht in weight. At 13,800 baht per one-baht weight, that makes 41,000 baht. I had a feeling gold would go up sooner or later, so I kept it." She smiles without humor. "That's why I stay at that bar—it's very lucky for me."

I feel like a naïve *farang* for the thumping in my heart, a sense of hurt. Some whores can affect you like that, even a part-time pimp like me. I don't want to think about her at that party; she's too beautiful. I watch a Thai couple walk past along the shore, the moon directly overhead now, a pure silver scythe. "You have no idea what business they might have been in, those middle-management-type men?"

She shrugs. "One of them who took an interest in me kept saying *tanakan*. I think that was the only word he knew in Thai."

"Bankers?"

"Maybe. Or maybe he was trying to say he'd just been to the bank. He was drunk."

"And the Chinese woman—she was the only woman there apart from you girls?"

"The only one I saw."

"She was arranging the party?"

"I don't know. We got there about eleven-thirty in the evening, so most of the party was over. We were the final show."

"Can you describe her?"

"She was the tall, willowy kind of Chinese woman. Hard to say how old because she'd taken such great care of her skin—you could see how much money had been spent on her. She was HiSo for sure. Very elegant. She spoke perfect English and not bad Thai. I don't think she was mainland Chinese at all."

By the time she has finished speaking, she is on her feet. Anyone spying on us would assume I had sat down to proposition her and she had refused after a short polite conversation. So she's not only beautiful and modest when off duty, she's a smart operator too. And lucky. That was a decent chunk of gold. I give her five minutes to disappear, so nobody thinks I'm following her, then walk along the road opposite the sea until I come to a guest house with a ROOMS VACANT sign. I don't bother to check out the room. When I lie down on the narrow bed next to the tiny window that overlooks the sea, I close my eyes, expecting to see Chanya there, where she usually is just before I fall asleep, nestled behind my eyelids. Instead I see Om.

When I wake up, a solid block of golden light is shooting through the window like something out of a space travel movie, as if a beautiful

Venusian is about to materialize before my eyes. It's quite blinding, and I have to draw the curtains for a moment, until I remind myself that light is good, light is what it's all about.

The room rate includes breakfast, which is laid out buffet style in a room downstairs. I'm the only guest up at this hour, and there are no staff. The coffee has been stewing all night on a hot plate, the imitation croissants are inedible, and the granola is old and stale.

I already paid for the room, so I'm a free man, walking along the beach at seven-thirty in the morning, wondering what Chanya did last night. I find a small café near the sea that serves real coffee and not-bad *pain au chocolat*. I ask the kid behind the bar if he knows anything about the mansions up on the hill—you can see the peak from this part of the beach, but not the houses—and he says no. He's a Muslim from Pattani, speaks standard Thai with a strong accent, and has only been here a week. The café was the only business he could find that was hiring workers and didn't sell alcohol. He confides how disgusted he is with *farang* decadence, especially the alcohol—and the sex. He's never seen anything like it. He understands why Allah sent the tsunami seven years ago, but nobody seems to have got the message. What will Allah do next, destroy the whole island?

I check the clock on my cell phone. Eight-thirty. If I take it slowly, I'll be at the police station around nine, when the two patrol cops start work.

I sense nervousness in the desk sergeant, which is not unusual. No provincial police force likes visits from the big city; very often the business models are incompatible. He cannot prevent me from seeing Constables Hel and Tak, but he is able to slow me down quite a bit. He says the interview room isn't ready, and the two cops are preparing to go out on patrol, so when the interview room is ready, they won't have much time for me, maybe ten minutes at best. I wonder if I should try to bribe him, then think better of it.

"Look, Sergeant," I say in my best let's-be-straight-about-this voice, "this isn't just any old murder. It's not sex-related, and it doesn't look like a drugs vendetta. When the story breaks, it will be all over the world. Everyone who checks the news on their Internet account will see headlines like 'MURDER AND ORGAN THEFT IN SUNNY PHUKET, THAILAND.' People very very high up in government will want to be sure the Phuket police have done all they can to cooperate."

He's about fifty and has been on the local force about thirty years, which in itself says *survivor with no scruples*. That character trait is confirmed by a sloe-eyed cynicism and a way of looking into the distance as if I'm a pain in the neck who has to be tolerated, but not for an unreasonable length of time. Now he turns his best blank stare onto me, lets a beat pass, then says, "Those houses have protection." He shrugs. The shrug is a reference to my future: do I really want to challenge the protector of the houses—or not?

I stare back without saying anything. I guess I don't always come across as a law enforcement fanatic, but I can get into the part when I need to. He shrugs again, picks up the desk telephone, speaks so softly I can't hear what he says, then leads me to an interview room and tells me to wait. About five minutes later two cops walk in: overweight, dumb, and probably honest in the context of local cops. The sergeant is with them and looks like he intends to stay during the interview.

"If you don't get the fuck out, I'll say in my report that you refused to permit these men to speak freely," I say in an even voice with a smile. That's quite a no-frills challenge, and the atmosphere congeals. He gives me that look again, with a touch of pity in it this time, but he turns to leave the room and closes the door softly behind him.

Like simple men the world over, Constables Hel and Tak decide to obey whatever superior is standing before them at the present moment. They look at me politely and expectantly.

"Just tell me all you know about the mansion on Vulture Peak," I say, already weary.

Hel and Tak look at each other. "It has protection," Hel says and looks at Tak, who nods.

"But do you ever go up there?"

"Only when someone invites us."

"About once a year."

"Have you been this year?"

"Once."

"When?"

"About five months ago."

"What happens when you visit?"

"A Thai man, a manager, welcomes us. He's very polite and makes us feel welcome."

"A really nice guy."

"Is he alone?"

"Twice he's been alone, three times there have been people there."

"What kind of people?"

"Chinese people."

"We don't know that."

"No, we don't know that. Looked like Chinese people."

"What were they doing, the Chinese people?"

"Playing mahjong."

"Not always mahjong."

"Sometimes cards."

"Gambling?"

"We don't know that."

"No, we don't know that."

I stare at them, then turn away to look out the window. It's frustration, not technique, that suddenly turns me on my heels to stare them in the face, one by one. "Where does the protection come from?"

"The army," Hel says, taken by surprise. Tak nudges his elbow. Hel stares at his partner, then looks scared.

"You don't know that," Tak says.

"Everybody knows it," Hel says.

"General Zinna, by any chance?"

Hel and Tak lose the color from their cheeks and stare at me as at a condemned man. "We don't know that," they say in unison.

I'm in a cab on my way to the airport when I remember I've forgotten to call Chanya this morning. She could be feeling a tad insecure, with me all alone in Phuket—always assuming those rumors are untrue. There's also something troubling me; I refer to a kind of telepathy between a man and woman who live together. In the back of my mind is that sweet shot of weakness I felt last night, that love-twinge which passed in the twinkling of an eye, but which remains as an afterthought. I have no intention of calling Om tonight or any night, but the memory of her sitting in that deck chair under the moon has yet to fade.

At exactly the moment I'm thinking that thought, my phone whooshes:

Hi there, you okay? C.

I text back: Sure. You?

Okay. Where did you stay last night?

Cheap hotel

Who with?

Alone

Don't believe you

14

Hong Kong is the world's biggest shopping mall, but the business of Hong Kong is China. Apart from a brief moment when the Chinese Communist Party was communist, it has always been so, from the nineteenth century, when Britain sent gunboats up the Pearl River to force opium down the lungs of twenty million Chinese, to the present day, when the gigantic container port of Kwai Chung sends goods to and receives goods from the mainland that, if spread out horizontally, would occupy a land area as vast as a medium-sized country, or if placed end to end would stretch around the world three times, depending on what statistic you prefer. After Mao's revolution of 1949, when the great expat party that was Shanghai finally came to a bloody end, the remains of the Raj continued its largely alcoholic contribution to world culture right here in the former narcotics entrepot, where the fortunes of a few were made out of the misery of the millions. From the start in the 1840s, if you wanted to be a real player, what you needed was a place on the peak called Victoria from which you commuted by palanquin carried by a team of four coolies who, for reasons of survival, were inevitable end consumers of your honorable product, with a life expectancy of maybe thirty years if they were lucky. (*The more one eats and drinks at the Hong Kong Club, the more of one's dope Johnny Chinaman has to smoke so he can haul one up the hill afterward, ha, ha. Can't go wrong, old boy.*)

The opium has gone and there is a funicular railway, but the ultimate proof of wealth beyond measure remains a spread on the peak, where you can rely on a refreshing breeze when everyone else is sweating down on the shore, and a Scottish mist weaves romantically over the hills during winter. Naturally, the first thing Lilly and Polly's grandfather did when he arrived with his factory from Shanghai was to buy a home up here, and it seems the property has remained in the family ever since. It was not difficult to find all this out by making a few inquiries before I left Bangkok, but I've not yet decided whether to forewarn them of my arrival, or to simply turn up at the door. Of course, there's no guarantee they will be at home: they could still be trading organs with *les misérables* at Lourdes, or playing roulette at Monte Carlo. I'm taking a flier, as usual.

The address I've been given involves taking a path called Stanley around the top of the peak. Naturally, those who live up here may use their cars to commute, but the rest of us have to walk. I find the house easily enough. There is an iron gate with a large red button to push and a microphone to speak into—and a speaker that says, "Yes?"

"Detective Sonchai Jitpleecheep," I announce.

Silence, then something clanks at the bottom of the iron gate, which begins to swing open so slowly, I am over the threshold long before it has reached the full compass of its aperture, whereupon it immediately starts to close again. I'm about twenty yards down a hundred-yard drive before I hear it clank shut. I ought to add that it's a magnificent day up here on billionaire mountain, with almost zero humidity, a cerulean blue sky against which contrasts perfectly the dark foliage of *bodi* leaves, ferns, and beech. The house from this side looks like a long half-timbered bungalow in the Elizabethan style, but a glance over the hedge reveals that the top floor of the house must be no more than a kind of lobby, for living quarters, tennis courts, a swimming pool, and what looks like a Chinese garden in the Ming style spread out about twenty feet below.

I must confess I was expecting, in the circumstances, to be greeted by a maid; instead an arched door (English green oak) has been left fully open for me to stride through. Inside: an intimidating selection of classic Chinese blackwood furniture stands on gray flagstones: stern chairs with curved backs, a student's bench at which would-be mandarins once knelt, a blanket trunk with mother-of-pearl inlay, a wardrobe in polished elm more than seven feet tall with great brass locks—and a collection of black-and-white photographs which form a family narrative that circumnavigates the long room. I would like to study the pictures, which from a quick glance seem to feature old Shanghai with the wealthy all dressed in top hats, monkey suits, and flowing dinner gowns and the poor in traditional Chinese peasant dress, but feel like an intruder who needs to identify himself before someone calls the police.

A second door, also oak and arched, also open, leads to a set of broad stone stairs that turn on themselves to land me on the ground floor. Corridors that must have been cut into the rock lead to the left and right, while an oval solarium of generous proportions, populated by a hundred varieties of orchid, invites me onward. The solarium is of the wrought-iron kind that reached a perfection of style a hundred years ago.

The main door is fitted with tinted glass, which throws a jolly collage of color onto the flagstones. I open it to emerge into the fresh air. The tennis court and swimming pool are on my left, the Ming garden with tiny humped stone bridges and trickling brooks on my right; the frozen psychosis of Hong Kong with its motherboard of steel and glass towers hums far below. At a marble table in the garden on the other side of the bridge, the Twins are sitting with a carafe of white wine and two glasses. One of them—I would not dare to guess which—is holding a revolver to her head while the other watches with considerable concentration. The one with the gun slowly squeezes the trigger until there is a click, then replaces it on the table. Jaw jutting, her sister now picks up the gun, holds it to her head, and slowly pulls the trigger until it clicks. She replaces the gun on the table. I am not surprised to note a sudden relaxation in the atmosphere, permitting them both to look up.

"Detective, what a surprise," one of them—the last to fail to die— says. They smile.

"Tell me it wasn't loaded," I say as I approach.

By way of answer she hands me the gun. "This is what we call our shrine."

When I spin the chamber, I see there is one cartridge in it. I look at the sisters, who raise their eyebrows. "It's a blank, right?" The eyebrows rise higher. I align the cartridge with the trigger and point—it must be the boy in me—at the crystal carafe. I already know the answer by the way they have both moved their chairs back, but I fire anyway. There goes the crystal carafe, as the shot echoes over the mountain. The last of the Chablis dribbles over the marble.

Suddenly I need to sit down. One of the sisters drags up a chair. "Do you do this often?" I say.

"Only when it's the maid's day off," one says. "That's why there was no one to greet you at the door. Very sorry, appalling manners and all that—but as you see, we were in the middle of something exciting."

Not for the first time in the company of these two, I am dragged into another world: surreal, exotic, rich, and mad. The scene is still playing in my mind: yes, the gun was loaded with a live shell; yes, each of them did raise it to her head and pull the trigger. But I still can't believe it; I'm tempted to ask them to do it again.

"I don't believe you play it every week. One of you would be dead by now."

They exchange glances. "That's true. You must be a good detective."

Silence. Now one of them says, "So, which do you think I am, Lilly or Polly?"

"I have no idea."

"Well, neither do we," they say in unison.

Nothing in my career as a cop, or as a human, has prepared me for this conversation. The beauty of the day here on the mountaintop, the ancient genius of the garden, the buzzards hanging in the air close to the peak, the sailboats and pleasure vessels in the harbor—it all seems to have taken on a darker hue, like a hallucination that has started to go wrong. "What do you mean, 'Neither do we'?" I say.

One of them—I shall have to call her Lilly or I'll go mad—makes a sulky face. "Sometimes I'm her and she's me. It's easy to get mixed up."

"You're a Buddhist," Polly says. "You must know there's no such thing as a self. Think of it: when you want to see yourself, you look in a mirror. You have a choice whether to look or not."

"But with us the other is there all the time in a mirror that follows you around. The same but different," Lilly says.

"It's not at all unusual for twins to go homicidal and want to kill each other," Polly explains.

"Oh," I say.

"It's a trick we discovered when we were teens. The Russian roulette. We both knew we would murder each other one day if we didn't do something—so we used the gun."

"It has a way of clearing the air."

"Sure does," I say. "You mean you were in the middle of an argument?"

"A serious one."

"What about?"

They exchange a glance. "Livers and kidneys."

"She bet five kidneys in a game of blackjack yesterday—"

"I did not. It was three kidneys."

"You use human organs as betting chips?"

"We use commodities. Sometimes it's gold, sometimes livers, sometimes kidneys, sometimes pig belly futures."

"I wanted to talk about something else," I say.

They look at me expectantly. I keep looking at the gun and the splinters of glass on the floor. I let too many beats pass and miss my cue, perhaps deliberately. Now that I've found the Twins, I realize that any meeting with them would be futile without more background.

Lilly says, "Let me show you around. We haven't taken you on the standard tour yet."

The other, Polly, remains at the table while Lilly and I climb the stairs to the top floor, where I came in. We start at the beginning of the photographic display, with a Chinese man in top hat and tails standing in a Chinese street that looks like circa 1930s. He is young, with a cigar in his hand and a shine in his eyes that promises a ruthless and successful future. "That's Grandfather. He was a very strong man— you can see it in his eyes. Strong men castrate their sons, a psychologist told us ages ago: that's what Peter the Great did to his son. That's what Grandfather did to Daddy. Daddy was an alcoholic and a gambler. Grandfather saw what a dead loss he was, so he put almost the whole of the property and his fortune in a trust a few years before he died. Daddy couldn't touch it except for living expenses, otherwise he would have gambled it all away.

"It still is in trust, otherwise *we* would have gambled it all away. That old bastard gave us such a piddling allowance, we had to scrounge around for years and years until we discovered organ trafficking. We knew at once we were just made for it. Imagine what it does to your worldview when you can see profit in everyone you meet. We felt the same excitement Grandfather told us about, to be perfectly placed in an industry that's about to take off."

"What industry was he in?"

"Armaments. At the beginning of the Second World War."

She gives me the big Chinese smile. Is she joking? Trying to scare me? Or is she just insane? Or—scariest of all—simply telling the truth? I see a world in which we size each other up not for sex appeal but for the resale value of our livers.

We stop in front of a cabinet in the same blackwood.

"Opium pipes?" I say. "With all the bits and pieces." Behind the glass must be the most complete sets I've seen, each one a work of art. I missed them on the way in. "They're exquisite," I say.

"They're called layouts. Each one includes two pipes laid on each side of the mother-of-pearl inlay. The bowls are made of Yixing clay. The miniature cupboard at the end is for the opium and whatever one used to thicken it, quite often just aspirin."

"They look well used."

"Mmm. Grandfather smoked every Friday night. He started in Shanghai, of course, and continued over here. In those days the British didn't take it seriously, even though it was already illegal. He forbade my father to smoke it, though. He said it was harmless so long as you were strong enough to use it sparingly. So Daddy became an alcoholic instead. Do you think that was an improvement? To die from opium addiction is, of course, a disgusting death—but not as bad as coughing up your own liver."

"That's how he died, your father?"

She twists her head to indicate she didn't like the question. "People with strong affections develop fetishes. I can't tell you how many Polly and I have about gambling. And the other things we 'do." A smile. "Grandfather loved everything to do with opium—he even grew poppies in the greenhouse. When you love something, you want it every way you can get it. But he was so strong, he never let the opium dominate. I have a luck charm tattooed on the top of my left thigh. Maybe I'll show you one day." She has come significantly closer.

There is a sound on the stairs. Polly appears, daggers in her eyes.

"You see what I mean about twins?" Lilly says. "Insanely jealous. She's not attracted to you at all. She just couldn't stand the thought of my having you. Isn't that right, love?"

Polly walks over to kiss me on the cheek. "She doesn't want you either. Neither of us likes sex. She's just provoking me. She's angry that I didn't die just now, aren't you?"

"Same to you with knobs on," Lilly says, and sticks out her tongue.

They are standing on either side of me, and the experience is making me feel faint. I am quite certain they know what they are doing. (I hope you will not laugh at me, DFR, when I explain to you that these women are not human at all. They are a variety of *pawb* or ogre that lives in human bodies, native to Southeast Asia. I didn't want to test your credulity by mentioning it before, but now I trust the matter is obvious. FYI, there are plenty of demons masquerading as humans all over the world, many of them in high places—political leaders, captains of industry; they are quite unaware of their true identity but often betray themselves by a tragic lack of depth.) The combined force of their malevolence is quite debilitating. I think the game of Russian roulette was set up for my benefit, a shock tactic to disorient me.

A buzzer sounds. They exchange a glance. Polly goes to the door to press a button. "Yes?"

"Polly? Lilly? It's Sam. Just popped by to say thanks for the other night." It's a woman's voice with a British accent.

Polly and Lilly share a glance, then Polly squeals into the microphone. "Sam! *Darling!* How *wonderful.*"

"I hope I'm not disturbing anything. My chauffeur just came back from the shops and—you know what gossips Filipinos are—he told me he saw the most *gorgeous* man standing outside your gates, so I won't come in. I just wanted to say *thankseversomuch* for such a *wonderful* party—you two still know how to throw them—and *how*, loves."

"*Of course* you *must* come in!" Polly squeals again into the mike. "Stop being so absolutely disgustingly polite and British. You know we both *adore* you to bits!" She presses a button, exchanges another glance with her sister, and shrugs.

The three of us wait in silence until there's a knock on the door. Lilly opens it, and a tall blond woman in her thirties enters, brimming with health, smiles, and money. Everyone squeals except me: "Darling!"

"Darlings!"

"Oh, darling, you look absolutely fantastic!"

"So do you two! *Ohmygod*, you're wearing the same clothes! It's like seeing double. And after all these years."

"Guess who's who," Lilly says.

"Yes, guess."

"A glass of Pimm's if you get it right."

"Two if you get it wrong."

Laughter. The woman called Sam throws me a glance.

"Oh, gosh, forgot to introduce you. This is—Detective—ah—"

"Jitpleecheep," I say.

The blond woman shakes my hand. Blue Brahmin eyes check me out: what caste do I belong to? I'm a cop and Eurasian, not her level at all. "*So* pleased to meet you."

"*Enchanté*," I say, Buddha knows why.

"Well," Sam says, "an absolutely gorgeous policeman who speaks French, only you two could pull that off. Where on *earth* did you find him?"

"He took us to Monte Carlo. Didn't you, Detective?"

"Well," Sam says again, definitively upstaged, "how *interesting*. Look darlings, I must be off. *TTD*, you know."

"Oh, it's always *things to do* with you. Won't you stay for a Pimm's, love?"

"I really can't, loves. I've got to go down to the snake pit to buy a birthday present for James. He's terribly sensitive about these things, and he *has* done rather well on the derivatives market lately, so he *does* deserve a little TLC."

"Are you going down into the city?" I say on impulse. "I'm going that way myself."

"Well, of course," Sam says, "I've got the driver waiting up top. Are you ready?"

"Oh, yes," I say, "I'm ready." I turn to the Twins. "Wonderful as ever." I kiss them each on both cheeks as they turn them.

"You don't have any bags or anything?" Sam says.

"Oh, no, he doesn't have any bags," Lilly says.

"How long have you known the Twins?" Sam asks. We are in the back of a long, low Jaguar with a polished walnut dashboard and a Filipino chauffeur in gray livery.

"About a month. You?"

"Ever since we moved here eight years ago. It's a village up on the peak, everyone knows everyone, and the Twins—everyone calls them that—grew up here. They're as much a fixture as the mountain itself. Our kids go to the same school they went to. Aren't they amazing?"

"Yes, amazing."

"Of course, being ethnic Chinese and speaking the lingo, they have *guanxi* coming out of their ears. Were there any servants there, by the way?"

I want to ask what *guanxi* is, but I've missed the moment. "No. It's the maid's day off."

Sam snorts and leans forward. "Did you hear that, Hill? They told him it's the maid's day off." Hill chuckles. She turns back to me. "They're notorious for not being able to keep servants. Wait till I tell everyone they told you it's the maid's day off." She gives a big, hard English laugh. "See, they use the same agency as we do, and Hill is in with the agent, so we get all the gossip."

"Really? I'm looking for a servant myself," I say. "Which agency do you use?"

She gives me her first frank expression: shrewd, penetrating, clever. "You're investigating them for something? The usual thing, I suppose."

"Yes, the usual thing."

She leans forward again. "Hill, do you have an agency card with you, so we can be of service to the police?"

Hill pulls a card out of his jacket and passes it back to her. She hands it to me. "Which unit of the police are you with? Fraud?"

"Not exactly. But if you have any information on how the Twins make a living, that would be helpful."

"Make a living? Well, they both have degrees in medical science, quite good ones they say. But nobody could imagine them working as physicians, not even them, so they taught anatomy for a few years at the Chinese University. That was hardly a living wage for them, so they went into business, some kind of China trade. No one seems to know exactly, but they travel a lot and are able to get hold of money these days. If you're not fraud, what are you?"

"Murder."

Silence. "I see. May I know if anyone up on the peak has been murdered?"

"Oh, I'm not based in Hong Kong. I'm from Bangkok."

"Oh," she says.

"What would 'the usual thing' be, by the way?"

She moves away to look out the window. "I'm sorry, I thought you were local police. We're in Central now—where would you like to be dropped?"

The domestic staff agent—a woman with a Filipina accent—will not give me the maid's name or telephone number, but when I say I'm willing to pay for information, she promises to pass on my own number. I take a stroll among the glittering caverns of Central, then take the Star Ferry to Kowloon. I'm staring across the harbor at the architectural hysteria of downtown Hong Kong when my cell phone rings. A young woman's voice speaks slowly and precisely in old school English: "May I speak to Detective Sonchai Jitpleecheep, please?"

She agrees to meet me this evening in the Neptune II bar in Wanchai.

. . .

The bar is an underground cavern that seems to be a Filipina hangout as well as a pickup joint for freelancers. I order a beer and watch the Filipino band get ready on the stage and wait. I gave the maid—her name is Maria—my description. After the band has started into a perfect imitation of an old Bruce Springsteen number, a woman in her midtwenties sits down on the stool beside me. She is heavily made up. I think she comes here to make some extra money now and then.

"Hello, sir. I am Maria."

I buy her a drink. She smiles and wriggles in a way that could be provocative, or not, depending on what I want. When I ask about the Twins, she asks about money. I pass a few notes in Hong Kong dollars under the counter. Then she starts to talk. It seems the Twins are notorious. They have to pay double the going rate for maids, and even then most quit after a month or so.

"The first thing that disturbs one is their fights, sir," Maria says. "They are quite bloodcurdling. Quite often one will run after the other with a weapon, a knife or some heavy object, and the other will have to lock herself in a room until the danger is past. Many a time I was frightened for my life. Then one of the former maids told me they have both spent time in mental hospitals. They are quite insane, sir, in my opinion."

"That's why the maids always leave?"

"Not exactly, sir. There is a room, sir, which they keep shut for the first week of one's engagement. Then when they have decided one is strong enough, they order one to clean it. I shudder when I think of it, sir." She shudders. "It is the most terrifying experience of my life." I wait for her to finish shuddering. "That room is full of human organs, sir."

"Human organs?"

"Yes, sir. The organs are embalmed in bottles on shelves, just like in a hospital or laboratory. They appear to collect them."

"They collect human organs?"

"Yes, sir. All with labels in Chinese characters. It is their hobby. They receive body parts and dissect them at home. They appear to be quite skilled. It would appear to be legal, however, otherwise they would not be so open about it. But that room is full of ghosts, sir. We Filipinas are quite sensitive to such matters. In my village in Oriental

Mindoro, there is a good deal of lore on the subject, so I know what I am talking about. Ghosts of those who have died violently and who are seeking a new bodily vehicle in which to express themselves. I have spoken to the other maids, all of whom agree with me on this point."

"I heard they often get into trouble with the police."

"That is quite a different matter, sir. It seems they are frequently short of funds and have recourse to fraudulent practices. However, they always seem to find the money in time to pay off the debt and avoid prosecution. In any case, they have *guanxi*, so they are able to get away with such things. That is all I can tell you. If you wish, I can ask some of the other maids to contact you. I am sure they will corroborate my evidence."

I pass her some more notes under the counter and forget to ask what *guanxi* is.

The bar is warming up. Since we have been talking, a number of Chinese women with mainland accents have arrived, along with more Filipinas and quite a few Thais. Some middle-aged men have dropped in after work in their business suits. It's almost like home. Maria seems to have a friendship with one of the men who looks like a British businessman and excuses herself. I watch the band get ready for their next number, which is vintage Beatles from *Abbey Road*. Then they play "California Dreaming" for the old folks before segueing into "Between the Moon and New York City," then a couple of Cantopop numbers I've never heard before, each song reproduced perfectly to the point of being indistinguishable from the original. While I'm listening to the music, a Thai woman in her early twenties approaches me. As soon as she realizes I'm Thai, she gives up on the proposition, and we talk about Bangkok politics and the proposed extension to the Skytrain.

I must have been enjoying myself because more than two hours have passed. It's about ten-thirty, and the bar has filled. There's plenty of light groping going on, but it's pretty tame compared to my mother's bar; couples disappear up the stairs to the short-time hotels just the same, though. I also climb up the steps to street level, where I'm immediately surrounded by four uniformed cops and an inspector, also in full uniform with resplendent stars and a shiny peaked cap. At about six foot, he is unusually tall for a local Chinese.

"Passport," the inspector says. I give it to him. He examines it, then jerks his chin toward a police van parked down the street. "I'm afraid I must ask you to accompany us to the police station," he says.

Now, DFR, a tip from a pro: the first thing you do when apprehended by police in a capitalist democracy, where everyone is equal under the law, is prove to them that you possess high monetary value and social status, whether you do or not. So when he gives me back my passport, I make a point of opening my wallet as if I keep it there, and allow the black Amex to fall out. I was afraid he might not know what it is, but this is Hong Kong and he is Chinese. He has instantly adapted his manner. Now we are walking together to the police van as if we are chums, and he gets in the back with me.

"It's a little thing, probably won't take up too much time," he explains, sitting on the opposite bench. "Just that some busybody *gwaipaw* British woman complained that you were impersonating a Hong Kong police officer. Of course, she was just trying to be important and collect gossip at the same time. You weren't, were you?"

"Of course not. If it's that HiSo woman in the Jaguar you're talking about, all I said was that I was a police officer, then when she asked more, I told her I was based in Bangkok."

"Good," he nods, "very good. Even if you're lying your head off, which you probably are, there's no way I can challenge that line of defense." He removes his hat and puts a hand on his spiky black hair, as if he enjoys the feeling of bounce. (I understand: there is something irresistible about the feel of spiky Asian hair when it's short. Whenever one of my mother's girls goes that way, we like to bounce our hands up and down on it; it has the feel of a soft broom.) The van trundles toward a set of lights. "Anyway, I don't really care if you were impersonating a police officer, I'm more interested in what you were doing with the Yip twins. So how about we do a deal? I'll pretend to believe you are not here on police business, and you'll pretend to believe I have a right to interrogate you about the Yips."

"That's what I call policing," I say.

. . .

At the station Inspector Chan does not lead me to the cells or the interrogation rooms, although they all look pretty comfortable compared to District 8, but straight to his office. (Such luxury: air-conditioned to exactly twenty-four Celsius, and he has his own door that he shares with no one. That's a tiger economy for you.) Chan hangs his hat on a hook so he can press a hand up and down on his spikes while he sits in his executive chair, opens his top drawer to fiddle with something, and stares at me. "You told the *gwaipaw* you were investigating a murder," he says.

"No, I didn't. I told her I was from the murder squad."

"So you're from the murder squad investigating tax evasion? Is that how Thai law works?"

"We already agreed I wasn't investigating anything." I stand up. "Where's your voice recorder? In your top drawer, by any chance?"

He smiles, takes out a digital voice recorder from a drawer, and lays it on his desk. "Just testing. Turn it off yourself so you feel comfortable."

I look at it for a moment as I sit down again. I say in a loud voice, "I am here in Hong Kong purely for private interest and have no professional purpose to pursue during my stay in the SAR of the People's Republic of China," then switch it off and give it back to him.

Now he's laughing. "Streetwise, that's for sure. Kind of third-world, though. You remind me of the sort of cops we had here under the British. They were so corrupt, everyone spent their entire working lives covering their backs. Had to—it was what the job was all about."

"And now?"

"Now it's all about *guanxi*—a different ballgame altogether."

I'm about to ask what *guanxi* is, when he stands abruptly and starts to pace with his hands in his pockets. "I'll be straight. I run the cops up on the peak, and one of my most important assignments is to keep an eye on the Yips."

"They are trouble?"

"They're gifted maniacs. Eccentrics of the old school, the kind of Chinese women the West doesn't yet know much about. Ha! A lot of *gweilo* have this fantasy our women are all submissive slaves who would still have their feet bound if not for Western enlightenment. Anyone who thinks that way should meet the Yips."

"Tell me."

"No. You first."

It may not seem it, DFR, but I'm in a tricky spot. Chan could easily find some excuse for locking me up and delaying my departure if I don't play his game, but on the other hand it has occurred to me that everything I've done that involved the Yip sisters has been either illegal or highly eccentric. I'm playing for time when I say, "They like to gamble."

Chan stops pacing and stares at me. "You don't say."

"I mean, they'll gamble for astronomical stakes on anything, like a fly crawling up a window."

"So would ninety percent of the population of this city. How d'you think we got so good at capitalism?" He is watching me with a slightly altered attitude. "They didn't invite you to Monte Carlo by any chance?"

"Monte Carlo?"

"From your body language I think they did."

"Did they invite you?"

"Yes, but unlike you, I didn't go. You went, didn't you?"

I'm fighting a blush. "It was part of an ongoing investigation I'm not at liberty to talk about."

He extends an arm in order to point a finger directly at me and says, "*Ha!* You did. You went. *Ha, ha,* you fell for it. Now you're pissed that you were not the only one. *Ha, ha.* They corrupted you in a heartbeat, *ha, ha.* Poor little Thai cop lives in a hovel and drives a clapped-out Toyota if he drives at all, dazzled by money and glamour—I'm assuming that black Amex is just on loan—from a wealthy superior perhaps who has a vested interest in the case? Now the Yips have you in the palms of their hands. *Ha, ha.*"

This guy sure knows how to irritate. I've never used soft-obnoxious as an interrogation technique myself, although I've heard of it. Just to spite him, I refuse to ask how many other men the Twins have taken to Monte Carlo over the years.

"D'you want to know how many other men have fallen for that?"

"No."

"Liar. I'll tell you. I keep records. You are the last of at least five we know about."

"Were all the others Hong Kong cops?"

He frowns and sits in his chair, puts his feet up on the desk. "No."

"But some were?"

"One."

"Did he live in a hovel and drive a Toyota?"

Chan stares at me. I know what the stare means because I've used it so many times myself. It means that if I don't tell him something useful, or at least a piece of gossip worth repeating, he'll hold me for the night out of pure spite. "I'm on a special assignment," I confess.

The phrase, hackneyed and overused though it is, seems to strike a chord in Chan. He raises his brows. "About time. That's what I've been trying to get at since we picked you up."

"But I mean, it's a *Thai* special assignment."

"Meaning? Don't tell me, let me guess. Meaning illegal, not at all the sort of thing cops do, but something you have to do to lick the ass of your superior?" He waves a hand. "We study Thai police as an example of how not to do things. Now I've met you, I know why."

I have to make a choice. On the one hand, I really want to get back to Bangkok; on the other, if I tell all, I risk getting snuffed by Vikorn. But I really want to get back to Bangkok. "It's to do with organ trafficking," I say.

To my surprise, Chan looks suddenly bored. "Really?"

"You know that's what they do?"

"Sure, but they don't do it in Hong Kong." He has suddenly and totally lost interest—or is he faking? "How far have you got?"

"Nowhere yet—I'm at the beginning."

"That's why you're here? Nothing else? No other dimensions to your investigation?"

"What 'other dimensions' could there be?"

"Not telling you." Chan bites his thumbnail for a while. "D'you gamble?"

"Not at all."

"Really? They say Thais are worse than Chinese. The million-dollar blackjack tables at Las Vegas are dominated by your people these days."

"The Thais who play at Vegas all have Chinese blood. They're Chiu Chow, from Swatow. They run the economy."

Chan assesses me with his eyes. "And you? You're half *gweilo*? A half-caste product of a GI on R&R from Vietnam and a Thai peasant?"

"The GI was a peasant too, from the Midwest. I have pure blood."

The volatile Chan seems to have decided he likes me for saying that. As an interrogator myself, I can see he has made a decision of some sort. He has changed his tone and manner by about a hundred and eighty degrees and speaks almost gently when he nods at the map on his wall. It is of Hong Kong Island, Kowloon, the New Territories, and the various islands that make up the Hong Kong SAR. Now he stands to walk up to it and points at a giant island at least twice the size of Hong Kong.

"Lantao Island. Heard of it?"

"Isn't that where the airport is located?"

"Correct. It's where you landed. Personally, I find it mysterious the way Lantao Island has become important all over again, thanks to the airport."

"Why, what was it important for before?"

"Opium storage. There were pontoons used as go-downs at all the western beaches — it's closest to Macao and the Pearl River. They had square miles of pontoons where opium was stored. You see?"

"Not really."

He is pointing at the jagged coastline of the island and showing how close it is to the mouth of the Pearl River. "The ships from India — Patna was the capital of opium — would unload onto the rafts, so smaller riverboats could take the product up into the heart of Canton."

I nod politely while scratching my jaw. Chan just doesn't look like the kind to carry resentment for the colonial debt. Nor does any other Hong Kong Chinese I've ever met; in this former colony, at least, the symbiosis between races was deeply satisfying to both. The locals made even more dough out of Hong Kong than the colonizing Brits, from opium to coffins: most of the caskets used during the Vietnam War were made in Hong Kong.

"Of course, like everything else in history, different generations have different interpretations. When I first heard about how grotesque the British narco empire was, I couldn't believe it. Then, soon after I made inspector, a very gifted Chinese academic from the mainland enlightened me."

The inspector is watching me closely, like a man dropping hints incomprehensible to the recipient. I have not a clue where he is going. To be polite I say, "What did this historian tell you?"

Chan screws up his eyes in a kind of concentration. "Oh, it wasn't that he was interested in the human suffering angle. He wasn't a historian. He was an economist."

He is waiting to see how I react, so I say, "An economist?"

"Yes. He said think about it."

"Think about what?"

"Think about why the British, who were quite fanatical Christians in those days, should have blackened their names and their souls for all time by becoming the biggest narcotics traffickers in the history of the world."

"So, what was the answer?"

Chan loses interest in the map and concentrates on my face. "Suppose, in the logic of empire, they had no choice? Suppose that in their time—we're talking about the early nineteenth century—there was just enough wealth and employment in China for, say, ten percent of the population. And most of the rest of the world, even working-class England, was in the same boat. The British were almost as addicted as the Chinese. You see, opium was even cheaper than gin. According to this economist, even the great Wilberforce, whom the Brits like to cite as the honorable Englishman who got slavery abolished, he too was an opium addict." He pauses. "Looked at from that point of view, the opium trade was not so bad. It was a way of keeping twenty million unemployed men docile. As soon as opium was suppressed, China tore itself apart in revolution—and the U.K. lost its empire."

"A modern Chinese economist told you that?"

"Yes, but only by way of illustration. After all, economists are there to forecast the future. See, his punch line was: the world economy has positioned itself in such a way that almost everyone is going to be unemployed by the middle of this century. The American sucker-consumer is now bankrupt for the next fifty years, and there's no way Asians generally are going to waste their money en masse on toys like iPods—hoarding is hardwired in every head east of Suez. Americans are strange people. They allow themselves to be bled white by gang-sters for generation after generation and call it freedom. But that bliss-ful ignorance may be in its endgame. The consumer economy is already dead—what we're experiencing right now is its wake. What do you think governments are going to use to keep everyone docile when the shit finally hits the fan?"

"Surely not opium?"

"No. Not opium. Opium is an ugly way of dying. How about cannabis? The Spanish used it in Spanish Morocco to keep the Riff tribesmen sedated. The best thing about it: young men delude them-selves into believing they're already war heroes. They don't need to kill anyone." He smiles. "When this economist came here and told a select group of cadres that the PRC was thinking of legalizing it within the next decade, everyone left the room to make calls to Beijing, to get in on the ground floor with one of the consortiums. Imagine the value of a license that permits you to sell marijuana to a significant portion of two billion people. Salivation in floods from Shanghai to Lombard Street." He pauses. "Of course, there will be other consequences of extreme poverty, worldwide."

It must be clear from my posture and my expression that I have no idea what he's talking about. He makes a decision, smiles at the same time as he loses interest in me except perhaps as a distant colleague to whom he should show hospitality. He puts an arm around me as he leads me out of the station. "If you stay one more night, I can get you invited to a box in Happy Valley on the finish line for the Wednesday-night races."

"Would that involve gambling, by any chance?"

We are in the police parking lot outside the station. He talks to a sergeant who seems to be running the cars. Chan makes a point of opening the back door of the cop car and says, "Remember, no one's elected in Beijing. That means they have time to plan ahead. They have teams looking fifty, even a hundred years into the future. They have detailed economic and social models. And they don't have democracy. They know what's coming next."

"Like what?"

"Like organs for sale on eBay."

"Okay."

"Bear that in mind next time you talk to the Yips."

"Okay."

"And tell me every damned thing you learn."

"Okay."

"Or forget about entering Hong Kong, or China, ever again."

"Okay."

Now my Chinese colleague makes an Elizabethan bow: "'Good night, sweet prince, and flights of angels sing thee to thy rest.'" He checks my incredulous expression. "See, Hong Kong was still a crown colony when I went to school. The Brits saw their culture as something to ram down the throats of wogs, chinks, and nignogs in far-flung colonies, so they could pretend to be improving instead of exploiting. Unselfishly, they kept very little of it for themselves. I know Shakespeare better than any Brit I ever met."

Now I'm in a Hong Kong police car racing to the airport. Once I'm in the terminal, I make a beeline for the computers that give free Internet access so long as you don't take more than fifteen minutes. It's takes less than one to access Wikipedia:

> **Guanxi** describes the basic dynamic in personalized networks of influence, and is a central idea in *Chinese* society. In Western media, the *pinyin* romanization of this Chinese word is becoming more widely used instead of the two common translations—"connections" and "relationships"—as neither of those terms sufficiently reflects the wide cultural implications that *guanxi* describes.

Closely related concepts include that of *ganqing*, a measure which reflects the depth of feeling within an interpersonal relationship; *renqing*, the moral obligation to maintain the relationship; and the idea of *"face,"* meaning social status, propriety, prestige, or more realistically a combination of all three . . .

As articulated in the sociological works of leading Chinese academic *Fei Xiaotong*, the Chinese—in contrast to other societies—tend to see social relations in terms of networks rather than boxes. Hence, people are perceived as being "near" or "far" rather than "in" or "out."

I have over an hour to wait for my flight, so I find a seat and close my eyes to try to work out what it is that's bothering me about the Filipina maid Maria. Something I left out, some subtle semaphore. I put the problem together with Chan's insults about Thai poverty, and I see where I went wrong. I call her, and she answers on the third ring.

"Maria, I hope this is not too late."

"Oh, no, sir. I am just in a taxi on my way home, so we can talk."

"Maria, would you trust me to send you a thousand Hong Kong dollars by Western Union? I have to apologize, you must have thought me very mean."

"Oh, no, sir. That's okay, sir. We have a very high cost of living in Hong Kong, that is all."

"Where d'you want the money sent?"

"To my mother in Oriental Mindoro, sir, care of the post office in our village. I think it better if I SMS on this number."

"Okay, I promise to send it tomorrow. Now, please, regarding the Twins, there's something you left out, right? Why is there such hostility between them? Why do they want to kill each other? They are beautiful, healthy, HiSo, rich, have the very best of everything. It seems unnatural."

"Yes, sir, *unnatural* is certainly the word that comes to mind, sir. So far as I am aware, there are three schools of thought, sir."

"Okay."

"The first posits exposure to the nefarious practices of their grandfather, who enjoyed having rivals tortured to death in front of him. There are two strands to this hypothesis, the first being that the girls themselves witnessed such atrocities, the other, more subtly, suggesting that they inherited the old man's sadistic gene."

"That's school one?"

"Yes, sir. The second school, inevitably perhaps in today's fallen world, posits a rape/seduction by the father, who was a known pedophile."

"Ah! And the third?"

"The third school, sir, takes this theme and adapts it to all that is known about them, their family, and the relationship with the father."

"Yes?"

"According to the third school, sir, they quite callously calculated in their early teens that it would be to their advantage to seduce their father themselves. I think the leverage that would have accrued from such a strategy is obvious."

"Wow! So, Maria, which school do you bat for?"

"All three, sir."

I pause. "All three?"

"Yes, sir. Of course, I am merely floating a hypothesis, but it seems to me to be consistent with the facts that they did indeed inherit the grandfather's hunger for absolute power at any cost, plus a dastardly capacity to enjoy the sufferings of others. I think they also seduced their father, and that the father immediately became addicted to their attentions. Naturally, after that moment they held the balance of power in the family and could get away with literally anything. I think they blackmailed him for every indulgence they could dream up while he was alive. At the same time the guilt he experienced as a direct consequence of his fatal weakness drove him to drink. I think that also was a part of the diabolical strategy they had hit upon."

"Murder by forcing the victim into a slow suicide by alcohol?"

"Exactly that, sir. On the other hand, I do believe the daughterly instinct remained present in a perverse and twisted way. They loved their father exactly for his weakness and indulgence, and each blames the other for his ugly death."

I let a few beats pass. An irrelevant but compelling question has floated into my head and will not go away. "Maria, if you don't mind my asking—what level of education do you have?"

"I have a master's in private and public international law, sir, obtained from one of our distant learning institutions. It is the enduring regret of my life that I lack the wherewithal to set myself up in practice, but it is not for me to question the ways of the Lord."

"Ah! I'm sorry. I'm sure you'd make a fantastic lawyer."

"Thank you, sir. That is most kind."

"Suppose I send an extra thousand Hong Kong. You have a punch line worth a thousand bucks, perhaps?"

She coughs. "They are cannibals, sir, and they use embalmed human penises, rendered tumescent by means of some kind of stiffening agent, as dildos."

I gulp. "Ah, what was that, Maria?"

"I think you heard me, sir, and I will not repeat it. Please ensure you keep your side of our contract. Good night, sir."

I close the phone, then it whooshes: an SMS from Maria with her account details.

I fell asleep on the plane and now we're just coming in to land. The lethargy of total disorientation makes me drag my steps all the way to immigration, then customs, where I snarled and flashed my cop's ID, because they look as if they're about to search me. In the cab on the way home, I loll in the backseat, where the latest radio reports of the Sukhumvit Rapist's adventures penetrate my dormant brain: a young woman's sobs and gulps fill the airways; at first they are indecipherable, only slowly the meaning of her words dawns on me: *"No, he didn't rape me. . . . Yes, I think he was going to but a noise disturbed him. . . . No, I don't have any physical injuries. . . . Why am I so distraught??? Because I was just this hour trapped in a dark alley by a seven-foot monster that looked like half-man half-monkey and it's scared the living shit out of me, idiot."*

15

Lek is normally the most self-effacing of assistants, with the discretion of a trusted servant. When he feels he has served beyond the call of duty and craves recognition over and above the usual, however, he acquires the characteristics of a neglected wife. He ambushed me as I walked into the station and hasn't stopped following me and talking for the past ten minutes:

"Talk about *footwork*, oh Buddha, you wouldn't *believe* what I've gone through the past two days when you were off shopping in Hong Kong. How you must have *suffered*, darling. I feel so *sorry* for you."

I arrive at my desk, pull back the chair, sit, and put my feet up on the desk while he stands beside me. "Tell me about it, Lek. What angle were you following up? I forget."

"Oh, *he forgot*. The maharaja of District Eight carelessly distributes duties, assigns tasks, and goes tiger hunting. You told me to check out the shareholders of the mansion in Phuket—you do remember *Phuket, Vulture Peak*? You know, *the case*?"

I let him have my best patrician smile, the kind that sends a message of infinite tolerance for the intellectual shortcomings of slaves. "Tell me about the shareholders."

"Well of course, *none* of them are in Bangkok—that would have been just too *easy*, wouldn't it? And when I checked out the registered home addresses, of course there are *no* telephone numbers."

"Where are the registered addresses?"

"Each and every one of them in Isaan, darling. And I don't mean urban Isaan, like Udon Thani or Khorat—oh no, nothing easy like that, I mean *deep country* Isaan, the kind of place that was genuine jungle with monkeys swinging from tree to tree about five minutes ago and even now is hardly more than shacks with corrugated roofs."

"Really?"

"Would I lie? Want to see the blisters on my feet? I nearly died of heatstroke about five thousand times. My expenses for bottled water alone will tell you what I've been through."

"Okay, okay, I get the picture. So, did you talk to any of the shareholders?"

"Depends what you mean by *talk*. There was only one actually living where he was supposed to live, and he was eighty-five years old, almost blind, and so deaf I got laryngitis from shouting at him."

"But he's the real thing, a shareholder in the Vulture Peak mansion?"

"Oh, yes, no doubt about it. He remembers signing his name and having his ID card photocopied—and that's as far as it goes. He's never been to Phuket in his life and has no idea he's worth maybe thirty million baht. And of course I didn't tell him, you know, just in case something goes wrong. I wouldn't want to get his hopes up, an old man like that. I felt so *sorry* for him and jealous as hell at the same time. Imagine, a multimillionaire, and he's living in a shack with no water or electricity."

"But who put him up to it? He told you that?"

"All he knows is someone came to see him one day and said they were an agent for a rich man who wanted to buy a mansion and they would give him twenty thousand baht if he signed a contract first, then another sixty thousand once the formalities had been finalized, on condition he kept his mouth shut. And he didn't have to do anything, not even leave his shack. So was he going to say *no*, a lonely old man starving to death? He couldn't believe his luck. He still hasn't spent all the money they gave him, says he can live on it for another year at least."

"When did this happen?"

"Just before the last official sale of the property."

"Can we trace the agent he's talking about?"

"Of course not, darling. That's the whole point, isn't it?"

"Anonymity?"

"My, you're quick today!"

"But the agent, was he Bangkok—did he speak to the old man in Isaan or in Standard Thai?" Lek scratches his chin. "You didn't ask?"

"Not in so many words."

"Lek?"

"Well, I didn't need to. Like I say, the old guy is nearly deaf, lived in Isaan all his life. I wouldn't expect he'd understand anything *except* Isaan."

"One of the documents he signed must have been a power of attorney."

"Right."

"So why was no power of attorney attached to the entry in the registry?"

"Want me to go and see that little tart of a clerk?"

"All the way back to Phuket?"

Lek taps his nose. "Not necessarily." I let a couple of beats pass and wait. When Lek is pleased with himself, he can't hold out for long. He sighs. "Well, I couldn't believe a little civil servant *ratlet* like that could afford the operation when I can't."

"You were jealous?"

"As hell, if you want to know. Anyway, I made inquiries."

"On the *katoey* network? And?"

"Just as I thought—he has a sponsor. A *farang* who hangs out in Pattaya. The tart flies up to be with him every weekend."

"You have the address?"

"How much do you love me?"

"For Buddha's sake."

"Well, you haven't been at all affectionate ever since you went to Dubai."

It's my turn to sigh. "I'll buy you lunch at Ma Ka's."

"Really? When?"

"Now. We'll eat, then get a cab down to Pattaya, check out the *farang.*"

"But it's not the weekend—the clerk will be in Phuket."

"That might not matter."

Lek raises his eyes. "Master, I'm so glad you're fully recovered, and I do hope you won't be abusing drugs again for a day or so. Please remember my career is inextricably bound up with yours."

"Any more sarcasm, and I'm not buying you lunch."

The difference between Bangkok and Pattaya, which is about an hour's drive down the coast, is quite simple from the tourist perspective: Bangkok has many industries, Pattaya only one. As a consequence, the mayor has persuaded the authorities to bend the rules somewhat. Whereas in Bangkok some attempt is made to keep the sex industry under control and restricted to certain well-known areas, in Pattaya it proclaims itself from the rooftops—or, more accurately, the neon.

When we reach the coast road the blatant bars compete for lurid attention: the Cock and Pussy, the Quickie, and one with no name but a sign on which a balding *farang* with huge beer gut and tufts of ginger hair is having congress with a shapely Thai girl, doggy style. Nor is the entertainment restricted to the conservative end of the sexual spectrum who still, quaintly, do it nature's way; the gay and the *katoey* market is so large, it occupies subdistricts in which an old-fashioned heterosexual lech may well feel unwelcome and out of date. Is it permissible for me to confess that boys for sale in underpants standing on stages fills me with a particular sadness that I don't feel in the case of tough girls happy to be in the business of manipulating a force of nature? (Sorry, DFR, but IMHO political correctness is soft fascism, and I'll have nothing to do with it.) I'm not in the best of moods when we stroll down the pedestrianized high street to a couple of lanes dedicated to transsexuals. I feel Lek's excitement to be in a burg dedicated to his own kind.

"Oh my, look at the money on *that* job!" he says of a platinum blonde with blouse-bursting breasts, silicone-enhanced buttocks, and cupid-bow lips leaning against a wall outside a bar named Love. "And to think he was just a humble farmhand humping rice up in Isaan only months ago."

"How d'you know?"

"Statistics, darling, statistics. I wonder how much cocaine *his* sponsor sold to pay for *that*."

This is Lek's moment, and I let him lead. He has counseled that rather than surprise the clerk's *farang* sugar daddy in his lair immediately, we would do well to make preliminary inquiries. Although the *katoey* market occupies many streets, long-term players tend to hang out in this particular cul-de-sac, which in comparison to the rest of the town appears restrained, even discreet.

Lek is fascinated by the platinum blonde, whether out of sexual attraction or an interest in the surgical investment is hard to say. He leads to the Love bar and gives him/her a friendly *wai* as we enter. It is early in the evening, and only a few *katoeys* are lounging among the tables and chairs. One of them rouses himself to cross the floor in a Marilyn Monroe walk to slip behind the bar.

Lek already knows the stage name of the clerk at the land registry in Phuket.

"Sally-O?" the *katoey* behind the bar says, and makes an exaggerated pout that includes placing an index finger along one side of his cheek and inclining his head while furrowing his brow. "Well, I *do* happen to know *one* Sally-O."

"Well, how many Sally-O's are there, for Buddha's sake?" Lek says.

"There's no need to have a tantrum, darling. Names come and go with the fashion. About six months ago every *second girl* was calling herself Sally-O—now you hardly hear it at all. Postsurgery names these days tend to be more *international*. Mon Amour is top of the pops, but Japanese Monicas are all the rage too."

"He's a government clerk in Phuket in his day job," Lek says, and describes the clerk. The *katoey* raises his eyes. I reach for my wallet and take out a five-hundred-baht note. The *katoey* sneers. I take out another five hundred but keep my finger on both notes after I place them on the bar. The *katoey* sighs. "I might be wrong, but the person you describe could be the Sally-O who is a regular at the Spank Me bar three doors down." He picks up the thousand baht and retreats to the far end of the bar, on which he leans in a way that showcases his implants.

Despite its name, the Spank Me bar is a no-frills place where the *katoeys* are dressed in jeans and T-shirts—enviably slim, with flat stomachs and breast sizes under control—and sport real smiles. The manager is also a *katoey*, but of the brisk business-minded kind. The bar is designed to make long-term players feel relaxed and part of a family. He guesses immediately that we are cops and sees the wisdom of cooperating.

"Sally-O? Sure, she comes in with her husband most weekends. When they're not on his yacht, that is."

"Yacht?"

"He keeps it at the Phuket Yacht Club. He used to be a keen sailor, but after his illness he sold the sailboat and bought some kind of floating champagne palace."

He takes in our incomprehension. "You do know who he is, don't you?" Lek and I shake our heads.

"Used to be quite famous, a third-division pop star, part of the wallpaper in the seventies, sold the fifties retro stuff, you know, Elvis-style glitter with silver pants that split and padded shoulders. Couldn't sing to save his life, but kids went for the glitter."

"Rich?"

The *katoey* thinks about it. "Hard to say. To me he's rich, but he was never top of the league—or the pops. And he had a lot of trouble with his health. Booze, drugs, dirty needles—he had a problem when he first started coming in here. He would drink and drink until he fell over. Then he disappeared for a few months, and when he returned, he looked like death. Liver failing badly. Then he got himself a transplant. Now he doesn't drink anything except fruit juice. You have to admire his dedication. It's all fear, of course. He was about as close to death as you can get and still breathe. He looks rough most of the time, but at least he can walk and talk. Sally-O is his long-term companion. I think they stay on his boat together a lot of the time, but they still need the bright lights."

"A transplant?" I say.

"Right. A transplant. All on the black market, of course, no questions asked—otherwise he would have gone back to England to have it done officially, wouldn't he?"

I let the strange coincidence sink in. "You don't happen to know who arranged the transplant for him?"

The *katoey* smiles. "All I can tell you is, it didn't happen here."

"Where?"

"I don't know where the operation took place, but I know he paid a few visits to Hong Kong, and one night he came in here with some kind of Chinese princess—I mean the real thing, money all over her, HiSo manners. Nice woman, knew how to charm, but way out of our league—out of his league too. I guess even aristocracy have to make a living these days."

"Was she tall, willowy, elegant with long hands?"

He laughs. "Exactly. All of those things."

"Did she speak Thai, by any chance?"

"Intermediate Thai with a strong accent, perfect English, and I heard her on the phone talking in Chinese."

"What is the name of the pop star?"

"Freddie Monroe. Named after that Hollywood woman, I suppose, the one who slept with John Kennedy—or was it the other one she slept with?"

"Would you happen to have his cell phone number?"

"Sure—so long as you don't tell him you got it from me. We survive here by discretion."

He takes out his own cell phone, presses some buttons and reads off the number while I plug it into my own. I think I've driven him as hard as I can, considering he is not a suspect and does not need to answer questions from a Bangkok cop when he surely pays protection to the local force. I chance just one more.

"This clerk, is he the usual run of *katoey*, d'you think?"

He frowns in contemplation. "There is no usual run of *katoey*," the *katoey* says with a kind of sadness. "For thousands of years young men have been volunteering for castration as a way out. To discover what kind of *katoey* you're dealing with, you have to find out what demon they're running from. Maybe they *do* want to be women, maybe they're simply gays looking for a higher profile. Sometimes it's pure money—modifying the body to please the customers. But most of the time it's a case of building a fantasy life until it's realer than the mundane. Taking control over your own identity right down to gender itself. Above all, *katoeys* are fantasists."

"Did Sally-O nurse a particular fantasy that you know of?"

"Sure. She thought she was the reincarnation of a fifteenth-century Chinese eunuch. Apparently there was a famous one who went to sea, but I'm not strong on history."

16

The mind tells you it has seen that mug a million times before, but it has to work at reconstructing it without the deep furrows, loose jowls, dreadful grayness of flesh, and yellow eyes that indicate a serious liver problem and remind one of death. Although he was no Beatle or Rolling Stone, nevertheless for a long fifteen minutes Freddie Monroe was once part of your internal wallpaper. In his younger form he leered and screamed at you from a billion TV sets; you have seen him on talk shows stoned and mumbling about his life and times; and once or twice you have seen him in police custody after a bust, although he always managed to avoid a prison sentence. He was never the serious artist, but he knew enough to forget to shave before every performance, grow his hair even longer than anyone else's, and wiggle his loins in that unambiguous way that even girls in their early teens understand.

He agreed to see us at his midrange apartment in a gated community on a hill a mile or so outside of Pattaya; it's not on the sea but gives a fair view of the Gulf of Thailand and the paragliders that crowd the air during most of the year. He walks with the aid of a walker, and there is a wheelchair in one corner of the room. There is nothing wrong with his legs, but any kind of physical exertion strains a fragile system and makes him breathless.

The flat is unexpectedly modest, with only a few memento pix of yesteryear in silver frames on a side table: Freddie Monroe wowing crowds of drug-addled kids; Freddie Monroe marching from gig to gig, carrying his guitar like a battle-ax; Freddie Monroe at a garden party thrown by the queen of England. There is also a strange oil painting on a wall, which I want to ask about when I find the opportunity.

After meeting us at the door on his walker, he has eased himself into an armchair with a sigh of relief. He is not especially concerned that we are cops; I guess the imminence of death occupies all his psychic space. In pride of place on a mantelpiece is a more recent photo of him in a florid beach shirt with his arm around the *katoey* clerk at the Phuket land registry.

He speaks as slowly as he moves. I think he has not the energy to lie even if he needs to. His account of himself is plain enough:

"This is my second liver transplant, and it isn't taking too well. The first, I had in the U.K. They frown a lot and wag their fingers and tell you what a bad boy you've been, but they'll generally find a liver for you. They make it clear it's a last chance, though. 'You're on your ninth life, mate, so lay off the booze and drugs.' I can't tell you how many times I heard that. But the thing is, what do you do when you've recovered and you want a life? Pub culture was *my* culture: down the boozer at least at the weekend. Without that I didn't feel like I was on my ninth life, I felt like I was already dead. So little by little I weakened, didn't I? Sal, my companion, nagged me about it. She's very warm and loving and didn't want me to die, but I didn't listen.

"So a few years later I need another liver, don't I? I thought, *This is it, I've really fucked myself this time*, but I heard about some setup on the Internet and sent them an e-mail. *Dr. Gray* was the name they used—a cover, of course. Next thing I know, a Chinese woman based in Hong Kong invites me to go see her. So I do, at her office over there: very elegant, very charming, very professional."

"What did she call herself?"

"Lilly. Lilly Yip. She said she was an agent, a go-between. Once she saw I was serious and had the readies, she came over here to check me out a few times. To cut a long story short, if I sold the big place I used to have here in Pattaya and my yacht—it was a two-masted classic schooner, won the South China Sea Race in the 1930s—I'd just have enough for the whole operation on the black market and to buy a floating gin palace, because I can't stand being without a boat and nor can Sally-O. I had best-quality surgeons, mind you, a proper setup in a proper clinic."

"In Thailand?"

"No. In China. I'm not saying where because I don't know." The effort is telling. He has to pause for energy.

"Did Sal—Sally-O—have anything to do with this Lilly?" I ask.

Freddie rubs his jaw. "Well, that was the strange thing. Sal was still a man at that stage, but he badly needed the reassignment so he could live out his true identity. I was very encouraging, and before I got sick the second time, I promised to pay his way—but then I found myself short of the readies and couldn't. This Lilly seemed to think she could help out. I didn't see the need, since there's nothing black market about gender reassignment. I didn't realize she'd got interested in Sal because of her job at the land registry.

"At that point it all went Oriental, if you see what I mean. They had a lot of private conversations I wasn't party to, and the next thing I know, Sal's taking the estrogen, growing breasts, and getting ready for the operation. When I asked him where the dough was coming from, he wouldn't tell me. 'Something Asian. Better you don't know' was what he said. Well, I wasn't born yesterday. I could see Lilly wasn't the kind to give anything away free, so Sal must have been doing something for it. And of course, you're cops, you don't need me to tell you how dodgy land transactions can be over here. And Sal working in the land registry in Phuket—I'm not giving the game away, am I? I'm not betraying anyone? I mean, this is stuff you would work out in three minutes, right?"

He gives Lek a particularly warm smile. I guess there are men who just naturally have a soft spot for the third sex.

"Did this Lilly say where the liver came from?"

Freddie looks uncomfortable. "Not in so many words."

"But?"

"Well, since she was Hong Kong Chinese and spoke Mandarin fluently, and since the operation took place in China—you know what they do with the bodies of executed prisoners . . . I didn't see what else it could be. I mean, the timing was all guaranteed months in advance, it wasn't like a last-minute traffic accident, it was all a lot more relaxed and sedate than that." He frowns. "I don't have anything to reproach myself for—the poor bugger was going to croak anyway, right? It wasn't as if they were killing him just for me. And if it hadn't been me got the liver, it would have been someone else, right? Not necessarily more deserving than me, either. I'm not the only bloke in the world fucked up his liver with booze and mainlining, am I?"

"Where in China did they take you?"

Freddie frowns again. "I already said I don't know. There was a lot of talk about Shanghai, so it could have been there."

"'Could have been there'? What does that mean?"

Freddie opens his hands. "I just don't know. See, once you've paid up the first slice of the money, they go to work on you, get you ready for the operation."

"Who does?"

"Actually, it was Lilly herself. She also sedated me before the flight. That way they could wheel me off the private plane into the operating theater—so I suppose it was near an airport. It was all done in the just-in-time-delivery style. Could have been any airport. I was totally out a couple of minutes after we got on the plane. I didn't know anything until I woke up in Phuket with a new liver."

Lek and I exchange a glance. I enunciate the words slowly: "You—woke—up—in—Phuket?"

Freddie doesn't understand the heavy emphasis, shakes his head, and shrugs. "That was part of the deal. After the operation they had me recuperate at some fantastic mansion on a hill there." He scratches an itch on his neck. "Actually, the mansion wasn't too far from where Sal works, so I wondered if there was a connection."

"But the operation itself took place in China, maybe Shanghai?"

"That's what they told me. That's what I paid for. It must have been China 'cause that's where they executed the prisoner whose liver I'm using."

A pause. "Where is Sally-O now?"

He stares as if the question is without meaning. "At work, of course."

I let my attention wander until it comes to rest on the oil painting. "Who's that a portrait of?" I ask.

Freddie turns to follow my gaze. "You don't recognize her? That's Sal in her ancient Chinese costume. She's dressed as a court eunuch in the late Ming dynasty."

"Right. Why?"

Freddie allows himself a shrug. "She's *katoey*, love. They're all a bit that way."

17

I tell Lek I don't want him to come with me to Phuket. He's already had a minor standoff with the clerk, and anyway two cops together look official and intimidating. I'm sitting at my desk in the open-plan office, thinking of a way to placate Lek, who has decided to sulk, and trying to decide whether to just show up at the airport or book the ticket using the Internet, which could easily take longer than simply taking a cab to the airport, when my cell phone rings.

"Hi, brother, how are things?" a male voice says in English with a Chinese accent.

"Inspector Chan?"

"The same. So, how're things?"

"Up and down. How about you?"

"I'm on vacation—holiday, as the Brits say."

I pause to stare at my cell phone. "Really? Where?"

"Oh, about a mile down the road from where you are now, assuming you're at the station."

"You're in Thailand?"

"You've been taking intelligence-enhancing medication?"

"But I mean, why?"

"To see a couple of people, you being one of them."

"You'll have to wait."

"Why?"

"I'm a busy third-world policeman. I have to cope with an existential reality that would have you messing your diaper, Spoiled Brat Hong Kong Cop."

"Hey—"

"I'm back in two days."

"Where are you going?"

"Not telling you."

The clerk's weekday pad in Phuket is in a back street on the third floor of an apartment building, but he's not in. I knock quite a few times and make all the usual checks for signs of life, but the place has a deserted feel. Of course he could be out on the town, but I doubt it. I remember those dark, unsocial eyes, the quick temper before he remembered he was a public servant—and the whole feel about him of a young man who might have had himself mutilated by mistake. It's a cop's hunch that sends me to the Phuket Yacht Club. I arrive at twilight with the last of the sun sinking like a plutonium rod in an asphalt sea. The bartender knows who I'm talking about.

"He comes quite often to spend the night on his sponsor's boat," the barman tells me.

"He takes care of it?"

"No, there's a full-time boat boy does that. He just comes and stays the night. If he's not working the next day, he sits on it staring out to sea. He doesn't like company." The barman coughs. "He likes to dress up when he's alone."

I have the barman point the boat out to me. It's hard to see clearly in the dusk, although the cabin lights are on.

"It's a forty-foot twin-screw motor cruiser made in Taiwan. The *farang* used to have something really special, a two-masted schooner about seventy feet long. All teak and oak, a vintage sailboat that won some kind of competition in the thirties. Beautiful it was. Broke the old man's heart when he had to sell it for some reason. Broke the *katoey*'s heart too. Actually, he wasn't a *katoey* at that stage—just a sad young man who thought he was a woman but wasn't sure."

I stare at the dark and silent bay for a moment. I was expecting the boat to be tied up to a berth on a jetty. I didn't expect it to be on a permanent anchorage. "How can I get out there?"

"You can pay one of the boat boys to take you out on a skiff with an outboard—or you can get someone to row you out." I suppose the last suggestion is somewhat exotic from the way he looks at me. Surely only a cop who wanted to retain the element of surprise, or an assassin, would go for the manual option.

"Can you find someone to row me out? It's such a beautiful evening, I don't want to pollute it with noise."

He gives me a cynical glance and calls to someone behind the bar. A robust boy about sixteen years old appears. The barman speaks quickly in the local dialect, and the boy answers back in a low murmur. I don't know how much he's demanding, but it's enough to make him shy.

"He'll do it for five hundred baht," the barman says, clearly expecting me to bargain.

"Okay, let's go," I say. Then I remember I have one more question for the barman. "Years ago, when the *farang* still owned the sailboat—did he have a lot of visitors? Boats like that are a great way of expanding your social life."

"Sure. Every weekend a small crowd would come out. Mostly they were middle-aged showbiz people from the U.K.—I understand he used to be some kind of pop singer. It changed over the years, fewer and fewer guests. In the end he had to hire crew just to grind the winches when he took the boat out. He was a good skipper, though, knew how to sail. Not easy with an old two-master like that."

"Were any of the people Chinese? I mean Chinese and female, who spoke Thai with a strong accent? Very elegant?"

"Her? Why didn't you say it was her you were interested in? Sure, she came out a couple of times. But it wasn't to socialize, as far as I know. Not the sort of woman you forget once you've seen her."

"So what was it for?"

"She's the one who bought the sailboat."

I let a couple of beats pass to let that sink in. "She only came on her own? Not with another woman who looked like her?"

"I only ever saw her alone."

"What did she do with the boat? I don't see any two-masted schooners out there right now."

"She had it shipped back to Hong Kong. That's money. Any normal person would have hired crew to sail it over there for next to nothing, but she had it dismasted and packed onto a container ship. I didn't see her as a sailor, myself."

It's a beautiful evening to be on the water. The moon is not yet up, the first stars are twinkling, and the water is so calm the kid's oar strokes are the only disturbance, save for small fish that jump now and then. The boy knows I declined an outboard motor because I want to retain the element of surprise, so he diminishes his efforts when we're about a hundred yards from the yacht; he doesn't want to give me any excuse to renegotiate his exorbitant fee. He lets the rowboat glide for the last twenty yards so we're almost at a natural halt when we reach the swimming platform. There is no sign of life anywhere on the boat. The boy whispers, "When do you want to come back?"

"I don't know. I'll flash a light or sound a horn—or maybe fire my gun." Of course, he has seen my cop's standard-issue pistol jammed down the back of my belt. He looks disappointed. "Don't worry, I'll pay next time you see me. I'm not likely to disappear, am I?"

He guides the boat around to make it easy for me to step onto the swimming platform. I climb up and sit on one of the padded seats where pampered guests drink champagne and tell the host what a wonderful weekend they're having. Just in case the clerk is in a homicidal mood, I've taken the gun out of the back of my pants. But there is still no sign of him, so I begin to wonder if the barman was wrong. Maybe the clerk slipped away sometime in the afternoon without being spotted and left the cabin lights on by mistake. If there were someone else on the vessel, they would have felt my arrival for sure.

Like any cop, I check out the whole of the top deck: nobody. By now I've made the boat sway left and right simply by moving around; you'd expect anyone on board to notice. I open the sliding-glass door to the stairs that lead below. When I duck my head to check out the salon, I see a human figure sitting motionless in an upright chair that is screwed to the floor with brass bolts. The figure is in a gray one-piece gown with extremely wide and long sleeves and a black hat with earpieces that stick out horizontally. It's the clerk, and I'm quite sure he is dead, because I've never seen anyone sit so stiffly for such a long period of time without breathing. He is also wearing a lot of makeup, mostly rouge and some kind of whitening cream. Up close, I see he has developed a thousand-mile stare. When I put my ear close to his nose, I hear the faintest inhalation and exhalation.

Now I notice the long opium pipe lying on the table, plus an oil lamp that has gone out and some transparent plastic squares. A black oily substance is sandwiched between them. When I bend over to sniff, I am able to confirm the sweet aroma of opium. Now I'm really stuck. Opium is so exotic these days, I don't think I've seen it in Bangkok since I was a cadet. I scratch my head. It's not at all the sort of expensive old-world habit you would expect from a lowly clerk in the local civil service. Nor is it a habit generally acquired by *katoeys*, who, if they use drugs at all, usually go for meth or coke. But then, *katoeys* do not normally dress up in fifteenth-century Ming gowns and winter hats, especially not in the tropics.

I fish out my cell phone to check the time. Seven forty-five P.M. The clerk would probably not have begun smoking until after dusk, so as not to be disturbed by boat boys and others. If so, that would give him about seven more hours of intoxication, on the basis that an opium high usually lasts about eight hours. I bob my head, trying to decide what to do. I don't really want to stay on the boat for another five hours, but on the other hand the weakened psychological state of the clerk after the collapse of his dream world could be useful. I remember him as a possible hard nut with a ton of resentment of one kind or another, who might be impossible to interrogate when sober. I find a flashlight in the wheelhouse and wave it in an arc in the direction of the boat boy, who rows over. I give him his five hundred baht and tell him I might want him in the morning. Then I sit at the bow gazing at the sky as the first of Orion's stars emerge with the moon.

I'm feeling Zennish. I remember a tale of a Zen monk who gave up his only robe to a starving and shivering old woman and wished he could share the moon with her as well. It's a great yarn, but it makes me feel ashamed because it's only about fifteen minutes since I dismissed the boat boy along with my last chance of making land before morning, and already I've started to feel bored. Well, it's more the *fear* of boredom: all those hours with nothing to do, no TV or radio, no podcasts, nothing to read, no one to talk to, no bright lights, no dope—only this silent and slow-rising moon.

I spend about an hour moving from below to above to below again. The clerk remains catatonic with a beatific smile on his face. When the boredom reaches an intolerable level, I shine the flashlight in his eyes: oblivious pupils the size of pinheads, behind which a soul gorges on bliss. I'm jealous as hell of his nirvanic state. I decide to go back on deck, out of sight of temptation. Now I remember to call Chanya. "Honey, sorry, but I'm in Phuket again and—" She's hung up.

Okay, I'm giving in, but let it be recorded that I held out for a full two hours before I found the clerk's aspirin, which I ground up, mixed with his opium, and smoked . . .

Take my advice, DFR: don't try it, so you'll never know how good it is. It is amazing. I see my life pass before my eyes without any anguish attached. Everything takes place against a backdrop of eternity; I see behind the surface of things, which dissolve into serene vistas where transparent archetypes from the origin of consciousness wait at crossroads in the middle distance. Colors acquire the reality of living creatures: imagine a mode of consciousness called Scarlet. Now my mother, Nong, and I are looking into each other's eyes, telling truths we've never told; it is as if our presiding angels have broken through and are talking to each other, silently. Now my long-lost father appears as a young GI, his face blackened for battle. He puts a hand on my shoulder and says, *Sorry*; I say, *Don't worry about it.* The source of pain is blocked; isn't this what one was looking for all along?

Dawn. The opium dream melts, leaving only the sound of running water. Well, maybe it's the clerk making the sound of running water in the galley below. I blink at a sky only recently illuminated: the mysteries of night still hang around in corners and cause everyday objects to glow sullenly.

"Want some coffee?" the clerk calls.

"Please."

Now he appears below, in a checked shirt and tight shorts: almost manly, no sign of the makeup. I find my eyes drifting to the area of his mutilated crotch, but catch myself just in time. He stares up at me. "You smoked my *fin*."

"I got bored waiting. Want to report me to the cops?"

He climbs the stairs and dumps a mug of coffee next to my elbow. Together we stare across the bay.

A couple of buzzards are already circling high overhead. Nothing else is moving. "You know why I'm here?" I say. We are both surprised at how normal we sound; like me, the clerk still has one foot in another world.

"Where do you want to start?" the clerk says.

"Start with the opium. I've been a cop in Bangkok for more than fifteen years. I haven't seen *fin* in all that time. Who taught you to smoke? Who gets it for you?"

The clerk stares at the ever-increasing glow in the east; already sweat has started beading on my forehead. Close up, the clerk, also, is looking a little worse for wear: the grayness of flesh that is said to accompany his hobby.

"*She* did," the clerk says. "You know who I mean."

"Do I?"

"She took you to Monte Carlo. I had a great laugh about that."

I blink into the sun and look away, thinking I really need to change professions. In less than a second a low-ranking clerk has turned the tables on me. It's quite a neat maneuver, too: if I say *How did you know?* then that's an admission. If I deny, then he knows I'm not leveling with him.

"Who did?"

He smirks at me. "You really want to play that game?"

"Okay. A Chinese woman, probably calling herself Lilly. Lilly Yip."

"Correct."

"Now you."

The clerk wipes his face with the back of his hand. "She's the one taught me to smoke opium," he says. "Isn't that what you asked?" Then he turns to look at me with eyes of infinite sadness. "She trapped me in a dream. I never would have cut it off otherwise. For ninety percent of *katoeys*, the operation is just a wish, a posture—we never really intend to go through with it. We simply need to be part of the conversation."

"She persuaded you to have your cock cut off? Why?"

"She wanted it. As a trophy. She has hundreds."

"That's all? Just to add it to her collection?"

"The thrill of the hunt, Detective. Like a python lying in wait—she saw me and pounced. Her speed is incredible." He shakes his head. "Don't you see? It's the ultimate proof of female power: to separate a man from his own cock. Ha, ha."

With the benefit of the narcotic, I see that the clerk is totally deranged. On the other hand, I have not emerged from that other universe myself; I am not yet restored to Social Man, more an electric storm of perception with no particular shape. "You're still in shock? You can't believe what has happened to you? But you wanted to be a *katoey*, that's what you told your lover, Freddie? You wanted to experience your true nature as a woman?"

"That's what every *katoey* says. Like I just told you, only a tiny percentage go all the way—most are safe because they don't have the dough. For the majority, gender reassignment is one fantastic topic of gossip that never fails. I told her I didn't really have the courage, that I was just a little fantasizing mediocrity like everyone else. She advised me not to think like that. She told me that successes and heroes are simply people who follow their dreams. That's why she introduced me to opium."

"Did she smoke it with you?"

"Sometimes. She used to spin yarns about how wonderful life was going to be after the operation. She knew all the *katoey* buzzwords and could play on every fantasy. And she made me feel so important."

We are standing together at the bow. The clerk's eyes are gleaming around the pupils but smeared at the edges. There is a kind of despair in his tone, which is nonetheless triumphant. "See, I didn't need to say it. For once I didn't need even to hint. She saw it in me."

"Saw what?"

"That I am the reincarnation of Zheng He, of course."

I look at him. For a second I see him through his own eyes: gathered behind him the greatest fleet the ancient world ever saw—probably the greatest fleet that was ever assembled before World War II. Lilly would have known about the clerk's Zheng He fantasy from talking to Freddie. "Of course you are."

"Oh, *you* can say that because you already know. But she *saw* it, without any prompting, d'you see? When a stranger recognizes your true nature, it's so liberating. It's a final proof."

"Final proof? But you're not entirely sure you've done the right thing! You're on the horns of a dilemma. Did you commit the greatest stupidity in the history of the world, namely let some sadistic, criminal-minded bitch talk you into having your balls and penis amputated, just so she has a new toy to play with for a moment before she chucks it in the trash? Or does that other, magical world really exist, the one you always longed for, the one she herself understands so well because that's where she lives most of the time? The world where Zheng He still rules, no?"

He is staring at me in horror. "Chucks it in the trash?" He has pressed his hands against both ears. The opium is still poisoning my blood, causing me to turn on him. I think I understand Lilly. The clerk is so completely lost, so utterly manipulable—I expect he triggered in her a primeval response to destroy. I too find contempt taking over. "But it was more than just your cock she wanted. She has a whole room full of men's embalmed dicks she uses as dildos—it's how she gets her thrills. Your manhood was just the icing on the cake. What she wanted was a whole castle. You got her Vulture Peak."

I think I have delivered an overdose of reality. The clerk's brain seems to scramble. He stares at me and blinks, then says, "Yes. I got her Vulture Peak. That's true."

"Want to tell me how it went?"

He sags against the outside of the wheelhouse, inhales. "It all started because Freddie needed a new liver and sent an e-mail to someone called Dr. Gray. Lilly Yip appeared. She spoke Thai and a lot of other languages. Of course, she saw I was *katoey*. And she saw I'd not yet had the operation. She seemed to understand craving. Somehow my whole focus was on that operation. I don't even know why, she just led me into this mind-set: I had to be released from being male. That was my only way out."

"So you both had reasons to bond. She offered the full *katoey* fantasy trip, including the operation, probably free of charge, and opium for life. In return you would help her screw the old man for more than half his fortune, and you would procure for her the most fabulous property in Phuket—somehow. What did you do?"

"Nothing very much. The place was already owned by Hong Kong Chinese. I happened to know who the real owner was—and the ghost shareholders here in Thailand."

"She must have wanted the property quite badly, to go to that kind of trouble."

"She did, but it wasn't really for her. It was for some conglomerate in China—a group she was involved with. And there was a Thai army general involved."

"Did she say who?"

"The general? No, never."

"The Chinese conglomerate?"

"There was a government ministry, and some banks too. They were some kind of lobby group. Lilly Yip seemed to need to keep them charmed. You know, entertaining your most valued clients. That's why it had to be the biggest palace on the island—a face thing. Actually, she's right, there isn't another property like that—probably isn't another one in Thailand."

"But that mansion, that's where Freddie woke up after his operation. You must have moved pretty quick."

"As I said, I knew the owner at the time. I was a clerk in the land office. I knew how to process a real estate purchase in an hour if I needed to. She'd already bought the place and owned it for more than a year before everything was ready for Freddie's transplant."

When I look into the clerk's smeared eyes, I see that exactly the same thing is happening to him as happened to me just now: an opium flashback, a sensation not of memory but of displacement in time: for a second I was nine years old again, and Nong was young and sexy, pulling out all the stops for one of her johns somewhere in France or Germany. (There were horse chestnut trees, empty streets black from rain, and old European houses built of stone that looked so solid. A strange light that had no origin permeating everything.)

Seeing the clerk lose control of his mind in the same way, I pounce. "But she included you in the house activities—she must have done. She had turned you into her best friend. No, let's put it another way: she had made herself your *only* friend, because she understood you so much better than Freddie did. Freddie is a useful sugar daddy but has no depth. The anguish of being alive is something he drowned with booze years ago—like a lot of Brits, he is just one long alcoholic escape trip. But you—yes, it would have been an important part of her plan to include you, to make you an intimate. Otherwise you might have reverted to *katoey* jealousy and tried to bring her down. You do have that vicious *katoey* thing, don't you? And let's face it, you've never been a man with a big social life."

"But I'm not a man," he says, "I don't need big face. I don't need a social life."

"But you need to be understood. We all do. For you, it must have been intriguing and terrifying."

"What?"

"To be understood by a woman, perhaps for the first time in your life."

Truth can be a radical interrogation technique, and I'm not sure this clerk will survive. He is grinding his jaw and seems on the point of tears. I think I've pushed as far as I dare and give him time. He stares and stares out to sea, as if the answer lies there. Finally, he starts to spill his guts.

"She is very skillful with the *fin*. She prepares the pipe with exactly the amount for the effect she wants. We became intimate very quickly—I don't mean sex, I mean something much deeper than that. 'Soul fucking,' she called it. I was pleased and flattered that such a woman would take an interest in me, even though I knew she had reasons. She had a way of using the *fin* to create a landscape. She introduced certain magic phrases when we were high, happy words like 'When we're totally free,' and 'Are you as delighted as I am to have found a soul mate?' The best was 'I understand you, Khun Sally-O. I don't like sex either, it's a bad joke. So much nicer to hold hands and be friends.'" He lets a couple of beats pass. "Pathetic, no? Not the sort of thing anyone would fall for without opium, right?" He sighs. "But fantasy is addictive. You know what she told me once? That she could only take about one hour of reality every day. The world was just too harsh. I can't tell you how wonderful it felt, to have met someone—a woman of all things—who understood me that well. *Me.*"

I let him stare out to sea for five minutes, then say softly, "Tell me what goes on at the house. What happens at Vulture Peak, Sally-O?" I'm afraid my use of his stage name might be too dramatic, too obvious. Tears appear at the corners of his eyes, but he seems to have regained some control.

"You're right, she was using me all along, wasn't she? Not a word, not a gesture, not a single second when she was not working me like a cheap whistle, right?" He gives a great heaving sigh. "I know you think I'm just the biggest sucker in the world, a total loser who let a female demon persuade him to have his dick cut off, but it's not that simple. There was something else."

"Tell me."

"She can divide herself in two."

"Huh?"

"Just like some Himalayan mystic, she can be in two places at the same time. She only did it to me once. I'll never forget it if I live to be a thousand."

"Tell me."

"It was very soon after the operation. She invited me up to Vulture Peak. She had the opium pipe already laid out. Maybe you can understand what that means to a smoker. You enter a room where there is a pipe laid out with opium—that means you enter a sacred place, a temple, an Aladdin's cave in which anything can happen. I was still very weak, and of course there was that hole between my legs that threatened to totally destroy my mind. And we smoked." He chokes for a moment, coughs, looks away.

When he looks back his eyes are streaming. "She'd already had it embalmed. Cock and balls, the whole set. Somehow she'd made my poor cock twice the size it used to be when erect. I wouldn't have believed it was mine if not for the birthmark on the tip. I guess she injected some clever embalming solution that set like stiff plastic." He suddenly looks directly into my eyes. "She took it out of a special case she'd had made for it, like a jewelry case. She said, 'Look, I can enjoy you whenever I want now. Your flesh has become my flesh. We are one.'"

I blink. "She used it?"

"Yes. She used it in front of me," he sobs. "Even though I was high on the opium, I knew she was doing that. I mean I knew I wasn't dreaming it. Then she left me, took my cock with her. I'm not sure what happened next. I found myself wandering around the house, looking for my cock and balls. I went into one of the bedrooms and found two of them sharing my dick. I mean there were *two identical Lilly Yips*. They were naked and both looked up at me at the same time. She—they—had a look in her eyes of a woman bloated on lust, as if she and her double intended to grind away at my poor cock for days on end, like hyenas with a kill. That blew me away forever. I knew I was her slave from then on. She even said it, after we fell out: 'So long as I have your dick, I have you.'"

"You fell out?"

He shrugs. "She grew bored with me. I had a tantrum, threatened to tell all I knew." He stops, searches my face. "I thought she was going to have me snuffed. I'm sure she thought about it. Then she changed her mind. We have an arrangement. I keep my mouth shut, she supplies me with opium. She's very regular. That boat boy you used, he brings it. That's how he knew to charge five hundred baht for a short trip across the water. She's got me under control. I guess I always was. You could say I'm a prisoner on parole with a location device. I'm allowed to be on the boat, at work, or with Freddie." He shrugs. "But when I call her, she tells me I'm the luckiest man in the world, I get the best painkiller on the planet free of charge for life. I think she really doesn't understand how I miss her. She is so exotic, so superior. No matter how she treats me, I know my fantasy life is safe with her.

I'm a *katoey*, after all. A snob. And I find it difficult to keep my mouth shut when someone like you shows up and wants to talk."

I am thinking, as I am sure you are, DFR, *Well, you're not keeping your mouth shut now, are you?* when I see the first boat moving from the jetty in the early light. I glance at the clerk.

"Don't worry. It's just the boat boy, bringing me my *fin*. I sent an SMS this morning, after I saw you'd smoked the last of it."

"That's a very efficient boat boy."

"He works for her, of course. She has that effect on anyone she employs. She pays double and expects one hundred percent loyalty and efficiency." We stand and watch as the boy rows toward us. He has about three hundred yards to cover, and he rows with steady, manly strokes that extract the maximum efficiency from each pull. As he comes nearer, though, I'm reminded of the wide innocence of those young eyes, the flawless flesh of youth, the unwrinkled face, the bloom in both cheeks. He was an undemonstrative young fellow when he rowed me out last night; this morning finds him quite lively as he ships the oars and glides toward us.

I'm surprised he seems to be aiming for the bow, though, where the clerk and I are standing, instead of the stern, where there is the platform to climb aboard. I guess he must get on well with the clerk, because he holds up a package in a black plastic bag and waves it. When I check the clerk's face, though, it is incomprehending, as if the boy is behaving in some way eccentrically. I'm still too distracted by the remains of the opium dream to react quickly. The clerk understands quicker than I, but not quickly enough. The boy drops the black bag to reveal a big handgun, some kind of Magnum, which he points directly at the clerk.

I did not detect a moment when those big innocent eyes lost their innocence; he simply aimed the way he had been trained to do; no doubt he telephoned Hong Kong for instructions after he brought me out last night. Lilly must have supplied him with some exotic bullets, because the one that hits the clerk in the throat causes his neck to explode. The bullet—I guess of the soft-nose exploding type—rips through his vertebrae; body and head hit the deck separately; the head rolls until it is stopped by the guardrail.

The kid is so shocked that he has decapitated a man with one shot, he is experiencing a kind of extreme ecstasy that could go either way: he can no more come to terms with the headless corpse—or the separated head—than I can. I'm so absorbed by the transformation that is taking place before my eyes (a million years of torment before this boy gets another chance at the human form, and on some level he knows it) that I fail to consider that Lilly might have had plans for me too. After all, I'm the one he was talking to.

The boy is recovering quickly, switching paranoid glances now, between me and the clerk's remains; but I'm like a blinded deer: I do not see it coming until it's too late. I watch in a paralysis of will while he raises the gun again and takes aim. There is nowhere to flee, the stairs that lead below are about six feet behind me. I know that if I panic and dash for cover, he will blow me away with that miniature cannon. And I left my gun downstairs with the opium pipe. But suppose I made it below, what then? I'd simply be a fish in a barrel for him to slaughter.

The moment freezes. Vikorn was right when he said I'm a steady hand in a firefight, but this is different. I'm mesmerized. The kid's reckless waste of his chance of personal evolution has totally thrown me. What, exactly, does a soul do when it has just condemned itself to hell? I'm locking eyes with the clerk and in some way his terror, confusion, pride, loss, and iron determination are penetrating my heart.

Then something goes wrong with the kid's body. He jerks, seems to experience a stab of unendurable pain, then jerks twice more before collapsing into the rowboat. I can see a pulsating fountain of blood spraying from his chest—pink, fresh from the lungs. Without thinking, I dive into the water. When I reach the rowboat, the kid has all but bled out. The best I can do is row back to the yacht, which I'm now sharing with two cadavers. Good morning, Phuket!

Back at the bow I search the bay with my eyes, paying special attention to a stand of trees somewhat to the south, not far from the road or the clubhouse. My heart thumping, my head raging with poisoned monologues by demons who stayed behind after the opium dream, I take out my cell phone and look for Chan's number.

He answers on the first ring. "Hi, Third-World Cop. Still alive, huh?"

"Thanks to you."

"Don't worry about it. Let's say I know the Yips. What happened just now could not be prevented—or it could have been if you'd let me into your investigation a little more deeply. But you didn't, so it had to be Plan B."

"You must be one hell of a shot."

"Not really. Modern technology, you know, a child could have done it."

"What d'you want to do now?"

"I want to go for a jolly on a yacht in sunny Phuket," Chan says in his best British accent. "D'yah think you could sail it as far as the jetty, old chap?"

"I'm not doing a damned thing till you tell me how you knew where I was."

"Cell phone. When it comes to women, you are truly pathetic. That was a woman you broke cover for, wasn't it? You just had to call her, didn't you? *She who has you by the balls.* There is only one transmission tower in the part of Phuket where you are. When the backroom boys in Hong Kong told me you were in the vicinity of a yacht club, I just knew you had to be under Yip surveillance. Funny how that popular holiday destination keeps cropping up in this investigation, no?"

"It's where the original victims were butchered."

"Exactly."

As it happens, I know motorboats (Florida Keys; the john saw it in his interest to teach me how to work the controls on his sixty-foot floating knocking shop, so he could take Mum down below for *boom-boom*). The clerk left the keys in the ignition, so I fire up the twin turbocharged diesel engines, roar across the bay, and (I blame the opium) nearly forget the most important lesson of all: boats don't have brakes. I manage to steer away from the jetty just in time to avoid staving in the bow, although I deliver quite an impressive sideswipe by the stern before I'm able to slow everything down by reversing the engines. Call me Captain Pugwash. To recover dignity I jump onto the boards like a pro, with a line in my hand, which I slip over a bollard before sitting on it.

Chan is wearing a short-sleeve shirt with tropical fruit all over, long walking shorts, and sandals. He is taller, slimmer, and fitter than I remember. In fact, he looks like an athlete as he strolls down the jetty with a large sports bag hanging from one shoulder.

"I tied the rowboat up to the buoy with the kid's cadaver still in it," I explain. "I had to put the clerk's head in the sink in the galley because it kept rolling around on deck, but I didn't move the trunk except to shift it out of the way of the anchor chain."

Chan skips lightly aboard to check out the headless clerk. "I saved your life," he says. "I'm not looking for credit, but isn't there a word for that in your culture?"

"*Gatdanyu*," I say.

"Meaning?"

"Roughly speaking, 'I owe you one all the way to death.'"

"Good," Chan says. "So let's go pick up the kid and do some serious evidence destruction. Otherwise the cops on this island will hold you for a year, until their owners tell them to let you go."

"Owners?"

"The Yips are big here, but the cops are controlled by some army general. I bet you can tell me the name."

"Zinna. How did you know?"

He seems to consider the question. "Fanaticism. One day very soon it will overtake you. Then you'll want to know every tiny thing about Vulture Peak. Just like me."

We hook up the rowboat to the stern and head out to sea. I feel dirty about what we are doing—in my own way I have always honored the deeper rules of law enforcement—but Chan is right: Zinna and the Yips would never let me off the island if they could find an excuse to keep me here. When we're about a mile out to sea, I watch him drag the clerk's body into the rowboat. He finds an adjustable wrench in the wheelhouse and unscrews the bolt at the winch that holds the anchor chain. He drags the chain and anchor across the teak deck to the rowboat and ties up the two cadavers with it, including the anchor. He is sweating from the effort, but won't let me help. The clerk's head is a problem, though. Chan solves it by putting it into a bin liner, then making a skein out of some rope to keep it from bloating and floating. Now he ties the skein to the anchor chain.

I jump into the rowboat and together we haul the corpses and chain overboard. Back on the swimming platform, Chan empties the Magnum's chamber into the bottom of the rowboat. Seawater floods in as if from spigots, and soon the boat also sinks. Chan jerks his head at the wheelhouse and tells me to make way.

"Where to?"

"Any position that gives a view of Vulture Peak."

Boats are very slow compared to cars. It takes more than three hours to round the various headlands until the mountain with the mansion comes into view. It's hot now. Chan and I are both stripped to our shorts, glistening with sweat. Whether out of some kind of respect for the dead, or a need to suffer, or because we are on serious business, is hard to say, but neither of us thinks of turning on the air-conditioning.

I drop anchor at the spot that Chan indicates and watch while he empties the contents of his sports bag onto a table. The main items are three light, hardened aluminum pipes that screw into one another. When put together with a few more parts, they transform into a single-shot rifle with an exceptionally long barrel, a high-tech scope, and a clever way of calibrating the angle of the shot to the finest tolerances.

"It takes time to aim. You were lucky the kid was so blown away by his first kill that he stood motionless for over a minute. Otherwise you'd be dead."

"You brought that from Hong Kong? I thought you were on vacation."

"Of course I didn't bring it from Hong Kong. Don't you know you can buy anything in Bangkok?"

We go out on deck, where Chan uses the sight from his gun to examine Vulture Peak. He seems fascinated.

"Don't you want to go up there to have a look?" I ask.

He shakes his head. "It's too soon. If anyone even suspects I'm here, we could blow the whole operation."

"What operation?"

He scratches his head. "If I'm right, then probably one of the biggest in the history of crime detection. But there's no way you would believe me at this moment. You might not appreciate it, but I've been working on your education since the night we met." He gives me a patronizing smile, then turns back to his scope. "And there's still a way to go. You examined the whole house up there on top of the hill?"

"Well, I took a look at it the day I was put on the case."

"And it's just a big house with bedrooms, a side lounge, deck, et cetera"

"Basically, yes, just that. Very fancy, but in the end just a house."

"Garage? There must be a garage."

"Yes, a big one carved into the rock. It would take at least three limos."

"And how was it?"

"Empty."

He nods.

I leave him to roast in the sun with his telescope while I retreat into the wheelhouse. It's been more than twenty-four hours since I was last in the world, so I switch on the radio. The story of the day is the Sukhumvit Rapist again, but with a difference. It seems he followed a *maichi*, a Buddhist nun, to her family home, where she was visiting, and tried to rape her. The *maichi*, though, had other ideas:

"He took all his clothes off and made signs for me to undress in front of him," the *maichi* is telling a press conference.

"Was he aroused?"

"Well, I'm not an expert, but I certainly got that impression."

Laughter.

"Then what happened?"

"I'm afraid I lost my composure and told him what I thought of him."

Snickers. "What did you say?"

"I said that I could quite understand why he would think of a nun as some kind of symbol worth violating, but he was wrong. As a *maichi* I'm as much divorced from the culture as he is. I told him that far from being a suitable target, I represent the only force in the world that could help or understand him. I probably despise the superficiality of a society that judges by appearances even more than he. I've certainly spent decades of my life thinking about it. Anyway, what could he possibly achieve by shoving his thing inside me and moving it in and out for a few minutes? I have no particular use for that organ at all, I would just wash it afterward hoping he hadn't given me a disease, then I would dissolve the whole incident in meditation. So what could he possibly achieve? I've never been pretty, and now I'm scrawny with a shaved head, so it wasn't as if he was going to possess a beautiful woman for five minutes."

"You said all that?"

"Yes."

"And what happened?"

"His thing went floppy, and he looked as if he was about to cry. I felt sorry for him. He put his clothes on and left."

Roars of laughter.

"So those Buddhist power words did the trick?"

"Oh, I don't think he paid much attention to what I was saying. I said it all looking him in the eye, you see? I wasn't horrified. My stomach didn't fall out at the sight of his ugliness. I told him by my body language that I knew he was not a demon, just another tormented human along with six billion others. I think that's what did it."

It's an amusing crime story so I go out into the blaze to tell Chan. He listens while he continues to check out the mansion in a kind of manic overdrive. I have to wonder if he is—well—a hundred satang to the baht. When I've finished telling the story, he says, "Does anyone know who he is?"

"No one knows for sure, but all the betting is on a young man who used to be Zinna's lover. We all thought he was attending a monastery in Cambodia, but it's looking like he decided to return to the world."

I tell Chan about Zinna and the tragic accident. He takes the scope away from his face for a moment. "Another transplant in China? Interesting, don't you think?" Then he returns to his distant surveillance of the empty house and, it seems, every inch of the mountain it stands on.

Part 2

18

When things go wrong between us, Chanya and I try to mend our relationship by going out to eat. We're both too shy to yell at each other in public, and we love food and wine, so there's nothing for it except to make polite intelligent conversation on all topics save the ones raging in our hearts. If we're still mad at each other after the cheese course, we tend to settle scores in the cab on the way home.

Tonight we're eating at a brand-new Italian place that's just opened on a *soi* off mid-Sukhumvit, impelled not so much by rage as by sadness that we seem to be drifting apart in separate rudderless boats. Chanya orders a Caesar salad, I order mozzarella with tomatoes drizzled in extra-special extra-virgin olive oil from some olive grove in southeastern Sicily; the bottle sports an explanatory tag with a coat of arms to prove it. For the main course we both order *fegato alla veneziana*, because it's almost impossible to get in the tropics. Chanya tells me to order the wine, in deference to the *oenologique* education I received from my mother's richest client, Monsieur Truffaut. But that was more than twenty years ago, and all the finest vintages have changed. Since we're eating on Vikorn's tab via his black Amex, I figure the simplest selection procedure is to choose the third most expensive Barolo, my thinking being that the two most expensive wines on any list are always irresponsibly overpriced by reason of glamour and cachet, but the cost of the third is probably fair value for an excellent wine. When the sommelier has me taste it, I'm fortified in my strategy and gaze at Chanya with triumph.

"It's good," I tell her.

"I can see that from the smug look on your face," Chanya says.

It becomes clear to both of us that the ensuing awkward silence can be relieved only by gossip, and the subject of that gossip is going to be the same as everyone else's.

"One of my women's groups has access to news stories the police try to suppress," she tells me as she sips the wine. "Apparently he brutally raped an army wife."

"He hurt her? So far he hasn't been violent. That story about the *maichi* almost rehabilitated him."

"I know. We were so proud of her, all the women at Uni sent her congratulatory e-mails. Such dignity, courage, compassion—a great example of womanhood at its best. I had an argument with a feminist who moaned that the *maichi* was a product of a medieval paternalistic exploitative system and she'd only prevailed against the predatory male by neutering herself. I was so mad I nearly punched her."

I sip the wine—actually, it's more a glug than a sip. "I agree. I felt sick in my heart after I heard the story. It made me realize how I'd strayed from the Buddhist path. Even my thought processes seem to have become superficial. I find myself fixating on things that don't matter, like a *farang.*"

"Yes," Chanya agrees. "I'm so glad you finally said it—all those eyes. You were really freaking when you came back from Dubai. But you're probably still not seeing the full horror—you're in denial, that's what makes people superficial. Look at the Brits, still in denial about the atrocities of empire and superficial as hell. They all watch *East Enders*, like Dorothy. That's not culture, it's despair in disguise."

Affronted by her lack of kindness, I return to an earlier topic. "So, the rapist—he beat up his latest victim?"

Chanya shakes her head. "I didn't say that."

"You said 'brutally raped.'"

She takes another sip of wine. "You can't do that to a terrified woman without hurting her, Sonchai, no matter how much KY Jelly you use. The harder the thrust, the worse the psychological damage."

I stare at my mozzarella and tomato salad, which has been drizzled with that deep green olive oil that looks so special. "I guess."

From the Sukhumvit Rapist, we move on to the extension to the Skytrain; then over the main course Chanya reports on Dorothy.

"You know what's amazing? She seems to have tamed Jimmy Clipp."

"Who?"

"You know, that American civil engineer who was in your mother's bar that night getting a hand job and then took Dorothy to the short-time hotel where she fell in love with him."

"She tamed him? What did she do?"

"Apart from threatening suicide about fifty times, I'm not sure. He's American, so maybe he's seduced by pubescent adulation. You know how they are."

That story sees us safely through the *fegato*, and neither of us wants to risk our waistlines on a sweet, tempting as they are (I have an almost insurmountable weakness for profiteroles, but with superhuman will I decline the whole desert trolley), so I pay with a dark flourish from BlackAm and add a hefty tip for the Thai man-and-woman team who have been trying so valiantly to follow the arcane system of HiSo *farang* restaurant rituals, not to mention forcing their tongues around such lingual torment as *profiteroles*, *Barolo*, et cetera: we tend to hold the *r* sound in contempt and whenever possible substitute the infinitely more elegant and playful *l*; few Thais can hear the difference. (The Balolo cost roughly two hundred dollars, by the way, DFR; I know you've been dying to ask.)

Chanya and I take a cab back to the hovel. We're silent for most of the journey, and my mind eventually flips back to the case. The deeper I sink into it, the less I am able to understand Vikorn's part. And now that he's popped into my mind, I realize the Colonel is the only remaining source of relationship-neutral conversation.

"He's a control freak," I tell Chanya as the cab turns into our *soi*. "For more than thirty years he has outmaneuvered, outcheated, out-witted, outflanked, outsold, outbought, and outkilled his enemies so that he could have total and absolute control of his kingdom. Now, suddenly, he decides to enter politics, we have three Americans running his life, and everything is in the hands of people in Beijing. It's not like him."

"Isn't it out of character for him to run for governor in the first place? It just isn't his style—he's way too shrewd to want to become a minor public figure. Is someone making him do it?"

"Force Vikorn to run for political office? Who in Thailand would have the power to do that?"

"Someone he owes a lot of money to—or someone with the power to blackmail him."

"Blackmail Vikorn? Vikorn in debt? He owns everyone."

Chanya shrugs. It's my problem, not hers. Then she says, "What about that Yunnan trip all those years ago? Something happened to get you all excited for a day. You were running around all over town and wouldn't tell me what it was about except that it was on urgent Vikorn business and that he was stuck in Yunnan with Ruamsantiah. Then it all suddenly faded, and next thing I knew Vikorn and the sergeant were back in town. I was sure there would be a coda to that one day. You told me Vikorn got himself into a tight spot and had to throw money at it. Maybe he still owes someone a favor?"

I blink. Stare. She points at my mouth, which is hanging open. I close it, give her one huge smacker on the chops, and say, "D'you know you are absolutely fucking brilliant?" I'm experiencing a non-narcotic ecstasy of the loving kind and cannot stop. "You're just the most fantastic wife a cop could ever hope to have. I just totally adore you to bits. You're just unbelievable."

She enjoys adulation as well as any woman, but she has known me for a long time. "Did I say something to crack the case?"

"Yes."

"So can I get laid tonight before you dash off to Phuket or Hong Kong or some other damned place?"

I hesitate—a bad mistake, which I have to cover by saying, "Sure," and placing her hand on my cock as an earnest of my troth. Once inside the hovel and naked, I make a supreme effort to dedicate all my energies to the task at hand and wait the regulation period of post-coital silence before beginning to make restless movements.

"It's okay," Chanya says with a sigh. "I realize I've had my twenty minutes. You can get on with your case now. I don't suppose you're going to tell me exactly what I said that's gotten you so excited?"

"Later," I whisper. "I'm just popping out to make a call, I want a good signal."

19

I have to tell you about the Yunan trip, DFR; it goes like this.

Colonel Vikorn was away on business with Sergeant Ruamsantiah. Only the inner circle, which is to say me, knew where they had gone: Yunnan, in southwestern China. He had never been there before, and my present guess is that he will never go there again. On the face of it, though, the intention had been a relatively normal meeting between high-end narcotics traffickers. It seems a Burmese general closely associated with, but not a member of, the ruling elite had perfected the black art of producing morphine from poppy and, when required, heroin from morphine. Vikorn was interested for two reasons, the first being that he could never obtain enough smack to match demand, the second that he had been trying for years to break into the Burmese wholesale market as a strategy for doing in his main business rival in Thailand, General Zinna, who had been pals with the psychopathic rulers of Myanmar for decades and derived most of his crystal meth supplies from there. Due diligence had revealed that General U-Tat was something of a rebel within the Burmese military but was too well entrenched in the Shan Mountains for them to do much about it. Clearly, this was a man to cultivate with a long-term view of using him to squeeze Zinna. Vikorn and Ruamsantiah set off together for Lijiang, leaving Manny and me at headquarters.

General U-Tat was not at the airport to meet them; instead they found one General Xie, of the People's Liberation Army. General Xie gave them to understand that his dear friend General U-Tat was dealing with a minor insurrection among the Shan tribes, which he was putting down with such speed and brutality, he would be able to join the party in not less than two days. In the meantime General Xie let it be known that he knew why Vikorn and Ruamsantiah had come to Yunnan, that he was himself a major shareholder in General U-Tat's enterprise and might even be the senior partner. As the days passed, the dinners grew longer, and the entertainment more lavish; opportunities to indulge in all the major vices were offered and, in the case of Ruamsantiah, accepted.

Then Xie announced that General U-Tat had successfully put down the rebellion but had sustained a minor yet debilitating injury to his left knee that made it difficult for him to travel. He would certainly not trouble Vikorn and Ruamsantiah to come into Burma, but would they mind meeting him halfway—at the village of Ruili, near the Yunnan-Burmese border? This would not be a sinister-looking jungle trek—there were modern roads and full communications all the way to Ruili, and for full security General Xie himself would escort them. The general had held a full inspection of the local garrison the day before and invited Vikorn and Ruamsantiah as guests of honor; they duly admired the general in full-dress uniform. Not that they trusted Xie any further than they could throw him, and not that General Xie thought he could induce them to trust him. It was more a case of the general showing how wealthy and powerful he was, and how well known, so he would hardly pull a fast one on them. For what? They were merely two Thai cops and had no money on them to speak of. What good could come from molesting them?

So when their car and escort were stopped just outside Ruili by masked men who held themselves very much like soldiers and seemed armed with standard-issue military weapons all of the same Chinese type and make, Vikorn and Ruamsantiah couldn't believe that they'd

violated the first rule of sophisticated professionals: never underesti-
mate the other guy's possible amateurism. They were kicking themselves.

"Suppose the general has been recording our conversations for
entrapment purposes?" Ruamsantiah whispered to Vikorn while they
were being professionally frisked by one of the masked gunmen.

"I'm sorry to have to tell you that our conversations together over
the past several days have been recorded. After taking legal advice, I
have reached the conclusion that I have no choice but to report you to
the authorities for conspiring to transport prohibited narcotics across
Chinese territory, a criminal offense with a mandatory death penalty,"
General Xie explained twenty minutes later, when they were in a
military-style cabin in an army camp less than a mile from the
Burmese border.

"How much?" Vikorn said.

"Two million dollars," Xie said.

"Okay," Vikorn said, concealing a smirk of contempt. In the general's position, he would have started at twenty million and stood firm
at ten. Two million? It wasn't worth bargaining about.

"In cash," Xie said.

"Ah!" Vikorn said.

"Used notes," Xie said.

Now Vikorn reassessed Xie. He had thought he was dealing with a
brain-dead thug, of a model not dissimilar to Zinna. Now he switched
models. This was classic Chinese small-and-medium-enterprises
thinking: modest returns with quick turnarounds and near-zero risk;
used banknotes were the caviar of money laundering. Smart operators
would give as much as a 60 percent discount for used notes.

"How often have you done this?" Vikorn asked.

"Not telling you," Xie said.

"More or less than ten?"

"More."

"More or less than a hundred?"

Xie could not resist a smirk.

"More or less than—"

"Can you get the money by tomorrow? The price goes up ten percent per day thereafter."

Vikorn thought about it. "You really need it for tomorrow?"

"Yes," Xie said, "I really need it for tomorrow."

Xie didn't know it, but Vikorn was giving him a chance to be reasonable. "Really really?"

"Yes, really really really. What's wrong with you?"

"And if we don't get it, you're going to have us executed for narcotics trafficking?"

"Sure."

"So we don't have any choice?"

"Right."

"Just tell me one thing. Are you really connected to a Burmese general named U-Tat?"

"He would corroborate if I needed him to," Xie said. "Or I'd send some men to talk to him. He does what I want."

"Okay," Vikorn said, "I can get it for you by tomorrow night. Before midnight, anyway. But I have to make phone calls."

"Only one," Xie said.

"Okay," Vikorn said with a sigh.

Which was when he called me.

"Hey, Sonchai, we've been kidnapped. It's okay, they only want two million dollars, but it has to be in used notes. I want you to get the money from the bank and bring it. You have to come alone, unarmed. Got it?"

I knew what to do. Once, a long time before, he had called me into his office and said, "If you ever get a call from me to say I've been kidnapped and held for ransom and I use the words *You have to come alone, unarmed. Got it?* you go to my bank—you know the one I mean?—and you tell them you want to speak to Mr. To on behalf of Colonel Vikorn."

The bank in question was a mid-ranking Chinese merchant bank based in Hong Kong with an outlet in Chinatown, not far from the

Chao Phraya River. I took a motorbike taxi and arrived within thirty minutes of putting the phone down on Vikorn. At the same time I used my cell phone to book a flight to Lijiang City. The travel agent doubted that I would be able to arrive before midnight the next day, but she would do her best.

The banking hall was of the Chinese-gaudy school, clearly intended to outmarble any rival in the area. When I asked for Mr. To at the information desk, the Chinese receptionist checked her computer and told me there was nobody there of that name.

"So, what are your instructions for when someone like me arrives and says I'm from Colonel Vikorn and need to speak urgently to Mr. To?"

She nodded and plugged the question into the software. "Just a minute please. I will try to get you Mr. Ng."

Within minutes a uniformed security guard led me to a private lift, which took us up to the top floor. When the lift doors opened, two more uniformed guards took me down a corridor, where a third man in a suit waited. He looked a lot more dangerous than the guards.

"Are you Mr. To?"

"No," he said with a smile.

"Ng?"

"No," he said, and knocked on a door. A male voice said something in Chinese. The man in the suit said something back that included the name *Vikorn*. The voice in the room said something that must have meant "come in." We entered. The man in the suit left, closing the door behind him.

It was a small room with a small desk crowded with old-fashioned file covers bulging with documents. Behind the desk sat a very thin Chinese man in his forties with thick straight black hair and a black moustache and a bright smile full of optimism. On either side of him sat two women who seemed to be secretaries. One was very thin and boyish, the other about thirty and voluptuous with black-rimmed glasses.

"Are you Mr. To?" I asked.

"No," he said with a sparkling smile, "I am not."

"Ng?"

He shook his head. "Not Ng either, but what can I do for you?"

I told him all I knew, which was almost nothing. He thought for perhaps two seconds, said, "Won't you please sit down," in perfect English, and stuck a finger in the air to shut me up when I tried to say something more. Then he spoke rapidly to the boyish secretary, who grabbed a pad and pencil and scribbled in Chinese script while he spoke. "Please tell me where you have been told to make contact in Yunnan."

"At Lijiang City airport."

The man who was not Mr. To nodded and seemed to repeat this to the secretary, who wrote it down. Then he spoke to the other woman, who took out a cell phone and used it to take a photograph of me. Then she asked me to stand up. She took a ruler from the desk and made a rough calculation as to my height. Then she seemed to describe me and my clothes to her colleague, who wrote down the details. The man stood up.

"Thank you, that will be all."

"D'you have the money now? I've got about an hour to get to the airport," I said.

He looked surprised. "Oh, no. You do not go anywhere. You stay in Bangkok."

"But Colonel Vikorn said—"

"No, no, no, no, no. You forget Colonel Vikorn. You stay here. Your job is over."

In addition to being a very skinny man, he was also quite short, but I wouldn't have disobeyed him for the world. He walked around his desk to escort me to the door and gave me a name card with no name on it, only a number. I looked at the number and said, "Thanks. Who should I ask for if I need to use it?"

"Ask for Mr. To," he said. Just before he closed the door on me, he added, "There will be no need to use it immediately. It's simply in case of unforeseen contingencies in the future. We like to be thorough."

The next day Vikorn and Ruamsantiah arrived back from Yunnan looking sheepish but somehow pleased with themselves. Neither would speak about their escapade save to say that they appreciated my help. They behaved as if nothing had happened, except that, according to Manny, Vikorn spent the whole of the next day at his bank, talking, I presume, to the man who was not named To.

It was a good six months later that the media ran a story about a Red Army general based in Yunnan who had confessed, under inter-rogation, to smuggling morphine into and out of China. The hook for the story was his execution by single bullet in the back of the head the day before. His name was Xie. It seems he had been held in solitary confinement for half a year, after a commando raid on his Lijiang City HQ by the army's internal security unit. The rumor that he had been holding two Thai fat cat narcotics traffickers hostage at the time was vigorously denied both by the army and General Xie (according to the army after Xie's death).

So, here I am halfway down our *soi* with my cell phone in my right hand and that nameless name card in the left trapped between the pinkie and the finger of the sun so I can use my left index to plug the number into the keyboard (because my model is too broad for my del-icate little Eurasian hand to hold and thumb simultaneously with the right—I knew you were wondering, DFR). "Hello," a woman's voice answers on the third ring.

"May I speak to Mr. To, please?"

Silence, then the ringing tone. When I try again, I get the engaged tone. On my way back to the hovel, I realize I left out the most impor-tant part of the formula: I should have said I was calling on behalf of Colonel Vikorn. Now there's only one man left to call, but it will have to wait until tomorrow.

20

By way of small talk I say, "Can you get me some more dope? I'm totally out."

Sergeant Ruamsantiah opens his cheroot tin and picks one of the thin dark sticks, which he holds to his nose and rolls as if it were a Havana. The girl behind the bar looks unhappy because he's already given her a big tip and a lot of smiles so she doesn't want to tell him he's not allowed to smoke in here, but Ruamsantiah takes out his police ID and the girl looks at it and grins. Everyone likes to have at least one cop as a friend. She even finds a butane lighter behind the bar, which she holds for him.

Now the sergeant is merrily puffing on the cheroot, making the other smokers in the bar jealous as hell. Nobody says *So how come he's allowed to smoke and not me?* because they've all guessed why the girl lit the cigar. One *farang* lifts his nose and tries to follow the fragrant trail as it diffuses. It's not often you see a Westerner awed by a local boy, but this guy would also love to be able to walk into any bar in town and light up without fear of getting yelled at. Maybe it would be less cruel if the sergeant were smoking something tiny and apologetic with low tar: the full aroma of the unfiltered cheroot is making that forbidden statement about power, manly badness, indifference to death—and to hell with the anal-retentive white mafia-esses who would like to kill anything big and hairy that has the balls to turn an entire bar into a crowd of passive smokers. After a few minutes the gasping *farang* can no longer maintain resistance; he goes out into the street for a puff on a Marlboro Light.

"Okay," the sergeant says, not noticing the distress he has caused. "Do you want export quality? It's quite expensive, even at cost."

"Can you get Thai sticks?"

The sergeant makes a face and frowns. "How many times do I have to tell you, they just don't make them anymore."

"But it's depressing," I say. "And it affects our international reputation. Thai sticks, from the best marijuana stock in the world, grown under tropical conditions and laced with opium—it was the greatest high terrestrial life had to offer."

"Too much fucking law enforcement," he says. "It's this *farang* obsession with detail. You have the law on the books, okay, that means you can control the trade and make sure only the more responsible traffickers survive, the ones who don't mind paying a little tax to the cops, which is like community service in advance of conviction. So why would you need a conviction? Why all the expense of a court case when the cops have already imposed the punishment? This is natural village capitalism. But nowadays, thanks to Pressure, they've got us checking every damned truck or car coming out of Isaan. It's killed businesses, broken up families, and destroyed the quality of our dope. It won't be long before they criminalize the chili in our *somtam*. This is not my fault. No, I cannot get Thai sticks, not even for you."

I use techniques drawn from Buddhism to cope with this depressing news. I focus on a beautiful beach on an ocean without a shore; it's better than one hand clapping. "Okay. Supposing I wanted to make some Thai sticks myself, how d'you do it?"

"Easy," the sergeant says. "Opium sap is water soluble, so the best way is to add a solution of sap and water while you're drying the weed. So when the weed is dry, it includes a deposit of opium. Set fire and inhale."

"So why can't they do that today?"

"They're balancing risk. If they get caught with cannabis, they're on the five-to-ten prison scale. If the dope includes opium, they risk the injection. Since *farang* these days don't know the difference, why take the chance? Want me to get you some raw opium so you can make the sticks yourself?"

"Sure," I say.

"Let me know how you get on—we might want to sell the product. We could even package it as a retro thrill, put it in a box with an old Chinaman smoking an opium pipe on the lid: nostalgia for the good old days, full of Eastern promise. Start off selling it at around the same price as that damned hay we're getting from Laos, then when they get addicted, charge like a wounded elephant."

"It doesn't worry you that a lot of people would become addicts?"

"If they become addicts, it's because they're suckers. Why should they be exploited by someone else's capitalism? Why not mine?"

"You ever think of getting a job on Wall Street?"

The sergeant is playing me along. He knows I didn't invite him out tonight just to ask if he can get dope. Dope is his sideline, an SME that he runs independently of the Colonel. I could have ordered some by phone. I think he knows exactly the question I want to put to him, but for some reason he slides away from me just when I'm getting close. "Sergeant, there's just one—"

"Tell you what," he says. "Shall we change bars?" He checks his watch. It's eight P.M. When we met at around seven-fifteen, the go-go bars were not yet in full swing. There were no girls gyrating around the poles on stage because they were using the stage as a table while they ate their evening meals, just like the *katoeys* in Nana. The bar we are in, which boasts no stage and traffics only in alcohol, is just a pit stop until the action starts. The sergeant lets me pay for the drinks with Vikorn's black Amex, then snatches the card when the girl returns it to me. He shakes his head, indicating naked jealousy. "What's it like, having one of those in your pocket?"

"It's better than a gun, a Ferrari, or an erection," I say. "You can take it into any hotel, office, or department store and get treated like the sultan of Brunei. Even ATM machines work faster."

Outside on the street we can hardly move for traders, tourists, pimps, and whores. Ever since Pat Pong achieved worldwide fame, merchandisers have been annexing territory, so now you have the whole street taken up with stalls selling clothes, watches, videos,

incense, and other tourist junk, which creates an interesting sociological study: *farang* who arrive in a family group for the safe, clean crime
of buying a couple of fake Rolexes to show friends at home maintain a
strict seclusion from those *farang* men who arrive as lone wolves and
hardly notice the stalls in the middle of the street because they're
focused on the girls in shiny swimming costumes and long silver
cloaks who beckon them into the bars. *Farang* wives watch curiosity
work their husbands' libidos, no matter how good a boy they married;
farang husbands don't notice the curiosity their wives also feel.
Respectable women, who would die a thousand deaths rather than sell
their bodies, wonder for a moment *exactly* what it must be like to do
such a thing. I see a mother cover the eyes of her son of maybe nine
years: too late, the kid saw his dad's pupils dilate in a most undadlike
way at a glimpse of a forbidden world.

Ruamsantiah pays no attention to the stalls, though, as he pushes
between bodies to get to the other side of the street where the Shangri-
La bar is situated.

Like my mother's bar, the Shangri-La is known for the extra care it
takes with the pay and selection of its girls. As a result, you have maybe
the most beautiful women in the world strutting their stuff and inviting offers: gracious smiles greet us at the same time as loins gyrate and
chests inflate. Ruamsantiah goes for the back seats and sags into one
with a sigh. I know he's been here before and that he was looking forward to this moment, which replicates an earlier moment, and so on
all the way back to puberty. "It's always the same," he says out of the
corner of his mouth. "There isn't a single one I don't want to fuck. I
could sit here all night and still not make up my mind."

"You remember the run-in you and the Colonel had with that Chinese general in Yunnan a few years ago?"

He orders a bottle of Mekong whiskey with ice and water on the
side, now brought by one of the staff, also a beautiful young woman
who can be hired, though for an extra premium because a replacement would have to be found to serve drinks. The sergeant gives her
a long, appraising look, accompanied by a magnificent smile, and
tells her to give the chit to me. He is pretending he didn't hear my

question. I groan. I won't get any sense out of him for hours, and we'll both be drunk by then. Such is his plan.

It's 1:25 A.M. The evening went pretty much as I expected, and now I'm in a cab on the way home.

Ruamsantiah kept inviting girls down off the stage and buying them drinks, so that after a couple of hours we were buying drinks for six girls, all of whom had lightly groped, and been lightly groped by, the sergeant, who with every grope given and received was that much further away from deciding which two he would take with him to the short-term hotel. He told me he needed to leave the bar for a while to clear his head, and we strolled across to Pat Pong II, where we climbed the stairs to the Wallabi bar. He sat in a corner where he got a blowjob by twin sisters who shared the labor fifty-fifty while he sent me to buy him Viagra. I walked across the street to the pharmacy where the owner, a Thai woman in her fifties, threw two blue pills into a tiny brown paper bag with a big sneer and charged five hundred baht per pop. I wondered if she'd ever thought of going on the game or trading in heroin to cheer herself up. How about body parts? By the time I got back to the Wallabi, Ruamsantiah had already ejaculated and the twins had disappeared somewhere to gargle with Listerine while he lit up another cheroot without bothering to flash his cop ID, because as a general rule the upper floors are lawless anyway.

The sergeant popped a whole Viagra when half is the recommended dose and ordered a beer while he waited for his next erection. I tried to start up the conversation I had invited him out for, but he was reliving the experience he'd just had and didn't answer while a smile of obscene gratification played over his lips. By that time I was resigned to playing his game, whatever it was, and even felt a certain relief when he reported the drug was starting to have effect and maybe we should return to the Shangri-La. I guess the chemical was building up quite a bit of steam by the time we got back to that bar, because with shocking speed the sergeant chose two of the girls he'd formerly been entertaining and had me pay for their services on the credit card.

While they were changing into street clothes, he leaned over to me and said, "Yeah, I do remember. How could I ever forget? It's at times like that you find out what leadership means. I was scared shitless, but the Colonel never turned a hair—didn't faze him at all."

Then he admitted he'd known from the start that I would want to talk about Mr. To, but he was afraid that if he spilled his guts earlier on, I'd disappear with the BlackAm, but now that the evening was building toward its second climax, he was ready to talk, and anyway he needed something to distract him while he suffered the sweet torment of gratification delayed: bar girls are known to take an age to put on the couple of bits of clothing they need to cross the street to the short-term hotel where they take them off again.

"But you *know* what happened. You went to talk to the bank's number-one enforcer with *guanxi* in Beijing. So there was the Colonel and me in a barrack cell, with armed guards outside, thinking this might just be the end, when there's a whole brain-bending show of the latest military disorientation devices going off outside the cell: noise, zinging like you wouldn't believe, flashes to blind you, quite a few real-sounding bullets from small arms, a few glimpses of some very serious-looking soldiers dressed in black, like Chinese special forces. Then our cell door gets busted open with a small explosive device, and we're dragged out and frog-marched to a light aircraft. I just have time to see a few bodies on the tarmac before we're thrown in the plane, and next thing you know we're over Thai airspace and about to land in Bangkok. On the plane they told us that a special services agent of your build pretended to deliver the dough about five minutes before the attack. They needed the evidence for the prosecution. But you must have guessed all that."

"Yes, I guessed all that. But the deal with To—that sounds like a very expensive operation. Vikorn must have mortgaged more than his Bentley."

The sergeant looked at me with a frank expression that seemed to ask for counsel: had I pampered, spoiled, and indulged him to the point where it would have been unreasonable for anyone to expect him to keep the secret—or should he have held out for more? I didn't know how to signal that I'd spent more than a thousand dollars on him, and no way anyone could seriously expect him not to share his most intimate secrets with me after accepting such hospitality, but he sagged anyway. "The deal? It was open-ended." I blinked. "You know how the Chinese work: they leave one enormous favor on the table, which they remind you of from time to time—until the moment comes for payback."

"Vikorn pledged to do just about anything, when the time came?"

Ruamsantiah shrugged. "We were in a tight spot. No matter what face the Colonel put on it, and he really is made of steel, there was only a fifty-fifty chance of getting out of there in one piece. Sure, he promised the world—because he knew that was the price."

"And am I right in thinking it's Beijing, through To, who forced him to run for governor?"

Ruamsantiah stared me in the eye for a long, serious moment; then his girls started to arrive, and he relaxed.

There are women so beautiful, the glittering bikinis they wear on stage only distract from their charms, and it's not until you see them in plain old skintight jeans, T-shirt, and flip-flops that your jaw really drops. I was jealous as hell of what he was about to do with her and for a wobbly moment wondered if I should use the BlackAm to hire a couple of girls for myself, but he had managed to choose the two most beautiful in the bar, so no matter what I did, he was going to end up as alpha-male apex feeder.

At that moment the sergeant and I were sitting next to each other on a padded bench with our bodies touching, so I was able to decipher his movements as he undid the waistband of his pants, reached down to rescue his member, which had stiffened in an awkward position and was now stuck painfully between pocket and inner thigh, then did up the button again, all while beaming with appreciation at the first half of his forthcoming orgy.

"Well?" I said.

Ruamsantiah stopped grinning at the girl in jeans and T-shirt long enough to say, "I don't know. Let's say I was very surprised when he told me he was going to run, and I came to the conclusion that it was not a decision he made all on his own. Khun To is a wild card, a money genius with *guanxi, ganqing,* and *renqing* coming out of his ears, but he may be out of control. They say he plays hard and weird."

Then the second girl arrived. If anything, she was even more stunning in her street clothes than the first, but my libido had switched off. I watched in a distracted way as he led them out of the bar.

21

So who says life is all bad? I'm up, washed and shaved, and ready to put on my organ trafficker's outfit to wear to the bank. Chanya can't resist ogling me, and to raise the libido level, I refuse to tell her where I'm going, even though the question that cracked open the mystery came from her. Yep, DFR, I am telling you to put that suspect list away now, because Jitpleecheep has solved the case. Excuse me while I go out into the yard in my shorts to do my victory dance. (It's from my Lakota incarnation: wood fires around the wigwams at dawn, a squaw who looked a lot like Chanya and another who looked like Om, white men with killing machines on the horizon, Red Horse and the braves grinning to crack their faces. *What a fantastic day to die!*) Chanya knows what I'm up to but takes no notice. She's seen it before.

Just in case you haven't worked it out, DFR, let me hand it to you on a plate:

The man who is not To (hereafter "Notto") is not only a high-ranking Hong Kong banker who runs the Bangkok office sotto voce in the Confucian style; he is not only an ace troubleshooter for said bank and whoever of its most highly valued clients may need him from time to time—I bet Vikorn has close to a billion tied up there for him to get that kind of service; but Notto is also the incarnation of *guanxi* with some of the oldies who run China. That much, I trust, is clear. So, when a very fat cat like Vikorn needs the kind of help he needed with

General Xie (deceased), dollar signs light up in Notto's eyes. Perhaps his first impulse was to charge the Colonel a few million for the hostage-busting service, but then he talked to Beijing, who had a better idea. Or maybe Notto had the idea all on his own and simply made a phone call to Beijing for approval. Either way, somebody senior saw a senior-size opportunity to make a lot of dough. Everyone knows how corrupt our civil service is (we came in *behind* Malaysia in the how-dirty-is-your-country statistics last year—which only leaves Cambodia, Burma, Vietnam, Indonesia, India, and Laos for us to sneer at), and everyone knows how lucrative for a merchant bank big infrastructure projects can be. Instead of bleeding Vikorn white in the old-style subprime-mortgage win-lose equation in which so many have lost their homes, they used the enlightened win-win equation that, as we know from the news networks, all of which are large corporations with vested interests, is saving the world. "You are the next governor of Bangkok," Notto said to Vikorn the day after he got back from Yunnan, or words to that effect. I imagine the conversation running like this:

Vikorn: What? No way.

Notto: Have you any idea how much a commando operation like that costs these days? Highly trained men, specialist equipment, state-of-the-art communications, stealth, airtight secrecy? And you know what, they're going to have to go public because someone in the foreign media got hold of the story.

Vikorn: You mean they weren't allowed to just shoot the bastard? I thought you said airtight security.

Notto: They charge a two-hundred-percent markup fee if they have to go public, whether it's their screw-up or not. It's to repair the army's tarnished image and pay for the legal expenses.

Vikorn: Okay, I'll run for governor. What do I have to do?

Notto: Nothing. That's what I want you to know. You do nothing at all except what our experienced team will tell you to do. You just obey them, and Bob is your uncle.

Vikorn: What experience do your *guanxi* have with
    democracy?
Notto: None. What do you think American friends are for?
Vikorn: So I'm governor of Bangkok, then what?
Notto: Then you extend the Skytrain and similar stuff.
Vikorn: Got it.

I'm pretty confident that's how it went, DFR—you agree? It's a wrap that explains everything, including the clumsy way Beijing and the Americans are going about the Colonel's election campaign, and including sending me on some photo-op in Dubai with those crazy Twins, but especially dumping those three bodies in that house on Vulture Peak. Can't you see the way the meeting went?

Linda: Ah, we do go along with the idea that the Colonel
    should be running a high-profile case at the time of the
    election.
Jack: Yeah, we all go along with that, right, Ben?
Ben: Right.
Linda: But we discussed it at length, and we don't know of any
    evidence that Thailand is a center for organ trafficking.
Jack: Yeah, that does introduce a, ah, what you might call an
    unwelcome variable.
Notto: Just a minute.
(Notto finds his cell phone and speaks into it. Perhaps he has
    to be patched on to a few other phones before he gets the
    right one. He speaks quickly in Putonghua. The Americans
    are all ears. Now Notto closes his phone and smiles.)
Linda: Okay, I guess Thailand is about to be a center for organ
    trafficking.
Jack: I didn't quite catch what he said.
Ben: Me either.
Linda: I didn't get all of it word for word, but the guy he spoke
    to runs the corrections services' pre-sales unit.
Ben: Pre-sales?
Linda: Yeah, pre-sales of organs of prisoners on death row.

Everybody wants fresh. I guess a few bodies with the organs
ripped out and delivered to a Thai location would be no
problem for him at all.

Jack (shaking his head): The magic of *guanxi*.

Ben: Right.

Linda (to Notto): You sure they won't be identified as executed
Chinese felons?

Notto: Yes.

Now I'm back in the hovel dressing and combing my hair, which
the victory dance disheveled somewhat, at the same time as I'm putting a few finishing touches to what, if I may say so, is an impeccable
piece of detection, when my attention is suddenly diverted against my
will. It's called possessiveness. I can't help it—with conjugal alien-
ation, I've become sensitive to little things, such as the fact that her
telephone just rang and she turned away from the door and began
speaking too softly for me to hear.

"Who was that, darling?" I say, putting on my Zegna jacket and trying to look as if I'm just making conversation.

"Ah, that was Colonel Vikorn, darling."

I turn, aghast and confused. Why didn't he talk to me? Controlling
myself: "Really, what did he want?"

"He wanted to know what you were wearing, so I told him."

"He wanted to know—"

My phone rings. It's Vikorn. "Why are you wearing that getup?"

"To go to the bank."

A pause. "Don't go to the bank. Isn't there a General Zinna line for
you to follow up?"

"Yes, but—"

"Good. Go see Zinna. And change out of that crap. He'll think
you've turned gay and try to screw you." He closes the phone.

Now I'm sitting bewildered on a chair. Chanya stands behind me
and strokes my hair, then starts to massage my head.

"You were spying on me," I say.

She giggles. "Honey, if you've worked out what I think you've
worked out, then d'you think Vikorn and the Americans would want

you making contact with the person I think you are trying to make contact with?"

"I'm a murder squad detective," I say. "I got carried away. For a moment I was a real cop."

"I understand that," Chanya says, still massaging. "But—and do correct me if I'm wrong—isn't there a genuine Zinna line? I mean, how is it that he has so many connections in Phuket? Isn't that worth following up?"

I hear myself saying, "Yes. I guess I'll have to make another trip down there."

She freezes for a moment, then transforms. At lightning speed she has processed the thought that I might cheat on her in Phuket, closed all emotional hatches, and refocused with 200 percent attention on her ambition. "Of course you will," she says, staring at the street. The massage is over.

Now my phone rings again. It's Vikorn. "Have you been to the morgue yet?"

"Of course I went to the morgue."

"I mean after the first time? Dr. Supatra called yesterday, I forgot to tell you. She says she has made progress with identification of the three victims."

22

In Dr. Supatra's underground lair, death imbues everyday tools with an outlandish dignity: giant pruning shears; those big handsaws normally used for cutting up logs; and rotary electric saws of various sizes. The one that gives me the creeps more than any other is the long-handled wire cutter, the kind you see in war movies when the sappers crawl on their bellies to cut through barbed wire: Supatra uses it to bust her way through rib cages. In the case of the three anonymous ones, though, there wasn't a lot left to investigate.

The doctor is in her office next to the autopsy room. She smiles when she sees me through the glass wall and stands to come to the door to greet me. "Detective, that software I told you about finally arrived. I'm halfway through. It's quite exciting."

She leads me to her desk and gestures for me to pull up a chair. She is finding it difficult to suppress a girlish glee in her new toy. When she jogs her mouse, a human head appears on her monitor in stark ghost white against a green background: eyeless, faceless, thin neck.

"It's the second girl, the thin one."

"I thought you said it was two men and a woman?"

Dr. Supatra shifts her gaze to something on the wall. "We all make mistakes. We thought she was a young male who had been castrated. It turns out she had very poorly developed genitals—not uncommon."

She glances at my face, then turns back to the computer. "Sometimes even the Olympic organizers can't tell a man from a woman. It's not always totally clear. She had no breast development at all." She pauses to look at me. "Of course, in reality sexual identity is merely another illusion we seize on in our pathetic need to be *someone*. You know that."

She clicks on the mouse, and a second portrait appears. "You see, the computer takes a three-D photograph of the skull, or rather a whole series of photographs turning three-hundred-sixty degrees, then puts together a three-D image. That's the easy part. Then we have to input other details, such as approximate age, genetic origins, et cetera. I wasn't sure so I simply clicked on 'Southeast Asian.'"

Now we are looking at a generic bald Southeast Asian with somewhat slit eyes, flat nose, and high cheekbones. It's a boyish face with no distinguishing features.

"That's as far as we've gone with that one. There's still a lot of data to input." She clicks on a side panel a few times, then types something on her keyboard. "I've reached about the same point with the other woman. But the man is nearly finished. Now, here is the untouched three-hundred-sixty-degree image of the male."

The screen is filled with another eyeless, faceless skull, somewhat fuller and stronger-looking than the other. At the next click we are staring at the skull-plus-eyes-and-skin phase. Once again the eyes are slightly mongoloid in the Thai style and the nose small and flared. I nod.

"Now, here he is after I've put in all the data."

The next window produces an individuated male face with black hair, oval eyes with black pupils, and a well-modeled nose, still small but slightly aquiline. My jaw is hanging open.

"What's the matter? D'you recognize him?"

"Can you squash the eyes a bit more, make them more Mongoloid—I mean Chinese, not Thai?" A few clicks, and the eyes stretch. "A moustache, tightly clipped, very thin, jet black, for the whole length of the upper lip." More clicks. "Make the hair a bit longer at the front with a cowlick that crosses his forehead from left to right, and a beauty spot just under his left eye." More clicks. I'm riveted by the screen. "Can you make him smile? The teeth are perfect, slightly large for the mouth, and brilliant white. Good, now darken his skin just a little, not Thai brown, but not Chinese porcelain either—between the two." I'm squashing my own face between my palms.

"Do you know his name?"

"Not To."

"Not To? You mean Notto, or his name is not To?"

"Yes. Can we work on the other two together?"

It takes about an hour, with Supatra constantly cross-referring to her base data to make sure I'm not straying from what is scientifically justified. Now we have Notto and his two female assistants, one hardly distinguishable from a boy, the other full-bodied and voluptuous with black-rimmed spectacles. I stand up and pace the room, throwing wild glances at the monitor, as Supatra clicks, and To with his two assistants appear one by one in a revolving show.

There goes my beautiful theory; I make a note of the life lesson: that's what you get from premature victory dances. "Can you do a group portrait with the man in the middle, the young woman on his right, the older woman on his left? Perfect." I am transfixed. As I pass and repass the screen, Notto's eyes follow me. I can almost hear him speak: *Oh no, you do not go anywhere. You stay here in Bangkok.* "Please print everything. I need copies of each plus copies of the three together."

"So, do you have a lead now?" Supatra says as I prepare to leave with the printouts.

"No. I have to start from scratch."

In the cab on the way to the airport, I fish out my cell phone and the card with the heart on it.

She answers on the third ring. "Hello, Detective."

"How did you know it was me?"

"I kept your number on my phone. I even put you in my address book under *Det*. Must be love, no?"

"Does your charm always work so well?"

"I don't use it on anyone else."

"Because you don't need to?"

"You sound excited. Are you going to tell me why you called?"

"I just happen to be on my way to Phuket. Want to meet me at the airport?"

"Anything you say."

She is waiting for me: jeans, T-shirt, flip-flops. Her hair is shiny and full-bodied, a black forest of unlimited fecundity. I am overwhelmed by tenderness. She sends me the same message with a touch of humor in her infinitely yielding eyes. If I were twenty, I would whisk her away somewhere—a lonely beach hut where we could live happily ever after until the world caught up. I take her hand, in flagrant violation of all the rules of interrogation, and lead her out of the terminal.

"I thought we were flying?" she says, leaning toward me.

"We are," I say.

The office for the helicopter company is about a hundred yards from the terminal down a service road. I already booked by phone, and the reception says the chopper is waiting. It's a small one with only four passenger seats. Now two pilots arrive and greet us with *wais*, and we're taking off in that oblique turning motion that reminds me of Vietnam movies. I think Om has been in the chopper before. She knows where we are going.

The entire journey takes about ten minutes. Now we're at the helipad on Vulture Peak, a giant H painted atop a mound in a circle of asphalt about two hundred yards from the house, concealed by shrubs. Om has turned to stone—this isn't the romantic assignation she had in mind—but she follows me to the house, slavelike. I use the key I obtained from the forensic team to open the magnificent door. When she has closed it behind us, I turn to look her in the eye.

"Why are you doing this?" she asks.

"You're used to luxury," I say. "I couldn't afford anything so grand myself."

She is bewildered but shows no sign of fear. I take her hand and lead her into the vast salon, with its tinkling streams and giant teak pillars. We cross one of the streams to the balcony. It's dusk; the sun's glancing rays have turned the sea to blue velvet. It might have been a Tantric moment—two spiritual beings joining our bodies for the salvation of the world—but it would have needed different bodies in a different age. When I put my arm around her, she sags against me, resigned to whatever male fantasy I have in mind.

"Which room do you normally use?" I ask.

"I don't know what you mean."

"For your customer. The one who brings you here. Which room is it?"

She stares into my eyes. "You're jealous? That's what this is all about? If you care that much, why don't you do something about it? Make me your second wife? Look after me? If that's what you want. I don't care about money, just so long as I have enough for my mother's medicine and some food. I'm not greedy. If it's just sex you want, tell me how you want it. I'll do what you want, so long as it doesn't hurt."

"How much do I have to pay?"

She turns away, humiliated. "Whatever you want to pay. Nothing, if it makes you feel better. Will it prove that I like you if I don't take any money? Okay, I don't want money."

"What do you wear, usually, when you come here? Does he make you change into anything?"

"He doesn't make me change into anything. It's not like that."

I'm grasping her wrists. "Not like that? Then what is it like?"

"What is it like?" From the wild look in her eyes, I guess that she has guessed: now she knows I know, but it's impossible to talk about: an emotional furnace. I'm sweating. She turns her wrists to let me know I'm hurting her. I let go.

My voice is quite hoarse when I say, "Do you want to take a shower first? There are towels and bathrobes in every room. You don't have to use the master bedroom if you don't want to."

She shrugs and turns away, puzzled. I watch her cross the salon and enter one of the bedrooms. I choose the master bedroom itself, which the forensic team have cleaned up in the neat Thai way. I wonder if I too should undress. May as well go the whole hog and shower under the great chrome splash shower, use up the last of the gel, grab a towel that the cleaning staff must have renewed, and change into a buff dressing gown with monk's hood. When I leave the bathroom, I hear her showering in the other room. I take out three photocopies from my backpack and lay them on the bed. The noise of the shower stops. She spends about five minutes drying herself, then walks through the door, also in a buff dressing gown, looks for me, sees me standing by the bed, and smiles. She has eyes only for me and does not see the three photocopies.

I know too much about whores not to understand that she is still clinging to the hope that I will provide a way out; *second wife* may not offer much in the way of status, but the income is usually regular, and the dignity infinitely greater than bar work. Her smile is frank, vulnerable, sincere. I wish she were more cynical; it would make what I have in mind a lot easier. When I stare at her, she pulls at the belt on her robe, which falls open.

I stride up to her and pull the gown off her shoulders until it drops to the ground. "Tell me how it is with him," I say. "Is it like this?" I slide my hands down her back, grab her buttocks, and press her pelvis against mine with as much harshness as I can manage. "Is it?"

She is shocked, disillusioned: her dream of a more dignified future has collapsed in less than a second. She shakes her head, tearful.

"No?" I hear the roughness in my voice. "Or maybe like this?" I fall to my knees and lick her nipples one after the other with pathetic gratitude. Her hand drops to my shoulder, then follows the line of my neck to my ear, which she cups and fondles. "Like this?"

"Yes," she says behind the tears, "like that."

"Every time? No dominance, no rough stuff, no fantasy?"

"Only the first time. Manu changed after the first time."

"Manu? That's his name? And you are the only one who can tame him?"

A shrug. "That's what he says."

I stand up and turn away from her. "Please get dressed," I say to the window. I hear her leave the room. Five minutes later she is back in her jeans and T-shirt, waiting for my next move. I point to the bed where I have placed the photocopies of To and his two women. She puts a hand over her mouth and closes her eyes.

"A lot of people use this house," Om says. "But they are all connected." She is dressed, sitting upright on one of the chaise longues while I watch her from a rosewood chair of classic Chinese design. There is a tinkling brook between us. "Manu's lover, that army general, owns it jointly with that Chinese woman, but he never comes. He uses it to maintain his connections with Beijing. Especially his banking and military connections. He and the Chinese woman put it at the disposal of that Chinese creep—that's his picture you put on the bed."

"Mr. To?"

"His name's Wong."

"You're sure?"

"Yes. My father was Chinese. That's why my skin is light. He was a peasant from Canton who fled the Cultural Revolution. He was quite old by the time he reached Thailand and married my mother. He said the only thing he could give me was his language. Cantonese. Wong was a Hong Kong Chinese, and so were those women he dragged everywhere with him, so they always spoke Cantonese. They didn't know I could understand everything they said. I never let on."

"Go on."

"What happened that night I told you about, it was all true, but it was only the first time. It seems I was a great success with the Chinese bankers that Wong was entertaining here."

"Wong was at the party?"

"Oh no, he was much too high up for that. He just made the place available and paid for the entertainment." She stares at the flow of pure water in the little brook between us. "I didn't even meet him until the next time."

"The next time?"

"Yes. Like I said, we were a hit. Especially me. Those were just peasant boys at that party who got recruited into banking—they'd never seen anything like it. Especially that little trick with the gold ring. The word spread. Wong's masters in Beijing were delighted, so Wong did it over and over again. Only this time he insisted on private rehearsals."

"I see."

"The Hong Kong Chinese woman was his face at the party, making sure everything went smoothly, but he planned everything."

"And he—"

"He never screwed me. He groped me a lot, but he was a born voyeur. He sat with his two weird women and watched me do things for him. Often he would have them film me while he masturbated. And every time what he wanted was a little weirder, a little more extreme. He got very aroused just having me as his creature, telling me 'Do this, do that'—all the time pretending it was a rehearsal, of course. He would turn bright red, and the sweat would pour down his face."

"And at the same time you were—I mean, Manu was your client?"

"There was overlap. That General Zinna called the bar one night—he'd heard about us from Wong—to say he had a special assignment, money no object. He told the *mamasan* about his problem, and she came up here with me the first night. Nobody knew how Manu would react. They kept him locked up in the main bedroom while they explained to me that he could be difficult. I got scared and asked if he had AIDS. They said no, nothing like that, no communicable disease—but he'd been in an accident. It would be better for both of us if I worked in the dark. So I did. He was like an animal at first, but I could feel his hurt. He had me every way he wanted, but he stopped being rough after a while. They paid me more money that night than I had earned for six months. I bought my mum a house. The *mamasan* said they were very pleased with me.

"Then the client—Manu—wanted me again. So the second time I told him to switch the lights on. It was a shock—I thought I was going to ruin everything by vomiting—but I remembered my vow to help all living creatures toward enlightenment, and that saved me. When he realized I could have sex with him knowing what he looked like, he just melted. He can't live without me. He's like a child with me." She looks me in the eye. "You know he can hardly talk, only whimper and blather? When he wants to tell me something, he has to write it down. The accident ruined his larynx almost completely." Om swallows and looks away.

"How many *entertainments* did you take part in all together?"

"I'm not sure. About ten."

"And the clients—were they always midlevel bankers?"

She looks away, bites her lip.

"Om?"

"No. But I told you, these were all people from the north, in the Beijing area. They didn't speak Cantonese so I didn't know what they were talking about."

"Always from the north, Om?"

She is holding out on me. She exhales. "No, not always from the north."

"So there were occasions when you did understand everything that was being said, when they assumed you could not understand a word?"

Reluctantly: "Yes."

"And what were they talking about?"

"It happened twice. Once it was a bunch of cops from Shenzen, the other time it was a group of prison officers from somewhere in Guanzhou."

I wait. It seems she has forgotten the question. "What were they talking about, Om?"

"Body parts," she says. She looks into my eyes. "That was the connection. Even when the group was from the north, I could understand some words. I didn't follow the story until the Cantonese-speaking groups came. Then I put the picture together. It seems there is quite an industry—everything that goes on in this house is connected. Even Manu—he is connected through his operation. He knows some of the players. He knew Wong, for example, who you call To."

I think about that. "But I still don't get it. What's the connection between a bunch of men on stag parties to Phuket and the organ-trafficking industry?"

"Exactly that. The parties were all for men who had had successful transplants of one kind or another. They were allowed to invite their *guanxi* group to celebrate their survival—'like being reborn,' was what they kept saying. Ordinary Chinese are just as superstitious as Thais. If they think some piece of good fortune has saved their lives, they feel obliged to share the joy, give thanks."

"Transplant operations made possible by removing the organs of people who had been executed . . . by that particular work group?"

She shrugs. "I don't know. When it was the cops, yes. I think they had a thing going, you know, if a fellow cop needed a fresh new liver, or kidney, or something, they would go and find one for him. Same with the prison officers. These were tightly knit male groupings, you know, with that thing men do: all for one and one for all." She scowls, then shrugs. "Survival."

I let about five minutes pass while she stares at the stream and twists a tissue into a knot and slowly shreds it over the floor. "So, Om, are you going to tell me who killed Mr. Wong and his two assistants?"

She stares down at the little pile of white tissue fragments on the parquet, then looks up at me. "You see, Manu thinks of this house as his own. He likes to feel he can sneak up here anytime he likes, like a wild animal with a secret nest. And he has all the keys. Of course he stays away when there's a party or something, but it's part of his relationship with Zinna that he can have anything of Zinna's—because of Zinna's guilt.

"One night I was here 'rehearsing' in front of Wong and the other two. They were facing me, and I was standing in front of the balcony, so I was the only one who saw Manu. He used his key to slip in, but he must have known there were people here because of the car outside. So he made no noise. I was naked, and Wong was telling me what he wanted. It was quite extreme, and I felt humiliated because of Manu. Manu disappeared for a moment, and I thought he'd gone. But it seems he just went somewhere in the house where there was a gun. It was a pistol.

"Suddenly he wasn't Manu the cripple anymore. I could see the kind of young man he must have been before the accident. He walked tall. I was sure he'd do something cruel to them, because he was in such a rage. But he didn't. He controlled himself. He was a soldier, so he knew how to aim a gun. He shot all three of them in the back of the head, one after the other in less than a second. It was an execution." Silence, then: "Who cares if people like that die? They were going to be reborn as pigs or insects anyway."

She is staring into space. I say, "The three cadavers were expertly harvested for all major organs, even faces. Who did that?" She stares at me until her eyes grow big, but she doesn't answer. "Who called a certain telephone number to bring in the experts? The ones who know how to extract valuable organs and sell them on the international market?"

She continues to stare, as if my question has no meaning.

23

I've hit the ground running. Vikorn called me about a minute after I landed in Bangkok and ordered me to take a cab straight to the police station. Now I'm knocking on his door. Now I'm taking a seat at his desk. The three Americans are here in their usual positions: Linda and Ben on the Italian sofa, the older man, Jack, on a high chair with arms. I tell the story of my trip to Phuket and Om's evidence. The Americans listen intently to every word; Vikorn nods now and then. When I've finished there is a long silence, then Jack says, "Linda?"

"I'm fortified in my original opinion," Linda says. "I say we keep the Colonel's name out of this. Let the detective carry on with the investigation if he wants to. I guess there are quite a few loose ends to tie up. Especially if we assume the perp, this Manu character, doesn't have the skill to remove organs from the recently deceased. But let him do it sotto voce. No publicity until after the election."

"Reason?" Jack says.

"If there's any relevant message at all in this case, it's highly confusing. You have a crazed killer whose life was destroyed by a medical procedure and who, in a jealous rage, murdered a high-level Chinese banker with strong connections in Beijing. That's going to be how the media present it and how the public receives it: the human/sensational angle. It's going to be hard to present the Colonel as a clear hero saving the country from the evils of organ trafficking. Mixed messages are always big trouble. I say we either get an organ-trafficking story with clear unambiguous lines, or we dump organ trafficking altogether as a campaign theme. After all, the Colonel's way ahead in the polls—we don't need any complications."

"Do we know anything about the bank this Mr. To worked for?" Jack says.

"An old-style merchant bank that was big on the mainland, then fled to Hong Kong after the revolution, then mended ties with Beijing and became one of its unofficial commercial arms," Linda says. "They are strongly connected to the Ministry of Correctional Services, which has been buying up a lot of real estate in Beijing and renting it out as office and residential accommodation. We think the ministry uses its real estate portfolio as collateral to borrow money from this bank at very low rates of interest."

"That would give them an edge," Ben says.

"Anyway, are we all agreed about Linda's point?" Jack says. "The detective here keeps his investigation under strict wraps until after the election? Or preferably, stops investigating until the Colonel is governor?"

"Too right," Ben says.

The three Americans look at Vikorn, who says nothing. The atmosphere has subtly changed. Something has triggered a new hostility from Linda and Ben toward Jack, who looks uneasy. We remain silent until Linda coughs. We all look at Linda.

"Ah, I'm afraid I have to ask a question, Jack," she says. "The preamble to the question is that from what I know of Correctional Services in Beijing, they don't get involved in small stuff."

"Right," Ben says.

"I mean, these are smart, ambitious cadres turned masters of the universe. They don't much care who runs Bangkok. These guys shoot for gold."

"Right," Ben says.

"I have no idea where you're going with this, Linda," Jack says, avoiding her stare.

"Where I'm going with this, Jack," Linda says with a crack in her voice, "is to point out that of the three of us, you are the one with strong, high-level ties with that ministry. 'Cause what I don't want is a repeat of the Sierra Leone thing and those blood diamond allegations that came just a little too close for comfort."

"Right," Ben says.

Now I understand that the balance of power has mysteriously shifted. Jack is rubbing a hand on one of the arms of his chair.

"I don't need the money, Jack," Linda says. "I didn't lose fifty million when Lehman collapsed and another twenty million with Madoff."

"Me either," Ben says.

"I stayed in cash, then bought gold," Linda says. "You do see where I'm going here, Jack? Me and Ben here, we're not desperate for the dough."

"I hear you," Jack says.

"Getting a third-world cop elected as governor of a little city nobody worries much about is one thing. Promising to take him all the way to leader of a country on behalf of a certain Beijing ministry with seriously powerful rivals in other ministries—I don't want to be on the Red Army's hit list."

"Me either," Ben says.

"Or worse, the hit list of one of the PRC police consortia."

"I hear you," Jack says.

"Next thing you know, we have the Yips up our asses."

"They're with Correctional Services," Jack says. "They would be on our side in that scenario."

"They've also done work for the police and army," Ben says.

"Not to mention regional bosses," Linda says.

"Look," Jack says, "I got the message. If I have instructions to take the Colonel higher, I'll do it on my own, okay?"

"Just so long as that's clear to everybody," Linda says.

"I'll second that," Ben says.

Silence. The eruption of aggression and distrust seems to have made them feel more at home. "So, who's going to check out this Inspector Chan?" Jack says.

Jack and Linda look at Ben.

"Okay," Ben says.

"And we need something real on the Yips," Jack says, recovering authority. "Ben and I tried to wake up our old contacts in the Company, but nothing doing. We need updating. I had no idea they'd gotten so big. Either the Company or the Bureau must know about them."

"Okay," Linda says.

The three of them stand on a common impulse and leave the room. Now it's Vikorn and me alone together.

Silence. "So, are you aiming to run the country? Is that what this is really all about?" He doesn't answer. "Nobody really figures you for governor—it doesn't make sense. You make more on heroin than you ever would peddling city construction contracts. Prime minister, though—I can see that might be a temptation. Is that the deal you have with Beijing?" He stares at me. "Which ministry is behind you?"

I shrug and get up to leave. When I'm at the door, he says: "Would you prefer Zinna?"

I stop short. "What?"

"There's been a last-minute addition to the candidate list. Check the lampposts tomorrow." Vikorn pauses to look at me. "He even has counselors. Two Americans. A man and a woman. They're said to have got people elected to high office in Africa somewhere. And, of course he's very well in with the Ministry of Correctional Services in Beijing."

"Who are his advisers? Ex-CIA?"

"Ex–World Bank."

I stare at him for a moment, shake my head, and turn the doorknob.

"What's your next move?" Vikorn says when I'm nearly out the door. He beckons me back in. I close it again.

"Next move? With regard to what? How can any cop investigate a case of triple homicide when my own boss doesn't give a damn because it isn't going to affect his election chances because he's given up on organ trafficking as a campaign theme? Anyway, we know who did it. If I arrest Manu, Zinna will go ballistic—is that what you want?"

"It's become important that you find out more," the Colonel says, making eye contact for the first time since I got back from Phuket.

"May I ask why?"

"I have a feeling someone in China has become aware of you. If they call, follow up on the contact."

I shake my head, shrug, get up to leave. At the door he stops me with a cough. He taps his nose. "I wouldn't let on to other detectives in other lands that you've found out who pulled the trigger—you know how lazy cops can get when they're certain who done it. There are depths to this thing designed just for you."

"Ah, okay."

"In fact, how about we make it an order. You don't tell anyone about the whore's evidence."

"Yes, sir."

I have no idea what he's talking about, but I nod knowingly, leave, and close the door behind me. Then I count to ten, and on one of those impulses born of long intimacy with an alpha personality, I silently turn the handle and open it a crack. Yep, there he is, the master of the universe, standing at his window puffing on a Churchill cigar.

24

I'm at one of the cooked-food stalls in the street outside the station when my cell phone rings. When I check the window, I see it is a "private number," meaning no one close to me: if it was Chanya or Vikorn, the phone would definitely let me know. I look at the screen for a moment and realize the phone is the only thing in my life that I have under control right now. It seems natural for me to exercise my sovereignty by pressing the "silent" button; now the caller is holding his/her cell to their ear thinking they're making a noise in my life when actually they're suffering from the great delusion of our times: that someone is listening. After a minute or so the caller gives up, and I restore the ring tone.

Now the thing starts again. I stare at the screen: "private number." I press "silent." The caller gives up. I restore the ring tone. The caller calls again. On the fifth attempt, I start to weaken. Suppose it's important? I check to see how long the caller is prepared to go on ringing into emptiness: three minutes this time. Maybe it *is* important? I decide to see if they'll go to nine attempts, nine being a lucky number over here. Yep. To fulfill my conditions for accepting their call, I decide they must wait until they're at two and a half minutes on the ninth call. Would you believe, they gave up after a minute and a half? Now I'm wondering who the hell it was and wishing they'd ring back.

I've finished my *somtam*, paid, and I'm strolling down the street—

when it rings again. I press the pickup button. Now a woman is speaking urgently into my left ear, but I don't understand a word. I scratch my jaw, trying to identify the language. It must be a Chinese dialect because there are a lot of x-type vowels, which can sound seductively soft one moment, then make you wonder if the speaker has a cockroach stuck in her throat the next. Got it: Shanghainese. I speak very slowly in English: "I do not understand a word you are saying," and hang up.

The caller must have my number on autodial, because it starts ringing again faster than anyone could plug the numbers into a cell phone. I say, "Yes."

"Is that the Honorable Detective Sonchai Jitpleecheep?"

Now the voice is male, Chinese. The English seems almost perfect, despite the literal translation from formal Chinese. "Yes."

"Honorable Detective, I am Detective Sun Bin from Shanghai Yangpu District, Thirteenth Precinct."

My heart has inexplicably skipped a beat. "Yes?"

"Detective, I am not at liberty to tell you how I obtained your private telephone number—"

"Inspector Chan of the Hong Kong police gave it to you, didn't he?"

"Ah, I'm not too clear about that. Detective, I am calling to see if it would be possible for you and I to collaborate on a matter of mutual interest."

"Really?"

"Yes. Detective, it has fallen to me to investigate a very sad and tragic case of triple homicide."

"Where?"

"In Shanghai, Detective. I have become aware of the similar circumstances in which three people died in a case you are brilliantly investigating for the Honorable Royal Thai Police Force."

"How did you become aware of those circumstances?"

"Ah, I'm not too clear, Honorable Detective. However, I can reveal that in the present case, which occurred in a luxury apartment building here, the victims were all shot in the back of the head and their solid organs were surgically removed with great skill."

He knows he's got my attention and lets the silence hang for a moment.

"What gender were your victims?" I ask.

"Two males and one female."

"Are you sure?"

"Sure."

I take a deep breath. "Do I come to you, or do you come to me?"

"In my humble opinion the honorable detective, who lives in a country which grants its citizens certain democratic rights, would find it considerably easier to obtain a visa for the PRC than your humble correspondent would find it to visit your honorable country."

"Where did you learn English?"

"Books and TV."

"You are a genius."

"Forgive me, but I cannot accept such a compliment from a giant in the art of detection such as yourself."

"Did Chan tell you to talk like this when you spoke to me?"

"Ah, I'm not too clear."

25

"Welcome to the Kingdom of Hu," Sun Bin says. He is short, slim, and wiry, with a thin face molded by mean streets.

I already know that *Hu* is the local name for Shanghai because I forgot to bring anything to read for the flight from Bangkok, so I was stuck with the in-flight magazine. That's about the limit of my knowledge, though. The airport is hypermodern, shiny and high tech, and so is the train into town. Then things start to slow down somewhat. I've never seen so many people crammed into the same space. They are everywhere, like a moving jungle where you have to negotiate your way around forests of Homo sapiens and avoid all bottlenecks. Sun Bin is a skilled guide, though, and demonstrates unusual talent for overtaking on bends and exploiting almost invisible openings in great walls of humans.

At the morgue he shows me three cadavers that have been mutilated in exactly the same way as the three on Vulture Peak. He watches closely as I become fascinated by *exactly* how accurately the atrocities have been replicated, down to the absence of faces and eyes. We exchange glances. I nod. He nods back.

Now we are in a cab on our way to some other part of Sun Bin's precinct. Now we are entering a high-end apartment building with a lobby to beat the Ritz, uniformed security, marble everywhere. Sun Bin flaps his wallet at the receptionist, who sees his police badge and nods. On the thirty-third floor we exit the lift and stride down a corridor until we come to a yellow tape stretched between two traffic cones. Sun Bin takes out a key, and we enter the apartment.

It is vast and must boast about six bedrooms. The floor-to-ceiling windows reveal a modern city like no other. In the distant days of aristocratic art, it was said that architecture is frozen music; I guess what I'm looking at is a pretty good three-dimensional representation of iTunes, with the great rap phallus of the Oriental Pearl TV Tower thrusting into the skyline, the Bolshoi-ish Exhibition Center, the orphic HSBC building, and the pop-songy Sassoon House in a riot of eclecticism. Sun Bin takes me into the master bedroom, where a tall figure in a floral tourist shirt and smart casual slacks is waiting, hands in pockets.

"Dr. Livingstone, I presume," Chan says.

"Fancy meeting you here," I counter.

He jerks his chin at the king-size bed upon which three life-size paper cutouts have been placed, to represent where and how the bodies were found. Chan and Sun Bin give me a couple of minutes to take it all in, then raise their eyes and wrinkle their brows.

"It's a copycat triple homicide, with Asian attention to detail," I advise.

"Laid out in exactly the same way as the bodies in Phuket?" Chan says.

"Exactly the same way."

"Same positions on the bed—I mean longitudinally, with heads pointing to the wall?"

"The same."

"And the bodies at the morgue?"

"In my opinion the injuries are identical to those suffered by the victims on Vulture Peak."

"In your honorable and expert opinion, would you say they were murdered by the same professional team?"

"Certainly."

Chan and Sun Bin exchange glances and let a couple of beats pass. "Want to bet on it?"

The two Chinese cops are looking at me with hardened expressions. Even Sun Bin, who has been the very avatar of Oriental hospitality, seems to have succumbed to a demon more powerful than himself.

"Maybe not," I say, mentally backing away from those two.

"I'm offering six to one these killings were carried out by a totally different team. Put in a thousand dollars, you get six thousand back plus your original bet. If you're so sure it's the same team," Sun Bin says.

"He wants me to open an escrow account in Hong Kong, so punters feel safe betting with him," Chan says. "He's already got half his precinct signed up."

"Why would you be so sure it's a different team that did it?"

Chan says something to Sun Bin, which I think must be standard Putonghua, because it doesn't sound like the Shanghainese dialect I've been hearing since I arrived. Sun Bin looks at me and smiles sheepishly. "I must humbly beg your pardon. The inspector here has reminded me that it is contrary to Confucian wisdom to take advantage of strangers. Naturally, we of the mainland need to take lessons from our Hong Kong brothers and sisters in such matters."

I have no idea if Sun Bin is serious or exercising a local form of sarcasm. Chan doesn't seem to know either and Sun Bin is unusually inscrutable for a Chinese. "You mean there are reasons for thinking this is some kind of revenge conspiracy killing for the murders on Vulture Peak?" I ask.

Now they are both staring at me. "In China, conspiracy theories are always well founded," Sun Bin advises with a smile.

I take a couple of steps back so that the two of them are silhouetted against the mad city on the other side of the window. I think I'm beginning to understand what are sometimes referred to as the "deeper" layers of the case.

"Would it be consistent with the new Confucianism to tell this humble stranger exactly what you two honorable forensic geniuses think is going on here?"

Both nod independently. "Come into the kitchen," Sun Bin says.

The kitchen is a fashion statement in stainless steel. It is also starkly empty except for a tablet laptop, manufactured by LG, on the stainless-steel island. The computer is plugged into a socket in the center of the island. The three of us pull up the stools that go with the island and watch Sun Bin jog the mouse and bring the machine to life. My eyes are swamped by a swarm of Chinese characters I cannot decipher. It's amazing to me how quickly Sun Bin can manipulate the 47,035 characters of his alphabet; it seems superhuman. Now we are looking at a split screen with a graph on one side and what looks like an address book on the other.

Chan and Sun Bin both stare at me as if I'm supposed to experience revelation.

"Start with the address book," I say. "If that's what it is."

"It's a list of suspects, except they are not people."

"So what do you have for suspects if not people?"

"Government departments, especially the uniformed services, large private enterprises, and some groups that are consortia in all but name but have no legal status."

"But there seem to be thousands of them."

Sun Bin nods. "That is correct. There are thousands and thousands of them. With two billion of us, everything is multiplied. It's logical, isn't it? In a country like America, with only three hundred million, you have—say—half a dozen suspects at the beginning of an inquiry. So we generally start with a hundred times that number. The increase is exponential."

"He's trying to impress you," Chan says. "He knows who did it, don't you, Sun Bin?"

"I'm working with a short list of ten," Sun Bin says.

Chan sighs. "He does everything by the book. Including the gambling. He has no emotional intelligence at all. Do you, Sun Bin?"

"None at all," he confesses. "When I was at school, everything was about industrial logic. Now when I start hearing about 'emotional intelligence' from foreigners like you, it makes me feel stupid."

"See what we have to contend with?" Chan says. "I live in Hong Kong, China, but to him I'm a foreigner. Sun Bin thinks Shanghai is *sooo* special, don't you, Sun Bin?"

"Shanghai is the eye of the storm called modernism," Sun Bin says.

Chan groans. "I've said it a hundred times. The Yips didn't do the

Phuket job, and they didn't do this one either. Just because I know that intuitively, and can't prove it, doesn't mean I'm not right."

"You have inherited from the British a tendency to overuse the word *I*. At the time of Chairman Mao, it would have been said that you suffer from bourgeois self-centeredness," Sun Bin says.

"It would have been said that I was a Capitalist Running Dog, and they would have shot me. But I think the West won that side of the class war."

"But your addiction to either/or strikes me as quite American monopolar, even British colonial," Sun Bin says. "It lacks a sense of the plurality of the modern world."

My eyes are flitting from one to the other, then to the computer and back again; at the same time I begin to see the China connection as an impenetrable wall. It's like being told that the answer to your question is to be found in the Library of Congress without anyone specifying the department, never mind the full reference.

"You mean there could be a third party?" I say.

"Third, fourth, fifth, sixth."

"Are there really so many skilled in the art of organ removal?"

Sun Bin seems embarrassed and looks away. Chan stares at me with his lips twisted. I have a feeling that I've transgressed some unwritten rule of local etiquette. Into the silence Chan says, "Hey, let's take a walk down Nanjing Road."

Sun Bin seems to have fallen into depression and says he won't come. Chan grabs a cab at the ground floor of the apartment building, and within seconds we are stuck in a jam. Chan tells the driver it's worth double the usual fare, which inspires the driver to take a few shortcuts. In the middle of the traffic jam, I ask why Sun Bin's mood suddenly changed.

"Everyone has mood swings," the inspector says, looking defensive.

"Okay."

Chan sighs. "He's shy of you because at least two of the suspect consortia are police. One of them is run by Sun Bin's boss. He may have to give up on the case."

"But if the Yips didn't do these three in Shanghai, what was the point of dragging me over here?"

"Two reasons. The main one is I talked him into it. But he chickened out."

"Chickened out of what?"

"My idea was that he would tell you everything. He wasn't supposed to just show you three corpses at the morgue. He was supposed to show you more than a dozen others—logistically, not all of them could have had their organs removed by the Yips. Nor could any one single agency be responsible."

"What are you saying?"

"I'm explaining what Sun Bin was supposed to explain. In every major Chinese city today, right this minute, the recently dead are having their organs removed by a skilled team under the protection of one consortium or another."

I let a couple of beats pass, unable to process this revelation. "And the other reason—there was some other reason why Sun Bin agreed to invite me?"

"He's desperate to go to Bangkok to get laid. It's tough in China at the moment, unless you're rich. Sure, there are women who will sleep with you, but it's a battleground—like sleeping with your enemy. He yearns for the sweet pussy of your medieval culture."

Chan is indulging in one of his smirks. I think I've begun to read him better. "You're lying, just to make some politically incorrect point."

The smirk broadens. "Of course Sun Bin wants to go to Bangkok to get laid, but that's not the only reason for getting to know you."

"So?"

"You haven't asked the only question worth asking."

"Which is?"

"All these human organs looking for a body, and all these terminally ill patients looking for an organ—where is the surgery done?"

I shrug. "Here in China?"

He nods. "Sure, some of it is, at the lower end of the market, but what about the Yips? They don't have a base on the mainland, probably wouldn't want one—the government is too capricious, it could change its mind about them anytime and clap them in jail. Nor can they afford to expose their upmarket Western clients to some makeshift surgery in a garage that might be raided at any time by a rival consortium—or even by the police on a legitimate law enforcement exercise."

"What are you saying? The Yips have a fully equipped surgery somewhere overseas, which they rent out to rival groups when they're not using it themselves?"

Chan smiles.

Now we are shuffling along Nanjing Road amid a great herd of humans, the slow pace set by the law of density. Inspector Chan ostentatiously takes out a small pillbox and pops something into his mouth. I guess there must be a message here, something he wants me to know, or he wouldn't take his medication so openly. I raise my eyebrows in case he is waiting for a prompt.

"Lithium," he says. "But don't tell anyone, or I'll be forced to deny it and sue you for defamation."

"You're bipolar, and you haven't told your superior officer?"

He throws me a glance, then jerks his chin at the solid block of people moving slowly forward in front of us, each one of them in a tearing hurry that they are forced to repress, like snails fleeing a fire. "Can you believe it? I live in Hong Kong, but I can't take crowds like this. I just can't."

I myself have felt the odd jolt of fear at being trapped on all sides by a slow-moving human tsunami, which might lift you up and dump you just about anywhere.

"I'm going to have to dive in here," Chan says.

He's referring to a Starbucks right on Nanjing Road. Inside, it seems almost as crowded as the street, but the Chinese patrons prefer to stand. Chan and I grab a spare couch; then I go to order two lattes, trying to separate merged flesh without being rude. Now I'm negotiating the press of customers with the tray and two lattes, catching sight of Chan from time to time between bodies; he has turned gray and looks awful. When I reach the couch again and sit next to him, he jerks a chin at the crowds on the other side of the window. I look on the solid block of people and remember how humid it is out there; the thought of going out into that urban "war of all against all" is daunting.

"I don't know if I'm bipolar or if it's something worse," the inspector admits. "Schizoaffective disorder and cyclic major depression are also possibilities. The shrink said he wasn't sure, but since lithium is the standard medication for all three, I may as well take it—or go to some expensive doctor who will end up prescribing the same thing after a lot of tests that would bankrupt me. No one gets cured of mental illness anymore. You are expected to make the drug companies richer by staying sick. Naturally, a citizen should feel privileged to be contributing to capitalism in however small a way." He sips his latte. "Personally, I think I'm just lonely."

"You don't have a partner?"

"Me? I'm too confused. Look, I grew up in a genuinely modern city, where nobody even pretends to know who they are. I could be gay. I've thought about it. It's true that I'm sexually aroused by young naked women, but on the other hand I can never convince myself that my sperm would be safe with them. Next thing you know she's had your baby, never wants to see you again, but demands child support for the next twenty years as an alternative for having you indicted for rape. At least with a man you're safe from that gambit." He shakes his head. "Cops know too much."

I freeze with the latte halfway to my lips because of the way he's looking at me. "You can't be serious?" I say.

"Why not? How d'you know it wouldn't work? Your wife wouldn't have to find out."

"You *are* serious?"

He shifts his gaze. "Just speculating. What d'you think of Sun Bin?"

"Ah, in what way? His sexual attraction, professionalism, mental health—my whole image of a modern cop has expanded since I met you."

"Yeah, you're kind of old-fashioned, even quaint. He's a homophobe. That's another reason why he's acting funny around you. He's not sure if you and I do it together or not, and if we do, would we want him to join in a threesome—that kind of thing. He thinks anyone from Hong Kong is fey and likely queer."

"Really?"

Chan jerks a chin at the window. "Look at that, will you? How can anyone take murder detection seriously, when the only rational reaction is to shoot half of them just to clear the street?" He frowns. "This is the way your head goes, sooner or later. It has to. We weren't designed for this." He sighs. "So, you really want to talk about the case?"

"Yes."

"What d'you want to know?"

"Everything you know."

"What will you do for it?"

"Nothing."

He grins. "Just testing. So, let's start with the Yips. Their grandfather was one of the biggest gangsters in Shanghai before the revolution. He got out of opium and into heavy armaments when he saw the war with Japan was inevitable. He didn't know a thing about armaments, just made a factory owner an offer he couldn't refuse and made himself gloriously rich. When he saw Mao was about to win the civil war in forty-nine, he put the whole damned factory on a ship and set up shop again in Hong Kong. Naturally, he made sure he brought the factory's general manager with him, along with the most skilled workers. But he kept up his connections to the Shanghai underworld, which quickly got itself party cards.

"His son, his only child, was sent to one of those British schools for colonial quislings, which turned him into a pedophile—a total no-no as far as the old man was concerned. So the son takes to drink after he's managed with great effort and years of trying to sire twin daughters, who are allowed to do what they like from the age of about zero. They're intellectually very gifted, but wild and compulsive gamblers, and the first big gamble of their lives—the big win that brings them all they dream of at that time—is to seduce their father when they are about thirteen years old.

"Naturally, the poor creep is instantly addicted to their little game—at the same time loathing himself from the bottom of his heart. They quickly drive him deeper into drink—and death. They teach anatomy after graduation for about a minute, then get restless and decide to use their grandfather's connections. Some of the mob from that time are still alive. Some are quite senior in the party. One is a party cadre in Correctional Services." Chan looks at me, waiting for comment.

"I see."

"No, you don't. You're stuck in the parochialism of a medieval culture. I'm trying to teach you third-millennium social reality here. Today everyone has to have an edge—even beautiful, highly educated women from the upper strata of Hong Kong society. And for those two that edge was always going to be crime." He stares at the street and adds in a sad tone: "Chinese are connoisseurs of power—we've been victims of it for five thousand years."

"You're not going to tell me these cases are really all about rival consortia with the best *guanxi*?"

"Those consortia have created identities. Those identities are at war—identities usually are. Any Chinese would understand that. Of course, what the war is *really* about . . . I guess you need to be not only Chinese but *mainland* as well. Shanghainese may be the only ones properly wired for this case. There are theories by Chinese academics to the effect that psychologically we Chinese are never far from the Warring States period, when the country was in total anarchy." He sips his latte.

"How exactly do the Yips get away with it?"

"I told you," Chan says. "They're with the Ministry of Correctional Services. You see, good doctors are a scarcity in China—no way they want to waste them on the dead. A reasonably gifted person with good digital coordination can be trained to remove organs without damaging them in about a week. When two pure-blood Chinese girls with degrees in anatomy turned up, boasting connections with high-level party cadres, were they going to say no?"

"No to what?"

"A couple of freelancers who preferred to do their own organ removal in order to maintain quality control for their *gweilo*—sorry, *farang*—clients."

I watch a local make her way to the counter, to see how it should be done. She uses her head as a wedge to break apart clumps of humans—none too gently as far as I can tell. "You mean they saw a business opportunity in the resale value of organs of executed felons, constructed a five-year plan, then borrowed money to set up shop, purchase equipment, and develop contacts—generally followed the capitalist blueprint for wealth down to the last detail?"

"Exactly right," Chan says. "Except, as usual, you have a bourgeois medieval running dog tendency to miss the macro point." He shakes his head at the crowds.

I think about his hidden meaning. "You mean it wasn't—isn't—just executed felons whose organs the Yips find irresistible? It's the freshly dead in general?"

"Do you think it is only the legally condemned that national and regional governments execute?"

I have not stopped staring at the crowds. Now I gulp and nod. The full ambit of the Yips' empire has begun to dawn. "Regional governments as well? Political rivals? Self-financing executions by a crack two-girl team?"

"Even Mao couldn't run China without allies. For allies, read 'regional warlords.' If Beijing is making money out of executed criminals, d'you think the regional bosses restrain themselves?"

I shrug.

"And have you thought what a perfect alibi a twin can generate—assuming nobody knows you're a twin? How intimidating that might be to an eyewitness, to hear respectable, independent witnesses from another hemisphere say, 'Yes, I definitely saw her in Paris or New York or San Francisco on that day when such and such an atrocity was committed in Beijing, or Shenzen.'"

"They made themselves irresistible to the wet department of every national and local government ministry?"

"Now you're getting close."

Chan seems to be silently urging me to work out the rest. The clue, again, comes from the crowds, who now look twice as desperate as before. "There are business rivals?"

"Worse. Take it a little further. Bear in mind, the Yips have been doing what they do best for almost a decade. They know how to turn 'I win, you lose' into win-win."

"You don't mean . . . a whole profession of competitive organ extractors using the Yips' business model, cutting corners and cutting prices, but needing to pay off the Yips for—expertise, foreign contacts, offshore surgeries?"

"Correct."

"All of them contractors to national and local government?"

"Not exclusively, but it's a good way to start, the way a lot of lawyers start their professional lives working for government prosecution departments, before they go private."

"And by selling the organs, of course—"

"You make your victim pay for his own assassination. The Yips had to stop charging for nonjudicial killings, which were thrown in as a loss leader."

"Because of the competition?"

"You got it."

"But they stayed way ahead of the game because of their superior access to Western markets, their perfect upper-class English and other linguistic skills, their contacts in high society?"

Chan looks toward the sidewalk, which is invisible due to the number of people on it. "But with a whole army of consortia breathing down their necks. Look how good Sun Bin's English is, and he's never had a native teacher, or even a lesson. Learned it all from books and television. It's despair that creates genius."

"Geniuses like the Yips?"

"Correct. But none of it stacks up unless you posit something special the Yips have to offer—something that makes them attractive to their competitors."

"The luxury 'offshore' clinic?"

"Right."

"So nobody really knows who removed the organs from those three on Vulture Peak?"

"I know who I think didn't do it."

"The Yips. What makes you so sure?"

"They took you to Monte Carlo. Suppose we speculate that somehow they heard about an atrocity that had occurred on Vulture Peak. The timing of the deaths is unknown—the bodies could have been lying there for days. What better witness to an alibi than the cop who would likely be investigating the case? That's why I thought you were such a sucker. There's also the added advantage of maybe being able to find out from you how the case stands from moment to moment. Expect more invitations to exotic jaunts."

"So why did they need an alibi? No Thai cop knew anything about them."

"Because they run Vulture Peak," Chan says, watching me watching the crowd, which has now ground to a halt in front of the café, blocking the exit right up to the door itself. "They knew that if you were worth ten cents as a cop, you would find that out sooner or later. That banker, To/Wong, had *guanxi* with the top brass of the Ministry of Correctional Services. He was in the Yips' own camp. On the other hand, anyone who wanted to set them up . . ."

"You mean they got word of the murders, but at that moment had no idea who did them? All they knew was that they would be suspects if anyone found out about their ownership of Vulture Peak?"

"It's a theory that fits."

"But they didn't invite me to Dubai. Vikorn sent me there to meet Lilly Yip."

"Exactly," Chan says.

Throughout this conversation an intense frown has appeared and disappeared on Chan's face. It is less than thirty minutes since he took the lithium, so I suppose the medication has not yet reached the bloodstream. I have a feeling that he is going to lose coherence any minute.

"Are you okay? You keep frowning."

"I already told you I'm nuts. I'm frowning to stop myself talking. If I let go of my will for even a second, I'll be babbling like a madman. You'll start to hate me." He gives me a look. "No wonder I can't find a partner, huh?"

"Well, before you lose your mind, tell me something. How is it that these warring tribes from the most populous nation on earth are interested in my boss, Colonel Vikorn? Why would anyone in China care so much? Why him for governor?"

Chan stands. I think he is going to the bathroom to talk to himself until the lithium starts to work. "You really think they would stop at governor of Bangkok?" he says, and starts to push through the crowd to reach the bathroom.

I sit with our half-drunk lattes for five minutes, taking in his last words. Then ten. I suppose I should go to the bathroom to check on him, and in any other city I might have done, but here the effort of crossing the jam-packed room is daunting. After fifteen minutes a man in a black suit and white shirt with a thin black necktie emerges from the throng. I think he might be the manager, but I'm not sure. "Your friend needs help," he says in English. He has enunciated the words perfectly, as if he consulted a talking dictionary before approaching me.

When I reach the bathroom, I hear a voice coming from one of the stalls. When I stand outside the stall, I can hear Chan talking to some invisible person with passionate intensity. He's speaking in Cantonese interspersed with English phrases like *top secret, damn and blast, I'll blow your fucking head off, terribly sorry old boy*. I knock. He forces himself to silence for at least a minute, then continues with his monologue. When the man in the black suit enters, I explain that the inspector has recently taken his medication, and he'll be fine in ten minutes. He takes fifteen before he emerges. He reestablishes dignity by ignoring me, steps up to the trough, and begins to pee. I take the hint, leave the bathroom, and wait for him by the glass door at the entrance to the café.

While I'm waiting, I'm watching the crowd: everyone except me has adjusted to the reality out there: men, women, and children, all have mastered the art of cramped behavior. I think: a state that executes its own people, having presold their organs to the highest bidder—it's like Moctezuma meets Margaret Thatcher. Or should we say that, thanks to the supreme power of the profit motive, state and antistate have become one? From Washington to New Delhi to Beijing we let gangsters bleed us white and the newspeak calls it freedom. Now *that's* modern.

Finally Chan arrives, and we open the door to brave the people, the humidity, and the heat. He doesn't speak until the crowd forces us to come to a halt twenty yards down the street. "We're all damaged," the inspector says, still gray from his internal ordeal. "That's why we're here."

As soon as the plane lands in Bangkok, my phone bleeps (I grew tired of being whooshed and reverted to factory settings, in case you're wondering DFR). It's an SMS from Vikorn, so I take a cab straight to the station. I'm expecting to have to address the Colonel's election committee, but when I arrive at his office, he's alone. He is sitting behind his desk and jerks his chin at me to indicate that I should sit in the chair opposite. These and other clues, which I have absorbed with the instinct of a jungle animal in the half minute since I entered the room, tell me all I need to know about his state of mind. While capable of tyranny of the cruelest type, Vikorn learned long ago that the only way to survive at the top of the greasy pole is to make oneself into a humble, if strategic, listener, from time to time. With the Colonel this involves a bizarre form of role play wherein he stares at you with wide-eyed innocence, as if you were recounting the most important, fascinating, and informative crime story he has ever heard.

At the end of my narrative he even adds an Isaan word which might be the equivalent of *wow, crikey,* or *jeez,* depending on which dialect you use. Now he stands and prowls to the window to stare at the cooked-food stalls, while somewhere deep in the brainstem he carefully analyzes my report and begins to reshape the case. After about five minutes he returns to his seat, where he rocks back and forth for another five minutes. Now he says. "So, it's already all over China, this industry? Apart from the three cadavers in the morgue at Shanghai, you saw no other hard evidence?"

"Not hard evidence as such. But that was a very upmarket condo— I mean, two little cops, only one of them local—in a multimillion-dollar condo in China; it looked liked the real thing. It looked serious. Why would they mislead me?"

He thinks about it and nods. "Hm. And the Shanghai cop, this Sun Bin. He seems honest?"

"Very. The kind of cop who martyrs himself for truth, sooner or later, whether he wants to or not. Couldn't deceive to save his life. Like me."

Vikorn ignores the jibe, if that's what it was. He pats the top of his head, normally a positive sign. Now his eyes are twinkling. "And somehow the Yips are facilitators, all over the country. How does it work?"

"According to the Hong Kong cop, Inspector Chan, they purchase fresh cadavers for their *farang* clients and also make available premises for organ-transfer operations beyond Chinese jurisdiction, presumably for rich or influential Chinese who don't trust their own medical system, while servicing their offshore clients on their own account."

He nods. Frowns. Rocks. Now he stands to prowl to the window again, shaking his head. "It's all a matter of timing," he mutters to himself. Finally he looks me between the eyes. "There's still something you're missing at that house. There must be."

"You want me to go down there again tomorrow?"

He shakes his head. "Things are moving too fast—and there's the election only a week or so away. Go now. Do not call me. Anything you see or hear, you keep to yourself until you're back in this office. No phone calls. Got it?"

"Do I at least have time to see my wife before I catch another plane?"

"No. Waiting is part of what wives do. Go see her when you get back—after you've reported to me."

26

I booked a seat on the next plane and took a cab to Vulture Peak. I don't know why I decided to climb up the iron stairs instead of having the driver take me to the front door: a hunch, I guess. Well, it was a bad hunch. The place is deserted, and I might just as well have taken the taxi all the way to the mansion. I spend a couple of minutes checking out the garage, which is cut out of the rock; access to the house is by a set of stairs that lead up to the deck. The garage is empty, not only of cars but of everything except a red fire extinguisher.

It's a beautiful evening on suicide balcony. There are some boats far out with their navigation lights bobbing, and the moon is a little fatter; under the balcony there is a nice black void, from which slapping sounds emerge far below. If I had the guts, I would slip under the safety rail with my legs hanging over, close my eyes, and meditate on the relentless invitation to jump made by the slapping waves.

Well, I do have the guts. There's that little hole that seems to open up in the area of the solar plexus when you slip under safety rails—I'm sure you know what I mean, DFR—and you wonder if maybe you really are crazy. Then comes the realization that it would be a mistake to fall asleep or forget you are sitting above a hundred-foot drop. Then, if you are a meditator, you remind yourself that you're going to die one day anyway and it's part of the path to experience that reality.

Sure enough, when I close my eyes I'm attacked by terror. It's been a while since I did anything like this. I try again. Best to let the fear in gradually, take a good look at it, let the higher mind deal with it. Good. Now, what do I see? The clerk dead on the deck of his master's boat, his blood splashed all over the teak, his head rolling. I slip back under the safety rail and pull on the handle of the big glass sliding door that leads to the vast lounge.

I'm tactile: I like to feel my way around before I turn lights on. Anyway, there's enough moonlight to see the outlines of the pools and the furniture—and two shadows sneaking down the hall to the front door, opening it silently, sliding through like ghosts, and closing it again. I run, stumble, fall, crack my knee on the floor, and make for the front door in a running limp, and fumble with the handle. By the time I'm outside, they have disappeared. I didn't hear or see a car.

Bad nerves cause me to fumble with my cell phone and my wallet where I keep the card with the heart. I listen to a recorded message in her soft tones. When I call the Chung King bar, I ask to speak to the *mamasan*, who says in a dry tone, "Om is not available." It's standard brothelspeak meaning *The girl you want is with another client*.

I turn around to face the house. From the driveway it looks as if it has only one story, because the land falls away on the ocean side. The design is so much the Thai temple style, it could almost *be* a temple. There's no light pollution on the Peak—everything is washed in moonlight. It's quiet too. It's entirely possible that a couple with reasons to keep their relationship secret have taken to meeting up here. Perhaps they heard the house was empty most of the time, parked their car by the seashore, and climbed up the back way, entering through the sliding door, like me. I imagine the man talking the girl into it and her pretending not to know what they would do when they arrived in the great mansion; but it doesn't fit. That was Om with her monster, or I'm a North Korean.

Before I return to the house, I walk to the end of the driveway, where it meets a one-lane road glistening with tarmac of the expensive kind that includes flecks of granite. Now I can make out the other two houses that are part of the development. They are both in darkness. I wonder who owns them and why they never seem to be inhabited. Back in the mansion I find a bank of switches near the front door.

There seem to be dozens of them, and for five minutes I have fun illuminating the pools without the side lights, side lights without the pools, the balcony without the house. Then I find the switch that turns on the serious lights that the cleaning staff need. Now the whole place is bathed in white neon, every flaw and defect clearly visible. But there are not many flaws—the place was very well put together by serious money. In the main bedroom all signs of death have been cleaned up by the forensic team. The white sheet covers the gigantic bed without any sign of recent frolicking bodies. The same is true of the beds in the other bedrooms.

The maid's room, though, at the far end of the house near the road, is a different matter: a small narrow bed with the sheets almost pulled off, a half-drunk can of beer, a glass with water and a smudge of lipstick. Odd, with so many grand bedrooms with grand beds to choose from, that a romantic couple should choose this little room—except that it's as far away from the scene of the crime as it's possible to be. And Thai girls are very superstitious. But in that case, why come to this house at all?

Proximity to sex and death has started a new continuum, which proves a relentless driver. I forget Vikorn and call a cab.

Down on the main street in Patong, business is booming. It seems a few more jumbos carrying a few more thousand tourists with an overabundance of single men have landed at Krung Thep in the past few days, with a sizable number of the passengers making straight for Phuket. The snake charmers are charming the snakes with added gusto, the *katoeys* are even more extravagantly made up, and halfway down the street one of the larger bars has set up a Muay Thai boxing ring where two battered fighters are slugging it out—or pretending to: no need to throw or take any serious kicks for a bunch of foreigners who don't understand what they're looking at.

In the Chung King I have to squeeze between girls and clients to reach the bar. I don't hold out any hope that Om will be here, but I ask anyway. This time the *mamasan* smiles: "She's just arrived. Over there." She points. Om is in a very short skirt with a skimpy silk blouse tied under her breasts that looks like it would fall open with a single tug; I'm pretty sure she's not wearing a bra. She is talking to a tall *farang*, her body language restrained although the smile is as seductive as usual. "He's not a regular," the *mamasan* says. "D'you want me to call her over?"

I do not say *You bet*, but she gets the picture. I'm surprised she takes the trouble to squeeze between bodies to reach Om and whisper a few words in her ear. Om turns immediately and smiles at me across the room. All this may not sound strange, DFR, but it is; my upbringing makes me abnormally sensitive to breaches of brothel etiquette. When Om arrives she puts a hand on my shoulder. I cannot resist placing one on her hip. Inexplicably we behave like old lovers, delighted to have come across each other again after a long break. I'm feeling bewitched when I say "I, I, ah—" and blush.

She smiles. "D'you want to pay my bar fine?"

It hadn't crossed my mind, but of course it's the obvious thing to do. If I pay her bar fine I own her for the rest of the evening. I can do what I like with her. I can even interrogate her. I say, "Yes."

She disappears for a moment to bring me a bill on a silver plate. I throw a thousand baht onto the plate without looking at her and wait. Ten minutes later she's in jeans and T-shirt when she brings me my change. Now I can hardly believe I'm walking down the main street with her, holding her hand. I can't believe how good it feels. How right.

"I have to talk to you," I say, after we've watched the Muay Thai for a while.

"D'you want to take me back to Bangkok?"

"The beach will do."

She makes a little pout of disappointment. When we reach the beach, we sit in the same chairs as before, looking out to sea. She waits. I ask for a cigarette. My hand is shaking a bit when I take it and let her light it. I remain silent for a long moment to give the impression of being in control. "Just tell me where you were earlier this evening."

She feigns surprise. "This evening? I've been—"

"Don't," I say, "don't spoil it."

"Spoil what?"

"Your beautiful face with a lie," I say with more tenderness than I intended and, surprised, experience one hell of a hard-on.

She takes a long toke on her cigarette. "Where do you think I've been?"

"Up on Vulture Peak. With a client."

She turns away to blow smoke into the black night. "Yes."

I take five minutes to reply. "Who was the client?"

"Who do you think?"

"Manu."

She shrugs.

"You knew it was me up there when you ran away, didn't you?"

A nervous toke on the cigarette. "I guessed. Who else would it have been?"

"You know I can arrest you?"

"For what?"

"Just about anything, from breaking into a house, violating a crime scene, to suspicion of murder—a triple murder. An atrocity of the worst imaginable kind."

She shocks me by bursting into laughter, then recovers. "I'm sorry."

"You have protection?"

"Yes."

"The army?"

She is quiet for a long time. Finally she says, "Detective, get out of Phuket. This isn't Bangkok. Nobody here will take you seriously. It was I who told the *mamasan* that if you came tonight, she was to let me know immediately. I like you. Maybe I feel about you the same way you feel about me. That's why I'm trying to save your life. There's a rumor going round that someone was murdered—a clerk from the land registry."

"So?"

"There are people who want to know who did it, and they're not cops who can be bribed."

I let that pass and go back to her earlier sentence. "How do you know how I feel about you? You hardly know me."

"I think I know men. Get out of here. Don't stay the night. Go back to your wife. If you can't get a flight, take a cab to Surat Thani and stay the night there. You have no idea how big this is. I haven't told anyone that you were up at that house tonight. But—"

"But *he* will?"

She lets the moment hang, then changes tack. "So what is this all about? I thought it was a murder investigation? So, the case is solved. You know who did it, because I told you."

I look away down the beach. "I suppose it's because you're a professional you guessed I'm married?" She doesn't answer.

I'm trying to puzzle it out, sending all the conflicting information into the great reservoir of consciousness the Buddhist theorists talk about.

It works. After a few minutes I think I have it. "You go to temple a lot?"

"Yes."

"You're devout?"

"I'm a whore."

"But you take the Dharma seriously?" She doesn't answer. "You would do anything, including screw me for free, so as not to have my death burdening your karma? But it is unusual for anyone to think like that—unless there are other deaths weighing on your conscience. Of course, if you were dragged into the organ-trafficking business, somehow, against your will perhaps . . ."

She's quiet for a long while. She seems depressed. "Please leave Phuket tonight." She stands and walks away.

I sit there for a few minutes, thinking, then give a good long sigh. I haul myself up from the chair and make my way to the main street. When I see a cab, I hail him and, standing in the road feeling a little theatrical, tell him in a loud voice to get me to the airport immediately. When we're out of the main street, though, I change my mind. "Take me up to Golden Goose temple," I tell him.

"I can't take you all the way up. You have to climb the last half mile."

"I know."

It seems like a long shot, but really it isn't. Of course, Buddhism is a science of the mind, so in theory it doesn't matter where you worship. It doesn't matter if you worship at all, so long as you follow the path. But I know sixty million Buddhists who don't think that way. Not a believer, from lowly farmwives to aristocrats, who doesn't have their favorite power center, that special temple that has always brought them luck, that particular monk who seems more enlightened than the rest.

The Golden Goose mountain is one of those places that have probably been sacred to humans for as long as there have been humans. I bet before Buddhism it was the center of an animist cult, and before that they probably sacrificed people up there. It's just such a perfect takeoff spot for the other side. And it happens to be held in respect by many of the ladies who work the night and need somewhere to go now and then to cleanse themselves.

The cab drops me at the end of the road, and I find the steps that lead up. It must be about one in the morning by now: the moon has completed more than half its transit. I'm tired, though, and the steps are steep. When I reach the doors of the temple, they are locked, but an old man is on guard, which is to say awake on a mat under an awning. I tell him I'm a former monk in need and give him a few hundred baht. He opens the gate and shows me a *kuti*, a monk's shack on stilts, which is empty, probably because it's the most decrepit they have. He says he'll tell the abbot about me in the morning.

I fall asleep on the bamboo floor of the *kuti* and wake up before dawn to the sounds of monks moving around. I find the temple building itself and wait at the back until it is full of saffron-robed men sitting on their ankles, like me. Soon we are all roaring out the "Homage to the Buddha" as if it's the first day on earth. For an instant I'm young, innocent, and high. When the monks have all gone on their alms rounds, I ask to see the abbot. When I describe Om, he knows who I'm talking about.

"She's the real thing," he tells me. "She comes here whenever she can and meditates. I try to persuade her to become a *maichi*, a nun, but she says she is her family's only breadwinner, she can't just leave them to starve. I tell you, that woman has the Buddha in her more than most of my monks."

"Does she talk to you?"

"About herself and her troubles? No, not at all. I have to drag it out of her. Even then she never complains. Like I tell you, she's the real thing."

I ask him about a certain day or night last month. He doesn't want to answer at first, but eventually he agrees that he has seen her upset once or twice. "Life isn't easy for anyone, especially the spiritually awakened."

To keep the conversation going, I ask him about *farang*. His temple has become world famous and is mentioned in all the guidebooks. He rolls his eyes. "I never know where to start. They're so programmed by materialism, they think they want enlightenment, when all they're really looking for is a new kind of gratification, a thrill they can't get from a pill or a bottle or a video game. When I try to explain that strong emotion is inherently unreliable and isn't what the Buddha meant when he referred to the heart, they think I'm being cruel. Thai monks may not be what they were, but they still have the perspective. For *farang* I despair. Hardly a one of them I meet who has a hope of being reborn into the human form. I see sheep and dogs of the future in designer T-shirts climbing up and down this mountain, getting in and out of the tourist buses."

"They're stuck in Aristotelian logic: 'A cannot be not-A.'"

"Tell me about it! The discovery of nirvana is the psychological equivalent of the invention of zero but vastly more important. Think of where mathematics was before zero, and you have the level of mental development of the West: good/bad, right/left, profit/loss, heaven/hell, us/them, me/you. It's like counting with Roman numerals."

I tell him about my time in a monastery a long time ago, when I was in my teens. My abbot was one of the most respected, and strict, in Thailand.

He shakes his head. "If I were to behave like that today, no monk would ordain with me. Everyone has gone soft. Can you believe there are abbots who spend fortunes on air-conditioning for the *kutis*, so the poor pampered little things can stay cool?"

We continue chatting for more than an hour. When I'm about to leave, his features change. A lifetime of ruthless discipline is suddenly written in those wrinkles—he has dropped the kind-uncle mask without a second thought.

"If you're not careful, she'll destroy you."

"Who?"

"Don't play games, you know who I mean. To love a woman for her body is no big deal—a man can get over it. But to secretly love a spirit as strong as that and think you can somehow own it—that's looking for serious trouble."

"But she's on the game," I blurt, and instantly regret it. I cannot stand his gaze and look away.

"Who isn't? Under materialism everyone is a whore. Go home to your wife."

"How d'you know I'm married?"

"If you weren't married, you wouldn't feel so tortured, would you?"

I walk back down the stone stairs. A delivery van has just unloaded some provisions. The driver agrees to take me back to the main road for fifty baht. Halfway down the hill we turn into a rest area to let a tourist bus pass. I look up at the windows, and for a brief moment I see dogs and sheep staring out. It's quite a detailed vision, very surreal. That abbot must be well on the way to Buddhahood.

At the bottom of the hill I wave down a cab and tell him to take me to the airport. When we reach a fork, though, I tell him to stop for a moment while I think about the case. Why, exactly, did I come to Phuket this time? Because the Colonel insisted that there was something I was missing. I'm not going to even try to figure out how he might know more than me, but I feel bad about returning to Bangkok with nothing much to report. So I tell the driver to take me to Vulture Peak again.

At the same time I'm wrestling with a nagging thought hovering just at the border of consciousness. It goes like this: I knew about the heliport with its giant H on that mound about two hundred yards from the house without thinking about it. That's how I realized there had to be a chopper service from the airport. But when I reflect, I don't understand how I knew about the heliport. So, I'm trying to think it through: I was in the registry with Lek and the clerk, examining the plans of the house, which are attached to the land registration, and I picked up on the fact that there is a tiny heliport not far away. What's wrong with that? Well, the plan was supposed to be only of the house and grounds, and yet it shows a heliport on common land quite a distance from the house's perimeter.

There is only one explanation. I call Lek to have him call the registry and check for me, but I'm confident I've finally got the picture: the registration, which at first glance seemed to be the official record of sale of one house, was in fact a record of a sale of the whole project, incorporating a total of three houses—along with all the common land. Instead of having the cab stop at the mansion, I tell him to keep going as far as the heliport, then pay him and get out.

Now I'm standing on top of the mound that forms the heliport to check out the other two houses. They were built as if to complement the main mansion. Each must have pretty good views of the Andaman Sea, but neither boasts that fantastic drop into infinity that the main property offers. I decide to ask the Buddha for help. I stroll up to each of the other houses with my mind as open as I can manage. As I suspected, it is the one on the right that causes the hairs to stand on the back of my neck. I'm not surprised it owns better security than the main property. It is surrounded by a wall about ten feet high with a gate that was originally a work of wrought iron in an open-scroll pattern, but it has been boarded up with sheet steel to prevent anyone from looking into the grounds. CCTVs perch on each corner of the wall, and more cameras are fixed to the house.

The sense of the sinister is so strong, I call Inspector Chan.

"I'm at Vulture Peak," I tell him, and explain my theory about the other houses perhaps forming part of the estate bought by the Yips.

"Perfect," Chan says. "Perfect. Where are you right now?"

"Outside the second house."

"Good. Is it far back from the mansion?"

"About three hundred yards."

"So it's looking down at a valley?"

"Not quite. There's a flat area."

"Examine the flat area. What's the vegetation like?"

I walk across to take a look, holding the phone to my ear. "Looks like it's been planted with grass and shrubs."

I hear a sharp intake of breath. "Okay, what about the contours? Is it unexpectedly flat, considering the shape of the mountain?"

"Yes. Why?"

"Fill. Landfill. Digging tunnels these days is easy with the right machinery, especially if you have plenty of dough and come from Hong Kong. The problem is where to dump the extracted material. What are the dimensions of the flat area?"

"More than a hundred yards long, about twenty wide."

He whistles. "Just what I thought. Except that I was expecting them to have dumped the fill over the cliff on the sea side. That's how I saw it, but I must have got that detail wrong. That's why I was checking out the cliff with my scope that day on the boat."

"You *saw* it?"

"I trained in the States for three months in the eighties. They let me take a remote viewing course. I've been trying to use it on the Yips for years. Recently I saw tunnels and landfill—and a lot of other things. But I didn't know where in the world they were."

"D'you want to come over here now?"

"No. This isn't the moment. If we raid now, all we end up with is empty properties that could have been used by anyone. You can bet the Yips have plenty of backup alibis. But they have to visit Vulture Peak soon."

"Why?"

"Because the clerk and the boat boy have disappeared. They need to know why, and they need to do the investigating themselves. They have no choice. I know they arrived back here in Hong Kong from a trip to Beijing yesterday, so they probably held consultations with their cadres. I have my nerds checking all flight bookings from Hong Kong to Thailand. It's important that I reach Phuket before they do, so as soon as I see they've reserved a flight, I'll get on an earlier one. Don't call me again. I'll send an SMS." He hangs up.

Now I'm all alone on the hill without a taxi. I shrug and call the chopper company to send someone to pick me up. At the airport I go straight to the computers to access Wikipedia.

Remote viewing (RV) is the apparent ability to gather information about a distant or unseen target using paranormal means, in particular, *extra-sensory perception* (ESP) or sensing with mind.

Scientific studies have been conducted, and although some earlier, less sophisticated experiments produced positive results, none of the newer experiments concluded with such results when under *properly controlled conditions,* and therefore, like any other forms of ESP, constitutes *pseudoscience.*[1][2][3][4] Typically a remote viewer is expected to give information about an object that is hidden from physical view and separated at some distance.[5][6][7] The term was introduced by *parapsychologists Russell Targ* and *Harold Puthoff* in 1974.[8]

Remote viewing was popularized in the 1990s, following the declassification of documents related to the *Stargate Project*, a $20 million research program sponsored by the U.S. Federal Government to determine any potential military application of psychic phenomena. Although one Stargate viewer was awarded in 1984 a *legion of merit* for determining "150 essential elements of information (. . .) unavailable from any other source,"[9] the program was eventually terminated in 1995, citing a lack of documented evidence that the program had any value to the intelligence community.[10]

Back in Bangkok I take a cab to the station and race up the stairs to Vikorn's office. He listens to my breathless report without comment, nods, and jerks his chin at the door as a sign for me to leave.

27

Today Chanya is *kikiat* and won't be doing any work of any kind. *Kikiat* is usually translated as "lazy," which is misleading because of the disfavor into which this vital component of mental health has fallen in the work-frenzied Occident; over here *kikiat* is not a fault so much as a frank statement of the human condition. To fail to lend a helping hand because you have something more important to do may provoke anger in others, but to fail to perform a chore because you are feeling *kikiat* will, in all but the most extreme circumstances, meet with an understanding sigh; indeed, the word itself has a kind of pandemic effect, so that one person declaring themselves *kikiat* can cause a whole office to slow down. You may spend a lot of time over here, DFR, learn our customs, know our history better than we do ourselves, and even speak our language, but until you have penetrated to the very heart of indolence and learned to savor its subtle joy, you cannot claim really to have arrived.

Naturally, now that Chanya has declared herself *kikiat* for the day, I myself am thinking of spending the next few hours in bed, calling in sick, and maybe getting up around noon to go to temple. After all, I'm the one who got back from Phuket yesterday. Surely I'm entitled to be idle too?

Now my hasty declaration that I too am *kikiat* absolves me from the duty of getting up to boil water for coffee, so we hang there in bed for an hour or so. Sometimes Chanya hooks a leg over mine; then after about half an hour I'll hang my leg over hers; about twenty minutes after that we will decide that too much flesh on flesh is distracting from the purity of our *kikiat*, so we'll turn aside from each other as if we've had an argument; then Chanya will turn back, or I will, and the first one to return to the flat position will hook their leg over the other's leg or body. We spent most of our honeymoon in this way, with breaks for beer, sex, and *somtam*. Of course, we went swimming in the sea from time to time, but too much exercise has a corrosive effect on *kikiat*. Eventually one of us will get up to boil the water, but we will do it slowly, drowsily, and resentfully, so as not to disturb the fragile condition. Communication is achieved by single words or, preferably, grunts. Try it at home, DFR—you'll find it a perfect cure for jogging.

After a while I sigh and put water in the electric kettle for three-in-one and grope around to see if there's anything to eat. Since she's been studying so hard, Chanya has developed a taste for fig rolls; I never paid any attention to them before, but recently I've developed an addiction myself; they seem to go with cannabis and coffee quite well. So I bring over the half-eaten packet with the two mugs of three-in-one while pointing the fan at the top of the bed. Normally, for sleeping, I turn it away from us, so the fact that I've now deliberately pointed it at the pillows, on one of which rests Chanya's dopey head, is a signal we are officially no longer asleep: a sort of indoor equivalent to sunrise. Chanya turns over with her face pointed at the pillow, but turns back after five minutes, yawns, and rubs her eyes. She sees that I'm still standing and jerks a chin toward her computer. "Guess what—my secret admirer sent me another message, even more explicit."

"Really?"

"Yes. I wanted to show it to you in the interests of a totally open relationship. You do get my drift, Mr. Phuket? Jog the mouse, and you'll see."

The voodoo works: now I'm very aware that my partner is as capable of cheating on me as I on her. I jog the mouse. Nothing happens. Chanya groans because she forgot that she had turned the machine off. Now she has to get up, sit at her chair, stab in her security PIN, and wait for the Internet. Now she enters her inbox and clicks on a JPEG attachment.

It is the same naked male body but a new clip: the penis periodically grows larger and larger until its tumescence fills the screen; then it bursts in an orgasm like a fireworks display and shrinks back to flaccidity. She makes no effort to disguise her fascination. I guess she must be as alienated from me as I am from her. So why am I angry? Why am I jealous? Why am I thinking of Om? I'm steaming but holding myself steady when I whisper, "Does it turn you on?"

"I'm not sure. It's silly, but I keep looking at it. I'm trying to understand." She turns just enough to give me a low-grade smile. "Trying to understand men. What it must be like with one of those between your legs. It has to be a different experience. With a woman, whatever way you look at it, it's a kind of absence, by nature passive, quiescent, an aching wound waiting to be sated. Psychologically it must be quite another experience to have something hard and tumescent to thrust into someone. I guess you'd want to rape first, ask questions later."

I put my hand on her shoulder and look down her T-shirt. She is not wearing a bra. I say, "He must be a volcano of rage and frustration."

She nods. "Perhaps. Or maybe he's just saying, 'Hey, I'm a real boy, this is what being male is all about. I'm sharing here.'"

"Only a woman would think so." I do not say: *a frustrated woman suffering from a serious dose of seven-year-itch. Like her husband.*

She turns to look at me. "Really? Why d'you say that?"

"Male virility is shy when it's real. That guy has a serious problem. Exhibitionism is for people who can't get it on any other way."

"Is that right?" She shrugs. "So, did you have sex when you were in Phuket?"

"No. I spent the night in a monastery."

She blinks at me. "Really?"

"Really. If you don't believe me, you can go ask the abbot of the Golden Goose."

"That one on the top of the hill? You really, really didn't go with anyone?"

"I really, really didn't."

"So why did I have such a strong intuition that you were cheating, or thinking of cheating?"

"I don't know."

We take our coffee mugs back to the mattress. Now she hooks her leg over mine and opens a *kikiat*-style discussion with the single word *Dorothy*. There is a protocol here: since I was the one who went on yet another exotic trip yesterday, I should be the one to humbly listen to local news as if it were the most exciting thing in the world. Chanya allows a good five minutes to pass before she says, "We're going to have to help her. Or I am."

"Oh? But I thought you said she had tamed her man and now it was all happiness ever after."

"I was being loyal. In reality no woman ever tames a man like that." A pause. "You see, I asked your mother to call me next time Jimmy Clipp turned up at her bar. Well, she called me two nights ago—while you were away, as usual. He's back with his buddy on weekend R&R. But when I spoke to Dorothy, she didn't know he was in town. She wasn't expecting him for a month. He told her he only gets one weekend off every three months, which is a lie. Generally he finds a way to get here every two weeks." She turns to me. "What should I do?"

"Nothing, of course. Let him have his fun and go back up north. It's not your business."

"I know, but he's not exactly trying to be discreet by going to your mum's bar. He'll make sure Dorothy knows he's back and ignoring her."

I'm quite shocked and raise my eyebrows. "Really?"

"You don't know anything about men. I was on the game for nearly ten years, Sonchai. This Jimmy Clipp is a classic: apparently kind, magnanimous, sensitive, great lover, still good-looking at fifty, extremely promiscuous. Such men are immensely cruel underneath. He'll find a way of feeding off her suffering." She flashes me a glance.

"That's why you're *kikiat* today?"

"Yes. I'm trying not to deal with it. At the same time I feel totally responsible. I should never have set up that night at your mum's bar."

"Why not? Dorothy's a sociologist. She's supposed to know something about human life."

"No, she's not. I've only recently realized what a freak I am. I'm a real person who happens to be studying sociology. Most of the rest are Dorothys—nonpeople who study people in the hope that one day they'll be people too. I handled it all wrong. Instead of being confrontational, I should have grasped the existential reality, namely that I was the educating mother, not her. I should have spent time teaching her how to have sex, introducing her to different men, how to get the best out of them—that's really why she's over here, I see that now. She wants to be a real girl." She tuts at herself. "To let the whole situation blow up like this—it's unforgivable on my part." She shakes her head. "But I didn't know. She's so big and dogged and speaks with *farang* certainty—I'd forgotten what a fraud it all is. I thought she was going to be the adult in the room helping with my thesis. I fell for the description instead of the reality—now I'm stuck with the mess on the floor."

(At this point, DFR, I feel it no less than my chivalric duty to warn that at times of stress my darling tends to revert—temporarily—to an earlier incarnation; no, I did not say *bitchy whore*.) "It's all because of her tits, of course."

"Really? I thought they were good enough for polite company," I opine. "Not your earth mother mammaries, I agree, but a lot of women are small and manage—like men."

"She's flat-chested. Worse, they're tiny and flat but still flop around like a couple of half-fried eggs. She's terribly self-conscious about it, which is why she wears a padded bra most of the time. Then she gets into a defiant mood and leaves it off so everyone sees what the problem is. Next day she's crippled with embarrassment. Of course, she's way too much of a feminist to have implants."

"Aren't you being a little premature? You haven't even spoken to her this morning."

Chanya closes her eyes and makes a screwed-up face to demonstrate psychic concentration. "She's already called five times." I frown. "I turned off the sound. Check the log."

I check her cell phone. The log shows there have been seven calls from the same number already this morning. When I read out the number, Chanya says, "Dorothy," and groans.

So I'm standing in the middle of the room still checking Chanya's phone and about to ask if she wants the profile changed so she can hear the ring, or if she intends to just disappear for the day as far as the world is concerned, when I happen to glance through the window and see a sky-blue Rolls-Royce with tinted windows and other accoutrements, which to the cognoscenti says *Five-star hotel limo*. Sure enough, when it stops, a chauffeur in livery gets out to open the back door on the curb side. For a moment I cannot make out the tall figure who emerges. Then I can. I say, "Wow, how about that," under my breath. Chanya hears but doesn't want any narrative of mine to interfere with her Dorothy narrative for the moment. "I think we have a visitor."

"Who?"

I watch a tall, slim woman in her early forties, a *farang*, cross the street. She's in jeans, T-shirt, and sandals, but her hair is well under control. "It's the woman I told you about from Vikorn's election team. Her name is Linda."

"Really? That superman woman who kicked the president of Russia in the balls?"

"Yes. That one."

There is an extra-soft knock on the door. I drag on a pair of shorts while Chanya goes into a corner to pull on a dress. When she looks ready, I open the door.

"Good morning, Detective. Sorry about this—I should have called. If it's even the teeniest bit inconvenient, say so and I'm out of here. It's just that—"

"You happened to be passing?"

She smiles. "Of course not. I called the station, and they said you were at home. I remembered your wife is an academic and maybe at home with you—I took a chance."

"You have something to say to my wife?"

"Nothing threatening. I'm here to ask for help."

Frowning, I ask her in. "Chanya, this is Linda, Linda, Chanya."

Chanya smiles graciously up at the tall American. She's embarrassed there's no chair to sit on—it's occupied by her thesis again. She makes as if to clear it and dump the manuscript on the floor, but Linda stops her.

"It's okay, I'll sit on a cushion. The last thing I want is to inconvenience you." But she remains standing with her hands in her jeans pockets. I think she's shocked that fully evolved human beings live like this, but way too much of a pro to show it. She turns to me and says, "It's about Colonel Vikorn." She turns to Chanya. "He's a great man but as elusive as the smile on a Cheshire cat. Sonchai probably told you, my team has been hired to get him elected governor of Bangkok. Translated, that means we're being paid quite a lot of money to be good old American control freaks. But he won't let us control him. Jack and Ben spent most of last night drinking with him, which has left them flat on their backs this morning. Apparently the Colonel has a hollow leg. Now I'm following up with a morning call to his most gifted detective." She smiles warmly at us.

We stare at her with bug eyes until Chanya remembers to say, "Won't you sit down?"

Linda sits on a cushion and leans against the wall with her long legs folded so that her face almost disappears behind her knees, while Chanya and I sit cross-legged in the middle of the room.

Linda does a cute little thing with her hands that ends up with the index fingers pointed upward and joined together. "I don't drink myself, which is why I let the boys do their bonding with the Colonel last night. No reason why I should play Big Nurse at your house though." At first I have no idea what she is talking about, until I realize that with supernatural speed she has taken in and registered a quite small reefer roach, which I must have left in the ashtray when I indulged in a joint after returning from Phuket.

Chanya doesn't get it so I say, "You want to smoke?"

"Why not? Let's us all do some bonding, hey? Been a damn long time, to tell you the truth. I was based in Kabul for a few months about five years ago, and man do they have some good stuff there. That was the last time, though. I'm wedded to the job."

"I see." I take our little plastic stash box down from a shelf. I'm thinking if she hasn't smoked since Kabul, that's going to be one high American. I start rolling.

She has impressive lungs. The joint diminishes by at least an inch with one long toke. She holds it well but splutters somewhat on the exhalation. To Chanya and me, it's like watching a thriller and trying to guess the ending. We keep quiet and are careful not to share glances: Linda is hyperobservant with a built-in cutting-edge mood detector. We wait. After about five minutes I deduce the silence must be dope-driven: *farang* don't tolerate it without assistance for more than a couple of minutes at a time. Is that not true, DFR?

Now Linda looks fondly at Chanya. "So, ah, tell me. I've always wanted to know. What's it like being a real woman?"

Chanya is startled but recovers quickly. "I feel like asking you the same question."

"Really? How about that. Well." Linda takes another toke. "Let me put it this way. When I started with the CIA, I studied Standard Arabic—most of us did. We got to study the history too. The Islamic empire, which was really the Arab empire, once stretched from Pakistan and western India in the east to Spain and southwest France in the west. The civilization they put together in Andalusia was fabulous beyond anything we have today.

"At its peak it was run by a guy named Abd ar-Rahman III, who built an amazing palace called Az-Zahra. After he died, somebody found a note of his that read—see, I remember it pretty much word for word: 'Fifty years have passed since I've been caliph. Treasures, honors, pleasures, I've enjoyed them all to the point of exhaustion. Princes admire me, fear me, and envy me. Everything man desires has been mine for the asking. So I've calculated how many days of happiness I've enjoyed during all this time, and the number comes to fourteen.'" Linda takes another long toke and hands me the joint.

"Well, I've had pretty much the best America has to offer. I've had any man I ever really wanted, any job. When I was young, I intended to travel and learn foreign languages, which I did. When I moved from the CIA to the private sector, I went from well paid to extremely well paid—you could almost say excessively well paid. I've known the best of the world, and you know what? I envy that old caliph his fourteen days, 'cause I can't remember more than a few hours of happiness myself, mostly when I've had the chance, which comes maybe once or twice a decade, to smoke some decent dope without risking my career. Too damned anxious staying ahead of the competition to even think about being happy—it would take up too much time." She smiles again at Chanya. "That's what being a fully liberated woman has done for me. How about you?"

I hand Chanya the joint, and she takes a few tokes before answering. "I'm Buddhist. We don't think that way. The question has no meaning for me."

"Uh-huh? How's that?"

"The kind of happiness you're talking about is a form of clinging—of greed, part of a cycle. Of course it leads to unhappiness in the end."

Linda stares at her. "Well, I'll be damned. I wish you'd been around when the Founding Fathers drafted the Constitution. They've got three hundred million of us chasing our own asses in the pursuit of that same happiness you Buddhists already knew didn't exist." She laughs. "I did always wonder why it was the *pursuit* of happiness—like you're never really expected to get there. Kind of a Godot thing right at the center of the American mind. The best is always yet to come, yet to come, yet to come . . ."

The dope has reached her, and now she's stuck in a vortex like the slow-spin phase of a washing machine. She shakes her head and smiles beatifically as if nothing unusual has happened. I think Chanya must be stoned too, because she gets a gleam in her eye and stands up.

"D'you get anonymous porn in your inbox, Linda?" she asks. "I got a prize yesterday. Want to look?"

Personally, I don't think it's such a good idea to show the American her porn collection. I guess she's decided it must be the way *farang* women bond these days. She goes to her computer and jogs the mouse. "Come and see," she says to Linda, who has to use the wall as support before she can stand. Now Chanya calls to me: "Sonchai, there's another one. He must have just sent it. Want to see?"

I get up to stand with the two women. Chanya clicks on the new attachment to the latest e-mail. It seems the anonymous one is smarter than we thought. He's not so much a random pornographer, more a focused campaign strategist. Now the image unfolds from the feet up, as before, and just as before, we are treated to a veritable fireworks display of male virility—but the revelation no longer stops at the neck; it continues unrolling until we have the full face.

Linda doesn't have time to reach the yard before she throws up; as a resourceful American, she manages to open the window just in time before emptying her stomach's contents. The room is filled with the sound of her retching while Chanya stares in fear and awe at the monitor, and I feel a strange kind of rage. At first I can hardly credit what I'm looking at. Then I have to shove a fist into my mouth. "Oh, no," I mutter. "No, no. It can't be." Can't be what? *Can't be a human face.* Well it is. A face put together by a demon, to mock our species all the way to annihilation. Nothing is aligned properly, the ears, the eyes, the mouth—especially the mouth—and it's hard to see anything that isn't scar tissue. There is no nose, only a hole, and a chunk of the upper lip is missing, showing crooked teeth and crimson gum. This is man inside out. If I was that young fellow, I'd probably rape anything that moved.

"Sweet Buddha, such suffering," Chanya whispers.

Linda has stopped retching but is still in cannabis-enhanced shock. She signals it's time for her to go, and I help her cross the road to the blue Rolls-Royce. I have to admire the strength with which she pulls herself together. Apart from one unplanned stumble, you would never know she was stoned out of her skull. I note, with an ironic smile, that her limo is parked under one of General Zinna's election posters. Just like Vikorn, he commands every third lamppost, but never the same one as the Colonel. I wait until the limo starts to move away and wave at the tinted windows. I'm a tad stoned, and I've got the munchies; I noticed we're almost out of both fig rolls and three-in-one, so I stroll down to the 7-Eleven to buy some.

When I return to the house, I see that Chanya is holding her cell phone and staring at the street. She clears her throat. Her voice quivers when she says, "General Zinna just called me. I could hardly believe it was him—he sounded broken. He said there's a risk Manu—apparently that's his name—is headed this way."

"Why would he be headed *this* way?"

She inhales. "Zinna is stuck in traffic. That's why he called. He said Manu is following up contacts with women he's met over the past few years. Apparently he met us once in Phuket—you remember, when we were celebrating our wedding anniversary, and we went to that five-star hotel for supper, and Zinna was there with his lover? He got our address from Zinna's address book. He said Manu is unarmed but very strong. It seems he's a big, muscular young man. He has already harassed a young army wife this morning, and yesterday he raped two women whose names also were in Zinna's address book. The general says it's all about Manu getting back at him for ruining his life. We should lock the door and protect ourselves." She nods toward the sink where a carving knife is prominent. "I stood here for a few seconds just now with that in my hand, but I felt foolish. D'you have your gun?" I show her the gun. "I don't want you to use it, Sonchai. Not to protect me. Protect yourself with it if you have to." She goes to the window and leans on the frame. "Such suffering. Dear Buddha. And I thought I had problems."

"He's a killer," I blurt. "He's the one who killed those three at Vulture Peak."

We stand at the window like two androids in a sci-fi movie and watch a late-model Benz draw up on the opposite side of the street. It's a convertible with the top closed: some kind of famous sports model. I can just make out a man in the driver's seat wearing a sports jacket and cravat, although I cannot see his features. He stops and sits in a composed posture staring straight ahead, no doubt with the engine running for the air-conditioning. He seems to be waiting for something specific to happen. We watch.

The man in the driver's seat shifts to pull out a cell phone from his pocket. He seems unhurried, even serene. Now he punches in a number and raises the phone casually to his ear. Then something clicks in my head, and I'm seeing him in a different light: a man in a daze.

"Zinna?" Chanya asks, squinting at the car.

"I'm ninety percent certain—" I stop talking because a five-ton covered army truck has appeared. The driver of the Benz moves the car forward as far as he can, so the truck can park behind him.

"It *is* Zinna," Chanya says, putting her hands on her hips and staring hard at the Benz and the army truck behind it. After a couple of minutes the man in the Benz opens his door and gets out. Yes, it is General Zinna of the Royal Thai Army, dressed in a sports jacket with brass buttons, open-neck shirt, and beige pants, hands thrust into his pockets; there's no mistaking that strut, nor the broad chest in a short body. He seems uncertain, though, as to what to do. His strut droops. When he approaches the truck a sergeant jumps out to give him a stiff salute, but the General in civvies only thrusts his hands more deeply into his pockets and stares up and down the street. He seems frustrated, helpless.

Now Chanya and I gasp because some army privates have emerged from the back of the truck with a net. It could be a fishing net for large fish, but to me it most resembles the kind of thing they cover ammunition dumps with in the jungle. About five of the young soldiers have rifles with bayonets fixed. Zinna stares at the bayonets for a moment, then starts to remonstrate with the sergeant. To my surprise, the sergeant remonstrates back, as if this is a private job he's doing for Zinna, and therefore he has civil rights here. I have the feeling he's protecting his men. No way will he tell them to put the bayonets and rifles away, and Zinna in civvies has no authority in this street at this time. The little General looks sad more than angry.

Now everyone suddenly turns to stare in the same direction, as if there has been a shout. Zinna seems scared and relieved at the same time. Now five of the soldiers run off with the net. There's a commotion loud enough for us to hear in the hovel—a kind of roar, half animal, half human—excited and scared shouts from the soldiers, a moment of panic—someone has got away—no, it's okay, got him—more commotion, *he's stronger than we thought*—yells as if someone has escaped again—another scuffle, this time sounding more controlled, as if the soldiers have had enough and have started to apply real will. Now a group comes into view. A human figure is trussed up in the net and carried like a wriggling mummy, howling hideously. Zinna has looked away, extreme grief on his face. The soldiers lift the captive up into the back of the truck. The howls cease. Zinna walks quickly to his Benz and drives off. The truck follows.

I have been preoccupied with the street drama and not paid any attention to Chanya for about ten minutes. Now I turn to look at her, and I see she has followed every nuance. She has covered her face and is staring at me in horror. I blow out my cheeks. She backs away from the window to squat against a wall, her hands still pressed over her cheeks, staring. I squat next to her. Now she puts a hand on my forearm and nods toward the street. The Mercedes has returned, and the driver is parking in the same space as before. Chanya and I watch as the General gets out, locks the car with a remote, and struts across the road. There is a knock on the door. *You get it*, Chanya's eyes say.

When I open the door, General Zinna is standing ramrod straight in the posture of a man of honor doing his duty. I give him the high *wai* at the same time as he *wais* me.

"Please forgive me for disturbing you," he says. "May I come in for a moment?"

I think that Chanya will remain squatting on the floor as a gesture of disgust, but thirty years of programming forces her to her feet with a high *wai*. Zinna isn't charismatic like Vikorn, but he carries a lifetime of military training and the brutal courage of a warrior. His head and face are huge with the crude power lines of a man who fights dirty, wins big. He looks us both in the eye once, then turns away to look out the window. "I think you saw everything, no?"

"We saw your men take someone away. Heard the howls," Chanya says, avoiding his eyes.

I watch Zinna while he takes out a pillbox. "May I have some water?"

Chanya finds some bottled water in the fridge, and we wait while he swallows the pill.

He stares at me with frank bewilderment. "You have no idea what shock and misery can do to your head. I suppose it's age. During the Communist insurrection I spent months in the jungle, fought hand to hand with bayonets, lived on a couple balls of rice a day, led my men to victory. To *victory*. I never thought something like this would happen to me. Never. In love there is no victory." He looks me full in the face. "He's broken me. A little private soldier from Isaan has brought me down like no enemy ever could." He stares out the window again. "I came to offer my most sincere apologies. I will do everything in my power to ensure nothing like this ever happens again. Even if it means . . ."

He and I both turn to look at Chanya. She puts a hand over her mouth. "I don't want anyone killed because of me," she says. "You can't kill a man as if he's a rabid dog."

The phrase has caught Zinna's attention. Perhaps he has used exactly those words himself recently. He is troubled and only manages, "No, no, of course not." He coughs apologetically. "Well, I must be going. Once again I am compelled to offer my humblest apologies."

We watch him leave. Chanya puffs up her cheeks, then lets the air out in a whistle. The raw fear has passed, leaving us in confusion. We are looking at each other as if we are both drowning, when my phone rings.

"Master, you are a total genius. Really, you blow me away with your brilliance. I just don't know how you do it. If Vikorn doesn't give you a promotion after this, I'm going to resign."

"Lek? What's happened?"

"What's happened? Well, you know how I hate flying, so I used the train and it took all night, but I thought you wouldn't mind because I arrived earlier than if I'd taken the morning flight—"

"Okay, okay. You got to Phuket, and you're now at the land registry?"

"It's exactly as you foretold, you witch. The reason that clerk was being so crafty was the whole purchase contract was a cover-up. Whoever bought the property made sure you'd have to spend days and days digging before you discovered that the transaction included those three houses and the common land. The whole estate."

I feel a twinge of excitement. "That's why they needed the clerk, the only reason they kept him alive. He's the one who did the paperwork, and so long as he worked in the registry, he would know if anyone was investigating the title."

"But why would they want to be so hush-hush? It's weird."

"I want you to dig further. See if there are any work permits for underground tunnels. If it was a big job, they would have needed legal cover—"

My phone bleeps. I see it is an SMS from Chan. I close on Lek and check messages:

Yips on morning flight tomorrow. I'm getting the red-eye around midnight. Arrive V.P. about four a.m.

I make the calculation in my head. If I'm to be there for Chan's arrival, I'll have to make my way to the airport now. When I close the phone, I have to summon the courage to look Chanya in the eye. "Ah, I know this is a bad moment, but . . ."

She stares at me. She's too far gone in rage and hurt to say *Great, I'm nearly raped by a monster, and all he wants to do is go visit his tart in Phuket.*

"I'll be back tomorrow for sure."

She nods in a state of collapse, apparently defeated by life itself; but summons the strength to whisper "Asshole" as I'm leaving with my modest backpack.

28

I miss the afternoon flight and have to take the early evening one instead. I don't want to use the chopper service in case a member of the Yip party has the same idea, so I take a taxi right up to the helipad. When I check out the other two houses, there is no sign of life. I'm curious about Inspector Chan's landfill theory and take a second look at the level area on the other side of the mountain. It's twilight, so visibility is low, but from certain angles it does seem as if a huge hollow in the mountainside has been filled in and leveled off.

I return to the main property, but I don't feel secure sleeping in it. I decide to wait on the balcony. After a while I realize I'm going to need some support for my aching backside, so I go back into the house to collect some cushions. It's been long day. I find the corner of the balcony that is in the most darkness and bed down. The moon has aged greatly since I started coming to Phuket on this case; it's only just on the eastern horizon when my eyes start to get heavy.

I awake because of a vibration that is shaking my body. The force is coming through the teak deck: footsteps, quite heavy. I freeze at the same time as I open my eyes and slightly adjust the position of my head so I can see who is there. At floor level all that is visible is a pair of legs dressed in fatigues tucked into army boots. If I turn my head a few degrees, I can see as far as a black T-shirt and a couple of brawny arms holding a combat rifle. I watch the rifle cover all sides and corners of the balcony in a professional sweep.

It must be quite late because the moon has reached far to the west and there is a quietness about the night that only occurs in the small hours.

If I dare to raise my head a couple inches more, I'll be able to see his face. As I try to do so, one of the cushions slips, making a faint catching sound on the wood. Instantly the gunman freezes, then crouches. Now he repeats the sweep of the balcony with greater concentration. The sound I made was so faint, though, it could have been anything, a rat or a mouse or even a cockroach. He relaxes again and stands up straight. But now I know who he is. I am surprised at how tall: at least six foot two, maybe more, with an athletic body.

He resumes his inspection of the balcony and pauses in the most westerly corner. Now, when I dare to raise my head, I see him in sharp black profile against the silver moon: the wrecked face, the missing nose, the lopsided mouth: it is the blunt face of a giant bat. In addition to the M16, he is wearing a holster with a handgun. Everything about him says *career soldier*. After all, this once was a young man so fired with military ambition, he was prepared to sleep with a general.

He remains illuminated by the moon for maybe five minutes, then crosses to the house, which he enters, closing the sliding door behind him. I roll over to the door and press my face against it. I am just in time to see him cross the vast salon and enter the hall that leads to the front door, and the road. When I reach the front door, I open it with agonizing care. He has gone, but I can guess where to. I scramble over to the heliport. Sure enough, he appears at the entrance gate to the second house and leans forward to press his eyeball into a security device. The gate opens, then clangs shut behind him. A light goes on for a moment, escaping from a crack where shutters join, then darkness. I am thinking: *Om must know this* and *Om never told me this* and *What else does Om know?*

· · ·

Rough hands shake me while their owner talks to himself in Cantonese. It's hard to see him clearly because it is still dark.

"Chan?"

"What are you doing on your back, Third-World Cop?"

"Waiting for you."

"So, here I am."

I groan. "It must be about five in the morning."

Chan checks his watch. "Four forty-two."

He is dressed in shorts and T-shirt with a soft sports bag. We enter the mansion, where he takes a pair of black coveralls from his bag and pulls them on. I take him across the common ground to the heliport and then to the other house. I watch while he walks around the perimeter, examining the walls and the CCTV cameras. He disappears behind the house, then reappears on the other side and walks quickly toward me.

"I'll have to make a move now, while it's still dark. If I set off an alarm, you'll have to cover for me somehow. Find some way of making it legal."

"There's no way to do that."

"Sure there is. The next governor of Bangkok will make it right—he'll have to if he wants to be prime minister." Chan touches my hand. "It's okay. I won't trigger the alarms."

"Sure?"

"I was in a tactical unit for six years. I know how to bypass security systems. This one is nothing special."

I wait on the heliport. It's not quite dawn but no longer quite dark when I see the main gate open and Inspector Chan appears, beckoning me to enter.

Chan closes the gate behind me. To my unspoken question, he says, "No sign of your friend. Maybe he left after his last patrol."

I look nervously at the CCTV cameras, but Chan claims to have neutralized them. Instead of the front door, he takes me to the back of the house and points to a shuttered window on the second floor. I stand while he climbs on my shoulders and manages to hoist himself up to the window ledge. His burglary skills are so well honed, he has opened the shutters and the window in moments. I walk back to the front of the house to wait. Now there is a sound of bolts, and the front door opens. With all shutters and doors closed, it is dark inside the house, despite that the sun has started to appear in the east.

Chan takes out a pencil flashlight. "I had to cut the electricity where it enters the building," he explains. He gives the impression of familiarity with the house's purpose. He traces the frame of the front door with his flashlight. "See anything unusual?"

"Looks like the doorway has been enlarged."

"Right. Why?" I shrug. "Hospitals also have extrawide doorways, to allow for the passage of gurneys flanked by medical staff." I flash him a look. "I knew three things: a place like this must exist; it could not be in Hong Kong or I would have found it; you would sooner or later lead me to it."

"What do you call your technique, parasitical policing? You could have admitted you were riding on my back."

He sighs. "Still the medieval mind-set, the fixed cosmology, the stunted Old Testament sense of truth and justice, right and wrong. Ever hear of cloud policing?"

"What?"

"It's going to be the next phase in humanity's descent. No one cop will have all the evidence — it will be shared out among significant players. A cop will need to maintain high-level contacts, like a diplomat. Guilt will be only one factor in any investigation and by no means conclusive. Negotiation, relative politico-socio-economic status, *guanxi*, all become relevant."

"Did you take your lithium yet today?"

He grunts. "You don't believe me."

I lose it and hiss at him, "What's to believe? Every time I meet you you're someone else."

"That also is a feature of modern policing. I believe we already touched on it. A fixed sense of personal identity will be a fatal impediment in law enforcement of the future. A murder squad detective will have also to be a murderer in some sense. See?"

"No identity, no loyalty, no rulebook?"

"Oh dear," Chan says, and shakes his head.

"You need to meet Vikorn."

"I have," Chan says with a smile. "Medium height, in his sixties, prowls instead of walks, a criminal genius almost on a level with Mao, if I was not mistaken."

I'm shocked. "Where?"

"China," Chan says. "Don't worry, he wouldn't recognize me. I was just some little cop in deep background." I scratch my jaw. "You need to stop trying to work it out. No one person has all the answers."

"Not even the Yips?"

"Those little girls? So long as they're allowed to be as naughty as they like, they don't ask questions either. They don't know."

"Cloud killing?"

"You could say that."

I follow Chan in his examination of the house. Now we are standing in what was once a bedroom with a view over the mountain. It is empty, like all the others we have checked: no people, no furniture. We return to the ground floor and notice a new hole in the wall. On examination it turns out to be a doorway that we missed because it is designed to be invisible when shut. It obviously leads to a cellar. We stare at each other: *Someone must have gone down or come out while we were checking the house.*

I watch Chan become seduced by the big black rectangle presented by the open door. It smells musty when we poke our heads into the cavity. A set of raw concrete stairs leads downward, like an invitation to sink into a lightless ocean of infinite depth. Only the inspector would find it irresistible.

"I'm going down," Chan says. He raises an eyebrow at me. "Why don't you stay here where it's safe, Third-World Cop?"

I groan and follow.

The underground room is a kind of operating theater. The stairs drop down into the huge chamber with—so far as I can make out—a dome-shaped roof. It is as vast as an emperor's tomb. Chan's pencil flashlight cannot penetrate from one end to the other. Little by little Chan edges forward while I cover his back.

There is a bank of refrigerators against one wall, shelves full of bandages, disinfectants, anesthetics, boxes labeled CYCLOSPORINE. There are five stainless-steel gurneys with drainage outlets, two operating tables side by side, red blankets, and some high-tech electronic gadgets on portable stainless-steel tables, including what I suppose are three heart monitors. It is cool down here, and there is a slight breeze from a ventilation system.

"They even have a backup generator," Chan says, pointing, "just like a real hospital. Look, see how close the two operating tables are? They wouldn't get away with that in a legal clinic—the donor and donee have to be decently separated. In the parallel trade, of course, it's all no-frills."

"So who are the donors?"

Chan stares at me in the gloom. "Don't you see? Anybody. Anybody at all. A young person coming home from school in India, a minor felon from China, a Western tourist led into a trap in Malaysia, desperate Africans without travel papers searching for work, unemployed Brazilians from shantytowns, orphaned kids in Isaan—in this business, nobody cares where the meat is grown, so long as it's still on the hoof and breathing when it arrives. Right now, I guess you could say we are in danger of becoming donors ourselves." I meet his gaze. "I told Interpol, but they didn't take me seriously. The Yips are too smart and the operation too big—it boggles the mind."

"Tell me how it works."

"Take Lourdes, the Yips' favorite hunting ground. They find someone with, say, terminal liver problems. In the course of a number of interviews, they dismantle whatever faith the patient has left in their god. Now you have a true citizen of the twenty-first century, a totally confused human soul with no identity, no direction, no faith, no religion, no politics, no instinct other than to survive. The Yips impose a culture of absolute secrecy, which is sealed by hints that if the authorities find out, the patient, also, will be an accessory to a serious crime. By this time, the patient, nailed to a cross of hope and terror—a real Christian at last—will do whatever they're told.

"They are given to understand they are being taken to China, where they will receive the organ of an executed prisoner who would have died and had his organs sold by the state in any event. That's the great Yip innovation. Everyone has heard of China's organ sales. Everyone with a serious problem with a solid organ has been through the thought process: *Well, I don't agree with it, of course, but if the poor bastard's going to die anyway, why should someone else get the liver?* And of course they tell the patient they're flying to China in a private jet.

"They are heavily sedated before they arrive at Phuket—as far as the patient is concerned, it could be anywhere, but they've been told it's somewhere in China, and they're happy to go with that. They have also paid a great deal of money by now, perhaps the whole of their wealth. They're committed. You could say they have finally become believers. They are already under the anesthetic when the chopper brings them up to Vulture Peak."

"And the donor?"

"Sometimes it really is an executed felon. Why not? The organ is popped into a chilled Jiffy Bag minutes after the bullet, but there simply are not enough legal executions to go around. The list of people in need of livers, kidneys, eyes, faces grows by the hour. In Shanghai you told me the Yips showed you some of the e-mails. And what happens when the disposable income of average Chinese and Indians reaches a point when, say, half a billion people are looking for organs to buy . . . perhaps even for frivolous reasons? You're a cop—you know to what lengths narcissism can drive people. What we do to poodles today we do to ourselves tomorrow. Suppose someone is sick of the face in the mirror and decides to buy another. D'you see?"

"Faces are still a challenge," I say. "It's going to be a while before someone can look at someone else's face and say, 'Gimme, or you will never see your daughter again.'"

"Sure. Personal computing, also, took a while to get off the ground."

I pause to take in the enormity of his argument. "I wouldn't want to be a film star in the economy of the future."

"Now you're getting the point. The human being has already been commodified by stealth. In the future everybody is viewed as an item for sale. Crowds become sources of stupendous wealth, so long as you can get away with murder—as the rich and powerful always do. In addition to corporate raiders, we already have organ raiders. Take the Yips. It's market logic: the only true god."

"The Yips saw all that?"

"Yes. When it comes to business, they are very mature and well ahead of the curve."

"But where does Manu fit in? He's not exactly a poster boy."

Chan nods. "Love." He smiles at me. "In the future love still exists, but it is twisted, thwarted, cowed by market forces. Only the strongest, and richest, can afford it."

"What are you talking about?"

"General Zinna. The Yips' setup here would be impossible without overwhelming political power and protection. They could never get away with it in Hong Kong—or even China. That's why I've been searching for this place for so long. That's why I got so interested in you, after I heard you'd been to Monte Carlo with them. The General runs Phuket. Part of the deal is that they take care of Manu. As soon as face transplants become more aesthetically pleasing, he goes under the knife again. Next time he will choose whatever face he likes— maybe someone he sees on the street, or a movie star on TV. In the meantime he is the organization's problem child, who has to be indulged."

As he spoke, Chan took hold of my arm. His flashlight had picked out a bank of refrigerators of the kind with transparent lids that open from the top. Corner shops used to sell ice cream from this model. At first I cannot see beyond the frost. Chan obligingly opens the lid of one of them, takes something out, brushes it off, and plays his light over it. "Of course, it's totally unusable. The flesh is dead, and all the cells will have been corrupted by ice. We're talking about a form of insanity, after all."

I am looking at the face of Mr. To, aka Wong; the moustache is a tad frosty. Chan gives it to me to hold, while he dips into the fridge and brings out two more faces. A quick brush with his forearm, and I recognize To's two women assistants. All three look pretty glum with drooping mouths, but I guess that's only to be expected.

"Let's get out of here," I tell Chan. "We have all the evidence we need now."

"Not yet," Chan says. "We haven't finished here yet."

He flashes his light around and finds another door, which opens onto a storeroom crowded with shelves.

"Embalming is big in the future—as a spinoff of the organ-transfer business."

"I didn't mind being brave when we had a good reason, but now we don't need to be, and he could be—"

He stops me by holding up a hand and nods at a set of shelves where bell jars sit in serried ranks. There is no liquid in them, however. As he passes the light from one to another, I see that each bears a label in Chinese script. He reaches up to one of the jars and takes it down to lay it on a metal table. "The labels are all names of previous owners." He lifts the top of the jar to pick up the embalmed penis. He reads the label: "An Chen Cheung."

He closes one eye while he strokes the cock. "Alas, poor Inspector An Chen Cheung! I knew him well, Horatio. A fellow of infinite lust. Here hung those famous testicles—quite sterile now. Here rises that cock he used to give pleasure to so many. There was hardly a woman he would not share it with, when asked nicely—and he was a handsome fellow." Chan smirks. He turns the set from side to side. "An Chen Cheung was a great cocksman—perhaps the finest on the force at the time." The smirk grows. "They took him to Monte Carlo. Of course, they didn't kill him there, they merely spoiled him. In the officers' mess one day he bragged to us that they offered him their dubious loins simultaneously in a threesome, but I have my doubts. In all my studies of the Twins, I've never seen any real evidence of copulation with a living male organ.

"Anyway, poor An Chen Cheung's mouth was bigger than his cock. He disappeared soon after the Monte Carlo trip—I always wondered." Chan holds the cock at arm's length to turn it under the beam of his contemplation. "He was a keen amateur sportsman. D'you think those mighty lungs are beating in someone else's chest? Are those twin kidneys still together, or have then been divided by the market, with one in Mecca and the other in Tel Aviv? Is one purifying the piss of a Jew and the other an Arab? And how about that miracle organ, the liver? Did they cut it in half and send the pieces north and south, one to Vladivostok, the other to Melbourne? Isn't globalism great?"

As a cop, I wonder most about the labels in Chinese. Chan reads my thoughts. "They must operate here in an atmosphere of absolute security. What do you know about this army general, Zinna?"

"The original gay bull—a control freak—uses the promotion carrot to seduce ambitious cadets. Very rich from the meth trade with Burma."

"Right."

"But why the labels on the jars?"

"Ever hear of good old-fashioned male triumphalism? You think women haven't always wanted a piece of that? These are trophies, my friend."

"Do they use *all* of them?"

"Sure. Can't you imagine the fights? 'I think I'll have An Chen Cheung tonight,' says Lilly. 'I've been thinking about him all day.' 'Oh, no you don't,' says Polly, 'I'm having him. Why don't you have Tom, Dick or Harry—have all three if you like.'" Chan looks at me. "Or something like that."

Chan's features have started to twitch. "Where's your lithium?" I say.

"I left it in my other bag, in the big house."

I'm thinking that this would be a good moment for Chan to take his medication. Too late. His gaze has morphed into the thousand-mile stare, a cold sweat has broken out over his face, and his lips have started to tremble.

"It's such a shame society has poured its disapproval over those of us with the bipolar gift. I've seen things, Detective, that no ordinary cop can see." He is shivering.

"Like what?"

"Like dawn on Andromeda." His teeth are chattering. "I've seen this new millennium laid out before my eyes in all its tragic futility.

I've seen our species descend to insect level in a prolonged orgy of nar-cissism which we will continue to call progress until we've descended into such a state of functional barbarism that we are all eating one another. I've seen the organ market rise in importance until it's bigger than oil. I've seen hearts and lungs for sale on eBay. I've seen women turn into men and vice versa. I've seen the average human reduced to a babbling idiot, so far gone he demands to be exploited. The false is to be preferred over the real—trash trumps excellence—truth is some-thing that only interests religious fanatics—science has to be applied to titillation and video games if it is to receive funding—soccer is the only world religion with any influence—the age of the little man, and woman, will be worse than anything perpetrated by a tyrant. I've seen the war of all against all—and I've seen the end. As the prophet said, nine-tenths of humanity will be destroyed.

"Why did I become a cop? Certainly the law has no interest for me, and detection is extremely boring most of the time—you are never permitted to prosecute the real villains. Only now and then the crimi-nal world turns up a prophet through whose eyes one may discern what happens next. What criminals do today, the respectable do tomorrow. Look how popular fraud has become on Wall Street. From that point of view, you could say I'm the luckiest cop on earth. I have in-depth knowledge of the minds of two of our greatest modern prophets, two spoiled girls who read the future better than any Internet entrepreneur and are probably billionaires as a consequence."

He inhales. "Like so many vocational cops, I was propelled by the heroic impulse. Make the streets safe for . . . et cetera. Bang up the bad guys . . . et cetera. Make sure they never again . . . et cetera. How cute. Now I'm forty-five years old. At my age guilt and innocence get turned on their heads. No authentic hero ever reaches fifty. I was sure the Yips would have a commodity shop like this—I *saw* it under-ground somewhere—but was it a paranoid fantasy? Was it my illness talking?

"Now there is only one more detail I need to know, then I'm out of here. I've come here to die, Detective. They can have my liver, my kidneys, my face, my cock—small prices to pay for liberation from their brave new world. What's your excuse for getting yourself carved up this day?" He glares at me with his lower lip trembling. "Did you ever read the Gospel of Judas?"

"No."

"You should. It's revolutionary. In it Jesus muscles Judas into arranging for his crucifixion sooner rather than later so he can escape the cloying human form and dissolve in a spiritual lake so pure not even angels have seen it. See, Judas was the only disciple who really understood him. I thought Christianity was strictly for children until I read that."

There is a click. The lights go on. Now the vast underground chamber is washed in neon. Chan's reaction is instant: he raises both arms. I follow his lead. Whoever made the click makes no further sound, so Chan and I are left to turn slowly around.

Close up, Manu is hard to look at. It is like seeing two different men in the same body: the perfect manly form of the tall, disciplined soldier holding a giant combat rifle, which is pointed at us; the maimed and frozen face.

The effect on Chan is electric. The expressions that come and go on *his* face bring vividness to the word *bipolar*. Now he has wrinkled his own features and is slowly lowering one of his hands. He points at Manu. "Translate," he hisses at me. Then: "I love you."

"He loves you," I tell Manu in Thai. There is no reaction from that Halloween mask. Only the eyes move. They glow with the dark energy of an edge dweller.

"I've been looking for you all my life," Chan says. "You are more of a pariah than I'll ever be. You are weirder than me, you live in an extreme atmosphere. I envy you above all men. There is no darkness you have not penetrated with your fearless gaze, no illusion you have not torn apart with your incredible ugliness."

I translate. Manu makes a gurgling sound in his throat. His eyes are sparkling, and I wonder if the gurgling is not a form of laughter.

"I understand you because I've aspired to be like you, but I don't have your courage. If I looked like you, I wouldn't have the strength to carry on. I would have done myself in right after the operation, when they gave you the mirror and came out with a whole lot of stupid excuses." Manu jerks the gun upward, as if encouraging Chan to continue. "But in my small way I too live on the other side. I'm a crazy bipolar—ask this guy here—he had to rescue me from a public toilet when I was having one of my raving sessions. See, I'm not so different. You could say I'm worse—if they could look at my mind they'd find it even weirder, uglier, stranger, more inhuman even than your mug. I admire you. The integrity of your suffering and isolation is beyond anything I've ever come across. You are urban man in his most pure form. I would be honored to be executed by a real man instead of slowly ground down into another clapped-out cipher. Why not make me your slave, keep me here with you in your underground lair, oh King of Hades? Or kill me right now if you like."

Manu shakes his head and turns his back. He moves like someone pottering around at home. We watch him go to the fridge where the faces are kept and lift the lid.

Chan does not take his eyes off that deformed figure. "You have to get into his mind," he whispers. "He's learned that without a face, he doesn't exist. Therefore he is invisible. Now he is making himself visible to us."

Manu has pulled out a face—it is To's—and slapped it over his own with one hand. It remains there for a moment while he turns to look at us. The gray flesh does not resemble anything living, more a macabre mask with drooping mouth. He cocks his head coyly, as if asking if we like his new looks. Then he turns back to the fridge, pulls off To, and puts on the face of the older woman who was To's secretary. He pirouettes and poses coquettishly.

"He's using us as a mirror," Chan explains. "Be polite." Chan starts to clap, and nudges me. I also clap; the lonely sounds are quickly lost in the huge chamber. Manu takes off the dead face and stares at us. He seems perplexed. Chan has twisted his features into those of a groveling sycophant. Out of the corner of his mouth he whispers: "He is going to become fascinated with me. I'm going to prove to him that I love him. That's your signal to run. Get the fuck out of here. This isn't your moment. This case belongs to me. Translate what I say until I tell you to go."

Chan drops to his knees. Manu's gurgling is an attempt to communicate, but I cannot work it out. Something in the sounds resembles

Thai words, but there is too much distortion to be sure. Now my mind has flipped to Om: I think of her making love to this monster, perhaps spending the night with him, seeing his face on the pillow, listening to the air passing through the hole that once was a nose. And now I understand what Manu is trying to say. "He wants you to kiss him," I explain.

Chan stands, embraces Manu, kisses those busted lips, and sinks his tongue into that mutilated mouth. Manu is holding the gun by the barrel while the stock rests on the ground. This would be a good moment to rush him. "Don't rush him," Chan says out of the side of his mouth. "Get the fuck out. Run. He's too far gone to care if you escape or not. I'm his next face. That's all he knows right now."

But there is no need to run. Manu seems pleased with Chan. He steps back from him and balances the gun against his stomach with one finger still on the trigger. With a single jerk of his head, he tells me to go. When I turn to find the stairs, though, he shakes his head and points to a door at the opposite end of the operating room. I have the feeling he is laughing at me.

29

At the far end of the room, I find a door that leads to a tunnel. It is brightly lit with sparkling white tiles and extrasmooth concrete. It is far longer than I expected. I must have run more than two hundred yards when I come to a door locked from the inside. It is wider than most doors. When I open the locks, I find I'm in a garage. After a moment of reorientation, I realize it is the garage belonging to the mansion. When I examine the door, I see that when shut it fits snugly into the wall and becomes invisible. I walk to the garage's entrance and find a button on the wall. The door folds upward. Daylight. I climb up to the balcony, go to the great glass sliding doors. Inside, the miniature stream is still tinkling over the feng shui master's lucky pebbles. When I attempt to take out my cell phone, I drop it three times. I sit on the floor and press an autodial number.

"Master, where are you? I've been so worried about you."

"Vulture Peak. Do you have the plans?"

"I have all the docs. It looks like they covered for the tunnels by obtaining a permit for full internal renovation and landscaping."

"Bring them anyway," I say, and hang up.

Now I hear the throb of chopper blades through the open doors of the salon. When I go out to look up at the sky, I see a small black dragonfly coming closer. I walk through the house to the front door and stand in the road to watch it land on the hillock. A diminutive figure in smart casuals with a small backpack emerges. It is Sun Bin. I wave at him, and he runs toward me. My teeth are chattering when I explain what has happened. He seems only half surprised.

"D'you have the plans to the underground system?" he asks.

"No, they pretended it was for internal renovation and landscaping. No tunnel plans registered."

He nods. "There has to be centralized surveillance connected to the Net. That must be how the Yips keep control."

"Chan's down there," I blurt, despite having told him minutes ago.

Sun Bin spares me a glance. "He has been planning this for years. He has his own agenda."

"Which is what?"

"Martyrdom, of course. That is his heroic nature. He was the most successful commander of special forces in the history of the Hong Kong police. He is a tactical and strategic genius. He can talk down would-be suicides and hostage takers like no one else—he understands criminals better than any cop I ever met. An enormous IQ of a hundred and sixty or something, but he uses it mostly to torture himself. He is capable of total identification with the perp." Sun Bin scratches his temple. "In other words, he's a total crazy. Sometimes he's Jesus Christ, sometimes Judas Iscariot. Whatever happens, it is because he has decided to make it happen that way. He used you as he used me. He's a kind of Sherlock Holmes on his last case—he confided to me once—but then he was in one of his bipolar moments, so it's difficult to be clear."

"Are you ever clear about anything?"

He shrugs. "For sixty years it was dangerous to be clear about anything in China. It still is. How do you break the habit of a lifetime? Tell me, how realistic is it to be clear about anything?"

"He planned it all?" I repeat, feeling morose. "What happens next?"

"Watch," Sun Bin says.

As he speaks, we hear the throb of chopper blades. In my confusion I assume it is Sun Bin's ride taking off; then I remember it took off as soon as he landed. When we go out on the balcony, we see another black dragonfly in the distance, coming closer. We go to the front door and watch from the road.

The chopper swings around to face into the wind as it lands on the big H. The first we see of a passenger is a long shapely leg. Another woman gets out on the other side. The gale from the blades sends the Twins' long hair fanning out behind them like black wings; they are squinting. Lilly—or Polly—bends into the bubble to say something to the pilot. They both carry large designer bags, which they hoist onto their shoulders as they run to the other house. We watch while one by one they bend to look into the biometric security device. The gate opens, they disappear. I'm thinking: *This has happened before. This is what happened when To and his two assistants were slaughtered. Now that the clerk has disappeared, the whole network is put on high alert and summoned to Vulture Peak.*

Sun Bin shakes his head at the chopper and retreats into the house. He takes a tablet laptop out of his backpack and lays it on a coffee table in the salon. It is the same laptop that I saw in that condo in Shanghai. He doesn't switch it on. "We need to look for an Ethernet jack. There has to be one somewhere."

"Why?"

"Because the people who use this house have to know everything that's happening in that underground network."

We divide up the house and search for an Ethernet jack. When we hear yet another chopper, we go out onto the balcony. This one is a hefty double-bladed army bird. It dwarfs the landing pad and creates a typhoon that bends bushes and small trees; twigs and leaves take flight. We retreat inside the house and watch from the window in the maid's room. First emerge the two *farang* election advisers, a man and a woman, who duck and run to escape the wind.

They wait while another figure emerges: squat, broad, indomitable, brutal. General Zinna is followed by his aide-de-camp, a tall, dark, handsome young officer. They walk at a smart pace toward the house. Zinna bends to offer his eyeball to the biometric gadget. The gates open, but when the rest of his party pass the gate, alarms go off. Zinna says something to his aide but does not pause in ushering the others into the house compound. The gates clang shut, and after a few minutes the alarm ceases. Silence.

Sun Bin and I exchange glances. Without a word, we go back to searching for the Ethernet jack. We're sweating with the effort and frustrated that we can find no leads, when there is yet another noise of throbbing blades. This time it is the little black chopper from the airport. We watch while Om gets out and runs for the house. She too has security clearance. The gates open when she puts her eye to the black box and clang shut behind her. We go back to looking for the Ethernet jack.

Sun Bin has an idea. "The kitchen."

"We already searched it."

"It has to be disguised."

Now Sun Bin finds the Ethernet jack behind the state-of-the-art coffee machine.

"Sneaky," Sun Bin says. He brings his laptop to the kitchen and finds a cable in his bag to connect to the jack. I wait while Sun Bin uses a software program to search for signals from the security system. Now we are looking at a set of sixteen boxes, each one showing green images from an individual CCTV camera. A couple of clicks on the mouse, and a new set of sixteen boxes appears. In all there are ten sets, making a total of one hundred and sixty CCTV cameras.

"They must be everywhere," Sun Bin says, looking around. When we examine one of the pages, we find a view of ourselves in the kitchen. We exchange glances. If the Yips have a laptop, which they surely must, then they will be able to see us. On the other hand, we can see them. They are under the other house in the tunnel system. They seem to be having an argument. Manu is alone in the operating theater, playing with his faces. We are unable to find Zinna or Chan.

"That tunnel system is vast," Sun Bin says, adjusting the program. "Look." He goes from page to page to show me the system, bathed in green light, which runs under all three houses. It's difficult to work out from the CCTV cameras, but it seems each house owns a tunnel, and each tunnel ends at the operating theater. We hear a voice calling from the balcony.

•   •   •

"Oh Buddha," Lek says. He is leaning against a wall of the house, breathless and soaked through with sweat. He is holding a large brown envelope.

"You climbed up the stairs?"

"The cab driver couldn't work out how to get here—all those lanes are *soo* confusing." He puts a hand on his heart. I take the envelope, which contains plans of the houses. In the kitchen the three of us pore over the details.

"So it works like this," Sun Bin says. "The donor and donee are brought here separately by chopper or car and taken into the other house on a gurney. The unwilling donor, who has been kidnapped, also has been sedated. He or she is probably already unconscious on one of the operating tables when the donee arrives. The donee is laid on the other one and hooked up to life support while the diseased liver—or another solid organ—is removed. As soon as the healthy liver has been harvested from the donor, it is placed inside the donee, who has been pumped full of cyclosporine. There is no life-support system for the donor, who is left to die.

"Later, the donee, who is only half conscious for the first few days, is told that they have been brought to Phuket to relax and enjoy Thai hospitality in accordance with the contract. Basically, they wake up in this fancy mansion with a new lease on life and maybe as much as half a million dollars the poorer.

"I would guess that for maximum efficiency the Yips would try to harvest as many organs from the donor as possible, so there are plenty of occasions when two or three patients are lined up to receive different parts of the cadaver: eyes, face, kidneys, sex organs, et cetera."

"*Charming*," Lek says. "So why were those three corpses left here on the bed in the master bedroom?"

"To and the two women?" Sun Bin looks at me. "What do you think?"

"I have no idea. It makes even less sense now."

"Unless . . ." Sun Bin says.

"Oh, no," Lek says. "You *can't* be serious."

I scratch my jaw. "It's the only explanation."

"Why not?" Sun Bin says.

"He's an ex-soldier. Tough as hell. Is he going to have the sensitive fingers of a microsurgeon?"

"Maybe not for working on the donee—but the donor is going to die anyway. What's to be careful about, so long as he doesn't damage the organ? Obviously, they must have trained him."

"Psychologically, it would make sense. Give a pariah work, a profession, something to be proud of. Bring him back into the economic system, pay him well. Maybe he owns a house, a car, and a bank account. What more could anyone want in terms of human identity?"

"Something that gives him face?" Sun Bin says. "That's sounds like a Chinese point of view."

"So after he shot those three in a jealous rage, he removed their organs—for what?"

"Practice, of course. And don't forget, he's an understudy to the Yips."

"But why didn't he do it in the tunnels?"

"He did. That's why there was almost no blood."

"So why did he then bring the cadavers back up here where they were bound to be discovered?"

All three of us are seasoned cops. We know the answer to that one.

"He's proud of himself."

"He wants recognition for his achievement, his mastery of a difficult and respected skill, his power over life and death. It's his final demand: that he be permitted to crawl out of his tunnels and reveal himself to the world as an expert surgeon."

"But he cut off the fingertips?"

"Just because he's insane doesn't mean he's stupid. His victim To was a real high-flyer. He didn't want him identified."

End of conversation. We are unable to look one another in the eye, because none of us has stopped thinking about Chan. I take over Sun Bin's laptop for a moment in my constant search for the inspector, who is nowhere to be seen. Neither is Om. As I continue to scroll from one green image to another and from one page to another, both Sun Bin and Lek become interested in the underground society.

"It's like they don't want to see him yet."

"Or maybe they can't get into the operating theater."

"There's been no contact with him so far."

"The Yips aren't even going in that direction. They're heading toward Zinna and his aide."

"That's a kind of communications center."

"That's right. That PC must be hooked up to the surveillance system."

We stare at the two soldiers and the two American advisers, bathed in green in the cellar of the third house, sitting at a table with a tower PC and a set of monitors. They also seem at a loss as to what to do next. Now the four of them look up. Has there been a knock at the door? The aide takes out a pistol and stands flat against the side of the door, then pulls at a couple of bolts. The door opens. The Yips enter, with Om between them. Om looks upset, frightened, and angry. The Twins and the soldiers remonstrate with her. She shakes her head with a wild look in her eyes. One of the Twins slaps her face. Om stares at her in disbelief. The four of them herd her back into the tunnel system.

Sun Bin has become adept at manipulating the software, and we are able to follow the progress of the group until they come to a steel door. It must be one of the doors to the operating theater. It seems that Om has decided to obey her captors. She knocks on the door and seems to be speaking, even shouting. We switch to the operating theater, where Manu has frozen with one of the faces in his hands. He replaces the face—it is To/Wong—in the fridge and walks to the door. In another square, Om is pleading with her face to the door. In the next square, Manu seems to be squealing in anguish, quite beside himself. He picks up a machine pistol lying on one of the operating tables and stands by the side of the door, then releases some bolts. The door opens. Om steps inside. Manu slams the door shut and bolts it. We watch while Manu approaches the camera and points his pistol at it. The square on the monitor is full of his destroyed face for a moment, then it turns black.

We switch to the screen where we can see the closed door to the operating theater, with Zinna, his aide, and the Twins standing outside. Perhaps they expected Om to produce a docile Manu within minutes. They seem to be fretting and arguing. Zinna's aide disappears, then comes back with a black backpack. He takes something out. It is another bag. From that bag he takes something that needs unwrapping. Now he is holding a black sausagelike object about twelve inches long in his hands. He kneels at the door to the operating theater and presses the puttylike substance around the edges of the door next to the locks. Now he takes some electric cable out of his backpack and presses one end of it into the explosive, then retreats while unwinding the cable. Zinna and the Twins retreat with him. Now they are back in the control room. The aide connects the electric cable to a switch. Sun Bin returns us to the door of the operating theater. We see a sudden cloud of dust envelop the camera lens. From the tunnel exit in the garage we hear a muffled explosion. All the screens go dark.

30

Two hours have passed, during which we've done nothing except stare at the blank monitor, wondering. Sun Bin owns one set of night-vision goggles, which he takes from his backpack and shows me. They consist of two heavy lenses that fit directly over the eyes and are held in place by a crisscross of straps over the head. He tries them on, then immediately takes them off. "It has to be dark for them to work."

I pick them up to examine them. They were manufactured by a German firm. "Made in China," Sun Bin says. "They're *my* goggles," he adds. "I should be the one to go."

I shake my head. "No way. It has to be me."

"Why?"

"*Gatdanyu*. He saved my life. I owe him."

Every now and then we return to the laptop to see if anyone has repaired the CCTV system. We are rewarded each time with a blank screen. Sun Bin and I think of Chan. Most of the time madness is an alienating condition; every crazy I've ever met has made me want to run. Except Chan. He has had the same effect on Sun Bin. "He's a kind of prophet," he says, "China style."

"China style?"

"In the old days, we were all crazy like that. He's so revolutionary, he could have been a Red Guard."

I take the goggles, go into one of the bathrooms, close the curtains, and turn out the lights. The goggles work fine, but the images are green.

I take out my gun, check the chamber, grab a handful of bullets out of my bag, and cram them into my pockets. I stick the gun down my waistband at the small of my back and start to descend the stairs to the garage. I leave the secret door wide open. Natural light only illuminates the tunnel for the first twenty feet, though.

I discover that the goggles need some vestigial light, but I don't dare use the flashlight that Sun Bin gave me. Deep inside the tunnel everything is pitch-black and I have to feel my way along the walls. I reason that if I can't see with these state-of-the-art German goggles (made in China), neither can anyone else. I also remember that this tunnel leads directly to the door of the operating theater, which Zinna's aide blew open. As I inch closer to it, I do not need visual clues. The stench of explosives, dust, blood, and guts is unmistakable. At the door itself I stumble over a body. There is no way of telling who it once belonged to, except that when I run my hand over it, I feel some long thick hair running through my fingers. I'm barely able to suppress the urge to flee: Panic Terror Claustrophobia. Any plausible excuse and I'm out of here.

When I inch my way into the operating theater, though, the goggles suffer overload and I have to rip them off. There is a single intense beam at the far end of the chamber, which is otherwise quite dark. Ever been scuba diving at night, DFR? Ever sink slowly down into that absolute liquid blackness that makes such a perfect proxy for everything terrifying, irresistible, and mysterious? If you have, you know how the mind goes when your underwater illumination focuses an intense lance of light into total blackness; it's like a Buddhist concentration exercise with heavy gearing. And the cavern is so long the figures at the far end are miniaturized in exquisite detail. I can even see the single tooth poking out of Manu's ripped lip as he bends over a figure strapped to a chair. In his big soldier's fist he is holding a blade so fine it disappears when the light catches it head-on. It is wider than a normal scalpel, a wafer of steel designed to harvest facial skin.

Both Manu and his victim are frozen, however. Well, I guess the victim doesn't have a lot of choice, but as I slowly draw my gun, knowing full well there's no chance of hitting him from this distance, I see that Manu has not moved an inch since I entered. My first paranoid thought is that he heard me and is about to drop the scalpel and grab a rifle, against which I have no defense. But he's not looking at me. He's not looking down the room in my direction at all. Something else grabbed his attention just as I entered. He's staring at a figure lying on a gurney next to Chan—I cannot be sure it's him, of course, because the head is turned away; I just know it's the inspector strapped to that chair and to my own shock I feel a weird, Chan-induced combination of horror, rage, and love. But what has caused the monster to pause in his black art if not me?

The three of us remain frozen in chiaroscuro, like in an old-style noir movie from the 1930s. I'm in a half crouch, pistol in both hands, elbows locked—a reflex of training, merely, and no use at all in this fix. And still Manu does not move, the glinting blade in his hand as steady as if gripped in a vice, those black shining eyes looking down the tunnel of light at the figure on the gurney. It is as if there has been an event too subtle to read, but too significant to ignore; something even more important than the theft of Chan's face. Then the figure on the gurney gives a groan that echoes through the cavern and makes the slightest movement of a hand. It is a beautiful fine female hand, every detail visible. I know that hand. I even share Manu's heartfelt care as he drops the scalpel, which clinks twice on the concrete floor, and goes to her.

Now is my chance. With gun at arm's length I dash down the chamber to a point where I can be sure of hitting him.

"FREEZE."

I might as well have yelled at a rock. I'm not sure he even heard me, despite that my scream echoes off the walls. I stare openmouthed as the monster picks up the figure from the gurney. As he does so I see that the back of Om's head has been smashed by something and her hair is thick with blood. And now comes the miracle: tears flow from those flinty black eyes and down the insensate cheeks as with infinite care he clasps her to him. She opens her eyes for a second, recognizes him, lifts a hand, finds the strength to caress his face once, then lapses into unconsciousness.

There's no question of firing now, because of the risk to Om—and because Manu pays me no heed. I might as well be a figure from a different dimension with a limited curiosity value but no power or influence. I have walked the full length of the cavern, and I'm right up next to him, maneuvering to reach Chan, who is strapped to some high-tech medical chair with his head and face held rigidly in a steel device with parallel struts and gleaming stainless-steel bolts. It is a simple matter to undo the bolts and the straps, all the while keeping my eyes on Manu, with my pistol at the ready.

"Don't kill him," are Chan's first words.

I had been too busy dividing my attention between his bonds and Manu's likely next move to notice what work the monster surgeon had already performed. Chan registers the sudden shock on my face before I'm able to dissemble.

"How bad is it?" he whispers.

"Anyone else would grow a beard—you though—maybe you'll start a new fashion. Better than tats and body piercings."

There is an exquisitely thin red line that runs with impressive precision the full circumference of the inspector's face, across the forehead just below the hairline, under the jaw and all the way sround in a circle; I guess faces can be removed like gloves when you've been trained by experts.

The inspector touches the incision with a finger and stares at the blood. "I'm disgustingly grateful to be alive," he mutters. "Given time I might even forgive you for robbing me of my consummation."

"What happened to Om?" We communicate in those extrasoft intense whispers that television naturalists use when they get up close and personal with dangerous animals.

"The girl? Those clumsy bastards used too much explosive. Bits of iron flew all over the place—one hit her in the head. Our friend went crazy. He's the best and fastest shot I've ever seen. They didn't have a chance, not even that young soldier. I tell you, I've never seen anything like it. No ordinary man can shoot like that. He saved me because he wanted my face. He was sure the girl was dead. So was I.

She isn't going to live long, though. Not with that much skull missing."

We are both fixated on Manu, who has not stopped staring at Om's unconscious face as he holds her in his arms. For a second the fascination of what he will do next quite eclipses fear. When he starts to turn toward us, though, I bring my gun up to a firing position. Chan holds my arm and shakes his head, even as Manu stares at us for a moment.

Telepathy is a curious phenomenon. Suddenly I know exactly what he is going to do, and so does Chan. I experience a despair that cuts deeper than anything a human can be expected to endure. But he does endure. He turns, quite as if we are not there, and carries her to the door where I entered. As soon as he has passed through to the tunnel, Chan finds a fuse box and the underground room is filled with harsh neon light. The bodies of Zinna (a single bullet in the forehead); his assistant, who managed to draw a pistol (stomach ripped open by a spray from an automatic of some kind); the Yips (one in a lake of blood from a heart wound, the other covered in fresh pink blood from the lungs); and the two Americans, also caught in a third-world disaster straight out of *farang* horror mytholgy. All dead. We have to step over them to enter the tunnel, which is now illuminated. We catch up with Manu, who is still carrying the wreckage of his love. I draw my gun again. Again Chan stops me.

"He's going to kill her," I say, suddenly angry.

"It's what she wants, fool," Chan says.

His words send a shiver down my spine, because of their surgical accuracy. I draw a breath. "Yes," I say, "I suppose."

After a few minutes we see the bright rectangle of the far doorway. When we reach the garage, we follow Manu up the stairs into the house.

Lek and Sun Bin are as transfixed as are we by the outlandish sight. We all watch, openmouthed, while the maimed giant takes Om to the edge of the balcony. With a skill made possible by his unusual strength and agility, he contrives to hold Om while he climbs over the guardrail. Now he raises her high in the sky with locked elbows as if offering a sacrifice to the gods, bends his knees, and dives with her in his arms.

Far below he is still holding her, motionless, both bodies broken. Her face, though, remains intact, her long black hair spilled onto the rocks and shining in the midday sun.

31

I have just finished making my report to the election committee. We are in the Colonel's office. Something has changed in the dynamics between the Americans and Vikorn. Given my in-depth knowledge of the Colonel, I would say that his strategy of playing the humble old man upstaged by the high-rolling ex-CIA professionals has run its course. He sits today in the only chair with arms, much in the posture of an emperor. The three Americans seem strangely cowed, and the older man, Jack, has been relegated to the sofa with the others. The atmosphere has hardened during my recital of the facts, but I have a feeling the balance of power changed some time ago.

When Jack clears his throat to speak there is a tone of resentment, even pique. "Well, I guess we missed a few tricks here," he says. Linda grunts. Ben looks at the floor. "Looks like you were right all along, Colonel."

"Yep. You sure played your cards close to your chest, sir. I have to admire you for that."

"Fact is," Jack says, warming to his theme, "you showed us the best double-double shuffle in the history of double shuffles."

"I'll second that," Ben says, shaking his head.

"Amazing," Linda says. "We thought it was the Beijing faction that was pushing the organ-trafficking theme to get you elected in an incredibly clumsy way, which was almost certain to backfire. I must say you made no effort to disabuse us of that mistake."

"Never guessed there really was an organ-trafficking syndicate operating right here in Thailand."

"Created and run by your archrival."

"All you needed was to have your man sniff it out. Now it's all over the media exactly three days before your inevitable election."

"Not only that, your only serious competitor gets himself snuffed by his own man. Nothing can stop you now. Either you're some kind of world-class genius, or lucky as hell."

Vikorn turns his head to look at me. "Isn't that what I told you when I gave you the case? That I wanted the sacred soil of Thailand to be free forever from this evil curse?"

"Something like that, Colonel," I agree.

Vikorn sniffs. Then, right in the face of these three resolute non-smokers, he takes a long, fat cigar out of his desk drawer and lights up. He prowls over to the window to gaze out onto the cooked-food stalls. After a couple of minutes he turns back. "Well, if you all will excuse me, I have the BBC in half an hour and CNN this afternoon—"

"Sure thing, Colonel," Jack says, standing. He walks up to Vikorn's desk. "By the way, I've recently started my own corporation—time to strike out on my own. After all, with my experience and contacts, I don't really need partners. You'll see on the card a list of affiliates, which enables me to cover most of the world. The affiliates are all run by the highest-caliber professionals, mostly ex-CIA or World Bank. I would be proud if you were to consider me one of your friends whom you can call on any time of the day or night."

Vikorn looks up at him, shrugs, and accepts the card. Linda and Ben seem to be hanging back. As soon as Jack closes the door behind him, they both stand with obscene deference.

"Ah, Ben and I talked things over, Colonel, and we decided we were both just the right age to start our own corporation and use our extensive contacts and knowledge while we still have the youth and vigor to represent our clients no matter how tough and demanding the assignment," Linda says.

"Damned right," Ben says.

Linda hands Vikorn her new embossed card (high-quality stiff vellum in cream and gray; very tasteful and discreet), then she and Ben back out of the room *waiing*.

Now there is only me left. With some ceremony I fish the black Amex out of my wallet and place it on the desk in front of him. He gives a nod and smile of recognition, clearly expecting me to leave the room immediately. Instead, I sit down again. Now the Colonel cannot understand why I don't just make myself scarce so he can prepare for the BBC. I will do so in a minute, but I have one last question. He stares at me, with perhaps just a touch of nervousness. Finally he says, "So?"

"There is only one thing, sir. That you answer the question you know I'm going to ask before I ask it." I smile.

I suppose if what I'm looking for is proof of life, I'm in luck. I've not seen him erupt for years now, so it's quite a treat, in a way, to watch the blood rise to his face and a furious sweat break out on his forehead. He is quite capable of grabbing his pistol and shooting me, so I stand up and make for the door. He is too quick and jams it with his foot. Iron hands grasp the lapels of my jacket: he crosses his wrists, and twists until I'm choking. "No, this whole case was not an elaborate revenge on Lilly Yip for humiliating me in a squalid little bet we had half a decade ago. Got it?"

"Sure, Colonel," I manage, half throttled. He throws me against the wall and jerks his chin at the door.

I leave the station and cross the road to sit at one of the stalls and order some *somtam*. Chanya and I are still working on our battered relationship, so I fish out my cell phone. "Hi, did you know it's Saturday? Doing anything tonight?"

She gives a token laugh. "Actually, we've been invited to a grand opening. Want to go?"

32

Vikorn's victory at the polls tomorrow seems assured. Tonight, though, Chanya and I have quite a different matter in which to invest our shock and awe. We received an elaborately embossed invitation to the opening party of a new bar on Soi Cowboy, just a hundred yards or so from my mother's. The name of the bar is Dorothy's, and the embossed invitation pictures her in a low-cut evening gown, sticking out her butt and baring enormous new mammary glands almost to the nipples. The invitations are signed "Dorothy and Jimmy."

The famous *soi* is exceptionally crowded. This is the first time a *farang* woman has opened a bar on the street, and everyone is curious, particularly the police and the mafia. When we have flashed our invitation cards at the first line of goons, a red velvet curtain is thrust back, and we find our two hosts on either side of the entrance. Jimmy is dazzling in a white tuxedo with plum cummerbund and bow tie—the knot genuine, the moustache immaculate, the smile Cary Grant. Chanya and I are fascinated to check out Dorothy's new tits: did she really have enhancements, or were they the device of the artist who produced the invitation cards?

She really had enhancements. I wait while Chanya embraces her; to do so, she has to lean over them. When it's my turn, I hug her close so I can tell if they're cheap silicone or upmarket saline pouches. They are saline pouches (about a gallon each would be my guess), skillfully sculpted to the contours of her body with plenty of wobble (but not too much). Dorothy smiles proudly and invites us to test them. I'm prepared to swear an oath that I wouldn't know the difference.

Jimmy Clipp smiles benevolently upon us. "Did you know they'll soon be able to do transplants?" Chanya and I share a paranoid glance.

Dorothy looks at Clipp in a fond but disdainful way, as a former slave might look at a master whom she has overthrown and bent to her use. "I've come out," she says. "This is the first day of the rest of my life." Clipp leads us to our seats.

The format is much like any go-go bar, with a central oblong stage and seats on either side. A switched-on young Thai man with dreadlocks, shades, and tats sits imperiously behind glass in the deejay's seat, right of the stage. On an elevated platform another switched-on young Thai works the spotlights. We are in the front row, and I watch while a great mass of *farang* men, mostly over fifty, slowly fill the bar. I have to wonder if Dorothy did not overinvite in her enthusiasm, for by the time they close the door, all the seats are full, and about fifty men have to stand in the spaces between the rows.

The lights dim. Dorothy appears on stage in a spotlight, which envelops and follows her. When I see she is holding a microphone, I whisper to Chanya that I hope she's not going to sing. Chanya nods in horrified agreement. Now Dorothy begins to sing.

"Ne me quitte pas, ne me quitte pas . . ." It's a sweet, low voice with perfect pitch. Krung Thep is not especially endowed with good cabaret, and she finishes to thunderous applause. We all stand up for an ovation. Dorothy bows humbly, then, when we've settled down, gives her speech.

"Thailand is the best and most mysterious thing that ever happened to me. I came here to teach, but I've not stopped learning since I arrived. Some of the lessons have been hard, some very hard. But this is a country that generously rewards those who put in the time and effort. When I first visited the red-light districts, I was horrified and disgusted. I started to change my attitude when I discovered that my brightest student was a former prostitute and proud of it. I want especially to thank Chanya and her partner, Sonchai, for being such an important part of my learning curve. I've grown and grown since then, and I will forever hold my brightest student as an example of female courage and resilience I cannot hope to emulate. I understand the empowerment of women in a different way, a subtler way, an Asian way, and I see that Thai women knew how to get what they wanted all along. They didn't need me. I needed them though—"

Dorothy stops, overwhelmed. Chanya stands up, all alone in the spotlight, gives Dorothy the highest of high *wais*, and bursts into tears in solidarity. I jump to my feet and find myself *waiing* Dorothy without thinking about it. Now every Thai in the room has felt the jolt and stood up in homage. The girls in bikinis, who have been watching from the dressing room, troop on stage, also *waiing*. Led by Jimmy Clipp, all the *farang* stand and make fumbled *wais*. Tonight everyone loves Dorothy, and Dorothy is very happy.

In the cab on the way home Chanya and I sit close without touching. We're hoping for something to trigger an emotional event while waiting for the lights to change. When the cab pulls away to make a right, it happens: Chanya claps one hand over mine, squeezes in a way that declares the channels of communication are now officially open, then removes her hand to indicate that no further intimacy shall occur until we've talked.

Many beats pass. "Look, let's get this out of the way once and for all. We'll tell each other the truth, then if either or both of us can't take it, we'll call it a day and separate. Okay?"

"Okay. You first."

"We'll toss a coin."

She takes out a ten-baht piece and spins it in the air, then lets it fall into the palm of her hand, then flips it onto the back of the other. Naturally, I lose the toss.

My turn to sigh. "I already told you, I didn't have sex with anyone in Phuket."

"Okay, you didn't have intercourse. She gave you a blow job?"

"Nope."

"Something sent you to the moon and back. You were in an incredible state when you got back one time."

"What was I doing?"

"You would sing that old Isaan song you used to like."

"Okay, a tiny thing happened. It's so tiny it's embarrassing."

"What?"

"I licked her nipples."

"How did her nipples get naked?"

I come clean and tell her the story of Om. She sits, stunned for a long moment, then says, "Maybe she was nuts."

"That too. Now: the cop?"

"He invited me to lunch. We had lunch."

"And?"

Chanya's speech has suddenly accelerated: "And then he invited me to a short-term hotel, *butwedidn'tdoanything.*"

"You went to a short-term hotel with a good-looking cop six years younger than you, and you didn't do anything?"

She is blushing and staring hard at the rearview mirror at the same time. "Okay, you really want to know? We were undressing each other, he started caressing me, and I realized the only reason I was doing it was because I was sure you were cheating on me and that you didn't love me anymore. So I apologized and said I would pay for the room but I couldn't go through with it. I decided I was past all that, I didn't need the karma of starting a whole complicated chain of negative events. I was bigger than that now. I decided to go be a nun instead. Or maybe just shoot you with your gun while you were asleep and claim you tried to rape me."

I'm staring hard at some people on the street, but I'm not seeing them. Waves of jealousy come and go. The same is happening to her. I'm surprised at how easy it is to forgive, however. I reach out to hold her hand. "So did he let you pay for the room?"

"Yes."

"What a cad."

"I can't get over it, the little shit."

She leans against me in a relaxed way and doesn't say anything more. After a while, just before we turn into our *soi*, I feel a tongue start to examine my inner ear. By the time the cab stops, I can hardly pull my wallet out of my Zegna pocket. As soon as we enter the house, however, we are possessed by a higher need. We each gather a bunch of incense sticks, light them, summon *samartit*, and bow three times to the gaudy shrine. A more thorough exorcism of the evil that so recently passed will have to await a visit to temple in the morning. Time for love.

DFR, I am yours in dharma, Sonchai Jitpleecheep.

ACKNOWLEDGMENTS

In the course of the narrative I have made use, from time to time, of both arguments and vocabulary found in the excellent pamphlet *The Last Commodity*, by Nancy Scheper-Hughes (Multiversity & Citizens International), and in *Commodifying Bodies*, edited by Scheper-Hughes and Loïc Wacquant (London: Sage Publications). Such use is entirely in the frivolous context of a fictional narrative, however, and cannot be construed as a representation of the serious purpose of these publications or their contributors.

A NOTE ABOUT THE AUTHOR

John Burdett was brought up in North London and worked as a lawyer in Hong Kong. To date he has published seven novels, including the Bangkok series: *Bangkok 8, Bangkok Tattoo, Bangkok Haunts, The Godfather of Kathmandu,* and *Vulture Peak.*

A NOTE ON THE TYPE

The text of this book was set in Electra, a typeface designed by W. A. Dwiggins (1880–1956). This face cannot be classified as either modern or old style. It is not based on any historical model, nor does it echo any particular period or style. It avoids the extreme contrasts between thick and thin elements that mark most modern faces, and it attempts to give a feeling of fluidity, power, and speed.

Composed, printed, and bound
by Berryville Graphics, Berryville, Virginia
Designed by Virginia Tan